A NOVEL BY SHEY STAHL

This book is a w[illegible], characters, places, and incidents are the product [illegible] the auth[illegible] imagination and are used fictitiously. Any resemblance to actual events, locales, or persons, dead or living, is coincidental.

The opinions expressed in this book are solely those of the author and do not necessarily reflect the views of NASCAR, its employees, or its representatives, teams, and drivers within the series. The car numbers used within this book are not representing those drivers who use those numbers either past or present in any NASCAR series or The World of Outlaw Series and are used for the purpose of this fiction story only. The author does not endorse any product, driver, or other material racing in NASCAR or The World of Outlaw Series. The opinions in this work of fiction are simply that, opinions and should not be held liable for any product purchase, and or effect of any racing series based on those opinions.

Published in the United States of America
ISBN-10: 1478374616
ISBN-13: 978-1478374619

Warning: This book contains adult content, explicit language, and sexual situations.

Cover Art: Allusion Graphics, LLC and Elaine York
www.allusiongraphics.com

Interior Design and Formatting/Proofing:
Elaine York, Allusion Graphics, LLC

Originally, I never planned to release this book. For me it was something I had to know. I needed to know where these characters had come from. So I wrote *Trading Paint* after I finished *Black Flag*. That's when I realized just how important *Trading Paint* was to the development of not only Sway and Jameson, but their love for a sport that consumes their lives both on and off the track. It was then that I knew, to appreciate all the books in the series, this one *needed* to be released as well. And without pushing from my friends Linda, Callie and Daina, it might never have been in print. So, thank them.

Please keep in mind while reading this book, it's told mostly through Jameson's point of view and he speaks racing. His thoughts and words are all directly related to his passion, racing. So, if you think, wow, there's a lot of racing in this book, it's because that's his thought process. It's his life and, in turn, how he communicates and what makes him Jameson Riley.

A special thank you to The Boy, Honey Girl, my parents, my siblings who tolerate me, my friends and my readers for making it possible for me to write.

For my dad, PJ. Without your knowledge of racing, stories of Republic and changing engines on the freeway, this wouldn't have been written. Thank you. You created a childhood I will always remember as one of the greatest times of my life.

A man is the product of his thoughts what he thinks, he becomes.

-Gandhi

Table of
CONTENTS

Magnuflux – Short for "magnetic particle inspection." It's a procedure where parts are checked for cracks and defects using a solution of metal particles, fluorescent dye and a black light. Surface cracks will appear as red lines.

Somewhere between leaving home to chase this dream, and now, I felt something missing. Her. The one who changed everything I thought I knew with one look.

For the longest time, I avoided the fact that I was in love with Sway for one simple reason. What if she loved me back?

If I didn't want to lose her, how long would I let this go on? I have only ever had physical encounters. So, how could I have more?

Just simply being my friend came with a price tag — imagine if she were more? How would that affect her life and how could I do that to her?

I knew my life would never be normal but I wasn't about to take any sense of normalcy that she had away from her. How could I? Sway never had a say in anything and Charlie proved that.

Was it fair that she would soon have responsibilities that no twenty-two-year-old should have?

No. The difference between her and me was that I asked for this. I knew the sacrifices I would have to make and was prepared for them from the beginning. She wasn't.

She had no idea of the pressure or opinionated populace that was out there. Being pessimistically jaded, I didn't want her to know that side of the world but I soon wouldn't have a choice and neither would she.

Bear Grease – Slang term used to describe any patching material used to fill cracks and holes or smooth bumps on a track's surface. Bear grease can also be used as a sealer on the track.

"Can I please race? Come on, Dad ... I've been racing quarter midgets for years and now midgets. I've already raced in about a hundred USAC races." I whined. "I just—I think I'm ready."

I didn't just think I was ready, I knew I was ready.

I'd been racing midgets in the USAC (United States Auto Club), a sanctioning body for midgets, sprint cars, and silver crown cars, for far too long and I couldn't wait to race full-sized sprint cars.

From the time I was little, they were the cars that caught my attention. They were loud and the fastest cars on dirt with their high power-to-weight ratio.

The sound produced by twenty sprint cars lined up on a track, revving their engines is definitely something you will never forget, especially when you're a kid. It shook the ground and filled the air with the sweet aroma of methanol. Sprint cars broad sliding their way around dirt tracks was enough to catch the eye of any kid but when you see one doing wheel stands inches away from concrete walls, again, it's something you'll never forget.

Briefly, his eyes focused on me.

"You're not ready," my dad said and walked into the race shop that housed his sprint cars.

I smiled following closely stepping over the tires and tools scattered around the concrete floor.

"Are you scared I'll smoke you?"

His head whipped around, his blue eyes narrowed. "You're an arrogant little shit. But, no, I'm afraid of your mother."

"I can handle that." I told him and confidently headed for the house. My mom was a push over for me and I knew it, as did she.

You hear people talk about when their career started for them or when they saw their first race but I honestly can't remember when that was. Racing has always been there, ingrained into my life in every way. My dad was racing before I was born so it's all I'd ever known. I'd been playing in the dirt of the pits since before I could walk.

I do remember when I got my first set of wheels.

I believe I was three, or just turned four. Sure, I had a badass big wheel that I'd perfected slide jobs on but I remember my first beast with an engine.

For my birthday that year, my parents gave me a cherry red 150cc Honda go-kart. That, combined with the perfect paved circle driveway, made my four-year-old world.

I had one rule: keep it on the pavement of our driveway.

Growing up with a dad who raced on dirt and that being all you had been subjected to was tall orders for a four-year-old wanting to be like his dad.

I had the quickest route around the circle panned out within the first day I got it and soon began broad sliding through the corners when I pitched it hard enough.

That red beast became my prized possession and, if you didn't hear the humming from the engine, you knew something was up. Soon after they bought mine, my older brother Spencer got one and, before long, we were holding races in our driveway and tearing up my mom's flowers while our little sister Emma acted as the flagger. We must have torn up every plant, every tree and every blade of grass in that yard before the summer was out.

The following year, once the weather had turned warm enough, we were back to doing the same thing.

That's when I decided some adjustments needed to be made to the kart.

Like adjusting the rev limiter to enable it to exceed its standard speed that clearly wasn't fast enough and ending up cutting the brake line instead. Yeah, at four I thought I was some kind of mechanic. It was evident by the gaping hole in the side of our house where my kart flew threw it that I was no mechanic.

After a while, the "keep it on the pavement" rule was out the window and I pretty much raced on any surface.

The following spring, just before I turned five, my dad took me with him to his race in Knoxville, Ohio, where he was racing on the World of Outlaw Tour; the premier division for winged sprint car racing.

That same weekend, Bucky Miers, my dad's long-time friend, let me tear it up in his son's quarter midget.

Two weeks later, we had one sitting in our driveway when we returned. Before long, we had outgrown the driveway and my mom had no landscaping left, so Dad hauled in a few truckloads of clay and made a quarter-mile dirt track in our backyard.

Naturally, I never got out of the car or off the track. Some nights I even fell asleep out there.

Originally, I was supposed to share the car with Spencer but once Spencer found girls and football he didn't care about racing like I did.

You could say my career started right there in my back yard in that quarter midget.

My racing teeth were eventually cut at our home track in Elma, Washington, at Grays Harbor Raceway on June 18, 1985, a few days shy of my fifth birthday, as I made my first start in a quarter midget race.

Elma is a 3/10 mile, semi-banked, clay oval track located off Highway 8 and it was fast — incredibly fast.

I still remember shaking from the adrenaline I experienced racing with kids twice my age as well as the sick but energized feeling in the pit of my stomach when I took the green flag.

By the time I was eight, I was running competitively and had won two USAC Regional Quarter Midget Championships, three track championships at Grays Harbor Raceway, and had won the Deming Speedway Clay Cup Nationals.

At the time, racing quarter midgets contained me and I soon became extremely comfortable in them but that also meant, in my mind, that I was ready for more.

I moved to full-size midgets at nine and now, at eleven, I was ready for something more which meant full-sized winged sprint cars.

The problem was convincing the parental units.

Most tracks were beginning to enforce age restrictions on full-sized sprint cars so I knew that parental consent was necessary. That left me trying to convince my parents of my plan.

It was time for the art of persuasion that I adroitly mastered.

"Mom ..." I cooed in my best compelling voice when I entered the kitchen. I had perfected it over the years for moments like this. "Dad said to ask you but I was wondering if it'd be okay if I raced tonight ... dad will be there." I offered.

She ran her hands through my mess of rusty colored hair, tilting my head to look up at her. Her fingers looped around the curls at the ends. "Honey ... I don't know about that." She said, continuing to do dishes while leaving me with soapy hair. "You know you have to be sixteen to race full-sized sprints."

"But, *mom* ..." I whined brushing the bubbles from my hair. "I've been racing since I was five. I'm eleven now, almost twelve, it's time I broadened my horizons." I grinned when she arched an eyebrow at me. "Besides, Charlie knows us and he said if Dad signed a waiver he'd let me race."

"Jameson, sweetie, I don't want you to get hurt. Sprints are a lot different from the quarter midgets or even those mini sprints and full-size midgets."

She was right.

Sprint cars pushed 120 mph at Elma some nights but I didn't care about that.

"I know that *but* I've been racing them out back for months now. My lap times are faster than dad's."

"Don't flatter yourself — you're smaller than him." She smiled. "Basic laws of gravity, son."

I had nothing left. I broke down into childish whining to prove my point which was somewhat revolting from a bystander's perspective, and I may or may not have resorted to the eye blinking that she loved so much.

Racing was my life and I knew that if I wanted to make a future in it, it was time to race with the big boys; at least that was my eleven-year-old logic.

After a good ten minutes of sucking up, Spencer, my older brother, walked in when I plopped down in a chair at the table.

"Just let the little shit race, Mom ... he's annoying when he doesn't get his way." He chuckled and shoved a cookie in his mouth. "Besides ... I'd like to see him get his ass handed to him out there."

Mom slapped the back of his head as he walked by. "Spencer, watch your language."

Spencer, now fourteen, thought he was God's gift to girls and football.

I had other ideas.

I threw a cookie from the plate in front of me at him, smacking him in the forehead. Although somewhat satisfying, it did result in a gladiator-style wrestling match between the two of us that mom had to break up with the hose from the sink.

"Stop it—both of you get up!" she yelled slipping sideways in the water. "Spencer, clean up this mess. Jameson, go talk to your Dad about racing tonight," She held up her hand to stop me from running into the race shop. "If you wreck, you're done."

"Uh-huh," I yelled over my shoulder as I ran to the race shop.

I told my Dad that Mom had said it was okay. He wasn't convinced and had an hour-long talk with her about it.

In the end, I was allowed with a few stipulations.

I was only allowed to race two races a month and I worked in the shop when I wasn't in school. I didn't care. I probably would have agreed to just about anything to get them to say yes. I wouldn't be allowed to race sprint cars at other tracks until I turned sixteen but only being allowed to race at Elma would be sufficient.

Later that night, I found myself at the track. As you can imagine, I was nervous. But I wasn't about to let them know that.

"All right kid, get in." I slid easily into the narrow cockpit. His head bent down near mine, his hands reaching inside to adjust my belts. "Remember, don't drive too deep into the corners. It'll flip ya' in a heartbeat. Find your lift point and feather the throttle accelerating through the turn. You'll have more control that way since the track is tacky."

Once I was on the track during qualifying and hot laps, I realized how different sprints were from midgets. With being heavier, the wheelspin and changes throughout the race, I was amazed at the differences.

Having spent every afternoon on our quarter-mile track practicing, I knew I was ready and I showed them.

I appeared confident on the outside but, on the inside, I was scared shitless as my dad explained the rules to me after the drivers' meeting.

"Pay attention, Jameson. This is different from racing midgets." He told me after time trials were finished.

I only nodded. I was overwhelmed but I wasn't letting on.

I didn't want to hear the words I told you so, which, by the smirk on his hard face, he was ready to say at the first sign of weakness.

Here we stood in the pits getting ready for the heat races. Pulling my racing suit over my shoulders, I looked up at him.

"All right," he began. "The top eighteen qualifiers will be split into heat one and heat two. You made fast time so you're in heat two. The top two in heat one, will move to the rear of heat two." He nudged my shoulder. "You following me, kid?"

Again, I only nodded. Dad had made it clear early on when I began racing that in order to race, I needed to understand everything; not just how to race. At times, it was overwhelming for a kid.

I had to know set-ups. I had to know handling, engines, *and* how to drive the car. He wouldn't let me slide with climbing in the car and driving. I had to know what to do if I broke it and how to fix it myself.

"The top eight cars from heat two will run the feature." He told me as I fastened my arm straps. I then pulled my helmet on and engaged the coupler.

It was show time.

When it came time for the feature event, the nervousness hit me like a ton of bricks.

Remaining moderately calm throughout the heat races, I presumed the rest of the night would be the same, but when twenty other cars pulled onto the track with me, I briefly contemplated backing out. That being said, there's also nothing like merging onto the track with the rumbling parade of twenty sprint cars. Right then my anxiety instantly vanished.

I did the only thing I knew when I got on the track with the other cars ... I raced. There was a stillness that washed over me and I blocked out everything like I always did inside the car. I wasn't sure if I was ready to run the top with the fast guys but when it came time to make a pass, I had no choice but to run the top as the groove on the bottom wasn't working.

With my heart pounding rapidly, I pulled a "Jimi move" as I called it and slid past three or four cars in each turn using the high side where the grip was.

Much to my surprise and probably everyone else at the track, I won. If you're surprised that an eleven-year-old kid could beat men who'd been racing for years and had ten and twenty years on me, imagine my amazement.

After the feature race and the trophies had been awarded, my dad caught up with me.

"Nice job, kid."

Hearing words of commendation from a World of Outlaw Champion was something any kid would want to hear despite him being my father.

"Thanks, Dad." I replied with a huge grin once we were back inside his car hauler loading. "Does this mean I can continue racing?"

"Yeah ... but school comes first." I started to walk away when he reached for the back of my suit and turning me back around to face him. "When you're not in school, you're helping out in the shop, *understood*?"

"Sure, whatever," I tried to play it cool. "I can do that."

"Go help Spencer load the cars. I'm going to go see Charlie." Without another word he walked off to meet Charlie who was standing outside the hauler.

When I thought about what I had just been allowed to do, it dawned on me that Spencer had never been allowed to do this. I always thought Spencer would show some interest and want to race, but outside of messing around on the track at home, he never wanted to race competitively. He'd rather work on the cars than race them, which was fine by me and good luck getting the football out of his hands.

Spencer and I spent more time checking out Charlie's daughter than loading cars, which was no surprise these days. I may only be eleven, but girls were *definitely* something I was responsive to. I was beginning to understand why Spencer liked the opposite sex so much.

Being eleven, almost twelve, I was launching into the teenage hormones and with that came strange ... urges or feelings, I guess you could say.

Girls, well they spurred these urges or feelings which, in turn, resulted in some fairly embarrassing reactions to my body, much like right now.

This was not something I enjoyed. Even at eleven, I wanted to be in control of everything and times like this I wasn't.

"Check her out," Spencer swooned. "She's growing up,"

"Dude, how have I not seen her before?" I asked peeking at her once again. I was never shy. I'm not sure that I even knew the meaning of the word but, for once, I was starting to understand the emotion that could be classified as shy. I think.

"You've gone to school with her since like the second grade." Spencer smacked my chest. "What's the matter with you?"

"I don't know. I've never seen her before."

If it didn't involve an engine, I hardly paid attention. I couldn't tell you half the kids who went to my school.

"I think she likes older men anyway." Spencer replied cockily with a nod.

I was about to respond when Dad called for us, "Jameson, Spencer—get over here!"

"Coming," we yelled as we jumped from the back of the car hauler. He reached for me by my race suit before I made it too far.

"Sway, this is my son, Jameson. I think you two are the same age." He shook my shoulders rocking me back and forth. "And this is my other son, Spencer. He's fourteen." He ruffled Spencer's hair. "I've got a daughter, Emma, who's almost ten but who knows where she disappeared to."

"She's selling T-shirts." Spencer told him smiling at Sway.

I rolled my eyes at him.

"It's nice to meet you both." Sway shook hands with us to which I smiled at her and, for good measure, I added a wink.

I couldn't have her thinking that Spencer was the better pick. Clearly, I was.

She was beautiful with her full lips, staggering emerald green eyes and lustrous flowing dark mahogany hair with hints of auburn that shone under the lights of the pits. I'd never seen such an innocent looking, but memorable, girl before. But I'd also never paid any attention to any girls until now.

"You did good out there tonight." She said, making eye contact with me, her cheeks flushed.

"Looks like you follow in your Dad's footsteps." Charlie slung his arm around Sway's shoulder. "You did good."

I laughed. "Yes, but I'm better than him."

Charlie and my dad both started laughing at my eleven-year-old confidence. I hardly thought it was funny. It was the truth.

Most everyone in the racing communities compared my talent to Jimi's. In the beginning, I welcomed it, as he was a legend in sprint car racing, but it soon became something I felt I needed to live up to and eventually surpass.

Something more than just my sprint car career started that night. A lifelong friendship was formed. After that night, Sway Reins and I were inseparable.

I had friends. Well, that was a lie. I *knew* other kids but to call them friends, I wouldn't go that far because we never talked outside of school or outside of the track. School friends were separate from track friends—it was just the way it was.

There was one kid, Justin West. We had started together in the USAC quarter midget and midgets. We hung out but outside of the track, we didn't see each other. He lived in Hillsboro, Indiana, so it was rare that we saw each other but being the same age, we shared the same interests, racing.

With Sway, it was easy to be around her. She didn't care if I wasn't at school, had a bad day or didn't want to see anyone.

I was incredibly moody and she understood that.

Sway was there on Saturday nights when I raced and helped me scrape mud from the car and made sure that I had tear-offs on my helmet. She was there on Sundays if I had a bad night racing the night before but, the best thing was, with Sway, we didn't have to maintain the relationship we had or even try because we were friends.

I thought for a while that it would be cool if I could call her my girlfriend but I saw what happened to all the girls my brother was friends with and then dated. It ended horribly and, worst of all, he lost the friend.

I couldn't lose Sway. Just her presence relaxed me in a way I'd never had before. And, best of all, she believed in me. I came to depend on her in a vital way.

Before that sprint race at Elma, I was usually only allowed to race twice a month. This was supposed to keep me focused on my schoolwork and not as much on racing.

During the summers I was allowed to race every weekend if I wanted to so that's when I began to shine.

The summer of '92, I again won the Clay Cup Nationals in Deming, the Northwest Regional Midget Championship and the Midget Championship at Grays Harbor Raceway.

By competing in a number of Western District Qualifiers, I was able to attend the Quarter Midget Nationals: The Battle at the Brickyard.

We went and my first time there, we won.

Right then, standing there being awarded the trophy, I realized this dream might be reality some day and became my only focus.

The deal with my dad worked well until being a teenager became a factor. I found myself partaking in the occasional acts of mischief at school and around town but racing was always number one to me.

As twelve turned to thirteen and thirteen turned to fourteen, my life became complicated and suddenly I had other interests knocking at the door.

Hormones were a factor but the drive to become a professional racer was still present and ruled over everything. I wanted more than anything to race and nothing else mattered. Not school, not friends, nothing. I wasn't living the normal childhood that's for sure.

While Spencer and Emma did, I didn't and had no desire to. I raced whenever possible. If I wasn't racing, I was learning everything I could from my dad and working on his cars in the shop. At times,

I guess I wanted to have a normal childhood life but I also knew this dream of mine wasn't something I could put aside. If I wanted to be the best, it would take dedication and hard work.

I remember when reality hit and dad forced me to decide, or at least he made the decision for me when he threatened to sell my car.

Sometime around fourteen, he left for Grand Rapids, Michigan, one Tuesday evening. My only chores were taking out the garbage and mowing the lawn. The rest of the time I was allowed to race on the track and do whatever I wanted.

Naturally, I didn't mow the lawn and the garbage made it to right outside the door.

I spent every night racing out there from dawn to dust. The only reason I stopped was from the lack of light. Don't get me wrong, I tried to convince my dad to install lights but he knew that would only result in me never leaving the track.

When the flashlights that Sway and I taped to the wings of my sprint car fell off, we called it a night and watched movies.

My parents returned Sunday afternoon to find me lying in bed eating Captain Crunch with a pile of garbage outside the door and a field of grass.

Let's just say my dad turned our house into something similar to what you'd see in the Civil War after he threatened to sell my car. I was not okay with that. I had a hard time drawing the line between racing and working. I knew I had to work around the shop but it was difficult to get out of the car and having unlimited access like I did, made it tough.

After a while, I understood that in order to race, I needed to show my dad I was responsible enough to handle a demanding schedule and put everything I had into it. What I wanted didn't come easy. To be the best you had to battle the best and to battle the best, you had to work for it.

I couldn't show up and race expecting to win. To win races everything had to line up, track conditions, set-ups, positions, and then the wheelman needed to be on his game. That's where my roughshod attitude to be the best came into play.

Eventually everything else began to slip away—the only things that mattered were working at the shop and racing on Saturday nights. I lost friends, gained some and then lost them once they saw I never made time for anything but racing.

One friend remained the same though: Sway. She was always there and if I decided to go racing instead of to the movies, she was there. If I decided to change my shocks out on Friday night instead of partying with the rest of our classmates, she was there handing me tools.

I never understood why she did it, but I was thankful she did. Every time I thought about giving up and living the normal teenage life, she was there to remind me why I was doing this in the first place. I began to realize that what I was lacking she had ... Sway believed in me. I wouldn't say that I didn't believe in myself because I did, but for the first time other than my parents, someone else believed I could do it and that was the push I needed.

She saw the potential and never let me forget it. She was my rock. She was dependable, supportive, not judgmental ... everything I wasn't for her.

I tried to be, but there was also that line again. I had a hard time drawing a line between racing and everything else.

The older I got, the harder it got.

Riding a wheel – This refers to wheel-to-wheel action in sprint car racing, usually disastrous when contact is made with another car.

Even though I was a racer and garnered respect from the other drivers at the track. Off the track, I was a normal teenager who, for the most part, thought of ways to get into trouble, hated getting up early and, of course, was infatuated with girls.

Being fourteen, I was hormone challenged as I called it. I had wants and as a teenager, those wants were hormone driven. Being someone who needed to be in control, I was not in control of my hormones so, as you can expect, I did not deal with that as well as I'd hoped for.

Most of the time I was able to push the thoughts aside and focus on the bigger picture: racing. It didn't stop the occasional fantasy of my best friend and me.

All that aside, I had a mission. I was determined to be the best racer I could be and was putting everything I had into accomplishing that.

The USAC Midget series opened in March of '95 in Chico, California. Racing was in full swing come April while I ran two USAC races a month and the weekly midget and sprint races at Elma. I had to be sixteen to compete in the USAC Silver Crown and sprint divisions so this left me racing only at Elma in a winged 360-sprint car.

I ended up catching a few outlaw late model races here and there when a car was available but I mainly stayed in the open wheeled cars.

Remaining focused, I learned everything I could from my dad. We spent many nights together going over set-ups and strategy. He constantly asked me, "Is this what you want?"

Without a fraction of a doubt, it was what I wanted. I never had to think about it.

I understood why he asked though as he had lived this lifestyle his entire life, like me. He began racing at a young age, like me. But, unlike me, he didn't have the financial support from his dad. Sure, grandpa was financially stable now being a lead manufacturer of sprint car engines. Back in the sixties and early seventies, that wasn't the case.

I had an endless supply of cars, parts and resources readily available when needed but that wasn't what I valued. What I cherished most was the time spent learning from him as well as reaping the wisdom of the sport that I loved so much.

To this day, I still remember the first sanctioned race I ran with my dad.

It was May 13, 1995.

He was racing in the World of Outlaws race at Bloomington Speedway in Indiana. I tagged along with the intention of watching and gaining pointers.

Sway came with us, as did my buddy Tommy, and older brother Spencer.

I only intended to *just* watch, but my dad had other plans.

When we pulled into the pit gate, he stopped at the credentials desk as he usually would.

"Hey, Natalie, how are you?" Dad asked handing his credentials to her. He scribbled his signature over the insurance and release forms before looking back at me in the back seat. "You need to sign this, kid." He pushed the clipboard at me.

I'm sure the surprised look on my face had something to do with Sway's sudden outburst of giggles beside me.

"I thought I was watching?" I asked hesitantly. I've raced sprint cars before but I had never been in a 410-sprint car.

The World of Outlaws ran 410ci engines in them as opposed to the 360ci engines ran on the Northern Sprint Tour, USAC sprint cars and local tracks.

Apparently ... he thought I was ready.

"If you don't think you can handle it ..." his voice trailed off when I glared.

Suddenly, I was nervous but I wasn't about to show it.

"I can handle it."

He laughed, as did everyone else in the truck. I signed the release forms and the liability insurance as well.

When we pulled up to the hauler, Sway reached for my arm before we got out.

I smiled looking over my left shoulder at her. "What's up?"

"Are you okay?" she returned the smile.

She was always checking on me. She also knew that if there was ever anyone I would admit that to, it was her.

"Yeah," I nodded.

I was more than okay. Sure, I was a little nervous but I was also humming with excitement at the chance to be behind the wheel of a 410-sprint car with my dad out there with me.

Dad and I had raced together at Elma messing around and on the track out back but never in a sanctioned race before. This was a points race for him and now his son would be out there with him.

I watched him squeeze into the cockpit of his double zero red sprint car, chuckling to myself that my six-foot-three dad was able to fit into these cars. Dad was burly and Spencer seemed to take after him in size. They could both be linebackers for the Pittsburgh Steelers.

Sway and I made our way over to the hauler where I got in my racing suit to take a few hot laps to get the feel of the car. I took four laps to get a feel for it.

The first lap, I took it easy and cruised around. As I came into turn three on my second lap, I threw it hard—sliding with ease through the ruts, feathering the throttle for control. Pushing the car hard through the corners, I ran the high line that I felt comfortable with.

I could feel the difference between the cars immediately. They were faster for one but the feel of the extra horsepower pulling me through the tacky clay was nice. Where the 360 sprints tended to get bogged down on the tacky tracks if you didn't adjust your timing, the 410 glided.

After my few hot laps, I looped back around into the pits to find Sway and Tommy grinning ear to ear.

"What?" I grinned back at them trying to contain my excitement. Useless.

They both laughed.

Before long, time trials were underway. I ended up qualifying for the A-feature behind my dad in the second row. For being my first time in a 410, I was content with that starting position.

This particular race, being a World of Outlaws event was a different format than USAC and the Northern Sprint Tours.

When the World of Outlaws lined up, they lined up four-wide and made a complete lap that way which was called the 4-wide salute to the fans.

I'd see it done many times by my dad and other drivers, but to do it myself, with my dad beside me, was tear worthy.

Here was the man I looked up to my entire life, racing beside me. I had no words for how I felt other than emotional.

Dad revved his engine beside me, jolting him forward a few feet. I did the same as did Bucky and Shey who were beside us.

When the race started, I held back for a few laps, watching my dad make his way to the lead position. I slid past Shey Evans with ease, and knocked off Bucky in the next turn. This left me right behind my dad coming out of turn two.

I think he wanted me to catch him; at least that was my theory. So, when he came out of three and went low, I saw my chance.

He knew it and I knew it.

I threw my car hard like I always did when he shot up and pushed against me, I knew he wouldn't give the position easily. That wasn't his style.

When you passed Jimi, you earned it. He could block with the best of them and could slip into a position faster than any other driver, making room where there wasn't. Other drivers called him "Shimmy Jimi" because one minute there wasn't room and then there he was in front of you.

The only problem with racing against your dad is that he knows what you do to outsmart the other driver. I also knew what he would do though, I knew where he was strong and I knew where he struggled. Turn four in Bloomington was his weak spot. While he ran high in three, he would swoop down low into four and ride the rail. Then he'd shoot up the track on the front stretch and nearly brush the wall with his right rear before hurling the car sideways high into one and two.

I watched him for about four laps before I decided to make my move. Yet another trait I learned from him over the years: patience in racing is your virtue.

When he guided the car low in four, on impulse, I went high letting my right rear bounce off the cushion. This gave me the extra boost needed to slingshot past him coming out of four.

I knew I wouldn't pull a slide job on my dad without him coming back for more.

I was schooled.

He shot back down on the inside and slipped past me going into one. This went on for about ten laps, every time I slid past him, he came right back, when the caution came out for a car that flipped on the front stretch.

This left two laps to go when the green dropped. With Bucky and Shey back in the mix, the greatest drivers in sprint car racing surrounded me.

Taking a deep breath, I told myself this was time to make my move.

Don't second-guess yourself.

When the green dropped, I came off turn four strong and went high into one and two. Dad didn't get as good of a jump on the restart as I did so this put me in line with him coming into three and four. I went low, he went high and I pushed against him taking his line.

If you could have seen my face under the helmet, you would have seen me grinning ear-to-ear.

I outsmarted the champion.

He didn't let me go far, he stayed right beside me, taunting me in each turn.

On the last lap, we took three and four again, neck and neck. When we came down the front stretch, my wheels came across the line not more than two inches in from his.

I smiled looking over at him and he raised his arm as much as he could, with the arm straps on, pumping his fist in the air.

I laughed.

Bloomington Speedway was essentially my dad's home track. He was born in this small midwest suburb in 1956 and raced here as a kid.

And his kid beat him.

This was pretty fucking cool. Not only would I have some serious bragging rights but I won my first Outlaw race.

Being fourteen, this was the coolest race I'd ever won. I'd won track championships, national and regional championships but to win a World of Outlaws A-Feature event in a 410-sprint car against your legendary father. That was cool.

When we pulled back into the pits, dad was out of his car as quickly as he could, Sway was jumping up and down with Tommy while Spencer offered a head nod, trying to remain cool about it. Being seventeen now, he thought he was a badass but I could see he was proud of me. Returning the head nod, I turned to Sway running to congratulate me.

"You were awesome out there!" she yelled launching herself at me.

"Fuck, yeah!" I screamed pumping my fist in the air when Dad sprayed beer all over us.

He was all smiles.

"Did you let me win?" I asked hesitantly when he pulled me in for a hug.

He pulled back ruffling my beer soaked hair. "Do you honestly think I'd let my overconfident fourteen-year-old son beat me?"

He had a good point.

"No."

"You earned that one." His smile said it all. "Remember it."

And I would remember it. Of all the races I'd ever raced in, all the championships I'd won, *that* win at that quarter-mile clay track in Bloomington Speedway stands out.

It was the day I grasped the meaning of the bigger picture and what I was capable of.

That was also the night I had my first beer—a well-deserved beer. Underage, yes, but it was a cause for celebration and that we did.

Throwing back beers with my idols was humbling even for a cocky kid like me.

My dad started racing when he was old enough to reach the pedals of his custom mini sprint grandpa designed for him.

My grandpa, Casten Riley, began racing with the moonshiners and rebels of the sport but never had a chance to race in any sanctioned race. When he was twenty-six he wrapped his car around a tree nearly paralyzing him and he never raced again.

Instead, he focused on building sprint cars where his real passion was and, once my dad was born, grandpa had him racing the cars as soon as he could reach the pedals.

Now, CST Engines is one of the leading engine manufacturers in the midwest for sprint cars.

While Grandpa built the cars from the ground up, dad raced them.

In 1978, he began racing the World of Outlaws series in Knoxville, Ohio. He'd won more championships and races than any other driver in the series.

I was surrounded by renowned greats.

Sitting next to me, Sway smiled while dad and Bucky swapped stories about their early days in the series.

"You're eating this up, aren't you?"

I smiled back at her nudging her shoulder with my own. "You have no idea."

I knew she had an idea of how I felt. She always did.

During the winter was the only time of year that our family was together and it was usually only for about two weeks before dad headed off to Tulsa for the Chili Bowl Midget Nationals.

I, for one, was in favor of the off-season that year. I hadn't realized how unending the season could be until November rolled around.

But just a few weeks into the off-season and I was ready for more. Funny how that worked.

That year I'd raced in nineteen sprint car races, four World of Outlaws feature events, and twenty-three midget races. I also ran the Clay Cup Nationals, Turkey Night, and managed to pull off a track championship at Elma and placed third in the Night Before The 500 at Indianapolis.

I was exhausted.

The winter of '95, my parents planned a trip to Jacksonville Beach, Florida, so we spent Thanksgiving there.

Sway usually went on family vacations with us because she was part of the Riley family. Her mother, Rachel, died of breast cancer when Sway was only six and she had no brothers or sisters. Her dad was raising her and managing a track on his own so she needed us.

Between ganging up on Spencer and Emma, my parents had basically told us to get out of the room just a few hours after arriving in Florida. That landed us at the hotel pool.

Wading around, Sway asked, "Do you ever think about what it will be like?"

"What?" My eyes caught a glimpse of girls walking in before I turned to Sway.

"Racing ... for a living ... do you ever think about it? I mean, you're good enough. You know that, right?"

"I know and I think about it all the time," I sighed leaning my chin against the concrete edge of the pool we were swimming in; my fingers traced the cracks watching the water seep into them. "I know I can do it ... that's not a problem but getting everyone, sponsors included, looking at me as Jameson Riley and not Jimi Riley's son is what's hard. Every track they constantly compare me to him. You saw how hard it was for me at the Dirt Cup this year."

Once a year, Skagit Speedway held the Dirt Cup. It wasn't a point race but a play date but a chance to prove what you had.

I did.

I won the 360-sprint division *and* the midget main events. After the race, another racer who was on the same circuit as my dad approached me.

It wasn't unusual for the Outlaw or NASCAR drivers to hang around these events. This year they had Dad, Bucky Miers, Skip Miller, Shey Evans, and Langley O'Neil from the Outlaw division. NASCAR rookie Tate Harris showed up along with Doug Dunham and Austin Yale; all great drivers.

I'd met Skip Miller once, with my dad, before at a race in Eldora, but I had yet to speak to him. I wasn't impressed once I did.

The conversation started fairly well with him congratulating me and, like always, I appreciated the praise from the drivers I looked up to but Skip had a different approach when he said, "I don't know that you'll ever live up to Jimi but you did good."

I wanted to say, "Hey, thanks asshole," but I wasn't raised that way and dad would beat my ass if I disrespected a veteran driver. And, one thing was certain, you don't piss off Jimi Riley.

The entire night was filled with comments like, *"Hey, there's Jimi's son,"* or *"Did you see Jimi Riley's kid in the last heat?"* I wanted to say, "I have a name you know."

I moved from my place against the side of the pool, kicking my legs out when I kicked Sway by accident and, like I expected, she smacked me.

"Is that such a bad thing?" she asked pushing her hair out of her face. She swam closer resting against the same ledge where I was.

"No ... dad is an amazing racer ... but I don't want to try to live up to him. He's a legend in sprint car racing. He's won more races than any other driver has on the circuit and won more championships than most people can ever dream about. It's not about being better than him, it's about making my own name."

"That's understandable."

I glanced over at her. "It doesn't sound dumb?"

"No," she ran her fingers along the dark grouted line in the tile. "I don't think it sounds dumb. Jimi is good but so are you. It's natural to want to be your own person."

I knew how good my dad was.

I came from a long line of racing blood so it was believed that Spencer and I would want to race. It was never expected.

When I took to it, I saw the excitement in their eyes, especially since grandpa's career had ended so suddenly.

As I said, it was never expected that I would race so when I decided that's what I wanted, they were pleased. In turn, I wanted to please them and be the best I could but I also wanted to have my own name in racing history. I didn't want to be another Riley in racing. I wanted to be Jameson Riley.

I've been on a number of vacations with the Riley family and they all include the same series of events: Emma packs way too much; Spencer fucks with everyone; and Jameson pouts because he's not racing and tries to find a racetrack. I end up sneaking alcohol to keep from going crazy.

At some point, Jameson and I would stay up eating Oreo cookies, our drug of choice, until three in the morning.

I've always welcomed the time spent with the Riley family if not for the entertainment value but for the chance to drink. I was only fifteen and drinking was unacceptable but it was something I enjoyed.

Who wouldn't?

I never went for the hard stuff, just beer. This somehow made me feel better about the choice.

"Jesus, Sway," Emma balked peering down at my legs. "Put some lotion on those lizard legs. They look like sandpaper!"

"It's just dry skin." I defended examining them. They did appear a little dry but I hardly thought comparing them to a lizard was necessary.

"It's disgusting."

"Not everyone is obsessed with lotion, Em." Jameson defended stepping from the pool to join us in the lounge chairs. "Her legs look fine." He glanced down at them and then averted his eyes. "I'll be right back."

Girls had been following him all day and now wasn't any different. He had a constant following of pit lizards on and off the track. A tall brunette without lizard legs walked up to Emma and I when he sauntered to the bathroom.

"Is he your boyfriend?" she gestured to Jameson walking into the men's restroom.

"He's my brother." Emma said making a retching sound in the back of her throat.

The girl's eyes focused on me.

"Me?" I pointed to myself. "No, he's not my boyfriend."

Not that I would be opposed to that with him but he was my best friend. I didn't see him in that light.

He was also a moody perfectionist asshole so how anyone could stand him was beyond me, but he was my best friend. If I needed a shoulder to cry on, he was there. He may be working on his race car at the same time but he made sure I had company.

The girl, who looked about sixteen, maybe even seventeen smiled and strutted toward Jameson, who was now approaching us, his shirt slung over his shoulder.

Manhandling sprint cars around a track for years provided him with a honed physique that most men would kill for let alone fifteen-year-old boys.

Jameson smiled at her but his smile faded when she began to speak. I had a feeling the dim-witted brunette didn't have much going for her besides looks.

It took all of two minutes for him to finally get away from her and, when he did, he glared at me. "Do me a favor," he huffed throwing himself into the lounge chair next to me. "Tell them you're my girlfriend." He kicked his long legs up. "That was ridiculous."

"So ... no date for you tonight?" I snickered.

"No, it's hard to believe some guys fall for girls like that." He sighed looking back at her. "She should be embarrassed for herself."

He ended up laughing with me after a few minutes but it took some convincing. This wasn't the first time this happened to him and wouldn't be the last. He'd never showed interest in girls but I also knew he had other priorities.

Jameson was all about racing and nothing else mattered to him.

I admired that about him.

As teenagers we struggled to find our identities and to live up to the expectations that our parents and teachers put upon us.

Jameson didn't. He knew who he was inside and knew exactly what he wanted. I couldn't decide on shit and I was lucky if I managed to pick out what CD I was going to listen to that day in under an hour. I also, for the life of me, could never manage to wear matching socks.

Expecting any of us to act normal on the plane ride home was downright absurd. Here you had Emma at fourteen, Jameson and me being fifteen, Spencer and his friend Colby at seventeen ... we were hardly in any position to conduct ourselves in a manner that was acceptable for society.

Nancy and Jimi were good sports until around hour three of

the six-hour ride when Jameson and I decided it was time to up the larking around.

While most of the trip was spent annoying Emma, we turned to Spencer and Colby when Emma burst into tears because we had replaced her lotion with glue again. No matter how many times we did that, we still found it entertaining and we did this at least once a week. It was funny.

Spencer, being a prankster himself, made it difficult for us to pull one over on him. This took dedication and research. His only weaknesses were girls and food.

We decided to knock off two with one prank.

When he went to the bathroom, we added a few drops of pink food coloring to his Pepsi and then convinced the girl next to us to come on to him. We were succeeding until it all turned on us.

Alley, a tall beautiful blonde, who sat on the other side of Jameson, was our decoy. Alley was awesome, witty, humorous, and could roll out the insults with the best of them. I knew I liked her when Jameson was fidgeting beside us and she turned to him.

"Will you stop fucking moving?"

"You stop moving." He shot her a glare. "I'm uncomfortable."

"Well, if you stop jumping around you might be comfortable. You're moving around so much you're about to throw your back out."

"What the fuck is wrong with you?" he asked her.

"What's wrong with me? You're driving me insane!" she exclaimed throwing her magazine at him. "Stop moving. You're vibrating my seat with all this moving."

"You enjoying the vibrating?" he teased.

Jameson couldn't help himself. He had a knack, like Spencer, for turning any conversation dirty if he needed to embarrass you.

"You wish shit head." She rolled her eyes. "Stop moving."

I laughed at their silly argument. After that, I befriended her as my cohort in my attacks.

I learned that Alley lived in Olympia, Washington, which was about forty-five minutes from Elma.

"Who's the ape in front of us with the pink mouth?" Alley asked eventually.

Jameson and I let out a childish giggle.

"Spencer, my brother," he replied.

"Why is his mouth pink?"

"We slipped food coloring into his soda."

Alley smiled and went in for the kill.

An hour later, Spencer and Alley were chatting and Jameson and I were not pleased. This did not work in our favor.

"That couldn't have gone any worse." Jameson finally said disgusted that Spencer was pulling out all the tricks for this blonde beauty.

I thought it was somewhat cute. Spencer has always been a chick magnet and had scored more than the whole football team with the girls. He was a god at Elma High School and everyone thought Jameson would live up to Spencer's reputation.

Jameson, on the other hand, could give a flying fuck about girls.

That was a lie. I saw that he looked at girls, particularly the ones at the track but he never showed a real interest in them and he never flirted.

At times, it was hard to tell if he was even interested in the opposite sex at times but after our few exchanges that we've had ... I'd say he was into the girls. It just had to be the right one.

We did our fair share of messing around because, let's be real, we were teenagers and we pushed boundaries.

I still remember the first time I saw him kiss another girl and I didn't like it. I don't know why, but I didn't like it.

It was at Elma, after a race he won and the trophy girl, Desy Miller, kissed him. The next thing I knew, the two of them were making out beside his car.

I didn't like her, but I didn't know *why* I didn't like her. Maybe it was her name?

I can only guess the real reason was because I hated trophy girls and I thought Jameson deserved better than a trophy girl. He needed someone who was stable and, in my book, trophy girls were not. They were clingy gold digging pit lizards and my best friend deserved more than that.

I remember approaching him as he loaded his car, Desy nowhere in sight thank God.

"Nice race," I said, congratulating him on his win.

Jameson closed the door to the hauler, looking over his shoulder at me before locking the door securely. "Where were you?"

"You were busy so I let you celebrate." I told him honestly.

He turned around completely and leaned against the doors, crossing his arms over his chest. Still clad in his race suit, he unzipped the top letting it fall from his shoulders and then tied it around his waist. "I was looking for you though."

"I was looking for you, too," I offered. "Where'd Desy go?"

He blinked slowly running his right hand across his jaw and then shrugged. "Home ... I guess. I didn't ask."

"Hmm," I said, and then walked over to the pit concession stand.

"Wait," Jameson yelled after me. "I'll help you lock up."

"You better, I'm not walking around by myself out here ... *in the dark.*" I insinuated.

"Good idea. You never know what kind of crazy assholes are around here." He laughed slinging his arm around my shoulder.

Just like that, we were back to normal.

With Jameson and me, nothing was complicated, so we thought, making it easy to be around each other. We never had to work at our friendship.

If he pissed me off, I told him. If he thought I was being a bitch, he didn't hesitate to tell me either and when you're struggling as a teenager to find balance and understand your complicated life with the added influence of hormones, uncomplicated is a blessing.

It still didn't change the fact that I wasn't keen on the idea of these others girls hounding him all the time because I saw through their cunning behavior. They were only looking for one thing, popularity. While Jameson didn't play sports and hardly attended any school functions, let alone school, he was popular among the female flock.

This didn't exactly make my life easy. They saw we were friends and did everything in their power to destroy that.

Hot Laps – A session held prior to time trials. During the sessions, each car is allotted three or more laps at speed to ensure their car is ready for qualifying.

During my junior year, I spent more time racing through the different sprint car series than I did attending school. I did fine balancing the two until the USAC sprint car division opened in Eldora that March.

From then on, it was racing every weekend and sometimes I'd miss weeks of school if I traveled to the Midwest or East Coast. I ended up getting a tutor so I could graduate next year.

Poor Sway had to be at school without me. We usually stuck together around there because, let's face it, Elma High School was not something you advertised attending and, at times, had some questionable attendees.

Tommy Davis, a good friend of mine from school, took care of her when I was gone and made sure no one messed with her. She took shit from girls at school for hanging around with me.

They all thought she was in it for the fame but that never mattered to her. She was good at avoiding them and could give a rat's ass what anyone thought of her. I loved that about her.

When Memorial Day weekend came around that year, Charlie let us kidnap Sway.

I was running in the National USAC winged sprint series that year which had a 37-race schedule. I couldn't compete for the title since I'd missed about four races so far because of mid-term finals at school but even with those four, I was running eighth in the division points and second to Justin West in the national points.

That weekend, while waiting for Sway to arrive, Spencer caught me inside the hauler getting ready for the heat races at Terre Haute. Dad had gone to get her from the airport so that left me anxiously waiting for her. It had been about two weeks, maybe longer since we had last seen each other and I couldn't wait to hang out with my girl. Shit, listen to me.

She's not your girl. She's your friend.

"Right." I told myself. The thoughts weren't lost on me that she could easily be considered my girlfriend to most, but it wasn't like that with us. Sure, being sixteen, I was physically attracted to her, but the feelings weren't romantic. I loved her as I would love any member of my family, she was part of our family and it was purely platonic, so I thought.

"What's with you two?"

"What are you talking about?" I asked looking outside once again to see if she'd arrived.

"I don't know ... you're a guy, she's a girl ... a *hot girl.*" Spencer implied.

"It's not like that with us. I don't know why but it's not."

"But, you find her ... attractive in that way?"

You have no fucking idea!

I laughed trying not to let on how attractive I thought Sway was in fear that my brother would give me shit.

"I'm not blind."

"Just ... be careful." He nodded. "It's easy to break a girl's heart that way."

That's exactly why I never pursued anything with her. I knew damn well where my interest resided and that was with racing.

Anything I had to offer *any* girl wouldn't be anything more than physical.

My desires … they were racing and racing only. I was also sixteen and I hardly knew the ways of the world but I sure thought I did.

Sure, Sway and I experimented with each other on occasion; kisses here, touches there and we had made out on more than once occasion but it never led to anything of substance and was usually ended quickly by one of us pulling away or Sway giggling.

There were a few girls I had also made out with from school or at different tracks where I'd been racing but that had never went anywhere either and it was usually kept PG-13.

The rumbling of my dad's diesel truck pulling into the pits pulled me out of my thoughts and I jumped to my feet.

Sway was getting out of the truck with my dad.

I smiled as did she and she ran full speed at me.

Launching herself into my arms, she whispered. "I missed you, Riley."

I pulled her inside the hauler when my dad approached the chief steward about a fuel problem my car had during pre-race inspections. They thought we were using some sort of additive in the fuel, which was not allowed in any of the USAC Divisions.

"So, how'd the race last night go?"

I grumbled for a minute before answering.

"Shitty. I wrecked with three laps to go."

"That sucks … does that mean we need to party tonight to get you in the spirit of winning."

"I guess so. I really missed having you around." I threw my arm around her shoulder.

Surprisingly, tears glazed her eyes.

"I did, too." She admitted softly.

My hand rose to cup her cheek. "Hey … are you all right?"

Sway, never being one to show a lot of emotion, chewed on her cheek for a minute before answering. "I just … it's not the same when you're not at school. Girls well, they … think I'm into you and constantly give me shit about it. It's annoying … sometimes it gets to me. That's all."

"Are you?"

"Am I what?"

"Into me ... I thought we were friends." I mumbled. I didn't want to hear she felt anything more than a friendship.

"No. I mean ... as friends. I don't have feelings for you if that's what you're asking."

"Good. Friends," I smiled and hugged her.

Glancing at the pit bleachers, I saw Amber eyeing me. Amber was Justin West's cousin who followed me around any race she attended. She was nice, I guess, but annoying. She was also fourteen. Being sixteen, almost seventeen, that was not an option to me. I didn't go for the younger ones. Besides, she seemed clingy, that was another trait that was not an option.

I pulled Sway closer. "Do me a favor this weekend?"

"Sure," she said without question.

"Will you pretend to be my girlfriend for a few days?" she started to object so I held my fingers to her lips and tilted her head at Amber. "You see that blonde over there?"

"Yeah."

"She's obsessed with me and I may or may not have told her you were my girlfriend the other day."

"You dirty fucking liar." She accused but laughed despite her scowl. "Sure, but if you molest me at any other time other than necessary, I will junk punch you."

I grinned. "So that's a no on sex then?"

Her expression was alarmed. "Deals off," she said beginning to walk away.

I snatched her hand with mine pulling her back toward me, she stumbled over the tools scattered on the floor and landed against my chest. "I was only joking."

"Good," she finally said.

We didn't have to do much pretending to convince anyone we were girlfriend/boyfriend and we did end up kissing a few times.

My male hormones peaked and attacked her in the back of the hauler at which point she had to push me off her, laughing. She thought it was funny; I did not. I was going through a rough time for sure.

I'd never spent so much time in the shower as I did during that weekend. Being able to kiss Sway whenever I wanted was a little much for me to handle.

The weekend of racing went good. I ended up with a feature win that night at Terre Haute and then two-second place finishes to Justin West at Lernerville and Grandview.

Justin was tearing it up in the USAC Silver Crown divisions with me. After his second championship, he caught the name "Wicked West from the Mid-West."

Another kid who was becoming a definite force was Ryder Christiansen from North Carolina. He was a year younger than us but had significant possibilities as a driver and frequently referred to as the "Beast from the East."

If you ever saw Ryder, at barely five-foot-two, he was hardly a beast.

I didn't have a name that I knew of, or at least they never told me what it was.

That weekend in Terre Haute also marked my first pit fight.

During a heat race, this kid from California, Bret Luther, kept clipping my right rear. I corrected it every time except the fourth time when it sent me into a flip.

This was not acceptable to me and I let him know it.

I should have known my chances of doing damage to a kid nicknamed "Bubba" were poor.

Me, being roughly six-foot-one now, had the guy on height but weight, not so much. I worked out constantly and felt comfortable with my strength but when you encounter a two-hundred-sixty-pound, seventeen-year-old kid, you shouldn't start a fight. I lacked any sane thoughts that night though.

Holding a wet towel to my bloody lip, my dad smirked. "You met

Bubba?"

"Thanks for the warning." I grumbled.

"No problem."

As my junior year progressed, I began contemplating the idea of a girlfriend.

Spencer had started dating Alley, the girl we met coming home from Florida so entertaining the idea of a girlfriend was something I thought I should try and, maybe just maybe, I'd stop thinking about Sway naked.

I could only hope for this at least.

Chelsea Adams was a girl I had been messing around with these days. We had a few classes together and she frequently hung out at the track as the trophy girl from time to time which is how we met.

I never looked twice at girls at school. At the track was different because I thought, "Hey, she's at the track so maybe we share the same interests."

I soon found out that Chelsea knew nothing about racing and hated it. This wasn't lost on me but she was attractive and willing to mess around with me so that satisfied that urge for a while and became a way for me to channel some of my hormone-driven thoughts away from Sway.

There was one problem with this. Sway hated Chelsea. So when I told her I wouldn't be going to Tommy's party that night, she wasn't exactly ecstatic with me.

Sway's reaction, "Are you ...?" her voice halted but I knew what she was asking.

"Yeah ..." I muttered unable to speak the words loud enough. "We're going to the movies."

I couldn't understand why it was so hard to tell Sway but I felt like I shouldn't be telling her this. Yeah she was my best friend but it felt as though I was cheating on her when I wasn't.

"Have fun," she simply said and walked toward Tommy who was carrying a keg into his parentless house.

I felt an unfamiliar sadness seeing her walk away that I didn't recognize. Was it wrong to see someone else? I thought we were friends. Did she want me for something more?

I hardly enjoyed the movies. Thinking of Sway's reaction had me puzzled and constantly assessing the situation like a goddamn girl. I almost checked to see if my balls were still there.

Chelsea had other ideas and we ended up leaving early and making out in the passenger seat of my car.

When she pulled her shirt over her shoulders, I stopped her.

"I need to get going."

Her eyes searched mine. "You don't want to ..." she motioned to my erection she was currently sitting on.

I did, believe me I did, but not with her. I felt nothing toward her besides physical excitement she was providing by writhing around on my lap. Other than that, it wasn't much more stimulating than the pornos I had stolen from Spencer's stash.

"No ... I have to get up early." I told her and drove her home without another word.

When I got home, I threw myself against my bed when I noticed my cell phone vibrate. I had a voicemail from Tommy.

"Sway is drunk off her ass at my house. Can you come get her? My parents will kill me if they find her in my room."

When I got there, Sway was sitting on Dylan Grady's lap, kissing him.

I was pissed.

Glaring at Tommy, I took hold of his jacket when he tried to run from me.

"What the fuck?" I shoved him against the wall. "I told you to keep an eye on her?"

"I did ... see," he motioned to her with wide-eyes. "There she is ... I've watched her the entire night."

Tommy has always been scared of me, for good reason. Right

about now he looked like he was about to shit himself.

It was hard not to chuckle when his appearance matched his hair color.

Tommy had this curly orange hair that looked like Carrot Top or something you'd see on a clown. I usually steered clear of orange heads because the orange hair just didn't seem right to me and usually meant the individual was off their rocker in some way but Tommy was cool.

I punched his shoulder. He rocked back on his heels reaching for the doorframe to steady himself. "I said *watch* her, not let her make out with that douche."

I strode up to them determined to give Dylan a piece of my mind. I stopped a few feet shy of them when I heard Sway whisper to him, "Let's go outside. I need some air."

They stood and walked outside. I don't know if she saw me standing there but I'm sure she didn't because she walked right past me and left with Dylan.

Frustrated, I left and told Tommy to keep her keys with him so she couldn't drive. I couldn't control who she left with but I wouldn't let her drive drunk.

I spent the remainder of the night replacing the rear axle on my car before tomorrow night's race at Elma while thinking of ways to convince Sway she could do better than Dylan.

I couldn't come up with anything. Nothing that made any sense at least.

I didn't want to stand in her way but I also thought she was far better off *without* someone like Dylan. Not understanding the pain I felt when I saw her kissing Dylan was also throwing me into a spin.

I'd never seen Sway kiss someone else other than her dad and it was also something I *never* wanted to see again.

Months passed and the school year progressed.

Sway never talked about Dylan with me and I never spoke about Chelsea. I guess you could say she was my girlfriend to the outside eye but I hardly admitted it to Sway or myself. Chelsea and I continued to go on dates, mess around, and then I took her home. It wasn't love; it wasn't even lust. It was filling a crack I knew was there but also refused to look to see how the crack originated in the first place.

Chelsea was all right, but she lacked a personality. Get her talking for more than a few minutes and you quickly realized the dye she used in her blonde hair had killed one too many brain cells.

I don't know if I need to point this out, but I hated high school, absolutely hated it. The high school experience alone is an emotional rollercoaster. Hell, our teenage years themselves were enough and then you add the pressures of co-existing together with a bunch of other crazy teens ... stupid.

All the hype around school was discussions of who was going to junior prom and with whom. I had no desire whatsoever to go to a high school dance. But, no, my mom was forcing me to go. Something about needing to be a normal teenager and I was only partially paying attention to her.

Sway and I had originally planned on going together when she backed out and said she couldn't. I knew it wasn't that she couldn't but that she didn't want to. We equally hated high school.

Knowing my mom wouldn't let me back out, I was forced to go with Chelsea.

The night of junior prom, I was pouting in my room while dressing in my tuxedo. The fact that I had to wear a monkey suit to the event was yet another bullshit tradition I was not so happy with.

I decided to call Sway to let her know how upset I was with her backing out. It went straight to voicemail so I expressed my concerns with: *"I hate you. Come rescue me."*

I wasn't sure how long I'd been sitting in my room sulking and wondering if I could make myself appear sick when I heard a tap at the window. I turned to see Sway standing there, balancing herself on a ladder.

My first concern should have been how in the hell Sway made it to my second story window but it wasn't; it was relief. I had no intention of going to that goddamn school dance nor did I want my pictures taken as a reminder that I was forced to attend in the first place.

"What are you doing?"

"You said you needed to be rescued. Are you coming or not?" Sway asked breathlessly. "The food is getting cold."

"You brought food?"

"Well, yeah, I was hungry."

"I haven't climbed out my window in years." I admitted climbing out nonetheless. After falling about five feet, I landed on my ass with Sway standing over me laughing.

"Smooth Riley. Real smooth,"

I glared at her brushing grass and dirt from my tux. "I should have changed."

Sway glanced my direction.

"Nah, you look good." She winked. "Keep it on."

That's when I finally looked at Sway's appearance. While she looked beautiful as always, I had to laugh at her attire. She had on a black tutu over her jeans. "What's with the tutu?"

"It's prom isn't it?" Her brow furrowed like I was stupid for asking. "This is my dress."

I shook my head. It fit her personality perfectly. She wasn't the type of girl to go for the gown. She was simplicity.

A few minutes later, we were sitting inside Emma's tree house eating Chinese food. I could always count on Sway to bail me out of situations like this. I laughed to myself at the thought of Chelsea looking for me at the dance but I was almost certain she'd find someone to dance with. There were times were I felt badly for the way I treated Chelsea but I was also well aware of the guys she flirted with, and did God knows what with, when I was out of town. I wasn't stupid. We were both using each other.

In the distance, we watched as Tommy picked up Emma for the dance. They were going as friends but that didn't stop me from threatening to cut off his balls if he tried anything.

Mom fussed endlessly over her dress while we laughed. I knew damn well I'd catch hell from mom over this but, like always, I didn't care.

As I took a bite of my egg roll, I noticed Sway gazing at Mom and Emma talking.

Unbuttoning the top buttons of my undershirt, I attempted to get more comfortable.

"Do you miss her?" I asked softly leaning into her shoulder.

"Miss who?" I knew she knew who I was referring to but was stalling. She fidgeted with the ruffles on her tutu.

"Your mom?"

Sway was silent for a long moment eating her noodles before sighing and leaned back on the wooden floor of the tree house. Setting down my food, I leaned back on my elbows to lay next to her.

"I miss her." She mused nodding once. "I don't remember much about her. I wish I did ... I feel like I'm constantly forgetting memories that I wish I wouldn't."

"What do you remember?"

We had talked about Rachel every now and then but it wasn't a typical conversation. Sway was a happy-go-lucky type girl and that's what I loved about her. It was refreshing. She'd rather have good memories than bad and she'd rather laugh than cry.

"I still remember what she smelled like." I watched her face closely as a tear slide down her cheek. "Bananas and coconut. It was a perfume she had I assume but I'll never forget it."

"I'm sorry," I reached for her hand taking it in mine intertwining our fingers together. "I shouldn't have asked."

"No," she wiped tears away. "I miss her. It's okay to talk about it. With you, I can talk about it."

"Come here," I pulled her into my arms trying to comfort her in any way I could.

Though I had an idea of the pain, I had no idea how much living without her mom hurt her. Other than my Uncle Lane dying when I was nine, we hadn't lost anyone in our family. My grandparents were still alive and, aside from my mom's parents who had died in a car accident on New Year's Eve when she was seven, I'd never had to deal with this kind of loss.

My mom did and I think that's why she and Sway got along so well. She understood what Sway was going through.

"Thanks for not going to the dance." She told me after a good ten minutes of silence.

"No problem," I chuckled against her shoulder. "Do you know what would make this night fun?"

"I could use some entertainment." She turned in my arms. "What did you have in mind?"

"Refilling Emma's lotions with glue again and cutting holes in Spencer's underwear." I stood to help her up. "Our usual madness,"

"Sounds like fun. Let's see what Hershey's up to tonight."

I laughed. "Remember to lock the gate this time." Hershey was old man Roger's cow. Sway and Hershey had a love-hate relationship. That cow fucking hated her. Sway thought Hershey was some kind of horse and tried to ride her every chance she could and, well, Hershey had other ideas about that. She took every opportunity she could to shit on Sway. Literally.

The following Monday at school I was faced with an angry Chelsea.

"Where the fuck were you?" Chelsea asked pushing my shoulder.

Sway, Tommy, Emma and I were all gathered around my truck before school began.

"What are you talking about?" I smirked noticing Sway moved from standing beside me to stand next to Emma.

"You stood me up at prom!" she yelled causing other classmates to turn and stare. "How could you?"

"I'm sure you made due." I retorted noticing a purplish mark down the side of her neck. My eyes narrowed at her and then moved to the mark on her neck and then back to hers.

She knew damn well I knew.

"Have a nice day, Chelsea." I winked and walked away to my first class.

Sway, laughing, followed Tommy and Emma toward their math class.

Emma began taking extra classes this year to graduate with us a year sooner so this put her in a few of our classes. That was fine until she ended up in my biology class.

Emma and I didn't get along for obvious reasons. Get two people together who have obsessive compulsive tendencies and then add the need to be a perfectionist ... we didn't mix. With her need to rub lotion on her body continuously and my obsession with anything on my skin, she made me crazy.

She bumped my elbow sometime before class began. "I need a pencil."

"So get one." I replied looking over my paper making sure I did it correctly.

"Hey, dumbass, that's why I asked you for one." She shot back kicking me.

Naturally, I kicked her back. And, before I knew it, we were kicking each other like a couple of kindergarten kids.

"No ... you said you *need* a pencil. Nowhere in that sentence did you say 'Can I borrow a pencil,' now did you?"

"You're an asshole." She whispered and walked away from me to retrieve a pencil from the teacher.

Chelsea caught me again after third period. "Did you stand me up for Sway?" her tone demanding and accusing. The way it always was.

Focused on my homework that I had failed to do the night before, I never looked up and I contemplated not answering her as well. I didn't feel the need to explain myself. I already had to tell my mom why and that was enough for me. In the end, Mom forced Sway and I to dress up so she could take pictures, either that or she threatened to sell my car.

Guess which option I chose?

I was in my tuxedo and forcing Sway to put that damn tutu back on within seconds. I'd grown accustomed to the tutu and found it incredibly adorable on her.

"Sway is none of your business." I answered, my jaw clenching tightly.

"I want to know where I stand with you. You're always leaving for her. I know you want her so why do you even mess around with me?"

"Why do *you* even bother with me? I know you see other guys."

Chelsea was silent for a moment, her finger drumming against her book. "Despite what *you* think, I do like you Jameson but you're taken."

I didn't get a chance to respond as Mr. Simmons walked in to begin class.

The entire hour-long class I contemplated what she said.

Was I taken?

I knew damn well what she referring to. Maybe I was taken but that still didn't change the fact that Sway was my best friend. She was not my girlfriend and I had no claim on her. Girlfriends complicate everything. You go from being friends and then once you slap the official title on it, things change. Emotions get involved, insecurities rule and feelings get hurt. I didn't want that with Sway.

I wanted the bond. I wanted the strong emotional connection we had and I didn't want it to end.

What if I hurt her? What if she didn't feel the same way and hurt me? Most of all, what if we did get together, I'm sure we'd have sex and then what? Would I feel the same way or was all this emotion for her because I couldn't have her in the ways I wanted? Infatuation maybe?

Once school ended, Sway caught a ride with Tommy and I, as

usual, headed to the track to blow off some steam.

Looking back on this time of my life, I hated being a teenager because, in the face of everything you're dealing with, you have emotions. The shitty thing about those emotions was not being able to decipher what in the hell they meant or why you felt that way in the first place.

Gauge – An instrument mounted on the dashboard, used to monitor engine conditions such as fuel pressure, oil pressure and temperature, water pressure and temperature, and RPMs (revolutions per minute).

"Where are you going, kid?"

"The track. I'm meeting Sway there. She's coming with us to Cottage Grove." I told my dad on the way out the door.

For my birthday last year, my parents bought me a car. I had to pay for half of it and whatever amount I was able to come up with they matched. All that hard-earned money bought me a 1967 Ford Shelby Mustang GT 500 that needed an engine.

Yeah, I was spoiled but I loved that car. A few weeks after I got the car, my dad went for a ride with me and squeezed himself into the non-existent back seat. He refused to sit in the front seat like a normal person would. Instead, he insisted I drive him around town like I was driving Miss Daisy.

Though I loved the car, it wasn't exactly practical. After four speeding tickets in two weeks, it was time to look for something else or I was about to lose my license.

Eventually, I traded the car for a truck, a 1996 Ford F-250 so I could haul my sprint car around.

Over the last summer, it was rare for Sway and I to ever be apart.

Chelsea and I dated on and off but I couldn't stand her longer than a few weeks before I was telling her to get lost. Then Sway would get to me again and I found myself looking to Chelsea or whoever was available as a distraction.

Sway never did anything to piss me off, quite the opposite. Everything she did turned me on.

I began dating girls in an attempt to hide the physical attraction I was feeling toward Sway and kept my distance from her and her body in fear that I'd slip and do something to ruin the intense bond we had. I could tell her anything, as could she. Having this intense bond meant I knew when something was up with her, like today.

Last night we were at the track for the Northern Sprint Tour and she had disappeared somewhere between the feature events.

I was racing but when I made it back to the pits that night, Sway wasn't around. I tried calling her afterward to see where she went but she never answered.

"Where'd you go last night?" I asked once she got inside.

Sway threw her bag on the floor and looked over at me. Her red puffy eyes focused on mine. "I went home. I wasn't feeling good."

I scanned her eyes, searching for the answer I knew they'd give me. She was lying and that's not something we did. We never lied to each other.

"Bullshit."

It took some convincing but on the way to the shop to load my car, she admitted she met up with Dylan Grady. I didn't feel the need to ask questions. The revolting nauseating feeling in the pit of my stomach kept me from asking what happened. It was comparable to the night I saw them making out at Tommy's party.

Dylan Grady was a player; had been and always would be.

Sure, he was popular and good looking as the girls would say but his popularity did nothing for his personality or lack of one. The fact that she was hanging around with him in general enraged me but I kept my cool. I wasn't her only friend and I wasn't her boyfriend. I had no right to dictate who she hung out with or where she went.

So instead of replying to her confession, I only nodded and drove to the shop in silence. When we got there, Sway went over to Alley, who was now living with Spencer, and Emma and began talking while Spencer, Dad and me loaded the car.

By the end of their conversation, Sway was crying in Alley's arms and Emma looked pissed. Emma may be the youngest of the Riley kids, not to mention the smallest, but she showed the biggest heart when she wasn't lathering herself with lotion.

If anyone crossed us, it was Emma who felt it and took action upon herself. If there is one positive thing I could say about Emma, aside from being ridiculously obsessive compulsive, it is that she would stick up for her family above all else.

"What are you doing?" I asked Emma as she rummaged around through the toolbox.

"Looking for a wrench," She seethed looking over at me. "I'm going to kill Dylan."

"Hold on there, why would you do that?" Spencer asked reaching for the wrench. I held her back from retrieving it again.

Her expression changed when she saw Sway approaching the shop. "He ... Sway ... *oh,* never mind." She finally mumbled when she realized she'd already given away too much.

Sway, in a slightly better mood and twirling a sucker in her mouth, bounded back inside the shop.

"You boys ready yet?" She chirped sitting down on the rear tire of my sprint car, with the sucker.

Holy fuck.

Distracted by the sucker around her lips for obvious reasons, I turned and made myself think of something else. Like why my sister wanted to kill Dylan.

Spencer drove up with Alley and Emma while Sway and I hauled my sprint car with my truck. I took the time to try to talk to her, after she threw away the sucker and I could look at her.

"Why did Emma want to kill Dylan earlier today?" I blurted out somewhere after we made it to Portland.

Sway smiled and looked down at her cut-off shorts, toying with the fringed fabric between her fingers.

"It's nothing Jameson, he's a jerk. That's all."

I left her alone, knowing my pushing the subject was bothering her.

Last night at Elma I had good run—not great—but good and ended up with a third place finish in the feature. Tonight at Cottage Grove was absolutely nuts. In the start, things couldn't have looked any worse, so I thought.

I was lined up fourteenth and fell back to eighteenth within the first three laps. Ryder, the kid from North Carolina, was racing side-by-side with me, taking every line I wanted. Every time I was beginning to make some ground, the caution flew and every time it took a few laps for my car to get into the groove.

My car was pushing which wasn't unusual when you're loaded down with fuel in the beginning laps. I hung on hoping the handling would improve once the fuel burned off.

The handling improved but my luck never did.

With nine laps to go, running in third, a bolt broke in the oil filter adapter base. Usually this wouldn't have been that big of a deal until oil shot into the header and the goddamn thing went up in flames. Luckily, I wasn't in it.

So there I was a junked car, a best friend—who'd said not more than two words to me since we arrived—and a drunk brother.

Later that night after loading up the car, we didn't leave right away. Instead, we stood around talking to Ryder and his team along with a few other drivers. I'd become friends with a few like Justin and Ryder.

Sway was around but I hadn't seen her in about an hour when I noticed her sitting on the back of my tailgate staring at her feet as she dangled them over the edge.

I excused myself and sat down next her. “You okay?”

“Not really.” She sniffed rubbing the sleeve of her navy blue sweatshirt across her wet cheeks. “But I’ll be fine.”

“Sway, what’s going on with you?” I asked softly as I leaned into her shoulder and then eventually wrapped my arm around her shoulders and pulled her against me.

Melting into my embrace, she was about to answer when a crowd off in the distance of the pits caught our attention.

Dylan frequently traveled around with the Northern Sprint Tour as his cousin, Nick Grady, raced on it as well.

There Dylan stood with his arms around some girl I’d never seen before, kissing her.

Sway sighed and looked down at her feet.

“Should have known,” She muttered hanging her head. With her head down, that’s when I noticed scratches and a bruise along the side of her neck.

“Is that what this is about? Dylan?” I asked, my voice rising with each word. “Did he do that to your neck?”

My jaw clenched as adrenaline began pumping.

“Jameson,” her voice held warning I didn’t appreciate at the time, “leave it alone.”

“I won’t leave it alone!” I shouted causing a few crewmembers of Ryder’s to turn and look over at us. “Something is up and for someone who swore to never lie to me, it’s pretty fucking evident you’re lying right now.”

Anger flushed over her features instantly. “You need to mind your own fucking business!” she pushed against my chest. “Just because you’re my best friend doesn’t mean you get to know everything I do or who.”

That right there confirmed my theory. She’d slept with him.

I sighed and hung my head, my gut knotted, as I avoiding her questioning gaze at my reaction.

I never thought it would feel like that.

"Why him?" My voice was soft and surprisingly calm.

"Why not?" she asked. "It's not like anyone else has showed any interest."

I was also to blame for this.

Most men that knew Sway also knew me and knew we were together more than apart. They steered clear of her, scared that I'd kick the shit out of them or, better yet, my beast of a brother would. She had no chance of meeting someone who would always be there for her if I didn't back away.

We didn't speak of Dylan again, mostly because I didn't want details. It was bad enough that I knew she was no longer a virgin and she gave it away to a guy like Dylan Grady. He wasn't gentle with her; that was apparent by the marks on her neck. Sway deserved her first time to be all that romantic shit that girls wanted and it wasn't.

When Spencer came to find us to leave, Sway was plastered.

Tommy had rounded up a case of beer while Sway sang "Total Eclipse of the Heart" at the top of her lungs four times.

When she began the fifth time, I removed her beer and politely told her she sounded similar to a dying cat and needed to get some sleep.

"I don't sound good?" she questioned, her eyes drooping.

"No, honey, you sound horrible and need to get some sleep." I told her carrying her to my truck.

Sway spent the remainder of the night with her head in my lap crying, while I drove the truck home.

I had no idea what to say to comfort her so I was simply there and never let my hand leave her back, hoping I was providing what she needed. I held her tightly. I wanted to lock my arms around her and never let go, never let her be exposed to any kind of hurt like this. She clung to me, her entire body shaking with her sobs.

I gave her everything I could that night by being there and holding her.

That following Monday at school, I had the chance of meeting up with Dylan. I would say this happened by accident but I'd be lying. We didn't know each other outside of the occasional "Hey" but he knew who I was.

I was pissed that he had the nerve to sleep with Sway and then never talk to her again so I opted for physical terminology. I think he knew exactly what I meant by that one punch to his jaw and never said a word to stop me.

The school had other ideas about this and suspended me for three days. It was fine by me. I had a crispy car to salvage and school was in the way.

This wasn't the first time I defended Sway's honor and it wouldn't be the last. She meant the world to me and I do anything for her. I kept my distance when she showed awareness in other guys at school or at the track in fear I'd hold her back. I did what any best friend would do. I was there when she needed me.

Since moving full time to sprint cars when I turned sixteen, I'd begun racing on the Northern Sprint Tour but I also raced occasionally in USAC races. I was doing anything to get seat time and log laps. I needed all the experience I could get and this, once again, led me to the Dirt Cup in Skagit the summer I turned seventeen.

It wasn't hard to make the change between midgets and sprints but there were differences to get used to. The biggest differences were the wings. I preferred running non-winged cars but I raced anything I could and that left me in a 360-Sprint my dad had built over the winter.

The difference between the non-winged and winged cars was the down force. You'd be amazed how much down force those wings produce effectively pushing the car around the track. There was not as much driver ability required once you add the wing. Take it away and you'd better hang on. They slide through corners easily and produce some of the best side-by-side racing around.

I enjoyed the side-by-side racing in midgets and non-winged

cars but I also loved the power the sprint cars provided. They were designed to go fast and that was exactly what they did but they could also cause some violent and brutal crashes.

Much like the one I got into that weekend at the Dirt Cup in Skagit, which is a 3/10 clay oval track outside of Burlington, Washington.

I preferred the clay tracks to dirt for obvious reasons such as the higher levels of grip it provided. The downside to clay though was it was an art to get the surface prepared. Too much water and the track was pretty much impossible to race on. Too little water and the track turned into a tire-shredding monster.

That night the track had tons of grip and it would be what most in the dirt world would refer to as "hookey" meaning the moisture content was just right.

With the surface exactly the way I liked it, I was running fast on the high line but this also meant I was dangerous.

There were a number of ways to get caught up in a wreck in a sprint car but some can be worse than others.

I took half the goddamn field out with mine when I was sent into a wheel stand after a driver moved up the track slightly and made contact with my left rear. My front end lifted and it was over. I tried to correct it with horsepower but it did nothing but let the staggered tires end my night.

My car turned hard on the left rear and flipped seven times ending up upside down on the backstretch, only on the *other* side of the catch fence.

Like I said, sprint car crashes are violent and happen so quickly that in the blink of an eye it's over.

When my car finally stopped flipping and the safety crew helped me to the pits, Mom, Emma, and Sway were huddling around me repeatedly asking me if I was okay.

If you were watching that wreck from the stands, it looked worse than it actually was.

"I'm fine." I announced pushing past them to assess the damage to my car.

The thing was, I wasn't fine. My head was spinning and seeing double vision was not normal, at least I didn't think so. Once the adrenaline wore off, I started to feel the pain. My neck was sore and extremely tender to touch, my head was pounding and I was positive I had at least one broken rib or two.

That night on the way home, Spencer drove and I laid in the back seat in Sway's lap. Times like this, it was easy to pretend we could be more than friends. With my head rested against her thighs, she played with my hair and I began to relax.

"Are you feeling okay?" she asked leaning forward to look at my face.

I flashed a quick smile and wink.

It wasn't long before I sat up. Not only was my head pounding worse by laying down, but I was also aware of what laying with my head positioned at an area where I desperately wanted a part of me buried in was doing to me. Currently my blood flow was being directed to a part of my body that wasn't allowed to make decisions when it came to Sway.

"You need to stay up," I told him gauging his unsteady demeanor once we made it into his room. Poor guy got his bell rung out there tonight.

"What are we watching?" I asked when he put a movie in and staggered back to his bed, collapsing against me.

I hadn't slept yet so why not stay awake all night? We did this a lot. More times than I cared for. He usually was so amped after a race that he couldn't sleep until the wee hours of the morning but now with a head injury he wanted to sleep.

I couldn't. I was a wreck.

We had just gotten back from Skagit and Jameson was in no condition to sleep with his concussion. He was loopy and the drugs we gave him were beginning to wear off.

Just so you know, a race car driver's idea of pain medication was a beer and three *Excedrin* ... not exactly healthy.

He was about to answer me when Emma came stumbling into his room singing "Take my Breath Away" at the top of her lungs.

I tackled her against the hardwood floor, "If you know what's best for you—stop singing that fucking song!" I seethed.

Jameson and I equally hated that song and she fucking knew it.

When I first met Emma, I thought, "*Oh, she's sweet.*"

I was wrong and understood why Jameson petitioned to have her auctioned off at the zoo when she was five. It was where the little weirdo belonged.

I finally got her to leave only after I threatened to dump out all her lotions and burn her favorite pair of jeans.

Relaxing back on the bed, I asked again. "What movie are we watching?"

"The Exorcist," he yawned, turning off the light on the nightstand, leaving his room dark and then patted his bed. "Lay down with me."

I panicked and voiced my concerns. I hated scary movies almost as much as I hated the word uterus. "It's evident that you forgot what happened when you forced me to watch 'The Shining' when we were thirteen so let me remind you, I pissed the bed for a goddamn week. I might add I still can't look at twins the same way ever again." I ranted while he rolled his eyes. "Oh, and let's not forget when we watched 'Jaws' and I couldn't so much as take a bath for months convinced a Great White would come up through the drain and bite my girly parts off." This time he chuckled. "Then there was the time you insisted we watch that ghastly movie with the birds in it and I couldn't walk outside without thinking a fucking crow was going to peck me to death. This," I pointed at the television, "is a horrible idea!"

"*You're* watching it."

"No, I'm not." I insisted crossing my arms over my chest. "I will not watch it."

I lost that battle real quick and we ended up watching it despite my attempts to knock him off the bed and burn the tape.

Later that night, securely in my own bed at home, I had never experienced being that scared in my life.

There I was, paralyzed with every light in my entire bedroom blazing with my window wide open.

Pulling the covers up higher and covering my face up to eyes, I searched the room wildly for any movement absolutely hating Jameson with every fiber of my being and wanted to kill the little fucker for making me watch that shit.

My paranoid self was beginning to hear things that weren't there and talking to myself.

That's when I heard my phone vibrating on my nightstand and answered immediately when I saw the name.

"I was worried about you. You seemed scared when you left." Jameson said softly his voice thick with sleep. "Are you okay?"

"Are you fucking kidding me? I hate you so much right now. Get your ass over here!"

I refused to sleep alone and since he made me watch that awful shit he was going to stay up with me until I could sleep again. Even if that was weeks from now.

I ran downstairs and was out the door before he even hung up. He met me at the end of my street seeing how our houses were less than a mile away and if you cut through the trees, it took only two minutes to get there.

Why I was running around at three in the morning should have concerned me more than the goddamn movie but I was a chicken shit and I needed Jameson.

I also wanted to kick the shit out of him.

"Sway?" he called from the bushes, hiding in the dark corner of the street.

"Why are you in the bushes? Get out here, asshole," I yelled, sad that I had been reduced to this, but extremely glad to see him.

I kept myself under the dim luminosity of the streetlights above. I had this crazy notion that nothing would attack me if I was lit up.

A few minutes later, we were settled in my bed this time.

"I can't believe a movie has me so freaked out," I mused ashamed of myself. "I feel like a dumbass."

He let out a nervous chuckle leaning back against my headboard.

"Well, I wouldn't say that I'm freaked out. Spooked?" he shrugged. "Yes. That was surprisingly ... believable. Who thought of that shit anyway? My God," he shook his head in disbelief. "I have some serious concerns about that director now. I mean, can he sleep at night after filming that?"

"Great, now I'm scared again." I started laughing at him as he leveled me a serious look.

We sat there laughing for a few minutes at how childish this was while he wrapped his arms around me pulling me flush against his body. It was comforting.

"That's nice. I think I feel better." I added after a few minutes of snuggling.

"Uh, me too, not too spooked anymore."

"How's your head feeling?" I reached out to run my fingers over the bruises forming on his forearms where he'd obviously hit objects inside the car.

"I'm fine, sore ... but fine."

You don't realize the dangers of racing when you're watching but they're there. A slip of an inch in a sprint car and you're flying through the air. I've seen Jameson wreck and I admit that it gives me a heart attack each time but I also know that he is doing what he loves. I was in no position to tell him to stop. I could only hope that he is safe.

We eventually fell asleep on my bed wrapped around each other because I refused to leave any space between us just as I did during the movie.

He didn't complain.

When we woke up the next morning, still wrapped around each other, Charlie was not so pleased that Jameson was in my bed.

"Sway?" he called out as he opened my door. "Oh, sorry ..." his deep voice trailed off but then he took a double take. "Jameson?"

Jameson, not completely awake shot up in my bed.

"Huh ... what ...?" he glanced around and then looked at me and back to Charlie and then moaned out in pain when he realized how sore he was as he tried to untangle himself from me.

Charlie chuckled but didn't look happy. "What are you doing here, Jameson?"

"Uh ... I was spooked?" he looked at me arching an eyebrow as if he needed confirmation.

"Yes ... spooked." I glanced to Charlie. "We watched 'The Exorcist' last night after we got home. It was a disaster. I don't think I'll ever sleep with the lights off again."

Charlie laughed again. "I almost shit myself when I watched that movie." He shuddered and began to leave before looking back over his shoulder. "Jameson, your mom called for you. I told her you weren't here but apparently, I'm wrong."

By the look on his face, I had a feeling I'd hear about this later.

When the door clicked shut, Jameson groaned again and leaned back on my bed before grabbing a pillow and placing it over his hips.

I giggled.

"Problems?"

"Shut up." He snapped and hobbled to my bathroom.

I made my way downstairs to see Charlie sitting at the kitchen table rubbing his head, his face buried in his hands. "You okay?"

His head shot up.

"Yeah, I'm fine." He cleared his throat reaching for his paper. "Listen, I don't want boys spending the night. I don't think that's a good idea."

"I know," I agreed pouring myself a bowl of Captain Crunch. "It wasn't planned. Like I said, we were a little freaked out by that movie."

"I know, but just ... be careful okay."

"It's not like that dad. Jameson and I are friends, nothing more." I said this as though I was trying to convince myself of it when really, I think I was.

I felt something for him but I had no idea what it was. I couldn't even decide on what to wear in the morning most days let alone decipher feelings.

Charlie looked at me for a long moment before narrowing his eyes at me. "Have you thought of college yet?"

I shrugged.

"Not really. It's a little overwhelming." I pulled my hair back into a ponytail before digging into my cereal.

"That's life, kid."

I snorted, bad idea with milk in your mouth. I ended up inhaling a crunch berry up my nose. "And I thought deciding on what cereal to eat in the morning was hard." I choked out.

He chuckled carrying his empty coffee cup over to the counter. "Well, kid, it's time I made it to the track. Some people don't have the luxury of sitting around all day eating cereal. *Some people* have to work."

"Some people will enjoy doing nothing today. Some people have fun."

I sort of zoned out reading the back of the cereal box in front of me as Charlie stared out the kitchen window.

"Hey, Sway ... is Jameson okay?"

"Uh ... I think so, why?" I looked up from the box glancing around the kitchen to see Jameson in the front yard, puking.

Concerned, I ran out there.

"Are you all right?" I asked frantically rubbing his back over his T-shirt.

"I think so ... my head hurts." He took in a deep breath before removing his T-shirt to wipe his face of sweat and puke.

"Maybe you should go to the doctor."

He slumped back in the grass. "I'm fine … it's just a headache. I guess I took a pretty hard hit last night."

I watched him for a moment. The sharp defined lines of his stomach contracting with each deep breath he inhaled and exhaled.

I've been around enough race car drivers to know they will *never* admit when they're hurt and will *never* go to the doctor. Most say it's nothing a beer can't fix.

"Maybe you should take a shower." I suggested. "That might make you feel better."

He finally smiled. "With you?"

And he's back.

"No," I laughed. "You take a shower—without me."

"Oh," he stuck out his bottom lip. "It might make me feel better."

"I don't think so, champ. That's what Chelsea and your hand are for."

I helped him to the bathroom and he tried to drag me in there with him laughing and I slapped him. He winced, I felt bad but not bad enough to get in there with him.

Jameson always teased that he was attracted to me but I chalked it up to friendly flirting. All guys did that, even Tommy flirted with me and I thought for sure Tommy was gay when I first met him. It didn't mean Jameson had feelings and it didn't mean I had any for him outside of friendship.

I was obviously no judge on attraction—Dylan would be a prime example. I thought he liked me, he said he did, we had sex and as soon as he pulled out, it was over. He never spoke to me again, just walked away.

I'd never felt so used, disgusting and dirty in my life as I did laying in the back of my old beat up truck half naked.

I don't understand why people can't decipher their emotions but I knew I couldn't and neither could any other teenager I knew.

I also didn't trust my feelings—look at Dylan. I felt something for him, so I thought and look how that turned out.

I had an attraction to Jameson as it was becoming apparent with my constant glances at his rock hard body but I also saw his desire to race. I've met a lot of racers at the track but no one ever showed the desire to be the best like Jameson did. He was focused, determined, and, above all else, he had the ability. That combined with his burning desire made him unstoppable.

He was a natural on the track. He was born to do this and I wouldn't get in his way and I *wouldn't* be a distraction.

I would be the friend he needed and not the distraction he didn't.

Dialing In – A driver and crew making setup adjustments to achieve the car's optimum handling characteristics.

My senior year I decided I was going to race with the World of Outlaws when they were in Skagit so that left Sway and I traveling together on a Tuesday night since the race was on a Wednesday.

After convincing Charlie that I needed her there, he agreed to let her skip school.

Spencer, Tommy and Emma also came along. This was our usual traveling team aside from Alley who decided to sit this one out.

We never had money to pay anyone who helped us since any money I did have went right back into my car. Tommy never once acted as though he wanted to be paid for helping. We did pay his way and fed him. If you knew Tommy, you knew that all he wanted was food and beer; money didn't matter. It didn't matter to any of us as all any of us lived for was the next race.

I always thought I was taking something away from Spencer and Emma being the only one who raced but I soon understood that's what they loved. They loved racing as much as I did and being the supportive family we came from, they did everything they could to help me.

I was loved, that's for sure, but that doesn't mean they didn't make me crazy. At the end of the day, we loved each other and they were the best fans I could ask for.

It wasn't unusual for Sway and me to be riding together in my truck and the others to ride in Tommy's car. I preferred it that way for less distractions but the trip there ended up being the worst distraction of all.

Just outside of Seattle, Sway was searching around in the backseat for a CD when she turned abruptly and sat back in her seat. I glanced around to see if she saw a cop or something but nothing, just open highway.

"Jameson, what's that smell?" she asked, her hand flew to her nose.

"Huh?" I didn't smell anything but her coconut perfume.

Sway slapped me. "Seriously, it smells in here. Roll your window down." She instructed rolling hers down frantically. She turned around again and stuck her ass up in the air digging around on the floor. "I still smell it, what is it?"

"I don't smell anything."

She huffed dramatically flopping back in the seat. She kept looking at me before averting her disgusted gaze out the window as a red Lexus flew past us.

I thought she'd moved on from the smell but then she groaned.

"Christ almighty, what the fuck is that?"

"I don't smell anything!" I snapped annoyed she was making such a big deal out of this.

"Of course you don't," she went back to searching around on the floor in the back seat, "you're used to it!"

A few minutes later, she pulled out a box I didn't recognize that clearly had something die in it. "Where'd that come from?"

"I don't know—your backseat?" Her eyebrow arched.

I smelled Spencer behind this one. He once put a dead rat in the vent in my bedroom and if you have ever tried to get that smell out of a heater vent, it is fucking hopeless.

When Sway opened the box, I nearly wrecked the fucking truck at the site of week old sushi covered in maggots and God knows what else.

When she puked on me after opening the box, I did wreck the truck in the ditch.

We sat there for a moment when I finally brought the truck to a halt on the side of the road, after barreling into the ditch, there appeared to be a stump that came out of nowhere. I hit that, too.

"Really?" I simply said when the airbag blew up in my face *after* the wreck.

So much for safety.

There I sat alongside the road in nothing but my underwear waiting for the tow truck while Sway laughed.

"I'm so glad you're amused by this."

"Me, too," she said, giggling again to the point she looked like she was crying. This was yet another instance in my life where I was not impressed with her lack of concern for me or my truck.

"I hope you piss yourself."

She stopped laughing altogether and looked appalled that I said that. "That's an awful thing to say. Why would you say something like that?"

"Oh, I don't know," I gestured to the no clothes and wrecked truck. "You puked on me and made me wreck *my* truck."

"Listen, asshole," she scowled, her mood completely changing from appalled to pissed shoving me in the chest, "*that* wasn't my fault."

"Really?" I challenged.

She shrugged carelessly as if this wasn't a big deal. "Well, maybe the puking part but you're the one who left sushi in your truck for a week! Who does that shit?" she held her hand up when I went to speak. "And, worst of all, you couldn't smell it! It was rancid."

"I give up!" I yelled throwing my arms up against the deployed air bag.

"As you should," she smiled triumphantly. "This is one battle you ain't winning, Riley."

When we finally made it to the track, I was not in a good mood.

This might have had something to do with the fact that my truck had a smashed bumper and reeked of puke but that's beside the point.

What was irritating me now was walking around the pits in my fucking underwear while other drivers whistled and made catcalls at me because I had no clothes to wear.

I found my racing suit so I had something to wear and then was met with Chelsea staring at me with her sister.

The day kept getting better and better.

"What are you doing here?" I asked zipping my racing suit. I told her to stay home but, no, she never fucking listened to what I said. I'm surprised she even listened to what track I was going to be at.

"I wanted to wish you luck." She cooed with a smile and wrapped her arms around my neck.

I sighed pulling her away.

"I need to get to the drivers' meeting."

I didn't have time for this shit today. A bad showing at a World of Outlaw race did nothing for your image in racing and nothing for my determination to step out of Jimi's shadow.

I needed to be on my game and with the way the day was starting out, I wasn't on my game.

"Where's Sway?"

"She's changing in the bathrooms." I kept walking to my car as they followed close behind.

A few drivers glanced at Chelsea. There was no denying that she was attractive but their attention to her didn't bother me.

Most of all, I *hated* when Chelsea came to the races. She spent the majority of the time bitching about dirt. Anyone wears anything white to a racetrack is asking for problems and she always did.

I made it about twenty feet from the pit bleachers where I stopped and signed a few autographs from some of the kids racing quarter midgets that night.

Chelsea sighed beside me, "Why do they always have to interrupt us?"

I scowled at Chelsea when the child frowned.

"Here you go, buddy." I handed him his program back and offered him my hat as well.

"Thanks, Jameson." He chimed skipping away, thankfully undeterred by Chelsea's comments.

Sway walked out of the bathrooms in fresh clothes before I could say something sarcastic to Chelsea. I may or may not have turned a hose loose on Sway when we got here to get even but, in my defense, she deserved it. I had to walk through the pits in my black boxer briefs because of her.

"I hope you piss yourself ..." Sway mocked walking up to me. "You're such an asshole."

"Do you always follow Jameson to his races?" Chelsea asked her as she wrapped her arms around me. "You don't have much of a life, do you?"

I wanted to smack her for talking to Sway that way.

"I was invited." Sway replied glaring in my direction. "Were you?"

Chelsea arched an eyebrow at Sway while running her right hand down my stomach—I caught it before it went further. "Well, I am his girlfriend."

Not that word again.

I groaned in misery. "Sway, Tommy is looking for you. Can you give him this," I handed her my credentials. "Chelsea, can I talk to you for a minute?" I asked once Sway walked away.

She smiled possessively. "Sure, babe."

Rolling my eyes, I walked with her toward the pit bleachers to get ready for the drivers' meeting.

"You need to stay in the stands if you're going to be here. Only crew members are allowed down here."

"What about Sway? She's not a crew member."

I lost it and threw my hands up in the air.

"Will you stop it?" I yelled. "Just stop! Stop acting so goddamn possessive over everything." My infuriated eyes focused on hers, wide with surprise. "Sway is part of my team. Every week she's out here helping me, what do you do?"

"I help in other ways ... ways she can't." Chelsea purred in my ear standing on her toes to reach around my neck. My harsh clipped tone did nothing to deter her. "Did you forget what I did for you the other night?"

I hadn't forgotten. Wanted too, but, unfortunately, I hadn't.

Until the other night, I had only kissed girls and maybe the occasional dry humping session but nothing underneath clothing. Against my better judgment, I let Chelsea jerk me off after we went to the movies. Since then, she thought she had some materialistic claim over me as though I was hers.

"Are you for real?" I snapped and then realized how childish this all was. "I have to go." I told her and walked away.

When I got to the pit bleachers dad was sitting there with Justin.

"Girl problems?" he asked laughing.

"Fuck you," was my reply.

Yes, I said "fuck you" to my dad. *That's* how annoyed I was.

I hated that I even had to deal with this shit in the first place. I pushed the thoughts aside when Clint, the chief steward for Skagit, rolled up on his 4-wheeler to begin the drivers' meeting. I focused on what was important, racing.

He talked about procedures for the hot laps, time trials, heat races and then the feature events.

I glanced across the track when he started in about cautions and what to do when the yellow came out, as if we didn't know. I watched as the stands began to fill with spectators.

The World of Outlaw series, being a premier division, drew in a hefty crowd. It wasn't unusual to see at least five thousand fans at the track on nights like this.

Looking over at my dad, he was hardly paying attention, having heard this a million times by now. Instead, he watched the water truck as it made continuous laps. The smells of the wet clay surrounded us mixing with sweet methanol.

Justin was yawning. Shey was glaring at Bucky who took his last cigarette and I was irritable with my leg bouncing obsessively against the metal bleachers.

I told myself I'd be getting away from Chelsea and her self-indulgent attitude as soon as possible but I wasn't sure I could.

She's exactly why I found Sway's company so refreshing. She never acted like that. Sure, she was my friend and had no claim as to who I kissed or flirted with but even if she did, Sway was above that, never juvenile. Chelsea was your typical high school girl.

My thoughts were focused once I slid inside my car. I qualified ninth for the main so that wasn't exactly positive but the track was exactly the way I liked it. After a few final adjustments, my car was perfect.

"Do you want to set back the timing?" Tommy asked twirling a wrench in his hands prior to the main.

I shook my head. "No ... it doesn't seem to be changing out there. Just leave it."

Usually if we thought the track was going to turn dry-slick, meaning the moisture had dried up, we would adjust the timing for less horsepower. If we had too much horsepower when the track changed that's when these monsters start with the wheel stands.

Sway, who I hadn't seen since I handed her my credentials, threw a bottle of water my direction and then walked inside the hauler.

"You need to sign the release form again before the feature. They can't read your writing. You're lining up behind Cody in the feature."

Visibly angry, I followed her.

"You okay?" I asked leaning against a stack of tires propped against the wall.

I watched her closely as she fumbled with a spare torsion bar laying on the counter. She was definitely angry but about what?

"Chelsea?" I assumed they exchanged a few words. This wouldn't be the first time.

Sway nodded with her back still turned. "She's a bitch. Don't worry about it."

I flipped out and punched the side of the hauler.

It was one thing to annoy me. It was something else entirely to involve Sway. While anger clouded my judgment, I didn't look at what I punched until it was too late. Instead of punching the plywood, my fist hit a metal beam.

Naturally, this pissed me off even more and I did the only thing I knew to do being seventeen; I threw a childish fit and started throwing shit in an attempt to ease my frustration.

It didn't. It only made me appear like more of an ass along with destroying about five-thousand dollars in race car parts.

Dad, visibly angry, caught me before I climbed in the car for the heat race. His face was a few shades lighter than his red racing suit.

"Get your shit together asshole," he went on furiously. "And you're paying for everything you destroyed." His eyebrow arched as his voice rose nearly to a shout. "Do you understand me?"

"Whatever," I replied. I was still fucking angry and didn't care. I had a quick fuse and it didn't cool off immediately.

He slammed me against the car and my head knocked against the top wing. His hands fisted roughly in my driver's suit before he pulled me closer.

"You will show me respect, Jameson." His usual bright blue eyes darkened as he glared. "I don't care if you think you're better than everyone out here ... you may be but if you don't get that smug fucking attitude of yours under control, it will all be gone before you know it!"

I pushed back against him as pain shot up my wrist from my hand that had punched the wall. I knew it was broken but I refused to acknowledge it.

Jimi pushed me back again. "I don't know what's going on with you but if you want this," he motioned toward the track. "Stop acting like a goddamn child!"

His hands dropped and he walked away without another glance.

I knew he was right but then again, I was seventeen. Like most seventeen-year old males, I didn't care what anyone thought.

I was black flagged four times in a matter of six laps before I finally wrecked myself and Justin coming out of turn three when I tried to pass him four-wide.

Justin was pissed and he had every right to be.

When he came to my pit after we made it back to the pits, I stood there. I had no excuse. It was my fault and I knew it.

"You know," his eyes met mine, hard and irate. "I take a lot from you out there Jameson. We're friends," Justin barked. "But that was bullshit and you know it!"

"I know," I dropped my head as Tommy and Sway approached us. They hung back trying to judge what Justin was about to do, his fists clenched at his sides.

I wasn't sure what he had planned. I was sure I could take him but seeing how it was Justin West, a kid I respected, I probably wouldn't have put up a fight.

Justin stepped closer, and for a moment, I thought he was about to punch me but then again, that wasn't Justin's style.

"You're talented, Jameson. I'll give you that." His head nodded at the mess in the hauler from earlier. "But your temper will destroy everything you've worked for."

He turned sharply and walked away.

Thankfully, he did because I was so pissed that I had ruined my chances of a good finish at a World of Outlaw event because of high school bullshit that I had taken it out on Justin, and that's not at all what I wanted to do. Justin was my friend and these days I had very few.

I sat there huddled in the corner of the hauler against the tires with my head buried in my hands for a good thirty minutes before Sway approached me when the feature was finished. She didn't say anything, just sat down next to me.

After a moment of silence, she sighed pushing her auburn locks away from her face and pulling her knees to her chest.

"I fucked up," I muttered watching her trace the outlines of a two-inch scar she had on her left knee from when she fell trying to escape from being chased by a bull the first summer we met.

"Who doesn't fuck up at one time or another? You need to focus." Sway said. "Too many distractions ... you know?" her knees knocked against mine.

"Yeah, I guess." I crossed my arms over my knees, resting my forehead against my forearms. "What did Chelsea say to you?"

"Nothing really ... normal high school insecurity shit ... the usual for her."

"Figures,"

"Why do you even bother with her?"

"I have no fucking clue."

I didn't have a clue either. I didn't love Chelsea. I hardly even liked her. There wasn't a single redeeming quality about her but yet I found myself giving in to her. I began to comprehend I was comfortable with her for some reason. I knew she was using me but it seemed tolerable because I was doing the same thing. No one would get hurt because it meant nothing.

Once we arrived home, my mom, who had stayed up, caught me before I made it into my room. Her face was the same shade as dad's was earlier which confirmed my theory he told on me.

"I will not have my son acting like a spoiled asshole all the time!" she said pushing me against the wall. I offered a grin down at her but that didn't work. "Your Dad told me what you did at the track."

"I'm not surprised."

"Jameson ... you need to pull your head out of your ass. Your Dad is trying to help you. Judging by that hauler outside, *you* need help!" She poked my chest before walking down the hall and slamming her door shut.

Dad strolled up the steps as I sat in the hallway. I had intended to go to my room but instead sat in the hallway.

He didn't say anything, just smirked, as he made his way past me to their room. It was late, at least two in the morning by now but mom always waited up for him when she knew he'd be home.

I never paid real close attention to the relationship they had but I knew it was a good one. I'd never seen them fight at least. She'd tell him to shut the fuck up at times but they never all out argued, at least not in front of us kids.

With the lifestyle we lived, you would think it would cause tension for them but it never seemed to, from what I saw.

Picking myself off the floor, I made my way inside my room and was asleep as soon as my head hit the pillow. I was exhausted.

I ended up working off *everything* I broke in the hauler that night and wasn't allowed to race the following weekend. Not because dad wouldn't let me but because my hand was most certainly broken.

I skipped school that week to get my car ready for Chico the following weekend. I had some shit to fix on it.

Sway stopped by after school on Thursday to help me when Chelsea showed up not long after that.

The door had been locked so I'll give you one guess as to who I have to thank for unlocking it. Spencer.

"So I'm not allowed to come by but she is?" Chelsea asked standing by the door.

I caught a brief glimpse of Spencer before I heard his annoying booming laughter as he trucked back to the house.

"I'd help you hide their bodies if needed." Sway said, with a smile and a deserving glare at Chelsea.

Chelsea looked ridiculous dressed in a white summer dress. But that wasn't what was so ridiculous. It was her attempt at looking like she was heading out for a strip club was with heels that could kill someone.

Sway, who'd been roughing tires, stood, and brushed the rubber shavings from her worn jeans.

"I'm going to go talk to Emma. I'll be back later."

My eyes shot to hers, frantically pleading for her not to leave me alone but she didn't. I growled at her, actually growled and then turned toward Chelsea.

"What do you want?"

"You,"

Chuckling to myself, I turned and walked back to my car.

She followed and approached me from behind. Leaning against my back, she wrapped her arms around my waist, slipping them down my hips.

I caught her hand before it slipped inside my jeans.

"I need ... you to leave." I told her trying to control my emotions and not freak out. "I have work to do."

"I can take care of you," she offered kissing down the side of my neck. It felt good, but it also felt wrong. While her touch physically felt welcoming, the emotions I felt weren't.

"I don't think so. I have a lot of work to do here."

"Are you really that mad at me? I only told Sway she should keep her hands off *my* boyfriend. I hardly think that's cause for the silent treatment."

I threw a nearby wrench across the shop, the crack it made when it hit the metal doors and forced Chelsea to step backward, her face frightened.

"Get the fuck out of here!" I yelled without turning around to look at her. "I mean it. You need to leave."

Her heels clicked loudly as she stomped away, slamming the door behind her.

I knew I would eventually turn back to Chelsea, as I always did but I also knew in that moment that if she so much as mentioned Sway's name again, I would have thrown the wrench bar at her.

I only wanted to race but because I was seventeen and my hormones seemed to rule over my actions I found myself wrapped up in the middle of this bullshit.

Something had to give and I knew what it was. Me. I couldn't take much more of any of this and it wasn't what I should be focusing on.

That weekend was our senior prom and after last weekend I wanted nothing to do with anything related to high school. I needed to be alone. Chelsea wanted me to go to prom and asked endlessly the following day despite my snide comments to her. I could care less what she thought. The one I was worried about was Sway.

I could tell Sway wanted to come with me to Chico but I didn't want her following me around and forgoing any normal high school experience. When Cooper Young came to me earlier in the week asking if I thought she'd say yes, I told him she wouldn't go, but after some convincing on my part, she said yes to him. I hated that she was going with him but on the other hand I would rather she went with him instead of Dylan.

The drive to Chico was not the same without Sway harassing me about my music choices although Spencer more than made up for it. I almost threw him out once we reached Portland and he stuck in a Britney Spears CD. Not having a pit crew this weekend, I endured it.

Justin, whose hauler was parked next to ours, approached me after I made it into the pits while Spencer and I were unloading my car.

"Hey, dude, can I talk to you for a minute?" he asked leaning against the side of my car crossing his arms over his chest.

I nodded. I hadn't said much to him since the wreck two weeks ago in Skagit. Part of me felt I needed to apologize, but the other part thought it's just racing. I never expected anyone to apologize to me after wrecking so why should he?

He surprised me though when we made our way over to the concession stands.

"Hey, Ami, can we get some service around here?" Justin teased handing her a twenty. "I'd like a beer." He told her with a grin.

"Yeah, sure," she smiled at Justin. "In four more years, sweetie,"

Justin laughed leaning against the counter. "Fine, then, I'll take a hamburger and coke." He nodded his head back toward me. "And whatever he wants,"

"I can cover it, Justin." I said, pushing his money aside and handing her another twenty.

"After Skagit ... you owe me. Just let me buy this."

I laughed. "So I wreck you and you buy me dinner. Isn't that a little backwards?"

"Probably,"

Ami handed us our food and we walked back to the haulers. "Listen ... I wasn't going to say anything last week ... I knew you had your hands full with ... women problems but I would hate for you to lose any chance at a sponsor because of it. They're not worth it."

"You have your fair share, too?" Justin was definitely a favorite among the women at the track. He usually had three or four around him at all times.

"Yeah ... after a while though ... they only want one thing,"

I nodded taking a bite of my hamburger and then a long pull from my drink. "They do complicate things, don't they?"

"That they do ... wait until you find one you love. That's when the shit really hits the fan."

"And I take it you found one?"

He smiled looking over his shoulder at the pit concession where Ami was. "Yeah, she's pretty special to me." he turned his gaze back to me. "Just remember why you do what you do. If you want it bad enough, everything else falls away. Look at Jimi, he knew what he wanted and look at him now."

Justin had dreams of racing in the World of Outlaw series someday so he looked up to my dad, as I did, but I wanted more than that.

I wanted to race sprints but I also thought maybe there would be something more for me out there. Not sure which way to go, I decided that, for now, USAC was the way after graduation. With three different series' to compete in, I could strive for the Triple Crown National title and that was where my interest was. Justin competed in USAC events as well but he attempted to qualify for *every* World of Outlaw race he could. Funny enough, he did qualify for most of them.

That night I broke the 410-Sprint track-record of 10.918 that was held by Tate Harris, a NASCAR Cup driver out of Charlotte, with a new record of 10.032.

It was a good night that got even better when I won the A-Feature with an entire lap lead on Justin. Compared to that weekend at Skagit, I was on fire. It took me a good hour for the adrenaline to subside and stop shaking from the thrill of the win.

Justin and I talked again after the race with Cody Bowman. Cody was twenty-one now so, of course, he brought us over some beer as we sat around the haulers.

"You two did good tonight," Cody said hunching over a stack of rear tires lined up right outside the doors of my hauler.

Justin glared toward Cody as they didn't get along. Not sure why. All I knew was if they were on the track together, one was trying to take the other out.

Cody left with Spencer after that to go check out a group of girls who had gathered near the gates. Though Spencer was now dating Alley on a regular basis, it didn't stop him from eyeing the opposite sex.

Justin watched me closely as I left a message for Sway letting her know where I had finished. I promised I would and knew that if I didn't, she'd have my ass when I got home.

"What's with you and Sway?" he asked patiently gauging my reaction.

"She's my best friend," I shrugged. "Not much to explain. It's not what you think though." I added.

Justin scoffed. "Yeah—sure,"

"It's not,"

"Really?" he countered. "I see the way you watch her ... she's more to you than that. You just haven't convinced yourself of that."

Was she more? Well, of course she was, but I was also not willing to take any chances.

What Sway and I had was good so why complicate it for the unknown because I was physically attracted to her?

No one seemed to understand me.

I had my reasons and they were mine. They may be wrong but they were still mine. Sway never asked me to be someone else. She never asked me to change and when the weight of the world was on me, she was there, lifting it away. But that's exactly why I wasn't willing to change anything. This worked for me. She was mine, just in other ways. My friend.

A friend was exactly what I needed right now. I didn't need complicated. I *needed* to keep focused. I *needed* to be the best. I *needed* unrivaled greatness and, to do that, I *needed* to be vigilantly focused.

Easier said than done when you're seventeen but I also knew if there was one thing I was good at, it was being focused on what I wanted ... racing.

Ignition – An electrical system used to ignite the air-fuel mixture in an internal combustion engine.

"Hey, you ready for tonight?" Sway asked approaching my locker.

Her hair was pulled back under her white Bowman Oil Racing baseball hat. The contrast against her dark hair made her green eyes stand out.

I smiled—so did she.

"Yeah, I'm ready. I need to be at the track after school and then I'll ride up with Spencer and Alley." I reached for my chemistry book before shutting my locker, turning to face her. "Do you need a ride?"

My perverted teenage brain instantly began contemplating all the ways I could give her a ride.

Damn it.

We began walking toward our chemistry class. I found the need to strategically place my book in front of me.

"No, actually—Cooper said he'd give me a ride." My stomach dropped at the thought.

I'll bet he did. I thought to myself.

I never cared for Cooper Young but I guess you could call him a friend. We grew up right next door to each other but when I introduced him to Sway three years ago, he slowly began showing interest in her. I knew it would happen eventually. Sway was beautiful and if I thought she'd stay single forever, I was being stupid.

One thing was true, I'd be having a talk with Cooper later today about keeping his hands to himself, something I should have done before prom but I had been distracted.

I hated to even consider where his hands could go, would go, or have gone. Cooper was a nice guy but I knew he had a thing for women and never dated the same one more than once, precisely why I didn't want him with Sway. He's not nearly as bad as Dylan Grady was, but he's close, and not what Sway needed.

When I said I didn't care if he asked her to prom, I never thought he would continue to hang around. Now that he was, I was cursing myself.

When I glanced over at Sway, I saw her lips moving.

Shit, she's saying something. Pay attention.

"Hey ... are you even listening to me?" She punched my shoulder.

"Yes ... sorry ... what were you saying?" I grinned trying to use my smile as a plea bargain.

"Asshole,"

"I said I was sorry." I opened the door to our classroom, watching her walk through.

The room was already half full with our fellow classmates, most of whom I had no idea who they were. I didn't go to classes often as I usually I had a tutor who came to our house, but during my senior year I did attend school more often.

"Stop thinking about racing and listen when your best friend is talking." She told me with a goofy smile. "Sometimes I wonder if you *ever* listen to what I say."

"I *do* listen to you."

"Really?" she took her seat next to the window dragging out her book from her bag. "Could have fooled me," I glanced at her book where she had stuck various racing stickers all over it and smiled when I saw my car number outlined in a *Sharpie*.

Chelsea walked in at that moment so I couldn't say much more. "Hey," I said in her general direction as she sat down next to us.

"Hey," she replied kissing my cheek.

I don't know why but I always felt uncomfortable when she did that in front of Sway. I still got a sick feeling in the pit of my stomach when Sway was around, as though my being with Chelsea was bad.

"You coming tonight?" Sway asked Chelsea biting on her pen.

I continued to stare unabashedly at Sway's lips curled around the pen, ignoring the fact that Chelsea was talking to me.

Fuck me! Look at those lips. Jesus, she is beautiful.

"Jameson!" Chelsea yelled directly in my ear.

I turned to her as Sway rolled her eyes.

"What?" I snapped opening my book to avert my eyes away from Sway and that goddamn pen.

I hate teenage hormones.

Sway kicked me under the table. "Jameson, I was saying ... it's just a bunch of guys up at Dayton Peak tonight, right?" she hinted.

"Oh, yeah, right," I caught on. "Yeah, Chelsea ... that's why I didn't say anything. I didn't think you'd wanna come up there if it was just the guys."

Chelsea smiled tenderly, her blue eyes focused on my lips. "That's not my idea of fun. If it's just the guys ... I guess you'll be there, Sway?"

Chelsea and Sway still did not get along. They never had and I doubted that they ever would. They were complete opposites. Chelsea was a girly girl and Sway spent most of her time at dirt tracks and cussed more than a trucker.

I never understood why Sway wanted to hang with a bunch of jerk-offs like us, but she did. Our idea of fun was hurling insults at each other and playing practical jokes that had a good possibility of someone being arrested or put in the hospital but I soon became aware that Sway enjoyed our type of fun, too.

Sway quirked an eyebrow at me and snorted, "I guess I'm just a *guy*." Her lips wrapped around that fucking pen again.

I reacted. Reaching across the table I snatched the pen from her hand and hurled it across the classroom. To my satisfaction, it slid under the heater vents in the back of the room.

She glared leaning in to whisper, “Was that necessary, asshole?” and then kicked my shin.

“Yes, it was.” I kept my eyes focused on my book.

“Well, I have plans anyway.” Chelsea piped in when Sway started giggling after she noticed I had a fuel pump in my backpack to give to Tommy’s dad.

“You couldn’t drop that off before school?” she asked ignoring Chelsea.

“I was going to but he wasn’t home ... so I brought it with me.”

“And, I assume you couldn’t leave it in your truck? You do realize everything in your bag reeks of fuel now?”

“Fuck no. What if someone stole it?”

She smiled widely as though this was amusing to her.

“Yes, because if I was going to break into your truck I would steal the fuel pump and not the hundreds of CDs you have all over the floor board. You know, they make these cool holders now for CDs. You should look into one of those.”

“Hey,” I flicked her hand that reached for the fuel pump. “Point taken—back off me, nag,” I grinned.

Chelsea moved from her seat to sit on my lap, which frustrated me, but I allowed it for God knows what reason.

Sway busied herself with pitching Tommy shit for passing out last night in her lawn. The black marker tattoo we added still present on his cheek.

“Fire crotch, you can’t hold your liquor for shit.” Sway kicked her long legs over the chair next to her.

Tommy’s head spun around to glare and motioned to me with a pointed finger. “Your boy there tried to kill me!”

“I had *nothing* to do with that,” I defended. “That was Spencer, not me.”

Sway and I started laughing at the memories of Tommy singing half-naked in her yard. We usually kept the drinking and partying to Saturday nights after races but last night “Fire Crotch” as Sway called him, lost his virginity to his longtime girlfriend.

When Mrs. Gunner walked in our conversations drifted away and Chelsea finally took her own seat. Like I said, we'd dated off and on and right now we were maybe on, maybe off. I hadn't decided.

Thinking back on it, dating Chelsea was more about letting Sway be her own person. I didn't want to stand in the way of her happiness and I knew I couldn't offer her anything more than a friendship and I sure as shit wasn't offering anything more than physical needs to Chelsea.

Chelsea was different from Sway in many ways. For one, Sway was a rebel and did whatever the fuck she wanted when she wanted, whereas, Chelsea was straight-laced. You'd think this straight-laced side would keep her from wanting to have sex, but no. We constantly had the same argument all the time. She wanted to, I didn't.

Now it's not that I didn't want to have sex because, let's face it, I was seventeen. I wanted to have sex in the worst way but I didn't want to with Chelsea. I was convinced that she had an ulterior motive, like trapping me, and I wasn't attracted to her in that way. Sadly, Sway was the one I wanted.

There were plenty of times when Sway and I could have acted on my hormonal flare-ups but she deserved more than that. Sway needed a man who'd be there for her, not one who wanted racing and racing *only*.

I knew I'd never give myself entirely to Chelsea or any other woman. Sure, we'd probably end up having sex ... I was a teenage boy, it was bound to happen. But I knew beyond high school, I didn't want anything from Chelsea. I'm not sure I wanted anything from any woman besides Sway—I needed her friendship.

Racing was all I wanted to do and that meant giving up a normal life and everything that went with a normal life. Friends. Girlfriends. Normal shit teenagers did.

Class ended and Chelsea was attached to my hip while Tommy and Sway pushed each other out the door.

"If you didn't fuck clammer last night, I'd think you were gay." Sway told him.

"At least I didn't spread my legs for Cooper." His smile widened. "He's probably slept with half the girls in this high school now."

Sway punched his shoulder, hanging her head dejectedly. "Fuck off, *fire crotch*!"

Without another glance, she trudged away, sadness evident on her features.

"What was that about?" I asked Tommy once we were outside. Chelsea was still clinging to my side.

"You didn't know she fucked Cooper after prom when you were in Chico last weekend?"

"Jameson, *come on*." She tugged on my arm. "Who cares who Sway fucks? Come on!"

"Come on what?" I threw my arms up, irritated. Not only was I irritated she was clinging to me but the fact Sway never said anything about what happened with Cooper had severely me pissed off.

"I thought we could go to my house for lunch." She smiled tugging again. "Please?"

I looked past her morosely to see Sway sitting on my tailgate, staring at her feet in the parking lot.

"I can't." I told her removing her arm from mine. "I have to drop my fuel pump at Frank's shop and then I need to stop by Glen's and pick up my springs before Saturday."

"You can do that tonight or Saturday morning."

"No, I can't. I race on Saturday in Cottage Grove. I'm leaving early Saturday morning before they open and I need to test the setup tonight."

"I thought we were going to the movies Saturday." She pouted in that annoying voice she had when she was trying to be adorable.

"No, I never said I was going. I told you when you asked that I had a race." My voice was getting heated. She never listened when I talked about racing which is why she didn't know I would be in Cottage Grove tomorrow. "It's not my problem you didn't listen."

"Can't you blow off the boys then and hang out with me tonight." She reached for me again. "Why do you need to race in Cottage Grove anyway?"

"Chelsea," I shook my head taking a step back. "I made plans with my friends tonight and then I'm leaving in the morning. I can't hang out with you tonight."

"So you're choosing your friends over me?"

"I shouldn't have to choose." I told her walking away.

"Lover's quarrel?" Sway teased with her head hung. I couldn't see her eyes with her hat on.

I pushed her off the tailgate. "Get in."

"Where are we going?"

"I need to drop off my fuel pump."

"Cool, Frank has my new shifter for the red dragon."

"I'm surprised that piece of shit still runs." I teased starting my truck. Sway grinned when I revved the engine for her.

"Don't knock the red dragon. She's reliable."

"Really?" I raised an eyebrow at her. "Is that why we had to walk home from the Ranch House Sunday night?"

"You watch—that truck will still be around when we're fifty."

"Yeah, as parts in a junk yard." When I glanced down at her legs she had put up on my dashboard, I noticed her pants were red by her pockets. "What happened to your pants?" I chuckled.

"Fucking fire crotch," She grumbled. "Asshole asked me to put some ketchup packets in my pocket earlier knowing damn well I'd forget about them."

I laughed. Those two were constantly at each other's throats. I was convinced Tommy was Spencer's long lost brother.

The rest of our lunch break was spent arguing as usual and dropping off parts. Once back at school, Chelsea found me and tried to invite herself to Dayton Peak. I knew damn well Sway would kill me if she came along, so I, once again, told her no.

"Jameson," Chelsea whined as we made our way out of our last class for the day. "Just come over tonight."

"Stop asking. I'm going to Dayton Peak with the guys." I threw my bag in my locker and headed for my truck.

"And, Sway ..." she added keeping step with me.

"Your point?" I shot back.

"You *always* choose her over me."

"Sway is my best friend ... you knew that going into this! Don't ask me to choose because you won't like the answer." I warned giving her another glare before turning toward the parking lot.

Chelsea did this shit all the time. She always made it seem like I wanted Sway instead, when I did, just not in the ways I should. Above all else, I shouldn't have to choose between Sway and anything. She'd never ask me to choose.

Charlie let me use the track on Friday nights to test out my cars before the next race so that's where I was every Friday night. It didn't matter what anyone else was doing; I was always racing. For a while, I was okay with that, but as my senior year progressed, I started to see the drawbacks.

While my friends had normal teenage lives where they partied, attended school functions, and had girlfriends, I didn't. Monday through Friday, you could find me at the track doing odd jobs for Charlie, my dad or racing. Saturdays were spent traveling to a race or preparing my car, and Sundays were spent heading home from whatever track I raced at and finishing up schoolwork so I could graduate. I didn't have a normal teenage life and I had few friends who understood the sacrifices I made.

Sway understood. If anyone did, it was her. She never gave me shit if I fell asleep while we were watching a movie because I'd spent the last few days traveling to make it home for school. That didn't mean she didn't fuck with me if I fell asleep, but she still understood.

Once I finished testing out my springs for tomorrow's race and got the setup dialed in, Spencer and I headed to Dayton Peak with Alley and Emma. Sway was already up there with Cooper and Tommy drinking, of course.

"Hey, Jameson," Tommy yelled as I stepped out of my truck, his words already slurring. I tossed my keys to Spencer knowing damn well I wouldn't be driving home tonight. "Get over here!" he motioned. "Sway told us you broke the track record in Chico."

I grinned. "So what,"

"So what?" Tommy repeated incredulously. "Dude, your dad has been trying to break Tate's record for years and then you act like it's no big deal."

I stood beside him. Sway threw a beer my way; I winked at her as I opened it. "It's not that big of a deal." I told them taking a drink of the beer and then sitting down next to Sway on the log.

She leaned into my shoulder. "How'd the springs work?"

"Good." I smiled. "I think I've got it figured out. I may need to make some air pressure adjustments but it's better than last week in Chico."

"When will you be back?"

"Sunday sometime,"

Sway nodded once and took a drink of her beer. I nudged her shoulder. "You're coming with me, right?"

"I didn't know you wanted me to."

"You *always* come with me ... aside from last week." I smiled.

It was true. Even if I was racing in California, we kidnapped Sway on the weekends. The one exception was last weekend and that was only because it was our senior prom, I refused to let her come. She needed to enjoy high school.

My eyes focused on her lips once again, wanting to feel them against mine. It'd been a while since the last time I kissed her and the magnetic energy screaming between us right now was enough to make me light headed.

I turned to drinking to divert my attention away from Sway. What caught my attention later in the evening was when Cooper started getting closer and closer to her. And by the end of the night they were leaving together, which pissed me off. I left after only three beers and I called Chelsea on my way home.

"I thought you were with the boys tonight?" she asked when she picked up.

"Do you want to come over or not?" I ignored her snide comment.

"Sure. I'll be there in ten minutes."

It wasn't right and it surely wasn't moral. I was using her for my own benefit. Chelsea was oblivious to the fact that I did not intend to date her beyond high school but that she was only fulfilling a need.

I watched Chelsea make her way inside my room, removing her clothes and lying down on my bed. I knew what she wanted.

I wanted it, too. I did. Sex was pretty much all I thought about when I wasn't thinking of racing.

Her face grew soft and persuasive. "Please, Jameson,"

My attention came gradually to what she said. "What do you want?"

"You," she whispered against my bare shoulder.

I didn't have any intentions of having sex with her that night but when I thought of the energy that hummed between Sway and me earlier and the way her eyes had sparkled against the flickering of the fire, I reacted to what was in front of me.

Yeah, I did it for the wrong reasons and thought of someone else the entire time but I did it anyway. Sway was out doing God knows what with Cooper, why couldn't I?

I wanted to stop, stop her, stop myself but I didn't. Stopping didn't seem like an option once I moved between her legs and my hormones took over and reactions seemed mechanical.

I heard her moan as I continued to push forward. She told me she was a virgin but she didn't feel like one with the way she moved against me.

Once again, I tried to stop myself but my need seemed to be stronger. I only realized this wasn't what I wanted when I stole a glance at her lust stricken blue eyes, wanting to see emerald.

The springs of my bed squeaked and my bed shook with what I *needed* and then I came. Groaning and clutching her tightly, my one free hand that wasn't holding her to me fisted roughly in her hair.

I regretted it before I even pulled out. Nausea rolled over me as I removed the condom and searched the floor for my jeans.

"All these months of asking—why now?" Chelsea asked pulling her jeans on.

I should have been embarrassed. I didn't last long with the memories of Sway in my head not to mention the fact that I was nearly eighteen and had never had sex before. There's no way I would have lasted long.

So many times, I'd imagined Sway in this very bed, showing her what I wanted to do to her. Repeatedly. That's all it took to become a trembling mess.

With my room still dark, I pulled my jeans up and slipped my shirt back on as well.

"Don't act like you didn't want to." I mumbled standing against the wall beginning to truly regret the decision and creating as much space as I could.

"Did you like it?" she pressed, her voice was shy. I felt bad for about a half a second.

"It was fine, Chelsea." I let out a sigh. "Listen, I need to pack for tomorrow so I'll see you on Monday." I told her throwing my bag on the bed to pack my clothes for Cottage Grove.

"Yeah, I need to go anyway." She leaned in for a kiss once she was at the door.

I leaned over and kissed her chastely.

When she left, I fell back against the wall. I knew having sex with Chelsea was a bad idea. I knew it.

Why couldn't I just have Sway?

She was perfect but, like everything else in my life, I wasn't what she needed so I stayed away. She didn't need someone who couldn't commit to her.

Thinking of what she and Cooper were doing right now made my stomach churn. Being the nosy fucker I was, I called Cooper to see where he was.

"Hey, where are you?"

He chuckled, his voice whispered. “At my house, where are you?”

“Home.”

He was drunk judging by his tone and talking to a drunk Cooper was about as easy as discussing politics with Spencer when he was drunk or sober. Damn near impossible to get a straight answer.

“Are you looking for Sway?” he finally asked when I hadn’t said anything.

Apparently, I’m not as sneaky as I thought.

“Is she with you?”

“Yeah, she’s sleeping right next to me.”

I punched the wall.

“You’re fixing that.” My dad yelled from down the hall. With a grueling 76-race schedule, he usually wasn’t home on Friday nights but the series had an off weekend.

Cooper laughed. “Is there something you need Riley?”

“Just tell her I’m leaving at five tomorrow morning.”

“Will do.”

I didn’t sleep well that night. Not only was I ashamed that I gave into Chelsea because I wanted Sway but I also hated to think that Cooper was with her right now. I needed to focus though. I had to keep my head clear for the race tonight. It was the Northwest Showdown Finals tonight and I knew I needed to be on my game. Cottage Grove was no Elma—the track was slick and fast. One mistake and the wall bit you hard.

“Did you tether the drag link?” Dad asked when I finished loading my car in the hauler that morning. It was early, *way too* early, but this is what a local racer’s lifestyle was like on Saturday mornings.

“Yeah, yesterday,” I pulled hard on the new torsion bar testing its resistance.

“What about your exhaust, did Charlie test it last night? The decibels need to be below ninety-five at Cottage Grove.”

“Yeah, it’s below that.” I told him closing the door to the hauler. He always made sure I had everything ready.

His eyes focused on the driveway and smiled. I turned to see what he was looking at after latching the door tightly and locking it.

Sway.

"Nice to see you among the living," I muttered walking to the front of my truck before tossing some tie-downs in the bed.

Yeah, so I was a little harsh and slightly annoyed. Sue me. I threw my bag inside the truck with a grunt.

Sway smirked kicking my ass with her foot, her flip-flop falling as she did so.

"Shut up, asshole." She reached down to put her shoe back on. "I'm here, aren't I?"

"Yeah, twenty minutes late."

"It's better than my usual thirty. I'd say I'm making progress."

Spencer walked up with Alley and handed us a bag of food mom made.

Sway sensed I was angry and cornered me between my truck and the hauler within the shadows of the maple tree.

"Sorry, I overslept. You'd think since you finally got some last night, you'd be in a better mood." She countered glaring at me but peeking into the bag of food.

"What are you talking about?" I leaned in and whispered in her ear not wanting everyone else to hear.

"You didn't think you could sleep with *Chelsea Adams* and her not tell me, did you?"

"I, uh ... what ... did she say?"

Sway handed me her phone and replayed the message Chelsea left her after leaving my house last night.

"We finally had sex! It was amazing Sway and he told me he loved me afterward."

"What the fuck is she talking about?" I barked causing Alley and Spencer to glance over at us.

I'd never told any woman I loved them aside from my mom.

"You tell me." Sway smirked. "You in love, Riley?" her eyebrows waggled.

"Fuck no ... she's out of her goddamn mind. I *never* said that," I hip-checked her knocking her sideways and turned to Spencer. "Get in."

"Don't shoot the messenger!" Sway teased tickling my side as she climbed over me to get to the passenger seat.

"You know there's a passenger side door." I told her when her foot was in my face. "It's easier."

"No, it's not." She turned back to look at me. "How else would I annoy you?"

"Good point."

Once we got on the road, the fight for who controlled the music was on.

"I'm not listening to this shit." She told me giving me the *hell no* look she had.

"Like hell, you're not. It's my truck. Driver picks the music."

The four-and-a-half-hour drive to Cottage Grove was spent testing out the new speakers in my truck and Sway and I arguing about which Pearl Jam album was the best. The same shit we did each weekend. Her arguments ended when I did my best impression of Eddie Vedder singing "Black." I knew how to make her speechless.

Once we were at the track, it was my turn to be speechless at how shitty things got and how it happened.

After the first heat race, Spencer found me back at our pit.

"Did you hear me? What's your temp at?" He panted heavily, his brow drenched in sweat. Tommy stood close beside him checking tire wear.

"I heard you. I was ignoring you." I told him pulling my helmet off. "Why are you all wet?"

He shrugged and I had a feeling I didn't want to know.

Shutting my eyes, I listened to the engine. There was a vibration I couldn't decipher and my temps were off the charts after my heat race. We posted the fastest qualifying lap but the car seemed to go to shit after that.

"210-240," I shouted over the rumbling before pulling the coupler out and letting the engine run out of fuel.

Spencer's eyes widened.

"Fuck, it's gonna blow. We can't run the feature with those temps." Spencer grumbled pushing his wet hair from his face.

"No, shit." I mumbled tossing my helmet inside the cockpit.

Figures this shit would happen when I needed to run good. This was a National event and placing in the top five in a feature was something that needed to happen.

"Jameson," Sway called out from inside the hauler. "You're in the next heat race."

"How?" I knew I didn't make the transfer spot.

"Shaley dropped out. Transmission's shot—you're in."

I nodded and pulled my helmet back on. "We need to run it. If it blows, it blows." I shrugged when Spencer began to grumble again about this being our last motor.

There was nothing we could do. Once the temperatures spiked like that, it was a given it'd blow, but you couldn't be sure when.

Surprisingly we did well in the second heat and advanced to the feature where the track changed drastically.

I corrected my line, searching for the new groove while gobs of mud flew, slapping my helmet visor. Coming out of turn two I yanked a tear-off in order to clear my vision; the narrow strip of cellophane fluttered away.

Depending on a track conditions, it varied how many I tore away.

Track conditions have a tendency to change quickly on dirt, so you come out of turn two and entering turn three, it's different.

Asphalt and dirt are extremely different. Dirt changes tremendously throughout the night whereas asphalt changes too, just not as drastically. You can actually feel it when asphalt was changing.

Dirt is weird. When most people think of dirt, they think it's the same everywhere they go.

Not true.

With composition of dirt being different everywhere you go, each track has a unique personality. Where some tracks dry up and resemble asphalt, others stay moist and sticky all night.

That night the track dried out so it was hard to find a line and setup my car worked well with. At tracks like Cottage Grove, I preferred running high and letting my right rear bounce off the cushion, jolting me forward. Sometimes this worked, other times it didn't. It seemed that any line I tried, my car would hang on.

That's the other thing with dirt, when the track changes, the groove changes and you have to find your new groove and hope like hell it has the same speed as the one you just had. You're constantly looking for the new groove and some racers don't even see the track changing.

We made it to the feature but the engine wasn't what took us out of the race with six laps to go. In my 360-Sprint I ran three brakes, every corner but the right. It was a trick my dad taught me that helps with cornering at tracks like Cottage Grove when the rails tend to get bunched up by the slower cars.

This obviously does nothing for your stopping power.

So there I was running second next to Justin West, when I leaned against him in turn one, couldn't slow down as much as I needed and took us both out and destroyed both cars.

I immediately got out, checked on Justin and apologized. I hated that I took him out in Skagit for a stupid mistake and now here I was taking him out again.

Now I'm not going to say I wasn't pissed. I *was* pissed. I hated losing. Anyone who tells you they don't mind losing is full of shit.

I walked back to the pits while they brought my car around. Looking over the smashed wing and front axle that was twisted around the side, I hated to think what it was going to cost to fix it and how hard my dad would make me work at the shop to pay for the parts.

Though my dad had money to fix the cars I destroyed, it didn't mean that shit came for free. I worked my ass off in that shop to be able to race. All that hard work didn't go without learning either. I could put a sprint car together from the ground up if need be and, to me, that was huge to learning these cars and how they handled.

In turn, I felt that it made me a better driver understanding things like that.

I took my time getting back to the hauler, watching the last few laps. Sway sat beside Spencer and Alley, biting her nails. She did this when she was gauging my reaction to something.

Flashing a smile at her, I looked over at Spencer.

"Car's done for."

"I see that." He muttered looking over the wreckage that pulled into the pits.

We ended up finding a hotel right outside of Cottage Grove for the night.

"Who picked this shit hole?" I asked afraid to remove my clothes or shoes for that matter.

Alley dropped her bag on the floor. "Since you three aren't eighteen yet, we did."

"You could have found some place—" I began but was interrupted by Spencer's glare to shut up. "Right," I mumbled understanding he had no choice in the matter.

Alley had Spencer by the balls.

"Where are we all sleeping?" Sway asked rubbing her eyes. Emma was already asleep on the couch leaving two queen-size beds.

"Alley and I will take this bed and you and Jameson take that one." Spencer said laying down on the bed.

We were all so exhausted by the time we reached the hotel. I don't think anyone had enough energy to argue, not that I would have argued sleeping next to Sway anyway.

"Keep your clothes on." I whispered to Sway when she began to take her jeans off. "This bed is questionable."

"Good idea." She smiled looking down at me.

We'd slept in the same bed together before on a few different occasions and I soon realized she liked to sleep in her underwear, no matter where she was.

Sway wasn't self-conscious at all, nor did she have any reason to be. She'd walk around naked in front of you if you didn't object. I didn't *want* to object, but for the sake of my self-control, I objected.

Once in bed, Spencer and Alley were fast asleep which left me wide awake staring at Sway.

"Stop looking at me," she whispered startling me.

"Sorry, you sleeping?"

"Yes, but I'm answering you ... *strange*."

"Shit head." I nudged her shoulder.

"Was it good?" she asked.

"Huh?"

Was what good? I wondered.

"Chelsea."

"Oh ..." Sway and I usually talked about these things but now I didn't know what to say and I was curious as hell as to what went on between her and Cooper last night. "No, it was quick though."

"Minute man, eh?"

"Not quite. I was thinking of someone else." I told her honestly praying she didn't ask who. Thankfully, she didn't and I'm not so sure she even heard me.

Her eyes drooped shut once before opening. "Well, she's a bitch, regardless."

"What did you do with Cooper?" I blurted out.

"*Uh* ... nothing much. We had sex a couple weeks ago and now he wants it all the time but," her eyes opened and she smiled. I could see a faint blush to her cheeks, "he sucks ... really, he does. It wasn't what I thought it would be. It just felt like movements you know, something to satisfy an itch."

"Well, he's still an asshole."

"He's your friend." She pointed out.

"He's still a dick." I repeated rolling over on my back to stare at the white ceiling.

"We should find new people to have sex with." She mused tiredly.

"Like each other." I breathed softly.

Her eyes were closed so I assumed she couldn't hear me. That wasn't the first time I'd made sexual innuendoes toward her but she never took me seriously. I was constantly telling her what a nice ass she had but she always blew it off as teasing.

"Yeah," she answered and rolled over, leaning in to kiss my cheek, her eyes closed. She intended to kiss my cheek but as she did that, I turned my head and our lips met.

The spark sent a jolt of electricity to the exact place I didn't want it to. Her lips stayed connected with mine before returning the kiss with another one, and then another as she shifted closer to me.

My hand rose hesitantly and cupped her cheek as I leaned in for another kiss, my lips parting ever so slightly, breathing her in. She felt amazing, she felt right. I wanted her *badly*.

I did the only thing I knew to do and that was to shift away from her, hiding my arousal. Sway didn't need this. She needed someone better and not Cooper or Dylan.

Hell, I would never think anyone was good enough for her, including me.

"Goodnight, Sway." I whispered and kissed her forehead once before turning away from her.

Through years of experience and extensive observation, I've determined my brother is clinically insane. At least that's the only rational explanation for his behavior that I could come up with.

First off, sleeping in a hotel room with Spencer was a risk in itself. Second, waking up alone in a hotel room with him was even worse. Just like any other volatile animal, you never knew when he'd attack and, for a reason unbeknownst to me, I was his favorite target, besides Sway. If he could knock us both down with one hit, he'd do so.

So, there Sway and I were, lying in bed, alone. Everyone else must have gotten up to eat breakfast.

Yawning and stretching I went to move my arms above my head when I realized I couldn't. They were handcuffed ... not to the motherfucking bed but, worst of all, to Sway.

This wouldn't have been so bad if I wasn't half-naked, as was Sway and Spencer fucking knew that. It's exactly why he did it.

He may be a deeply troubled sadistic asshole but stupid was not one of his qualities.

This was not the ideal situation for a number of reasons ... all that flooded through my stupid teenage brain were pornographic images of Sway in handcuffs and all the things I would enjoy doing to her.

Consequently, this resulted in an embarrassing reaction that I couldn't cover up because my hands were handcuffed.

Thank God for the blanket.

I pulled on the chain, the clanging of the cuffs hitting against the metal framed bed caused Sway to stir.

"What the fuck?" she shouted realizing her hands were cuffed.

The sequence of emotions that displayed across her features would have been entertaining if we weren't handcuffed.

"Fucking Spencer," She grumbled and slumped back against the bed.

If there is one positive thing I can say about Spencer, it's that he never does anything half-assed. The crazy son of a bitch had somehow removed my jeans leaving me in my boxer-briefs.

I moved my legs to relieve the pinching on my wrists when the blanket slipped off both of us and pooled on the floor. This also wouldn't have been so bad until my reaction to the pornographic images was revealed.

There was no way to hide it.

I was mortified. Sway was entertained.

"Uh ... are you okay?" she asked in between giggles.

"I'm *so glad* you're entertained by this." I replied not so calmly.

"I'm sorry, it's just ..." her giggles prevented her from finishing.

I did the only thing I could. I kicked her.

"You know what ... you suck."

"Yeah, you wish right about now." She cackled.

That did nothing for my problem, nothing at all.

The next fifteen minutes were spent with Sway making every sexual reference she could possibly think of. I tried to kick her off the bed and finally resorted to curling into a fetal position and trying to hide myself from her.

Spencer eventually returned to see the results of his handiwork and gloat in his glory.

While laughing, Spencer choked out, "Wow there, little brother, happy to see us?" and then proceeded to pat down his pockets searching for his phone. I could only assume that he planned to capture this on film.

Fortunately, for me, he couldn't find his phone, which happened about four times a day.

Spencer has waged mental warfare on me for years and, at some point, you'd think he'd move on, but he hasn't. Every chance he got he would take a picture of his fucking dick and send it to me. Just so we're clear, I did not enjoy this.

The happiest day of my teenage life was the day he moved in with Alley. The worst day was when he still came over *every* goddamn day. Other than sleeping at their apartment, they were always hanging around the house—it was unacceptable to me.

Getting him to release us was a chore. It took some major persuasion by Sway to get this accomplished.

I didn't have the energy to chase Spencer out of the room once I was released, but Sway did.

When she returned all sweaty and panting, I bolted for the bathroom. The reactions I was having to her this morning were alarming.

The entire trip home Spencer made references to wood and said the word "hard" any chance he could. Sway provoked him which was another part of the day that was unacceptable to me.

At one point, when we stopped for lunch, I pushed Sway against the side of the restaurant when everyone else walked inside.

"What's *up*?" her eyebrows waggled, grinning lasciviously.

"Shut up, already," I groaned. "It's not entertaining."

"Oh, yes it is." another grin. "It's *very* entertaining." She shifted her weight from one foot to the other, her fingertips touched to her lips as though she was contemplating. “Now tell me, do you always have this much of a reaction in the mornings or was it just in my presence?”

I couldn’t tell if she wanted an honest answer so I started to panic. “Yes ... wait, what?”

“I’m being serious,” her eyes narrowed and she was being serious. “What’s with you? Why are you acting all weird ... so I saw your morning wood, *big* deal?”

“Big?”

Her face flushed and her eyes darted to the concrete. “Like you need to be told,”

“Ego boosting is always good.” I suggested and leaned back against the brick wall.

“Like I said, you don’t need to be told but, yes, you’re rather *large* Riley.”

Spencer walked and looked at us. “Hey, assholes—get in here.”

Sway reached for my hand when I groaned. “*Come* on, let’s eat.”

“You need to stop it with that shit.” I hissed and smacked her ass causing her to yelp.

“Or else what?” she challenged opening the large glass doors to the restaurant.

“You don’t want to be on my bad side ... I’m your best friend so I know all the ways to get you back, and I know all the things you are *deathly* afraid of.”

“You wouldn’t ...” she knew damn well I was aware she was afraid of clowns and could wreak havoc on her with them if I wanted to.

“Watch me.” I smacked her ass once more, this time my hand lingered a little longer than necessary.

As teenagers, we want to see ourselves as some kind of renegade, or rule breaker, a badass. That’s exactly how we want to see ourselves—it’s cool, right?

It’s bullshit. We’re just as vulnerable as everyone else, probably more so with the addition of the teenage hormones that controlled our bodies and ruled our decisions.

Either way, we want to take risks and prove to everyone that we are those renegade rule breakers we think we are. With any risk, there can be reward but then there can also be fallout. Then what? All I knew was I wasn't willing to take the risk when it came to Sway. Losing her friendship wasn't an option.

As a teenager, I took risks every day. It was part of being that teenage badass we all wanted to be but some risks you don't take out of fear of the unknown.

The funny thing with risks was that even if you're not willing to take them, they're still tempting, like the last cookie on the plate. After a while, your self-control gets the best of you and you reach out for the cookie.

High Heat – Above normal tire temperature that's usually around 260 degrees.

Toward the end of my senior year, my life had turned crazy and it was only May. I was racing at different tracks around the Northwest every weekend and when I wasn't racing, I was working in the race shop or doing homework to graduate in a month. I couldn't fucking wait. I also couldn't wait to get away from Chelsea. Since we had sex, she pretty much stalked me.

I had no time for anything; barely enough time to sleep and if it wasn't for caffeine, I'd be asleep right now as I tried to focus on my mid-term final.

Sway kicked my leg under the wooden table we sat at during our political economics class. As I thought to myself why I would ever need to know anything about political economics to better myself, she whispered, "Wake up."

I shook my head, trying to focus but the late nights getting my car ready for the next weekend were taking a toll on me and my attention span.

Once school finals were over, it was time for the World of Outlaws race in Chico and then Cottage Grove followed by Elma and Skagit. It was a busy week for my family and a chance at seeing my dad for more than a few days at a time. He was usually on the road beginning in March and ending in late November so we welcomed the chance at finally seeing each other when he was home.

Since I was competing on the Northern Sprint Tour this year, I had to make all four races and place. I ended up driving down to Chico to meet up with Dad and his teammate now, Bucky.

Bucky was a good wholesome guy. He'd do anything to help you out if it was in his power, so I wasn't surprised when Spencer and I pulled into town and Bucky was standing there with my dad and an older gentleman dressed in a black suit.

Spencer and I got out and approached them. Bucky smiled at me and gestured toward the man.

"Jameson, this is Walter Gains. He's the president of Bowman Oil. He'd like to talk to you about sponsoring your car next year and running the USAC Silver Crown series full-time."

I'm sure my eyes widened. Dad and I had frequently talked about my plans for next year once I graduated and I'd made it clear to him I'd be racing. I still didn't have a plan in place but I knew, just as he had done, the real challenge was in the Midwest and East Coast. Those are where the big boys are.

I reached for his hand. "It's nice to meet you, Mr. Gains."

"Son, call me Walter and let's talk."

Walter and I talked for a good hour about my plans for next year. I told him I'd planned on heading to the Midwest to try my luck out there with the open wheel guys and, in turn, he offered up sponsorship on a silver crown car as well as a sprint and midgets if I chose to run them.

In racing, sponsorship is necessary. Without it, there's no way for you to do this. We need sponsors to help foot the bill. In turn, we plaster the sides of our cars with their names, promoting their products. Why? It's simple, exposure. Race fans see the products that we use and want the same thing.

Unsure how to adjust to this information, I called Sway from a payphone outside of Chico while my dad and Spencer ate dinner.

"What's up?" Sway asked.

"I got sponsorship for next year." I blurted out.

"No, shit?" she asked her voice excited.

"Yep,"

"That's awesome, Jameson. I'm so happy for you."

I felt a twinge of homesickness hearing her voice. It'd been almost two weeks since I saw her and, to be honest, I missed her. I also hadn't seen her since she felt me up in the hall way but things like that never kept us from being friends. We did that shit all the time. I'd felt her up on more than one occasion and frequently slapped her ass. That was us.

"I wish you were here. I miss you." I told her in a sudden onset of word vomit.

"Well, yeah, I'm worth missing." She giggled.

"You are."

The line was quiet for a moment before she sighed.

"I miss you too. Tommy isn't as fun as you and it's not nearly as entertaining to make fun of him when you're gone."

"Come see me then." I suggested. "Bring Tommy."

"In Chico?"

"No, in England ... yes, Chico."

"But you're only there for tonight and then you'll be in Cottage Grove."

I laughed; she knew my schedule better than I did. "Right, well then come to Cottage Grove,"

There was a long pause before she spoke. "Okay, Tommy and I will drive down tomorrow morning."

That satisfied me immensely. No matter how much time I spent doing what I loved, I still missed my friends and the normal life I had when I was with them.

The following night we were in Cottage Grove where Tommy and Sway met up with us. Sway found me prior to the main putting my racing suit on.

I was only in my underwear when she opened the door.

"Oh, my God," she stepped back. "I'm sorry. I thought you'd be dressed by now."

"It's okay, Sway." I laughed. "It's not like you haven't seen me in my underwear before."

"True," she mused stepping inside, closing the door behind her. Without averting her gaze from my stomach, she smiled.

"See something you like?"

"Get dressed. I came in here for a reason."

"Oh, yeah, what reason would that be?" I pulled my racing suit up over my shoulders after slipping on my lucky t-shirt Sway gave me.

"I was ... uh ... shit." She laughed. "You distracted me."

Turning around, I faced her.

I smiled. She smiled.

"I distract you?"

"Yes ... sometimes." Her face lit up. "Oh, right, I made you brownies ... that's why."

"Brownies, you say," I looked around for them. "Where are they?"

She squinted at me in the cutest way.

"Tommy ate them on the way here."

"You let Tommy eat *my* brownies?"

"I'm sorry ... I was distracted by some asshole on the freeway and, well, he ate them." She shrugged indifferently. "They were really good though."

"I thought you said Tommy ate them."

She smiled. "He had some help."

I was silent for a moment staring at her. I wanted to kiss her badly. I wanted her. I wanted her against my car, against the side of the hauler. I wanted her. Having sex with Chelsea only amplified my hormones. I knew what sex felt like and now it was pretty much all I wanted.

My willpower was vacillating; I could go either way. My hormones ruled and I stepped closer to her, my hand curled under her chin and before she could pull away, I kissed her.

She responded, kissing me back, her lips moving in sync with mine, our tongues gliding together. I smiled against her lips as my body pushed her against the side of my car, trapping her.

We kissed for a moment before my need peaked and I knew she could feel the results of this. Turning away from her, I mumbled a "sorry" before bracing myself against the wall. She left me weak.

"Now I'm distracting you." She said hanging her head, she looked confused, just as confused as I was. "I should get out there before Tommy gets himself in trouble." She leaned into me again and kissed my cheek. I wrapped my arms around her once again to feel her warm body against mine. "Good luck. I drove all the way down here ... win for me tonight."

I nodded arrogantly.

"I will, honey." I vowed with a wink.

I could feel the energy humming between us, building over time. I knew she was attracted to me, and, me, well it was beyond attraction now. I was pretty much obsessed with her to stalker levels.

It was hard to get the thoughts of Sway out of my mind that night but, once again, when I slide inside the narrow cockpit of my car, I was vigilantly focused.

That's not to say I didn't imagine her throughout the race. I could still smell her perfume on me and taste her mint gum.

Damn it.

I groaned pushing the thoughts aside and focused on the race.

I was running a different shock package tonight that I hadn't used before but my worries were eased when I easily slid past the top three cars in the second corner. I was leading on the first lap. The race stayed green for the entire 40 lap main and I never saw another car besides the few lapped cars I passed.

After collecting my trophy, I made it back to the pits to see Sway, Tommy, and Spencer waiting. I let the car idle before revving the engine twice for Sway and then letting the fuel run out.

She smiled launching herself at me when I pulled myself from the car.

We sat there chatting when Bucky approached.

"Hey, kid, you did good."

I smiled. "Thanks, Bucky."

Bucky motioned with his head for me to follow him, so I did.

When a guy like Bucky Miers wants to talk, you listen.

We walked through the raucous of the pits. Sprint cars were being loaded into haulers and trailers where others were being torn down for inspection. Drivers and crews mingled with fans who had made their way from the stands. The smells of the heated rubber of tires and sweet methanol mixed with beer and dirt. It was the smells of a dirt track on a warm summer night.

"I've had some conversations with Walter Gains about you. Will you drive a midget car for me on the USAC series next year?" He looked my direction. Dark lashes shadowed his almond-shaped hazel eyes. "I have eight races scheduled and need a driver."

"I thought Justin was going to drive for you."

Last week Justin had told me he'd be driving for Bucky next year.

"He is ... but on the Northern Sprint Tour and half of the Outlaw races. I need my USAC car running, too."

I nodded but didn't answer him right away.

USAC had three different divisions. I knew I would already be running the USAC Silver Crown and Sprint Car series with the help of Walter and Bowman Oil but that would only be for thirteen Silver Crown races and thirteen Sprint Car races and it wasn't a full sponsorship. I had a lot to think about. I could be their puppet or I could go on my own.

Bucky and I talked more and I told him I needed to think about it. I wasn't sure what I wanted to do and, instead of making a snap decision, I decided to think it over.

Trudging back toward my pit, I glanced around the pits one last time as the haulers and trailers filed through the pit gates on the way home. The lingering smells from the cars were replaced with the thick pungent smells of the diesel from the trucks.

When I got closer to my pit, I noticed Sway perched upon my car, sitting on the edge of the right rear tire, laughing at Tommy dancing around.

She was beautiful.

Her hair shined under the lights, auburn highlights sparkling with the light breeze reflecting the light. She caught me staring at her and smiled, motioning for me to come over. I did.

Slinging my right arm over her shoulders, she leaned into me.

"You smell like racing." She said breathing me in as though the scent was pleasant to her. I had yet to change out of my racing suit.

"Well, I did race. I won by the way."

"I saw." She smiled looking up at me. "I watched every lap."

"I don't doubt that." I returned the smile. "Let's party. We are graduating in two weeks and I won."

Sway jumped off the tire. "Don't have to ask me twice."

Getting drunk was exactly what I needed. I wanted to forget everything for one night. I didn't want to think about racing, sponsors, school, Chelsea ... nothing. I wanted to have fun. I wanted to be a teenager.

And, we were teenagers.

We did stupid shit, drank too much and ended up together in a sleeping bag. Too drunk to function, we ended up kissing some more. I felt my way around her soft body as did she. Her smooth hands crept under my shirt and then removed it. I didn't stop her as I was too busy kissing her.

But it never went past touching and kissing. It never did. It seemed like we both wanted to. The desire and temptation was there but, then again, there was hesitation ... from both of us. I don't know what it was but it was there. It was as though we both saw the boundary. There was an imaginary line surrounding us and we both knew what happened if either of us crossed over.

We all ended up camping in a field that night. Sway and I were in one sleeping bag and, oddly enough, Tommy and Spencer were in another. Not sure how they ended up that way as the night was seemingly a blur but when they awoke and found themselves snuggled together, they were alarmed to say the least.

It was a good joke for the entire trip home. I even took a picture for future blackmailing. And, like usual, Sway and I never spoke about our kissing, that imaginary line we had developed, or what it meant.

Once we got home, graduation was approaching fast. I couldn't wait. The other important event was our senior prank.

The night before graduation, we finalized our plans.

When Spencer graduated, he stole Sheriff Stevens' car, took it for a spin around town and then returned it.

I decided that I would race my sprint car through downtown Elma one last time, for old time sake.

At the Homecoming football game earlier in the year, Spencer and I took a pair of 360 sprints onto the running track around the football stadium.

Jimi was not happy about that.

Knowing that, I knew he wouldn't be *happy* about this either but, come on, a kid has to get his kicks somehow.

Sway was amused immensely at the thought of Stevens having a heart attack at the sight of my 800 horsepower sprint car broad sliding down E. Young Street toward his house.

She couldn't stop laughing as she push started my car with the Red Dragon.

We installed a 2-way radio in my car to communicate while she told me when and where the police were. The goal was to make it past the Sheriff's house and then back to my house before he caught me.

So, there we were pulling out of my driveway onto Cloquallum Road.

All I heard on the radio were Sway's giggles which made me laugh.

"Focus, Sway," I said, between my own laughs. It was that funny to us. "We have to focus if we want to pull this off."

"I'm trying ... ah, *shit*, I can't breathe." She said breathlessly trying to catch her breath.

"*Stop* laughing. This is supposed to be sneaky."

"All right, let's do this!" she shouted gaining focus. "Clear. Go!"

I took off like a rocket down Cloquallum, turned onto Elma McCleary Road past the racetrack and the Rusty Tractor restaurant. Cars on the road stopped, people looked, and bystanders on the streets covered their ears at the roaring of my sprint car.

I laughed.

This was more amusing than I thought it would be.

Throwing my car sideways onto Oakhurst Drive, my left rear bounced up on the sidewalk and knocked over a stop sign. When I came flying down E. Young Street, I threw the car into the sheriff's lawn where I did a burn out, hopped the curb and then made my way back the way I came. The same onlookers watched as again I made my way back.

The Sheriff speeding past me going the opposite direction would have been humorous except for the fact that he was chasing my dad's brand new Aston Martin Vanquish with Emma driving. A car he wouldn't even let my mom drive, let alone any of us kids.

When I pulled into the driveway, my tires smoking from the burnouts, Sway ran over to me. "Did you see Emma?"

"The shit is about to hit the fan." I told her not so calmly. "Help me get this in the shop. If Jimi sees my car out, he will know damn well what I did."

It took us a good twenty minutes or so to get my car back inside the shop when Emma came walking down the driveway, crying, without my dad's car.

Sway walked inside to find Spencer. We were going to need help with this one.

Emma threw herself face down into the grass.

I wandered over to her, not sure how to comfort her but I thought I'd give it a try. Emma and I never had heart-to-heart talks but I did protect her. She was my little sister.

"Where's dad's car?" I asked standing next to her.

"The impound. I panicked when the sheriff turned his lights on and saw your sprint car going down the road doing a wheel stand."

I smiled. That was the best part.

"Why were you in his car in the first place? You have your own?"

"I wanted to see Nathan tonight and dad wouldn't let me." Nathan was Emma's boyfriend who dad did not approve of.

"So, you took his car ... a car he specifically told you not to drive, to see a boyfriend he doesn't like?"

"I know!" she wailed.

I dropped down beside her. "Um, you need to stop that." I awkwardly patted her back. This was not what I had planned at all. I was no longer thrilled with my prank on the sheriff and now I was worried about Emma. Something I never did.

"Now what do I do?"

"I don't know." I said, unconcerned with her problem. "That's not my responsibility."

"Will you come with me and talk to him?"

"No," I answered. "You tell him. I terrorized the city in my sprint car. I doubt I'm on his good side."

"Please, it will be better if you're there."

"I highly doubt that. Did you not hear what I just told you?"

She started to cry again as Sway walked up.

"What did you do to her?" Sway asked.

"Why do you automatically assume I did something?"

"Because you always make her cry,"

"He told me he wouldn't come with me," Emma wailed. "Please, come with me?" Emma begged.

Thankfully, we were saved by dad yelling, "Emma, get your ass in here!"

Jimi wasn't happy.

"Sucks to be you," I told her and nearly carried Sway with me to get away from her. I'd been there before many times but I was not about to tell my dad that I wrecked his car, Emma did.

Besides, when he found out about my leisurely drive through

town, he wouldn't be happy.

Hearing Jimi screaming from twenty feet away, *outside*, I began to feel bad for Emma. Against our better judgment, Sway and I decided to try and get the car out of impound with the help of Spencer.

In Elma, we didn't have impound, we had the sheriff's back yard. This was worse than an impound lot for one reason, his wife.

That crazy old broad had chased me down the street with a shotgun when I was nine years old for digging up her flowers with my go kart. Seriously, I was nine years old. Like I knew any better, and who the fuck did she think she was that she could chase a child with a gun?

The nut was off her rocker, I was sure of that.

That's what caused Sway's hesitation.

"I don't know about this ... it seems wrong." We both stepped over the ruts my sprint car left in their front lawn.

"No one is going to give a shit." I told her cutting the lock with a pair of pliers I brought with us before stuffing them in the back pocket of my jeans.

Sway sighed undeterred by my harshness. "But what if the police come?"

I gave her a look of disgust.

"I'm sure they have bigger problems, Sway. And, let me remind you, that it's the sheriff's house. Cops won't come, he will."

She rolled her eyes. "Even better,"

While I didn't get along with Mrs. Stevens, Sway didn't get along with Sheriff Stevens. This was mostly because he hauled her in for everything from branding cows, to spitting on his squad car.

For being seventeen, Sway had been arrested by Stevens twelve times in the last two years. It became a joke to us as to what we could do to get arrested in this pacified town.

So far we'd paintballed his house, spray painted Mrs. Stevens car with camouflage paint, branded old man Roger's cows, let out a herd of cows in downtown, and our most recent prank was letting loose in the town with sprint cars. Oh, and you can't forget the time we took them to the school or the many times we stole his squad car and parked it on the other side of the street to confuse him. He thought he was getting senile.

It paid to have a brother who worked at a hardware store part-time and could make spare keys.

So while we retrieved Dad's car from impound, Spencer kept watch down the street.

After a minor incident where I lost my footing and fell about ten feet, causing Sway to laugh so hard she almost pissed her pants, we were just about home free.

Falling ten feet and thinking I broke my ass wasn't the worst part. The worst part was with all Sway's cackling, she woke up their fucking dog who I was sure woke up the old hag.

In the end, we ended up getting the car and were on our way to get Spencer at the end of the street when we saw flashing lights pull up beside him. Turns out, because Spencer was standing on the corner, some chick thought he was casing her house and called the cops on him.

While we were in all reality driving a stolen car, I didn't stop for him.

"He's going to kill you." Sway said giggling.

"Will you stop fucking laughing!" I turned down Hurd Road, my eyes darted around looking for any sign of the Sheriff. "This is not funny."

Her fist rose punching me triggering the steering wheel to jerk. "All I can do is laugh because you constantly get me into these messes."

"Um, I hate to burst your bubble but this was your fucking idea. You're the one who wanted to help Emma."

"So we helped Emma but got Spencer arrested, nice work!" she huffed crossing her arms.

This was most certainly not going to go over well with my parents and I felt relieved when I pulled down the circle driveway to see dad's truck was gone. I snuck out back pulling his car Aston Martin into the race shop so I could fix the dent Emma put in the door.

I felt pretty good walking into the house. Not only had I

successfully boosted my first car and raced my sprint car around the city but Spencer had been arrested. This pleased me.

When I rounded the corner, Jimi yelled, his face turning red, "You kids are assholes! I can't believe this shit. One kid wrecks my car, the other breaks into the impound lot after taking his fucking race car for a joy ride around town, and the other … Christ," he glanced around the room. "Where the fuck did Spencer go?"

"Jail," I answered sheepishly securing a position against the wall a good distance away from him in case he decided to throw something at me.

"Jail?" Mom asked looking over at me. "Like in prison?"

"Well, no, not like prison. Like in the county jail," I clarified with a chuckle. "The sheriff picked him up."

At that moment, if possible, dad had steam coming out his ears when I held my hands up. "It was a total misunderstanding." I added.

Just when I thought it couldn't get any worse, Sway walked in, not knowing my parents were standing in the living room.

"That was a close one but I don't think—" she sighed when she saw my parents. "*Shit.*"

I hid my head in my hands.

Not that my parents or Charlie ever got terribly upset about the shit we did around town but they weren't happy about this one. It was classified as breaking and entering *and* stealing a vehicle.

Seventeen and we already had a B & E and boosting on our records, awesome.

It's not like that was our first run-in with the law and I doubted it would be our last. The next day, it was all over the paper that the Riley kids terrorized the town the night before graduation.

We got a kick out of it. Parents did not.

Loading – Weight at a given tire position on a car due to aerodynamics, vehicle weight and lateral G-forces in a turn.

Graduation day finally arrived.

My only thought was that I would be free. No more wondering when I could leave this shady Northwest town and pursue my dreams, this was it. I would be able to do what I've been working for all these years which is to run all three series in the USAC divisions.

I decided I was going to race Bucky's car for him in the USAC Midget Series and then I would get seat time in both the USAC Silver Crown and Sprint Car divisions with the car dad gave me with the sponsorship help from Bowman Oil.

This wouldn't pay for everything but it helped. Dad agreed to provide the cars but I had to pay for what sponsorship didn't cover.

I had money saved up from my winnings over the years in the various races and, of course, mom deposited money in my checking account, which I hated, but to make this dream come true, you needed money. Racing ain't cheap.

My dad provided a few cars and a hauler for us to use but everything else I had to take care of.

Even with my dad's help, it's impossible to do this on your own so this left me searching for more sponsorship; sponsorship he could help me find.

Once we found sponsorship to help us then this goes back to exposure for the sponsor.

How much exposure could I provide them?

You have to sell the product for them. You need to show positive publicity and win. The more you win, the more exposure they get, in turn, this promotes sales for them.

Here's the thing though, when you're seventeen, you don't care about any of that. You just want to race. You don't give a shit about the expectations they put on you or that glaring spotlight from the media. But I tell you what, that harsh criticism stings each time you have a bad night at the track.

You're there to race and that's all that matters.

When you have a sponsorship, that's not all that matters anymore. Suddenly it becomes a job. Something you did for fun becomes your means of income and something you're expected to do and do well.

You're a puppet for them.

My plan was to leave that weekend. We graduated on Wednesday night. I left right after graduation that night to make a race in Cottage Grove and then was back in town by Saturday night for our graduation party. Come Monday morning the following week, we were heading to the Midwest.

Cottage Grove ran on Friday so it was before the graduation party Spencer forced me to have since mom and dad were leaving right after the race that night to make it to Williams Grove for a race dad was scheduled for.

I stopped by the track to see Sway after I got into town Saturday. She didn't come with me to Cottage Grove so I was anxious to see her. I didn't ask anyone to come with me to Cottage Grove besides Spencer because, really, I wanted to be alone. I needed time to think not that Spencer allowed that. Next time I knew not to invite him.

Once I got to Elma, I thought about hauling out my car and gaining some seat time but I decided against it and opted to watch. It'd be good to have a little break before my schedule was so tight I could barely make it from city to city.

Approaching the fence at Grays Harbor Raceway and hooking my fingers through the chain links, I thought back on the first race I ever raced here.

I watched closely as my dad used the same techniques he'd taught me over the years to pass in a spinning drift off the corners and then bouncing his right rear off the outside cushion to get that added boost needed to slide past Shey Evans.

Dad always made it look so effortless.

"Will I ever be as good as you?" I asked myself silently.

I heard gravel crunching behind me before Sway appeared and leaned against the fence beside me.

"You already are." She said, answering my silent question.

The corner of my mouth twitched into a smile knowing she knew exactly what I was thinking. Turning away from the track, I sat down with my back against the chain link fence. When the cars would roar out of turn two, the dirt sprayed past us throwing chunks of mud over our heads.

"You nervous?" Sway asked after a moment of silence. She had a larger chunk of mud between her hands, rolling it through her fingertips.

"I wouldn't say I'm nervous, anxious, I guess."

For so long I knew exactly what I wanted, but it never crossed my mind that wanting something and needing something are two different things. Just because I wanted this didn't mean I needed this. Did I want this lifestyle forever?

I thought I did ... I knew I did. There was no question I wanted to race.

Sway smiled patting my knee. "You were meant to do this," she told me smiling. It was like we always had some unspoken language with each other.

When the races got underway, I made my way into the grandstands, my hood pulled over my head. I knew if the locals recognized me, they would be hounding me. The metal bleachers were filled with local diehard fans, kids squirming around in their parent's arms, teenagers strolling, and women with barely any clothes on.

I glanced around for Sway but couldn't find her. I wanted to watch with her but I knew she was busy. Usually on the weekly races, she was kept busy with making sure all the drivers signed in and staffed the ticket booth at the pit entrance.

Two rows down, I could hear an older man talking with his buddy next to him, who I later recognized as Travis Shin. He paid in pennies each week to get into the weekly races.

"You hear Riley's kid is leaving town?"

"Did you really expect a kid like that to race here forever?" the man chuckled. "His kid's got more talent than all ya'll out here put together."

"You're right man, he'll go far."

I shook my head, leaning back on my elbows, my feet kicked out on the metal bench in front of me. I'll never understand why everyone had so much faith in me. I was a seventeen-year-old kid. Sure, I had talent, but what made them see greatness out of me?

"How's it feel?" I heard Charlie's rough low voice from behind. "I don't think I've seen ya in the stands since you were just a little guy running around with skinned up knees."

"Yeah ... it's a strange feeling."

He took a seat beside me when the heats ended and throngs of people headed for the concessions.

"We're gonna miss you around here." Charlie said looking the direction of the pits.

I swallowed, nodding my head.

"It will always be my home track." I offered.

Charlie nodded as well. "I know."

We sat in the stands for the remainder of the heat races and features.

Before long, fans were leaving, cars and haulers were loading up, and eventually the lingering drivers left. Even after the lights in the infield went black, we still never said a word, just stared into the blackness.

When I stood to leave, he pulled me into a tight hug, "Take care of yourself kid and, remember, I'm trusting you with my daughter. Take care of her."

I wasn't much of a hugger but I wrapped my arms around him.

"I will."

I asked Charlie about a month ago if it would be all right if Sway came with Spencer and me. After a two-week debate, he finally agreed.

I left after that and headed home to where I knew our house would be teeming with high school graduates. I was looking forward to letting loose one last time with everyone but I also couldn't wait to get the fuck out of here.

Pulling down our long circle driveway, I laughed. Spencer must have invited the entire fucking high school, and then some. Walking inside, I realized I had no idea who half the people were. I knew Sway though and found her off in the corner dancing with Tommy to some rap song. They appeared to be having a good time so, instead of interrupting them, I made my way into the kitchen to grab a beer.

Another thirty minutes later and three more beers ... I was stumbling into the living room, once again, to find Sway and Tommy. Tommy excused himself to find his girlfriend while Sway threw her arms around my neck.

Sway and I had danced before but this time we were drunk and I was horny, *very* horny.

So, when *Bust a Move* came playing through the speakers I wrapped my arms around her waist, pulling her against me.

"Dance with me." My hands reached down and cupped her ass pulling her against me.

"You are so drunk," she slurred against my shoulder wrapping her arms around my neck.

"I know," was my only answer as we moved to the pulsing beat. Out of the corner of my eye I saw Chelsea come through the door but, being impaired by alcohol, I kept Sway in my arms.

Sway didn't seem to notice and just bounced around in my arms dancing to the music.

Chelsea hadn't seemed to notice me—how she couldn't have noticed was beyond me—it was my house. Maybe she thought I was still in Cottage Grove ... either way, she didn't notice me.

An hour later Sway was passed out on my bed so I planned on sleeping in the guest bedroom. I was far too horny to sleep next to her.

Stumbling down the hall, I entered the guest bedroom to see a couple going at it. Averting my eyes, I mumbled "sorry," when I caught a glimpse of the girl.

Chelsea.

"Shit, Jameson, you could knock!" Colby shouted covering her with a pillow. It was too late. I already saw it was her.

I laughed.

"Funny you should say that *Colby*, it's my fucking house!" I barked slamming the door shut.

Not wanting to be bothered and knowing Sway was far too gone to bother me, I went back into my room and fell asleep on the floor. I was amazed I could sleep, I thought this would bother me but it wasn't *anywhere* near the anger I felt when I found out Sway slept with Dylan. I didn't understand why, but this confirmed my theory that I felt nothing toward Chelsea. I wanted happiness for Sway, whereas, Chelsea, I didn't care.

I always knew she was messing around with other guys but I never thought it would be someone I knew. I think that's what bothered me the most. Yeah, I never showed much interest in Chelsea, but Colby knew we'd been seeing each other. I couldn't even call Chelsea and me together though. It was more about the occasional encounter.

The next morning, the day before we left, I was in my room packing when Sway came strolling in holding a bowl of cereal.

"When do you leave?" she asked throwing herself down on the bed.

I laughed. She was dressed in one of my t-shirts and sweat pants that were entirely too large for her.

I grinned. Charlie and I hadn't told her yet.

"What do you mean *me* ... you're coming with me."

I heard the clank of her spoon when she dropped it in the bowl and turned around.

Her wide eyes caused me to laugh. "What? When were you going to ask me?" her expression turned sour.

"What do you mean ask—I thought you wanted to come?"

"Well, yeah ... but you could have asked me first." She huffed. "Like Charlie will ever agree to it. I start college in the fall."

I didn't forget. I knew she had a full scholarship to Western but I was hoping she would delay starting for a little while. I knew I could do this but I didn't want to without her.

Sitting beside her on the bed, I fumbled with my racing gloves in my lap pulling the velcro back and forth. "I already asked Charlie two weeks ago. He said yes."

Sway glared arching her eyebrow at me. "Did he now ... and when were you going to ask me?"

"I'll ask now if you want."

"Yes, yes, ask me." She motioned with her hands for me to continue.

"Uh ... so do I get down on my knee?"

She glared. "This isn't a marriage proposal, asshole. Just ask."

"Sway," I grinned. "Will you ... come with me?"

She contemplated for a moment and then sighed heavily rolling her eyes. "I guess so."

"Wow, *try* to control your excitement a little. It's overwhelming."

Despite her sarcasm and lack of enthusiasm, I knew she was excited. Sway loved road trips about as much as she loved flip flops. This was a lot by the way.

Giddy about the potential road trip, she left to go pack as well.

Not more than five minutes after she left, Chelsea showed up. I'm sure Spencer let her in which pissed me off. I specifically told him not to.

She knocked and walked in like she owned the place, which I'm sure she thought she did after last night.

"Where were you last night?" she asked smiling at me from the same spot on my bed Sway was just sitting. "I called you last night. When did you get home?"

"Really ..." I laughed darkly. "Was that before or after you fucked Colby?"

Her eyes widened in surprise.

"I ... uh ... how did you ... I thought you were in Cottage Grove?"

"So, you thought I was in Oregon and fucked my brother's best friend, in *my* house?" I hedged. I turned around to lean against my dresser with my arms crossed over my chest.

"I'm sorry ... I just ..." she stammered bringing out the tears.

"Don't act like you're sorry." I snapped stepping closer to her. "I knew you fucked around but in *my house* ..." I shook my head. "That's low even for you."

She reached for me but I shook my head and stepped back.

"I'm sorry. Please let's talk about it." She begged pleading with her reddened eyes.

I looked at her finally. For the life of me, I couldn't understand *why* I was ever with her.

"There's nothing to talk about." I finally said evenly.

"What do you mean there's *nothing* to talk about?"

"That's exactly what I mean." The fact that I was moderately calm about this confirmed my theory that I felt nothing for her. She tacked on the name girlfriend to our relationship but then she felt it was okay to sleep around when I was gone. She had another think coming if that was her theory on all this.

"So, that's it ..." She laughed sarcastically. "You know, Jameson, it's not like you're perfect. I know you slept with Sway."

"What are you talking about?" I scoffed. "I've never slept with Sway."

"You did last night ... I saw her leave this morning."

I let out a sarcastic laugh. "You know, Chelsea," I stepped closer to her so she could feel my breath against her face. Reaching up, I angled her chin up to look me in the eye. "It *is* possible to sleep in the same room with someone of the opposite sex and not fuck them ... but you wouldn't know how to do that, would you?"

Her eyes flashed anger.

"Fuck you, Jameson!" she shouted pulling away. "Fuck you and your racing! You're never going to make it out east with that temper of yours. You'll fuck it all up."

I laughed despite the anger raging inside me. I wasn't sure what else to do. She knew goddamn well I would make it. Undisputable, my anger could potentially be a problem but she was trying to piss me off.

She then decided to up the sermonizing by adding, "You're always going to be considered Jimi's kid. I'm not stupid either, you can deny it all you want but I know you've been fucking around with Sway."

Never in my life had I wanted to hit a woman like I did right then. Not only was she knocking my skills on the track, but she was accusing me of something I didn't do. Wanted to, but didn't.

"Don't turn this around on me, Chelsea." I yelled after her as she stormed out of my room, my fist connected with my bedroom wall. The gaping hole in the sheetrock confirmed my anger problem was still present. I would need to work on that.

Surprisingly, once she left, I went about packing again as if nothing happened.

Trying to pack proved to be difficult because everyone stopped by that day to say goodbye to me. Some were enjoyable and others were not.

Tommy cried, actually cried, and then when I told him to meet us in Vegas, he was fine again. Tommy knew sprint cars and he specifically knew setups. I needed him.

Cooper stopped by and that was awkward because we hadn't talked since I found out he had slept with Sway.

He said he'd come watch races when he could and to keep in touch. I said I would but I wasn't sure that I would. I seemed to guard myself with anyone who showed an interest in Sway. I know now why I did, but back then, I didn't.

I nearly lost all control when my mom came for a visit. She spent most of the time in tears and crying about her baby boy leaving home and some shit about a nest and birds and I frankly stopped listening at one point until she started to make sense.

"Don't forget where you came from." She told me pulling me into a hug, an excessive amount of tears falling from her eyes. "Above all else, do this because you want to not because you can."

I'm not sure what she meant by that, but I listened. I think.

The next was Spencer.

I always felt bad ... what Spencer and Emma wanted was usually put on the back burner because of my racing.

"We do this because we love it." Was all they ever said to me when helping me out at the track. When it came down to it, they loved their odd jobs with my makeshift team. Emma had the negotiation skills of a great debater and Spencer could lift a fucking Buick if needed.

They were perfect to have around.

Emma on the other hand, I refused to let her come. Yeah, she graduated early with us but she was also sixteen. I didn't want that type of responsibility. I could handle Spencer and I could handle Emma, but not together. They fed off each other and I was the only normal one, stuck in the middle.

Later that night, as I expected, when dad arrived home from Grand Rapids, he made his way inside my room.

He didn't say anything for a good ten minutes and when he did speak, it was quiet.

"Is this really what you want?" he asked. "I only ask because you need to think this through. This isn't about doing something you love anymore. It becomes your entire life."

I knew what I wanted. I didn't have to think about it. I'd spent the last seventeen years thinking about it.

"Yes." My voice was confident and unwavering, just like my decision to leave home.

He sighed with a nod of his head, his tired eyes found mine. “There’s going to come a time in your life when you’d give it all away to feel.”

Huh?

I think he knew this was lost on me, so he continued. “I’ve been in your shoes. I know what you’re feeling ... you think I don’t, but I do.” He said. “It’s not easy to feel and it’s not easy to let a woman love you—at least not one who you are afraid to lose.”

Jimi was always cryptic when speaking. Half the time, us kids had no idea what he was talking about. Now wasn’t any different.

“Someday you’ll understand.” He said before leaving my room.

I nodded at everything he was telling me. He thought I loved Sway, which I did but not the way he thought. I loved her friendship. I couldn’t see myself loving her any other way. Sure it would be easy to but that wasn’t me. I had no intentions of having that type of relationship with anyone. I didn’t want the responsibility of it. From what I’d seen of relationships, I never wanted that again. They were complicated and required attention, attention I didn’t have.

Right now, all that mattered was seeing how I compared to those beasts from the east.

Scuffs – Slang term for tires that have been used at least once and saved for further racing. A lap or two is enough to "scuff" them.

The morning we left, I took my time loading everything after I got back from seeing Charlie and Sway. Charlie informed me that if anything happened to Sway, he'd kill me.

I loaded the car that morning and everything else we were taking with us.

To save on money, we only took one 360-sprint for now and then the others would be stored at the race shop my dad had built in Mooresville.

This would make it easier when we needed to pick up different cars.

Spencer and I had the car loaded with spare parts and engines by nine that morning. Sway showed up not long after that with two bags.

What girl could leave home for five months and take only two bags for clothes? Sway could. This confirmed my theory that she was pretty much the coolest girl I'd ever met.

While my parents made sure we had everything and harassed us about safety and food, Alley showed up. Spencer and Alley were inseparable these days, which meant she would be coming with us.

I was okay with that, only because we needed all the help we could get. Standing around the driveway after everything had been loaded, we went over the schedule with my parents so they knew where we would be and when. You could see the hesitation and anxiety in their eyes. They wouldn't have told you but to let their two sons travel across the country with no supervision was a significant risk for them, particularly when you are talking about the Riley boys.

Despite our argument yesterday, I never thought I would see Chelsea again but she showed up carrying a bag.

"What are you doing?" I asked glancing down at her bag and then leaned back against my truck. My arms crossed over my chest.

"I'm coming with you." She told me throwing her bag at my feet. "I'm not letting you go that easily … if Sway is coming, I'm coming."

"Do you really think after yesterday, I would ever want to see you?"

"I'm your girlfriend."

"Who fucked around," I hastened to add.

"So did you."

Anger surged through me. I shoved my hands in my pockets.

"I never slept with anyone else, Chelsea."

"But you kissed Sway." Her eyes had tears in them as she examined my gargoyle expression. I lost my temper in front of everyone. My family was standing not more than twenty feet away and I lost it.

"Why do you always bring up Sway?" I seethed my voice just below a shout. "I'm fucking sick of it! Do you want to know why I'm friends with her?" I didn't wait for her to answer. "Because, unlike you, she's not a vindictive, fucking, insecure bitch."

"I'm not insecure. I know that I'm attractive."

Rolling my eyes, I shot back with, "What do you want? Why are you even here?"

I wasn't upset that she slept with Colby, I was relieved. It was a way out for me. What I was upset about was her accusing me of sleeping with Sway.

"I'm coming with you." Her eyes found mine.

"No, you're not."

"What are you talking about?"

"I forgot ... you're like twelve fucking years old." I sighed and stepped closer. "No, you're not coming."

She stomped her foot as I knew she would. "I'm coming with you!"

"No ..." Jameson told her and hung his head. His temper seemed to be diffusing ever so slightly but I could still see that he was on edge.

Why Emma and I found this so entertaining was beyond me but I couldn't stop laughing. Probably because I hated Chelsea and I knew she used Jameson for her own popularity.

First came the rage, she slapped him so hard that his head jerked back. His cheek turned pink but he cracked his neck glaring at her and stood straighter, stepping closer to her as if this was his warning to her not to do that again.

Then she hugged him and from the grim expression he wore, it was just as painful. We couldn't hear anything else they were saying as Jameson was blocking our view but I could tell he wasn't happy. I got bored and made my way inside the shop to say bye to Jimi.

"Hey, Jimi," I greeted leaning up against the toolbox in the far right corner of his race shop.

"Hey, sweetie ... did you already say bye to Charlie." He looked up at me from his place against the sprint car.

He was down there checking tire pressure and the stagger on the car Jameson was taking. I knew we'd be back in but it was still hard to say bye to everyone. We were doing something we'd never done before. Four kids were heading into the unknown to experience life. Jameson and I weren't even eighteen yet.

"Yeah, I said goodbye this morning. Jameson came over and talked with Charlie for a little while and then we left." I laughed. "I think he wanted to warn him that if anything happened to me, he'd probably kill your son."

"Sway ... I'll kill Jameson myself if *anything* happens to you."

I only nodded, tears threatening. Jimi and Nancy were like my adoptive parents and seeing the emotional side of Jimi was a little much for me.

"You make sure he's careful out there." Jimi requested pulling me into a warm hug. "Keep him focused. He depends on you and sometimes you seem to be the only one he'll listen to."

I had to laugh. "Jameson doesn't listen to anyone, Jimi."

"I know."

We exchanged another hug and before tears could overcome the two of us, Jimi made his way inside the house to comfort Nancy. She wasn't doing so well and carrying around a book full of Jameson's baby pictures.

I hid in the race shop for a while trying to compose myself when Emma walked in.

Emma was similar to Jameson in the sense that when she wanted something she knew she couldn't have, her shy side came out. The Riley children were not shy by the way, it was all an act. "Um ... I was thinking since I graduated early I could, you know ... come with you guys."

I laughed. "You don't have to ask me. You need to ask Jameson."

"I thought maybe I could come along. He won't even know I'm there."

"Doubt that." I snorted. "You need to ask him."

"Ask me what?" Jameson came inside the shop with an arm full of tie downs. How he got away from crazy lady was probably a miracle. "Shit." He cussed when he tripped over a pair of shocks Spencer left lying on the floor.

"Emma wants to come with us." I said.

"Absolutely not," He didn't even think about it as he straightened his stance. "Hell, no," as he tossed the tie downs inside the hauler.

"But I want to be with everyone." She begged.

I started to feel for her. Emma didn't have any friends besides us and now that everyone was going with Jameson that would leave her with Jimi and Nancy.

Jameson leaned against the sprint car and crossed his arms. "You're not coming. I don't want that type of responsibility. It's bad enough I have to worry about Sway."

"Please," she cried.

I laughed. This was pathetic. "Let her come, Jameson."

Jameson was quiet and then pinched the bridge of his nose and huffed. "Fine, but I have rules."

"I'm listening." Emma perked up.

"You listen to what Spencer and I tell you." His eyebrows arched in question at her.

She nodded while I giggled next to them.

"No dating racers."

Emma frowned. "Lock me up why don't you?"

"Don't come then." Jameson challenged.

"Fine, but I get to pick the first hotel." She beamed and ran to her house to pack.

"I thought we were done with her." Jameson sighed tipping his head toward me standing shoulder to shoulder with him.

"She's your sister. She's not going anywhere."

"This is going to suck."

"What did Chelsea say?"

Jameson hung his head. "Uh ... she broke up with me."

I couldn't tell whether this bothered him or not, so I didn't say anything. Jameson knew how I felt about Chelsea so he didn't need to hear it again when he was clearly having some mixed emotions about this, so I didn't say any more.

I thought he would have been glad to get rid of her seeing how he wasn't even considering letting her come with us.

An awkward silence crept over us when he took a deep breath and smiled. "You ready?"

"Sure, let's do this."

"You sure?"

"I was until you said Emma could come."

"Hey, asshole ... you told me, too." He said glaring.

An hour later—an emotional outburst from Nancy—Emma carrying her entire bedroom outside and Jameson throwing everything out of his truck—we were on our way to California.

The plan was to race in Chico this Saturday night, then Vegas the following Tuesday night and then we'd be off to the Midwest.

I thought Jameson would be excited but instead he was quiet. He didn't even fight me when I turned on Gary Allan.

Once we stopped to eat, I decided to have a heart-to-heart with him while everyone else argued about what hotel we'd be staying in.

I pulled him aside. "What's up with you?"

He shrugged and looked down at his feet. In the distance, a group of kids around our age piled in the back of a Jeep with a boat attached to it. They were doing what every other teenager would be doing this summer, spending their time at the lake.

"Why does something have to be wrong?" there was a sour edge to his voice I hadn't heard in a while.

"Are you upset about Chelsea?"

"No." he answered immediately. He sighed and sat down on the curb outside the Denny's where we stopped at. "I'm not upset."

"Then what is it because this mopey side is not something I'd expect from someone who just left home to follow his dreams." I sat down beside him bumping against his shoulders.

"I just," he drew in a deep breath. His shoulders slumped forward letting his head fall into his hands. "I guess I feel like my entire family is risking everything for me to do this and what if I can't? Sure, I guess I can compete with the guys around Washington, but out east ... it's entirely different out there. They eat, sleep, and breathe sprint car racing."

"And you don't?" He made no attempt to look at me so I continued. Placing my palms over his shoulders, my head dipped to meet his weary gaze toward the parking lot. "Jameson ... ever since I met you, racing's all you've done. Spring breaks, you were in Eldora with your dad. Summer vacations, you were racing at different tracks around the West Coast. Friday night football games, you were preparing your car for Saturday's race or working in your dad's shop. Senior prom you were in Chico. Graduation you left early to make a race in Cottage Grove."

He finally tipped his head and looked over at me, his cheek resting against his forearm. "Do you think I can do it?"

"Yes," I told him confidently. "You're an amazing racer. Don't think of yourself as Jimi Riley's kid because I have no idea who that is. I only know Jameson Riley. You can do this. What I'm trying to say is that you gave up a normal childhood because you believed in something, yourself. You have this dream that means everything to you and I will not sit back and watch it pass you by."

He grinned. "You gonna force me to race?"

"If I have to,"

"Really?" he challenged with another grin, this time it was full of mischief.

I held up my hand. "Don't even think about it."

He had me thrown over his shoulders before I could even finish my sentence and swatted my ass once. "You were saying?"

"Fuck off and put me down."

"I don't think so. Let's go eat."

The rest of the night Jameson's mood improved immensely and when we were lying in bed that night, he finally talked a little about Chelsea. He was always so guarded when it came to his feelings about her.

"So she broke up with you?"

He blinked his eyes slowly as though he was gauging my reaction or something. "Yeah, I didn't give her an option. When I told her she wasn't coming, it pretty much forced her to."

"You didn't want her to come?"

"No, she ... I just didn't," his voice changed so I decided not to pressure him anymore.

I always knew when his tone changed that he didn't want to talk about something.

Rolling over on his stomach beside me, he tucked his arms under the pillow. "What about you, are you going to miss Cooper?"

"Hardly ... after I told him I didn't want to mess around anymore ... he stopped talking to me."

"Figures," Jameson grumbled rolling his eyes. "Told you he was an asshole,"

"Yeah, well, where were you at prom to warn me?"

"Sorry," he wrinkled his nose. "I'll screen your future boyfriends."

"Good, wouldn't want any more assholes."

"I don't think that will be a problem ... I probably won't approve of anyone. You're special to me Sway and you deserve someone who will put you before anything else."

"Have you been reading Hallmark cards or something?"

He laughed, *finally* laughed. "No," his eyes found mine. "I want you taken care of. I won't settle for anyone but the best for you, honey."

I felt this weird sensation when he spoke the words "*I won't settle,*" as though I was hoping he would say it was him. I didn't know how I felt about Jameson but I could feel *something* happening between us, something intense but I also felt that maybe it was just me. I decided not to look too much into it because, really, he didn't need this. This summer would be hard on him and I wasn't here to complicate things. I was here to support him and that's what I would do. I would be the friend he needed.

I could feel the tension building within him. A crumbling pressure. Now that he had sponsors, this wasn't for fun any longer. He needed to perform. But with anything that builds with pressure, the constant loading needs to be released at some point and, with Jameson, you didn't want to be around when that happened. He could put a volcano to shame with the way he could erupt without the slightest trace of warning. I was waiting for the explosion.

I laid awake most of the night, as did Jameson. No one could sleep with Spencer and his goddamn snoring. I was ready to kill him around two that morning.

"This is ridiculous!" I yelled covering my face with a pillow.

Jameson laughed beside me. "Let's go swimming."

That sounded like a wonderful idea to me. I jumped out of bed with more pep than necessary and was in the pool before he even made it to the door.

"I take it you wanted to swim." He laughed stepping into the water. I looked away since he was in fact in his underwear.

So was I but I think I was more distracted by him.

He swam closer, smiling at me.

"You're wearing your underwear." His smile grew wider.

"I'm wearing my bra and underwear." I repeated when his hand reached out and grabbed my ass. "What's with you?"

"Sorry." He gave a shy smile pulling away. "I'm horny."

"Then maybe you should go take care of something."

"Or you could?" His eyes looked down my body, well the half that wasn't in the water.

I slapped his shoulder, laughing. "I don't think so. You swim over there, I'll swim over there."

I pointed to opposite ends of the pool.

His eyes, those piercing green ones that screamed sexy, scanned my body again.

"Sorry. It's been a while." Before I could say anything, he swam to the other end of the pool.

We could hear Spencer snoring from inside the room. "I don't know what's more disturbing," he began glaring toward the room. "The fact they can sleep through *that* or that we have to spend the next five months with it."

"This is going to suck."

"Yeah, well, I may kill him or Emma by the end of this."

"You concentrate on racing. Ignore them."

He smiled from across the pool. "They're a little hard to ignore."

I swam closer when he held up his hand and chuckled.

"You better stay down there."

"Still having problems?"

"Yes."

We spent about an hour out there in the pool before we fell asleep in a pair of lounge chairs next to the pool.

When we woke up, he was still having issues so I suggested a cold shower, which he took me up on. He tried to get me to join him but eventually he took it *alone* to bleed his pressure valve as Jimi called it.

"What's with him?" Emma asked when we were eating breakfast that morning.

"Spencer snored all night."

"I didn't hear anything." She smiled. "I slept great."

"Figures," I muttered taking a drink of my orange juice.

Jameson plopped down beside me in the booth while Spencer and Alley, I assume, made use of some alone time in the room.

When we finished eating, we walked the mile back to the hotel room hoping Spencer and Alley were done. The thought wasn't lost on me that this might have something to do with Jameson's anger. His brother was getting some and, well, he wasn't.

"I'm thinking of getting my nipples pierced," Emma said to no one in particular.

Jameson started coughing loudly.

I smacked his back.

"Emma ..." I glared in her direction as she skipped along the sidewalk, pleased with making her brother uncomfortable.

Jameson pulled his cell phone out from his jeans.

"What are you doing?" I didn't need to ask, but I did.

These last few days if Emma did anything to annoy him, he called home to try and convince Jimi that Emma needed to come home.

"I'm not going to deal with this shit," he grumbled.

Emma being Emma, reached for his cell phone, retrieved it, and chucked it across the busy street.

"I'm sorry," she offered when a truck smashed it.

"Listen to me," Jameson growled at her while I held him back. "I let you come with us ... I won't feel bad about killing you."

"I said I was sorry. You don't have to be such an asshole all the time."

"Emma," I interrupted. "I would quit while you're ahead."

She didn't. Emma never did. I think she lived for the moment when Jameson blew up, and that he did.

The race in Chico was cancelled due to a rain out and that did nothing to help his anger. Then, to top it off, Bucky called and wanted him in Indianapolis for a Silver Crown race in four days.

He was already scheduled for a World of Outlaws race that same day in Grand Forks, North Dakota, at Rivers City Speedway.

With the way the schedule was this summer, he was racing three times a week *and* on Saturday nights.

I wasn't sure how long he could keep up with it, but judging by his temper flaring in front of me, the outlook was not positive.

"Jameson, calm down," I urged when he started loading everything into his truck to leave.

He was slamming doors, throwing parts ... just being the usual hotheaded Jameson.

"Calm down? Do you realize what you're saying?" his voice had that same sour edge it did the first night.

"Since Bucky is paying you, just skip the Outlaw race."

"I knew I shouldn't have agreed to this," he ranted ignoring me. "I don't want to be their fucking puppet. I want to race."

"I know but you can't back out of it now."

"I realize that, Sway."

"Well, if you do, why are you throwing such a fit?"

Jameson hurled another bag in the back of his truck. It made a loud thud as it hit the bed.

"Just get in the truck. We don't have time for this shit," he huffed throwing another one over his right shoulder. "Where the fuck is everyone?"

Anyone who knew Jameson knew to stay away when his temper was surging. They were safely in the hotel room. "They're in the room." Without another word, I climbed inside the truck.

"Get out here! We need to go!" Jameson yelled at the room. "We have two days of driving."

I got back out of the truck when he turned over the toolbox

spraying tools throughout the parking lot.

A jet would be nice right about now. I told myself but then focused on the bigger picture, getting Jameson to calm down.

For one, I was not riding next to this crazed asshole for two days and two, well, I didn't have a number two. I knew I wasn't going to put up with his shit tonight.

"Jameson!" I grabbed his arm shoving him up against the truck. His hard eyes looked anywhere but me but eventually focused on mine. "Remember why you're doing this."

When his breathing had returned to normal, I knew the pressure release hadn't been discharged nearly enough. This was only the beginning.

Yes, there were times when I wanted to punch Jameson for his outbursts; his lashing out at track owners; the temper tantrums in the hauler ... I wanted to remind him how lucky he was to have these opportunities because not everyone can race, but I never did.

Why?

Because he knew. He knew because those same outbursts, the lashing out and the temper tantrums were *why* he was doing what he loved. It was because he believed so strongly in what he was meant to do that if he was black flagged, he took it personally. If he was wrecked by another driver, he questioned them. And, if he didn't win, he took it hard. All that emotion molded him to what he was becoming.

The greatest driver he could be.

That emotion made him real but, more importantly, it made him Jameson Anthony Riley.

Adhesion – The "stick" between two touching objects.

"Give me that."

"No ... I had it first."

"I don't care, it's my truck ... give it to me." I barked and ripped the last energy drink from Emma's hands.

"God, you're such an asshole."

We were only two days into the road trip and I wanted to kill myself. Emma sent me to epic levels of madness with her constant talking and stealing my shit. Alley was acting like my mother. Spencer, on more than one occasion, made a wrong turn and Sway, well, my dick was the only part of me that was annoyed with her.

We had to make it to Indianapolis by Wednesday so Spencer drove. If they would have allowed me to drive, we would be there already but I'd also probably be in jail for speeding.

I spent a lot of the time with my headphones on so I didn't have to listen to Spencer and Alley arguing. They got along fine most of the time, but you put them in a car inches from each other for fifteen hours a day and you wouldn't act normal either.

Sway and I slept a great deal—most of the time on each other. We took my truck, a four-door Ford F250 so there was plenty of room in the back for us to sprawl out, until you accounted for Emma but we usually forced her to ride up front with Spencer and Alley.

Sleeping on Sway was doing nothing for my self-control, nothing at all. On top of that, I couldn't do a goddamn thing about the constant hard on I had for the simple fact that everyone was around, all the time. When we stopped in hotel rooms, they were there.

I had a feeling Sway sensed this when she curled up in my lap for a nap before we reached Indianapolis and she felt the rock hard bulge under her head.

She giggled as always, "I think I should sit in my own seat."

I groaned pulling a pillow on my lap and stared out the window. She was wearing just a flimsy black tank top. Her bra was showing and this didn't help.

"Good idea," I mumbled refusing to make eye contact with her.

Getting Sway's body out of my mind was a challenge that night, but once I pulled into the pits, the smells of methanol and dirt calmed me and I was able to focus on the bigger picture and not think with my dick.

I wanted to ask Sway so badly if we could have sex. Maybe that would subdue the need for her but, then again, what in the hell would that solve besides complicate things.

That night I raced in Indianapolis at the Lucas Oil Speedway, which is a 2/3 mile asphalt track. It had been a while since I had raced a Silver crown car so it took a few hot laps to get the hang of it. There was always a learning curve when you switched divisions but the good drivers adapted quickly. You had to or you had no business switching it up.

The biggest difference was the weight and the way that weight changed during the hundred-lap race. When you loaded the cars up with fuel to make it the entire feature, you had seventy-five gallons of fuel that wasn't there at the end of the race.

Another difference was that a Silver crown car has a two-speed gearbox and an Indy-style had a handheld starter. In order to fire it up, one of your crew members would start the car after you're buckled in and then you're on your way. If you stall in the race, you have to be pushed off.

Along with being heavier, they have smaller engines, a larger wheelbase and never run on a track smaller than a half-mile.

They took some getting used to. Not only did you struggle to push around a heavier car, you usually had to do this for a hundred laps. I was used to racing forty-lap features so I had some conditioning to do.

As soon as I pulled onto the track, everything felt right and that was a good feeling to have after the last few weeks. I was prepared both mentally and physically. I was unstoppable.

During hot laps, I was smooth, my lines were perfect and I knew I made fast time without even hearing it. When I slowed to a dawdling pace and made my way in the pits, I overheard the announcer.

"Ladies and gentleman, with a lap of 11.918, your new track record was set by a kid who has never seen this place before, Jameson Riley driving the 9R Bowman Oil car!"

I grinned, as did Sway and Spencer who met me at the trailer.

That was about the only good thing that happened that night. In the heat, I blew a tire. Fixed that, but in the main a driver from California, Alex Reed, kept pushing against me and eventually just drove me straight into the wall with eight laps remaining.

I had nowhere to go and ended up getting tangled with Ryder Christiansen and Cody Bowman (his uncle Walter owned Bowman Oil, my sponsor, but wouldn't sponsor him), two guys who were also competing in all three USAC divisions for a chance at the Triple Crown, the champion in all three divisions.

After ninety-two laps of leading, I was beyond irritated with this guy.

I was pissed by the time I made it back to the pits, my thoughts raging and uncontrollable. I had a wicked temper and this wasn't helping.

I didn't even want to look at the car when I got out, knowing damn well there was a lot of shit broken. I had no idea what I was going to tell Bucky or Bowman Oil. First car they provide for us and it was junk now.

Having dreamt about this for years and now that I was starting out, I go and destroy my car on the first night. Well, I didn't, this Reed fucker did.

Pushing a USAC official out of my way and throwing my helmet at him was not the brightest move of the evening, but neither was shoving Alex when I found him standing next to his car.

Next thing I knew, we were in an all-out pit brawl and I still didn't feel any better.

Alex wasn't much bigger than me but I got a couple good hits in before the officials separated us.

Sway and Spencer were in my face immediately.

"Jameson, calm down!" Spencer shouted pushing me back away from Reed and to our hauler.

"You'll never be the driver Jimi is you little shit!" was Reed's attempt at defusing the situation.

This only pissed me off because I was tired of hearing that, goddamn it.

"I seem to remember being in front of you asshole before you took me out!" I knew I would have won that fucking race if it wasn't for him.

More race officials and his crew surrounded us now and I knew my chance at doing any more damage to him was over if I didn't want to be suspended.

It took Sway a while but she eventually got me to calm down enough to get inside the truck and head back to the hotel.

I was still irate when we walked inside. The others stayed in the parking lot while I stormed inside, Sway following close behind.

"Jameson, don't sell yourself short. You won't always be referred to as Jimi Riley's son."

"I just—" I tried to interrupt her but she spoke over me.

"Stop acting like a fucking child about this!" she threw the magazine she'd been holding on the bed and stormed off to the bathroom, slamming the door behind her.

I stood there, confused, severely pissed off, and strangely *guilty*.

Yelling at a closed door made me feel slightly better.

"I don't need your goddamn guilt trip on top of this shit right now!"

I glanced down at the blinking message on my new phone from Bucky. USAC had suspended me for two races for shoving an official.

I left after that and slept in the back of the truck. Missing two races would put a huge hit in the points for the national title and I'd miss the start of Indianapolis Speed Week.

The entire thirteen hour drive to Dodge City, Kansas, to race in the Boot Hill Showdown with the World of Outlaws, Sway and I didn't say one word to each other.

She gazed out the window in silence.

I decided it was time to apologize when we stopped to eat outside Dodge City around eleven that morning.

I hated the excruciating silence between us but, more so, I hated that I took my frustrations out on Sway. She didn't deserve that.

"I'm sorry," we both said at the same time as we stood outside my truck in front of a restaurant.

She laughed reaching up to nudge my shoulder. "I shouldn't have yelled at you. I know you have a lot going on."

I shook my head, my eyes focused on my feet. "I shouldn't have acted like a dick and I need you to keep me in check sometimes. You're my best friend and I know I take you for granted at times. I just ... can't do this without you."

"Then don't be an asshole."

"I'll try not to."

By four that afternoon, the pits in Grand Rapids were filling in and it was time for the drivers' meeting.

Sitting there listening to the chief steward describe the rules at the track I began to wonder why they had these meetings. I mean, sure, some needed it but really, it annoyed me to attend these. Did the other drivers not understand what happened when the caution came out of where to look for your car number on the pit board?

Perched on the back of his ATV reading notes, the stalking man looked toward my dad and me. “Some guys have been cheating lately and dropping weight throughout the race.”

I don’t know why he was looking at me. I never cheated. Well, that was a lie. All racers have cheated at one time or another but I will say that I don’t blatantly do it. Everyone stretches the rules as far as they can, without breaking them.

“You need to number your weights prior to the main. If you drop them, it’s a thousand dollar fine.”

I shook my head. We already had our weights numbered but the fact that this jerk was implying that *I* was cheating angered me. I hated being accused of, he wins because he cheats.”

That night I made fast time with the help of Tommy who had arrived earlier in the week to help us this weekend. Dodge City was a two-day event and I needed a good setup with the way the track changed constantly, so that’s where Tommy came in.

I caught a touch of his conversation with dad and Shey prior to the heats, “If you don’t want to change your weight distribution, but only make a stagger change, you need to turn your adjusters to bring the car back to the original weight that you recorded with the other set of tires. You need to record the number of turns you made to the adjusters so you can recreate the adjustments at the track when you change tire sizes.”

These two always cracked me up when they talked setups. Tommy listened intently and dad, well, he was in heaven.

I understood setups and could manage on my own but I also knew to concentrate on racing. I needed to focus on that alone. I learned from Jimi with that outlook.

He was a one-man team until he got big sponsorship and now he just showed up to race. That’s what he was paid to do and it was easier on him in many ways. It still didn’t stop him from helping us but he had a good group of guys working on his cars and, in turn, they helped us.

Dodge City is a 3/8 mile dirt track that was tacky and the way I liked it. Then, right in the middle of the damn feature, it would turn into a tire-shredding monster.

Dad was also racing tonight since it was a regular scheduled point race for the World of Outlaws, which meant mom tagged along to see us. Originally, I wasn't supposed to be here but since that asshole USAC official, I wouldn't be able to compete until the division was in Bloomington. This left me in one of dad's 410 cars for the next two days. It was fine with me for the most part ... I love sprints. Although I was a little irritated with what this would mean for my chances at the Triple Crown.

Halfway through the heats, it was as though I was playing ringleader to these assholes, the assholes being my family and friends. I stood there next to my hauler leaning against a set of tires looking over my tire pressures Tommy had jotted down for me earlier and wondering if I could make any changes before the feature.

Kansas was not the place for us, entirely too boring which meant my crew turned to drinking. Once we got to the race that night, I seemed to be the only sober one as I never drank until after the race.

Thankfully, Spencer and Tommy could still function enough to help me with the car. Emma and Sway were another story. I also wasn't happy about Emma drinking this much. For one, she was sixteen and two, I despised a drunk Emma even more than I did when she was sober. Hard to believe, I know.

I insisted Spencer and Tommy stop drinking when I cut a tire down after the first heat and it took them a good fifteen minutes to change it.

Spencer dropped down in the chair beside me.

"I can't believe I got sober for this shit." He didn't seem amused that Alley was now giving him shit about being drunk most of this week.

Not much later when I was getting ready for the feature event, I caught a glimpse of Sway and was somewhat concerned.

"Uh, what are you doing?" I asked alarmed she was holding a hammer.

"That asshole shot me with a staple gun!" she wailed holding her thigh and pointing to Tommy. Her thigh was, in fact, bleeding.

I turned toward Tommy. "Where the fuck did you find a staple gun?"

He shrugged moving me in front of him as a shield.

"Does it matter?" he asked frantically tugging at my racing suit.

"Apparently, it does," —I gestured to Sway— "She's about to kill you," I told him laughing and moved out of the way.

By the looks of Tommy sprinting through the pits with Sway hot on his ass, I was on my own for the setup during the next race. There was never a dull moment when Tommy and Sway were at it.

Dad caught me when the horn sounded for the drivers to get to their cars.

"Hey," he greeted with a smile. He'd been in non-stop hospitality events since he arrived. "How'd ya do in your heat?"

"Second," I told him.

"Did Tommy set back the timing? It's changing out there." He looked over his shoulder at the track.

You could see the black shiny spots forming on the front-stretch that meant the track was drying out and resembled asphalt.

When the track turned black like that, the surface had become hard with very little loose material. The moisture evaporated off the first inch of dirt creating less grip. When that happened, you wanted a softer setup while the track was in that phase reversing the split in the front springs. You could move the weight up to the right of your car and that provided you with more bite where you needed it.

"You should soften the right rear sprint, too. It will help."

I nodded. "I think Tommy and Rick did ... but Tommy was also being chased with a hammer so ..." I shrugged. "He might have forgotten."

"A hammer; like an actual hammer?"

"Yes—a hammer,"

"By who?"

"Sway."

He smiled and reached inside my car to check the ignition timing. Sure enough, Tommy had.

"Well, good luck kid. Hope you get a good finish." He patted my shoulder; his chin came up arrogantly as he smiled.

"You mean, I hope you finish *but* behind me?" I laughed sliding into my car.

"Something like that."

Just when you think that you have a handle on the ways of racing and you begin to think to yourself, "Hey, I can do this!" you race with Jimi Riley, the King of the World of Outlaws and he quickly shows you that you know nothing.

He had been racing in this series for twenty years and some seventeen-year-old kid wasn't going to pull one over on him more than once. I was able to in Bloomington when I was fourteen but I knew I'd need to up my game if I thought I could win tonight.

I know I've said this before but sprint cars are violent cars. It takes extreme technique and throttle control to get these beasts to maneuver the way you want, and one slip and it is over. But in the same sense, you push the car to the edge of control where they hover on out of control and that's where they will handle the best.

Ten laps into the A-Feature and the track turned into that tire-shredding monster I talked about.

There were more cautions thrown that night than in any other race I'd been in and you couldn't see shit, just a dirt cloud.

Shey Evans flipped on the backstretch and took out five other cars. A rookie in the series blew a tire and ended up in the guardrail after collecting Justin West, and me, in the same corner. The feature event was taken by the only driver who finished ... Jimi Riley.

"What's the matter ... couldn't stay out of the guardrail?" Dad teased when I tossed my broken top wing inside the hauler.

He kissed his trophy just to rub it in some more.

I smiled and hung my head.

So far, this was turning out to be the summer from hell.

I couldn't catch a break for anything.

I sulked by myself in the trailer for a good thirty minutes before I heard Spencer stick his head inside, "Hey, dipshit, let's go. Mom and dad want to take us to dinner."

Jumping up, I followed. There were two things that would improve my mood right now, food and, well, sex. Since I wasn't getting any sex, I decided food would do.

Sway sat beside me. I jammed my foot pretty good when I smashed into the guardrail so she felt the need to constantly ask me if it was okay. It was annoying but I tolerated it only because it was her.

We also usually shared food so it was easier to sit next to each other anyway.

I groaned when she wasn't quick enough to take the foods I didn't like.

"Take the carrots before they mix with the others."

I hated carrots so Sway usually took the liberty of eating them for me. She detested tomatoes so I retrieved those while she took the last remaining carrots from my plate.

Dad watched in humor from across the table. "You two are something else." He mused taking a drink of his whiskey.

Never failed, dad always had whiskey around. I wouldn't say he was an alcoholic but he was surely borderline by some standards.

"What are you talking about?" I asked pushing the cucumbers toward Sway's plate.

"You two ..." he motioned with a head nod at Sway and I. "Do you ever eat a meal without eating from each other's plates?"

Now that I thought about it, no, we didn't. That was us.

Sway giggled picking at my plate.

I ordered a steak with steamed vegetables and wild rice to start, then, I had a milkshake, most of Sway's fries, four glasses of water and, well, half of Sway's hamburger and half of her milkshake. She had a huge eye for food but could never eat everything she ordered. I wasn't even sure she was a hundred pounds; she was a tiny girl, not as tiny as Emma but small for her height. Emma was a human version of an Umpa Lumpa and still couldn't ride on the rides at Disney World.

"Do you guys have enough money for hotels?" Mom asked shuffling money at us. Spencer grabbed the money while I pushed it back toward her.

"Yes, mom, we have plenty."

We didn't but I was tired of my parents funding everything. I didn't feel the need to tell her that half the time we were sleeping in the truck, she'd probably have a heart attack if she knew that. I glared in Spencer's direction when he told them we stayed in the truck a few nights to save money to buy a new set of tires.

Feeling full and having Sway next to me, I felt comfortable and sated. In the booth we were in, she was right against my side, our bodies touching ... feeling every intake of breath she took. My arm was thrown around her pulling her even closer. Every so often I would lean down and whisper something in her ear, usually making fun of Spencer or Emma. She would giggle.

This went on for probably an hour, chatting with my parents and keeping Sway close to me before a few girls who didn't look much older than me approached our table holding a picture of Jimi.

"Hey, Jimi," a tall blonde said to my dad as she placed her hand softly on his shoulder.

His head whipped around to find the girl leaning against his chair. My mom, always the optimist, smiled at the girls. I'd seen those looks before. They wanted more than talking.

"Hey, girls, what can I do for you?" he asked shaking their hands when they held them out for him and introduced themselves.

"Well, I'm Cassie and this is my friend Alyssa." Cassie smiled again at dad. I admit that she was pretty but not something I would ever look at twice. "We were wondering if we could get an autograph from you ... and your son, Jameson. Maybe a picture, too?"

This surprised me for two reasons: they had yet to look my direction and they knew who I was.

Clearing my throat, I nodded when Cassie arched an eyebrow at me.

I felt Sway's body tense when I untangled myself from her to stand.

Dad and I took a few pictures with the girls and, in the end, they stuffed their numbers in our back pockets before disappearing toward the bar.

Dad reached into his pocket and threw the number on the table.

"They were bold," he said tucking mom into his side and kissing her forehead.

I knew this wasn't the first time this happened to him. Jimi Riley was the king of sprint car racing. Not only was he a king of sprint car racing but with piercing blue eyes and black messy hair, he had looks going for him, so I've been told. My mom never paid a mind to it though. She always smiled and looked the other way as if it wasn't happening. Don't get me wrong, he had never once acted on the advances that I knew about and I doubted he ever would. Mom was it for him. I watched for years the way his eyes lit up each time he saw her and the way she grinned like a schoolgirl every time he whispered in her ear. After twenty-two years of marriage, they were still madly in love. Seeing that type of devoted love made me hope one day I'd find that but I also knew my love for racing overstepped that.

I wasn't looking for love. I was looking to make a name for myself that didn't include being Jimi Riley's kid.

When I started the summer my dad provided us with five sprint cars and deposited money in our accounts but we still had to work within a budget. Racing is not cheap.

Cars were upward of forty grand each and when shit breaks, it's expensive.

Knock off a wing like I did in Williams Grove and that was $600.

Front shock in Terre Haute was $900. An engine after the race at River Cities Speedway was $10,000. A broken left front axle at Columbus was $200. And a driveline after Eldora was $1500. I kept waiting for the priceless part like the commercials but it never came.

As you can see, racing couldn't be done without sponsorship. For me, sponsorship didn't even cover all that shit.

By the time August rolled around that summer, it was apparent a change needed to occur. Either that, or I was done racing sprint cars and needed to find a job to support my racing hobby. I couldn't rely on my dad's financial support forever and I didn't want to. I hated that he was even paying for as much as he did.

I was still racing in the USAC divisions for Bowman Oil and Bucky but that wasn't enough. To get to where I wanted to be, I needed as much experience as I could get.

Funny thing was I didn't know where I was heading. I knew I wanted to compete for the Triple Crown this year, but next year I hadn't given much thought to it.

Again, I just wanted to race.

Open wheel guys usually go one of three ways: Indy, IRL, or NASCAR.

Being an open wheel guy, Indy appealed to me but I was curious about those stock cars. I liked racing the outlaw late models so I thought for sure I'd like those stock cars as well, although I'd never raced them on asphalt yet.

After Knoxville Nationals in early August, I was heading to Grain Valley, Missouri, to race in a USAC Silver Crown race there on Saturday afternoon.

So far, I was fourth in the USAC Sprint points, second in the Silver Crown, and first in the midget series ... this meant that overall, in the National Triple Crown points, I was third behind Justin West and Tyler Sprague.

I was confident going into Grain Valley and that was exactly the mentality I needed to win there, and I did.

The following week I raced in Sun Prairie. I won both the midget and sprint race. It seemed that even though I was destroying a lot of cars, I was beginning to win. This was a good thing because I needed the money to pay for all that shit I broke.

Sleeping in my truck was getting old fast. I was at my wits end with my sister and Alley constantly bitching at me and I frequently found myself offering Sway my sweatshirt so she'd cover up. It was going on six months since I had sex and I wasn't sure how much longer I could go.

After the race in Sun Prairie, all of us, including Tommy who had been traveling more often with us, headed out for a night on the town. It had been a while since we had let loose since I raced sixteen days in July and already thirteen in August and we still had another week to go.

"What is that smell? Roll up the damn windows!" I barked plugging my nose as we rolled through the farm town.

It smelled like shit at the track and it smelled like shit at the hotel, so naturally, it smelled like shit at the bars.

"It's shit, I think," Sway said rolling up her window as we pulled up to a bar.

"I'm not going in there," Emma announced.

"Good," I replied sarcastically. Emma kicked at me from her place on Sway's lap. "Kick me again and I will throw you out of this fucking truck." I warned not looking at her but checking my voicemails on my phone. I had three revisions to my schedule that Nicole from Bowman Oil sent me. They had me racing in LaSalle and Terre Haute on the same day ... I was sure that wasn't going to work unless I could be in Ohio and Illinois at the same time.

"Can we even get in there?" Sway asked pointing toward the Canary Grill we sat in front of.

"It's Sun Prairie, Wisconsin, and I doubt they check IDs," Spencer said from the front seat. He sighed looking at the bar. He looked defeated. "Let's pray they don't."

After four speeding tickets in two weeks, I was no longer allowed to drive. My license was suspended. Bullshit if you asked me but I wasn't about to argue with the cop who pulled me over for doing 110 in a 45.

I think I got off good considering he could have thrown me in jail for that one.

No one was making any attempt at getting out so I did. I, for one, was tired of being cooped up in a car with these assholes and needed to get away. I didn't think this bar would sell us any alcohol, but when I walked in, there was a large USAC calendar on the wall. I had never used my connections for anything so far, but right then I did. I don't believe in using your popularity or who you know to get anything in life but there are times when this will work to your benefit. When you're eighteen, in a bar, and surrounded by your annoying family, you'd use your connections to get alcohol any way you could.

"Can I help you, honey?" an older woman behind the bar asked. Her skin looked like leather, and judging by the numerous tattoos covering her body, I doubt she cared what her skin looked like. Her voice was rough, marred by the years of smoking, I'm sure.

Spencer and Tommy walked up behind me.

"Hey, Jameson," Spencer pushed against my shoulder with his. "Sway said to tell you that she'd find you later. She and Alley went across the street."

"For what?" I turned to ask him. I did not like the sounds of that.

What in the hell could she need across the street?

"Hell, I don't know, they said they'd be back." Spencer replied holding his hands defensively near his face. "Emma went with them."

"Calm down, Riley," Tommy said throwing his lanky arm around my shoulder. "Let's get drunk."

"Riley?" a younger version of the leathered woman asked. She too was just as rugged but probably twenty years younger. "As in the USAC driver?"

Spencer pushed me toward the bar and I hit the edge with a huff and tripped over a few stools in the process. Graceful, right?

"Thanks, asshole." I muttered at Spencer before flashing the girls a smile and finding my footing. "Yes, I'm Jameson Riley." I held my hand out to them.

They shook it and the alcohol flowed from there.

The younger leathered girl was flirty, and I had a few drinks by then so I flirted back. Sway walked in about the time, Tessa, the leathered tattooed girl was showing me a tattoo of a dragon on the inside of her upper thigh. By now, she was sitting on my lap while I downed my fourth Jack and Coke.

Sway smiled when she approached and then walked past us to sit at the bar with Tommy and Spencer. This left me alone with leather Tessa. "Hey, I live close," she began leaning closer to me.

I knew what she meant by this but I also knew that I was getting hammered and this girl had been ridden hard in her short years. Who knew the diseases she had and was willing to share. I was not about to leave with her.

Soon my brain caught up with my all too willing dick and we pried Tessa off my lap. "I need to be getting back to my friends." I told her when she tried to push me back down in the chair.

"I'll show you a good time," was her attempt at convincing me to stay.

"I'm sure you would, but I really need to be getting back."

"You don't want any?" she tried again.

"Have you met my friend Tommy?" Tommy was recently single and needed some so I thought this would be good.

Turns out, Tommy was interested in Tessa. They left together not more than ten minutes after meeting each other.

This left me, drunk and horny, molesting poor Sway on the dance floor as we danced to some country song. Her head rested against my chest, her arms wrapped tightly around my neck. I breathed in, inhaling her rich intoxicating scent.

Sway sighed contently and pulled me closer. I wasn't complaining so I wrapped my arms around her tightly. "Sing to me," she whispered.

My lips brushed against her forehead before moving toward her ear. "I don't know the words but I'll try ..." I felt her smile against my chest as I began singing in a low voice.

I realized right then this wasn't the song for us but Sway had other ideas and asked if I wanted to get some fresh air with her.

"Let's go outside." I glanced around the bar. Tommy was gone, Emma was talking tattoos with the older bartender and Alley and Spencer were making out in a booth off in the corner.

Once outside Sway pushed me against the brick wall and her mouth was on mine in the next second. Her kisses were slow, patient and testing. Mine was frantic, desperate and uncontrolled. I wanted her so bad right then.

I picked her up, her legs wrapped around my waist and I spun her around so her back was against the wall. I let go of everything I'd been feeling those last few weeks and kissed her. Everything rose to the surface, displayed in ways I couldn't and didn't want to control. She met me as an equal, touching, kissing, and moving. The feel of her against me consumed me with pleasure. My hands greedily searched and settled on her ass.

I was operating on pure instinct and want.

I moaned against her lips, parting them ever so slightly as I settled into the juncture of her thighs. Sway gasped and, at that sound, I was brought back to reality and jerked back away from her.

"Shit ... I'm sorry. I ... shouldn't have ... sorry."

Sway shook her head, her breathing ragged. "No ... it's okay ... I think it's the beer talking. I didn't mean to attack you," she said straightening her shirt.

"It happens," I shrugged running my hands through my hair and then adjusting myself. Sway giggled, of course, and pushed against my shoulder.

"We should get back to the hotel. I'm tired."

After that kiss, I was not tired and in definite need of a pressure valve release.

I laid awake most of the night trying to decide what it was that I wanted from Sway.

Did I cross the line?

Sure, I wanted something physical, look at her! She's beautiful but I wasn't willing to give up anything. There's a reason why I kept her at bay. It wasn't that I thought I was happy alone; it was because what if it all fell apart, then what?

I shook my head infinitesimally at the thought.

I rolled over and watched her sleeping, only she wasn't sleeping, she was staring at me. I knew something was wrong with her by the sighs that broke through over the humming of the air conditioner. I was on the verge of asking her what was wrong when she sighed again, our eyes meeting. Even in the dark, it was easy to see the glowing of her eyes.

I smiled hoping it would ease whatever was frustrating her, but it didn't and she turned away facing the wall.

It annoyed me that she didn't return my smile to the point where I didn't sleep at all that night and was left with my own annoying thoughts.

I was not taking any chances with her. I needed her and, for now, I would get what I could. Even if it was drunk kisses and groping here and there, was that enough?

I had no solutions to this; no easy answers, and nothing was simple because nothing is ever simple. Just when you think something, life throws you a curve ball and you're stuck looking for that next perfect pitch to hit your home run.

So, was it enough?

Not really, but it had to be. Anything more wasn't an option.

I wanted one thing and one thing only: that USAC Triple Crown title.

Chassis – The steel structure or frame of the car.

By September, with two months to go in the season, I was driving anything I could but still focused on the Triple Crown title.

USAC ran on both dirt and asphalt tracks and the schedules were usually split evenly with thirteen races on each in the midget and sprint divisions. Some teams would only run the pavement tracks where other teams only ran the dirt.

Then there were teams running both, and only managed to be competitive on one, never both.

We ran them all with the help of Bucky Miers and Bowman Oil.

Between fighting the changing weather conditions throughout the season, we dialed in setups for each surface that worked well for us.

Because of that, we stood out, as did Justin, Ryder and Tyler. They were all winning but I was holding my own with the beasts from the east and feeling good about it.

The thing you don't realize when you're running all these races, fighting to make it to each town and a different track each night of the week, was how draining it was.

It's different from the stock car tours because NASCAR usually raced on Saturday nights or Sunday afternoon.

The USAC divisions and The World of Outlaws raced multiple times throughout the week and at different tracks each night.

I went a step further and raced anything and everything I could. It wasn't uncommon for me to get into a midget, sprint and late model all in one night. It was all about seat time to me. Wherever there was a seat, I was in it, learning.

That's not to say there wasn't a transition period between each series though.

Midgets are lighter than sprints and Silver crown cars are heavier than sprints. Then you have a modified or a late model that was an entirely different beast that weighed about 2,400 pounds and handled completely differently from any open wheel car.

When constantly changing divisions, there were nights when I never got the hang of it and then there were nights I seemed unstoppable in anything I got into.

Most of the time I was racing our own cars my dad had, but other times I was racing for guys like Bucky and Bowman Oil or Ron Walker. When I raced dad's cars, we worked on them and if changes needed to be made, we made them. If something broke, we fixed it.

One night while racing at Sunset Speedway on the West Coast, a third-mile red clay track in Banks, Oregon, we blew the engine in our outlaw late model we were running and needed an engine. We didn't have any spares that night because that was our spare in the car. I blew the original one up in Chico the night before.

Thinking our night was done for, I sulked for a good hour before Sway came walking into the pits holding a set of keys, dangling them in my face.

"What's that?" I mumbled cracking open another beer and leaned back in the lawn chair I'd set up beside my truck.

Her smile widened as though I was her favorite flavor of ice cream. "Keys ... what does it look like?"

I cleared my throat. "Whose are they?"

"Does it matter? He offered up the engine in his Mustang for you," Sway stared at me.

I stared back wondering how the fuck she got him to offer up the engine in his Mustang.

When I didn't move, she slapped the beer out of my hand while kicking my shin.

"Why the fuck are you still sitting there? Get up."

Spencer and Tommy were already pulling the engine out of my car and preparing for the transfer.

At Sunset Speedway they liked to water the track prior to the main and then pack it down again to provide more grip for the cars. By doing that, it created better racing with a tacky track.

So there we were riding around the track packing it down for them, really just messing around, when I noticed a lot of the drivers slowing in turn four and revving their engines. Took me a good ten laps of them doing this before I figured out what the fuck they were looking at.

There was Sway, Emma, and Alley sitting in the pit bleachers. The guys were staring at them. I chuckled to myself as this happened more times than I could count.

When we got back to the pits and began lining up for the main, a couple of the local guys were standing outside their cars when I walked up and caught a part of their conversation.

"Did you see the one in the black tank top with the jean shorts on ... I think she was the one with the reddish brown hair?" the driver of the number eight car, Mark Bayne, asked the driver of the six car, who I thought was Greg Ackers but I couldn't be sure. I had never seen him race before.

Greg said, "Yeah, I did see her ... I saw her earlier. She's with Riley, I think. His arm was around her at least."

That's right. I thought to myself.

"Nah, I think that's his friend," Mark said.

"Fuck that," another asshole said, walking up to them. "I'm gonna take her home tonight."

I sure as shit wasn't going to allow that to happen. I watched to see what car he got into and then decided to make sure he had a tough race.

Turns out, I didn't have to, he wasn't that great of a driver and turned himself around.

I never did have the balls to ask what Sway did to get that guy to offer up his engine out of his brand new Mustang.

After the race (that I won), we sat around drinking beer with the Mustang guy and, by that time, I was three sheets to the wind and could give a flying fuck about how the engine came about with the trophy girl sitting in my lap.

"We should change out the engines. We'll be here all night if we don't get started soon." Tommy said, removing the beer from my hands but left the trophy girl there.

And, for the record, I couldn't tell you her name.

"We ain't changin' shit," I told him with a lazy grin. "Give 'em the car."

And, we did. The Mustang guy, Patrick, got to keep his car *and* my 800 horsepower outlaw late model, all for letting me run that night. I even went so far as to hand him the trophy afterward and the trophy girl once I was done with her.

I hated to admit it but I was at a stage in my life where I had a sex drive. I was eighteen, with wants, desires, and downright needs.

That need was being intensified by my best friend, who I couldn't have.

All this resulted in me taking this trophy girl to the men's bathroom when Sway disappeared with Emma.

Still not knowing her name, I never even asked if she wanted it. I assumed that's what she wanted. It was what they all wanted.

So there we were in the bathroom, locked in a stall.

Her legs wrapped around my waist, her kisses just as frantic as mine. The problem was that I felt nothing.

When I kissed Sway, I felt everything. Each kiss I felt with a burning desire for more.

This wasn't like that, but it was providing a distraction.

I hesitated not knowing if this trophy girl wanted this or not but I figured when I unzipped my racing suit down to my waist and pushed her panties aside, that she would have stopped me if it wasn't what she wanted.

She never did stop me, and, Jesus Christ, she was loud.

I think you could hear her moans outside. I was thankful Spencer had stuffed condoms in my racing suit.

This being only my second time, I only lasted maybe three minutes. I don't think I knew what the fuck I was doing but, judging by her screams, she seemed to enjoy it.

I set her down when I finished. Pulling my racing suit back up, I tossed the condom in the toilet.

She smiled and kissed me again. "Thanks, Jameson. That was amazing."

I untangled myself from her and smiled.

"Thanks," running my hand down my jaw I smiled at her. "See ya around."

Looking back on those times, I'm ashamed at the way I treated them but it is what it is. I wasn't going to provide them with anything and I think they knew that. No one climbs on a man's lap in the pits and asks for a ride without knowing it's a one-time thing. At least this was my reasoning behind it.

When I got back to my trailer, Tommy was loading the rest of the tools by himself.

"Where is everyone?" I was surprised to see Spencer wasn't helping.

Tommy's head shot up when he heard my voice.

"Oh ... well, Sway left with Emma. Said something about being tired. They caught a ride back to the hotel with some guy and then Spencer and Alley are over there somewhere." He gestured to a field on the other side of the track before throwing my helmet inside the truck.

I wondered who Sway left with first and then felt bad because, for my own needs, I left Tommy to clean up by himself.

"Here, let me get that." I told him carrying the chairs toward the bed of my truck. "Did you see who Sway left with?"

"No, didn't ask." Tommy let out a grunt as he pushed the toolbox on the trailer. "It was another driver from the looks of what he was wearing. It might have been Justin, I think, or maybe it was Ryder? Hell, I don't know."

"You okay?" he seemed irritated.

"I'm tired."

I knew the feeling.

I was still amazed at the shit all of us did just to race. Yeah, I was the one driving the car, feeling the adrenaline rush but we all had the drive to go racing and would do whatever it took to make it to the next track.

Take Tommy, for example. He didn't have to be doing this but he traveled with us helping in any way he could for what, a hamburger here and beer there? He never asked for anything. He just wanted to be there. But all that took a toll on us by the time October rolled around. We were all tired. We worked well together but we definitely had our moments.

I had two of the best guys around working on my car each week. Alley did my schedule and talked to track owners and sponsors because I couldn't, without saying something stupid. Emma could sell crack to a nun so she handled the promotional side of the sponsorship and any media events, and then there was Sway ... she was there to keep me sane.

Later that night, I voiced my gratitude to Sway.

"Thanks." I told her as we slept alongside Nehalem Highway that night.

She left with Justin, which made me feel better. I nearly had a heart attack thinking she'd left with one of the douche bags who had been eyeing her.

"No problem," she mumbled curling up with her head in my lap.

We slept this way a lot. All our money either went to food or racing parts. We didn't have money to stay in hotels every night so we made due with sleeping in my truck most nights.

Recently we had purchased a few tents and sleeping bags, which helped so we weren't all sleeping in the truck. Tonight, Sway, Tommy and I were in the truck, Emma was in the back of the truck and Alley and Spencer were sleeping in the tent.

Sway didn't mean anything by it, I'm sure, but her hand rested against my upper thigh as she curled her arm under her head for a more comfortable position. Inadvertently, she had caused a rather intense reaction between my legs that was starting to throb painfully. I'd just had sex not more than a few hours ago but, with Sway, all she had to do was touch me innocently and I was hard.

She must have noticed, she had to have noticed, because she sat up, pulled her jacket from the floorboard, curled it up in a ball and placed it on my lap.

I couldn't take it.

"I need to get up Sway. I'm not feeling good," I lied pushing her away gently.

She sighed and curled up on the seat.

I got out and walked it off. I couldn't believe the reaction she had on me. One simple touch and I was aching with need for her. Knowing exactly how men think, I chalked this up to wanting her because I knew I couldn't, right?

Isn't that how it worked? The problem with that was letting go, I couldn't. I couldn't let go because of the possibility that it might not work. I needed my support system now more than ever. What's the most important part of your car? The chassis ... without it, you'd be dead. It supports you when pressure is put upon the car when you wreck. That was Sway. She was the steel cage protecting me from the blunt force of myself.

By the time the Triple Crown Nationals rolled around, we'd all been on the road for fifteen weeks. I wouldn't say I was tired because I'd had a lot of fun on this trip so far but I was confused. In those fifteen weeks, everything I thought I knew about Jameson and myself had changed on me, over the course of 107 days, that night in Eldora changed things for me.

I saw the warning signs.

I got jealous when the pit lizards lingered too long. I got jealous when he glanced at women. I got jealous when he left discreetly with some and downright angry when anyone said anything derogatory about him. I had no idea what all that jealously meant until the last night of the Triple Crown Nationals.

Sitting in the stands, much like the night I met him for the first time, I watched as they announced his name over the loud speaker. During their salute to the fans he messed around, revving his engine and throwing the car sideways in the turns to rouse the fans. He knew how to put on a show. He had recently gotten the name Mr. Excitement in the USAC divisions by the fans because he'd wait until the last few laps and either let another car catch him or make his move on another to kick up the crowd.

Watching closely as he waved to the crowd, my thoughts swirled around wanting those very same hands touching me. Just the same as any other night, the same thrill shot through me when he revved his engine and the same erratic beating of my heart was there when he took the green flag.

One would think someone who was only eighteen years old would show some sort of rookie mistake but he didn't. He rocked the house that night. His agile movements, his alertness, his adroitness shined.

Even Tyler and Justin, the only two who could stop him this season couldn't touch him that night. He was in a league of his own.

I stayed in the stands until he took the checkered flag. Even when he did, I stayed back and simply just watched his unpretentious but confident side emerge in victory lane.

He glanced around when Tommy and Spencer darted down to the track. I thought maybe he was looking for me but I couldn't be sure. He took his picture with the trophy girls and received his check for winning before making his way into the pits. I decided to catch him at the trailer to congratulate him when the trophy girl made her way there as well.

Lately, this would have infuriated me but seeing Jameson smile the way he did when he saw me, I realized, at the moment, what I felt for my best friend was way more than friends now.

When he kissed me, it shook me to my core. I was weak and I'd never been weak. I was independent, but when he kissed me I was reliant and helpless.

Pit lizards surrounded us when Jameson hoisted himself from the car, his face flushed and his eyes glowing.

"Come here," he mouthed.

Naturally, I pushed forward and approached his car.

I smiled, probably a sappy puppy smile but I tried to fight any emotion that would give away that I was most likely in love with my best friend.

"Good job," I reached up to wipe some dirt from his cheek.

He leaned into my hand covering it with his own. He didn't say anything but he stared into my eyes for a long moment before chuckling. "I can't believe I won Nationals."

"I can."

The party in our pit that night was insane as it should have been. He had just won a national event and that was huge. Even though I felt my feelings shifting, I knew Jameson's weren't. When we kissed later that night, the uncertainty was clear. Even when we ended up falling on top of each other sitting by the fire we camped out next to, he tried to get up many times but came back again.

Once again, we slept in the same sleeping bag. We seemed to do this when we were drunk. Trying to avoid my own internal deliberation, I got so drunk I blacked out.

All I remember was making out with Jameson and when I woke up my bra was off, though my pants were still on and intact. My shirt was another story, as was Jameson's.

Both of us were confused as to what happened but I was relieved to know that I didn't have sex with him, at least we didn't think so considering our pants were on. I later got a laugh out of Jameson when he admitted he needed to change because it was apparent he had gotten pleasure out of whatever we did in that sleeping bag. This entertained me. Poor boy had been so sexually deprived that he probably came just from making out. Not to say I didn't because I probably did, too.

As usual, we never talked about what happened in the sleeping bag and, by the next weekend at the Williams Grove National Open, we were back to being our usual selves.

I think that's what I was beginning to love most about him. We had a good relationship and didn't even need to try. We could get drunk, fool around, and we didn't need to explain. It was just friends being comfortable. I knew we needed to have boundaries and I was certain we would never have sex, but we were sexually comfortable with one another as well as being able to not have to try. We were friends in his eyes but I saw more to the mystique that everyone else saw.

I saw Jameson Anthony Riley, my best friend, who inadvertently and unbeknownst to him, I had fallen in love with. I think.

Being in Williams Grove that weekend meant Jimi and Nancy were around. I thought I'd hidden my newfound knowledge of loving my best friend fairly well. I told him to fuck off on more than one occasion this weekend but, *apparently*, I didn't slip this past Nancy. How could I? She herself loved a racer.

"I've seen that look before, sweetie." She said to me as we watched Jameson and Jimi during hot laps.

I hid my face in my hands. "I'm so stupid."

"You're not stupid." Gently she rubbed my back. "I've been there before."

I had heard from Emma how Nancy and Jimi fell in love but I didn't know everything. By her expression, I was about to find out. I loved Nancy. I felt at ease in her presence and now wasn't any different. She had a way of calming your nerves and you didn't even know it until you sighed happily. She was literally like a breath of fresh air.

Tucking a loose strand of her rusty waves behind her ear, she smiled. “Do you want to hear how we fell in love?”

I nodded and positioned myself so I could hear her better. With the cars on the track, their roar could be deafening at times.

“My childhood wasn’t the greatest. After my parents died, my aunt Mae moved us to Elma where she met Terry, the owner of Grays Harbor Raceway before Charlie bought it. So like you, I grew up around Elma.” I knew this already as she’d told me once before as did Jameson. “So when I was seventeen I was running the back ticket booth when the sprint car guys of the Midwest were in town. This was before the World of Outlaw series was formed. There I was, working the booth when a handsome driver approached. I’d seen my share of roughed up drivers, so to see a handsome one I was looking.” She smiled again, her eyes lighting up when she looked over at Jimi sliding past Shey in turn three. “I watched him race in the heats and then made my way to the pit concessions. Jimi came over for a beer. I wasn’t sure he was twenty-one so, of course, I carded him. I handed him back his ID and beer to have him keep a hold on my hand and say, “Does this mean I get to take you out later.” We went out later that night and I was sure when he left town the next day that he would forget my name. I didn’t see him again for four months and, by then, I was eighteen. He came to town again for the track championship night but he wasn’t racing. I couldn’t figure out why he drove across the United States to not even race.”

I smiled warmly. “He came for you?”

“Yes, he said he knew what he wanted and that was me.” Nancy put her hand on my back again. “Once the Riley men figure out what they want, they’re persistent and relentless.”

I knew this well. This season couldn’t have begun any worse for him when he started USAC and now, look at him: two points out of the lead in the Triple Crown heading into Pontoon Beach with six weeks to go. I had no doubt in my mind he’d pull this off. When he wanted something Nancy was right, he was like any other Riley, he persevered against all odds.

"I won't say anything," Nancy offered observing me watching Jameson sign some autographs in front of the pit gate. "But once he figures out what it is that he wants, I get to say I told you so."

"I'm sure he doesn't feel that way," I responded disheartened.

Nancy laughed quietly. "I know my son. Of all my children, I can read him the best."

I was about to tell her she was wrong when Emma dropped down beside us in the bleachers. "I swear to God, the longer we are around each other the more I want to kill him. He's such a jerk these days."

"He's not that bad," I replied gazing at him like a goddamn idiot. A few pit lizards had surrounded him when he got out of the car.

"Bullshit, he's not that bad. That asshole punched Trace!" Trace was another midget driver that Emma had been hanging around with. She apparently didn't get the memo when he told her she wasn't allowed to date other racers.

"Why do you think we intended to stop having kids after Jameson? He's been that way since he was a baby. You should have seen the fit he threw when we took his bottle away."

"What do you mean intended to stop having kids?" Emma asked skeptically.

"Emma," Nancy sighed but had a wide grin as if she'd won the lottery. "You were an accident."

"I was?" she balked.

I laughed, scratch that, I fucking fell over laughing hysterically. Not because Emma was an accident but because of her expression of pure mortification.

Emma leaned over and pushed me off the bench. I landed on my ass, still laughing next to the bleachers. "You bitch."

"Emma, watch your language."

"What's up asshats?" was Spencer's greeting to us.

Nancy shook her head. There was no hope for us. You'd think truckers raised us all but when you grow up at dirt tracks, cussing is part of the game. "He's in a mood tonight," Spencer said nodding to Jameson who was still signing autographs and glaring at another driver, Alex Reed.

"Isn't that the kid who wrecked him in Dodge City back in June?"

"Yeah," said Spencer before standing. "Come on, Sway, he wants us to get him away from them."

"When did he say that?"

"Five minutes after they surrounded him ... I thought I'd take my time though." Spencer found it funny when the women mauled him.

I shook my head. "And you two wonder why he's such an asshole all the time."

Later that night, prior to the B-Feature, Jameson found me inside his hauler avoiding the pit lizard convention outside. "Where have you been all night?" his voice was laced with tetchiness.

"I ... was with your mom."

"Oh, I didn't know she was here."

I wasn't surprised he didn't know. He'd barely been able to leave the hauler tonight and when he did there was a crowd surrounding him.

My eyes found his. "Are you okay?"

"I'm fine," he let out an enervated sigh. This season had done a number on him. "Only six more weeks,"

"Yeah ... then what?"

"Home for a few weeks and then off to California for Turkey Night and then back to Eldora in February."

"Have you thought about Australia?"

Bucky had been pressuring him to go to Australia right after Turkey Night to race in their sprint car series for the winter. Sprint car and midget racing was huge down there.

"I don't think I'm going to. Maybe next year. I need to regroup." He stepped closer and threw his arm around my shoulder. "You know," he smirked. "I always race better when my good luck charm gives me a kiss."

I giggled. "What kind of a friend would I be if I said no?"

"Clearly not a good one."

"Fine ..." I acted like this was no big deal but any time Jameson had kissed me these last few weeks, it was all I could do not rape him.

"Try to control your excitement just a little," he derided.

"Oh, sorry," I threw myself into a balls out kiss.

I knew anytime I put everything I had into our frequent boundary pushing, he panicked and pushed me away. I tested him.

I wrapped my arms around his neck and wiped that goddamn smirk off his face. His tongue was the first to brush across my lower lip. Within seconds of his tongue entering my mouth, he let out a groan and pushed me against the side of his hauler, his strong hands moved from my hips to my thighs and pulled me up around his waist.

Instinctively, I wrapped my legs around him and felt what I was doing to him. I was counting down the seconds before he put the brakes on and wrenched himself away but it took more time than usual. This time he let it go on and I was the one to stop. He needed to focus and not be doing this. Jameson had enough distractions lately and making out with his best friend should not be one of them.

"Jameson ..." I breathed in his ear but he didn't stop, instead he pushed me back further, grunting as his hips met mine. "Stop," I said, softly, and I'm not sure he heard me because he didn't stop.

I pushed against his shoulders only to have him push back against mine and wrap his arms around me tighter. He strained closer and moved his hips again.

As much as I enjoyed it, we did need to stop or I knew where this would be heading.

"Jameson, you ... I need you to stop."

I moved my mouth from his gasping for air only to have his lips travel to my neck, kissing and sucking along my collarbone. Running on instinct, I wiggled against him because this felt so good I couldn't stop myself, his hips twitched forward and the sensation caused us both to gasp, that brought him back to reality.

His face was pure mortification as he stumbled backward against a set of tires. "Shit. I am so sorry, Sway. Fuck!" he cursed himself. "I can't believe I did that ... Jesus Christ, what the fuck is wrong with me?" he punched the side of the hauler before storming out, cursing at himself.

Well, then.

I slumped against the side of the hauler, confused.

I knew Jameson well enough to know that he was just horny. Being on a road trip with all of us didn't provide much time to bleed his pressure valve as Jimi would call it. I knew he'd slept with someone a few weeks back, but other than that, the poor boy was in a constant state of arousal. I couldn't blame him. He was eighteen. It had nothing to do with me. I was just there and I was safe. He didn't have to worry about me wanting more or expecting anything from kissing. There was only one problem with that situation. I didn't know what I wanted anymore. For so long I was all right with that but now, I didn't know. I had begun to analyze everything.

Eventually when I heard the cars lining up for the feature event, I made my way outside. Jameson's car was lined up but he wasn't. It was just Tommy and Spencer standing beside it.

"Where's Jameson?" I asked looking around.

"Who knows," Spencer grumbled kicking the rear tire and then gestured with a head nod to the pits. "Asshole told us to line his car up and then took off the other direction."

Tommy looked perplexed. "We thought he was with you."

"I was with him earlier but ... he left ... I haven't seen him in probably thirty minutes."

Right when we were starting to get nervous because the rest of the Outlaws were making their way onto the track, Jameson came running from the bathrooms, zipping his driver's suit as he slowed to a jog. Without looking my direction, he hoisted himself inside his car. I watched him lock in the steering wheel before sliding his gloves over his bloody knuckles. Before putting his helmet on his eyes met mine, he mouthed "sorry" and then winked.

I gave him a smile and winked back before mouthing "good luck."

I had no idea where he disappeared to but I assumed he did some speed bleeding with either some pit lizard or himself. I hoped it was himself but doubted it. This made me sick to my stomach to even think about and, frankly, ready to vomit so I pushed those thoughts aside and focused on making fun of Tommy, always a good time.

"Looks like fire crotch got a little too much sun today." I slapped the back of his red neck.

"That's it!" he shouted chasing me toward the pit bleachers. "And you wonder why I shot you with a staple gun!"

Being distracted by Tommy was good because when Jameson won the race, I saw the girl I assumed he fucked somewhere in the pits sitting on his lap.

When he saw me, he removed her but I knew, a girl always knows. I was observant enough to know that he was hanging on to his sanity by a thread and I wasn't helping.

I didn't believe in regretting anything in life but I was wise enough to master avoidance and denial, two of my best traits I thought.

Take a Look – This happens when a driver, who's following another, darts out and takes a look in front of him. He may or may not make the pass. Sometimes it's used to make the car in front nervous.

It seemed in our rush to make it to a different track each night that this had us making silly mistakes here and there ... and then there were the mistakes we had no control over but were forced to fix.

There's no worse feeling, as a driver or crew, than spending fifty hours a week preparing a car for the next weekend to have it break and have to start all over again the next week, praying it doesn't break again.

And, when it does, it's crushing for everyone involved.

After the Triple Crown Nationals, still wanting seat time, we had the bright idea that I was going to run the Wild West Showdown, which was a six-night international driver challenge at six different tracks.

By the fourth night in Chico, I was beat and so was my engine. It blew up halfway through the feature race that night.

Now usually we would have time to change the engine prior to the next race but with the Showdown, they had racing in Chico on Wednesday night and then Skagit on Thursday, that's a thirteen-hour drive. So, ordinarily, we would have time to stop and change out engines in the sprint car we were running that night but, as luck would have it, we had to haul ass to Skagit to make it there in time for the race. It was around two in the morning when we left Chico after sleeping three hours alongside the highway. This left one option. We changed out the engine on the back of the trailer, going down I-5 at 70 mph. Not something I would ever do again with Spencer driving.

Tommy, and our other buddy Scott Pricket (Scooter), who we had met during the season, and me were hanging off the side of the open trailer changing out engines while Emma and Sway handed us tools we needed through the back window of my truck.

We weren't using my hauler this week but an eighteen-foot open trailer and it wasn't safe to be hanging off the side of it.

"Hand me the 9/16 wrench," I told Scooter reaching my hand over the roll bars and holding on with the other to the torsion bars. He didn't answer so I peeked my head up making sure he hadn't fallen off the side. "Where's the wrench?"

"Uh ..." he looked around beside him. "I think it's in Woodburn. Do you still want it? We could turn around," he suggested with a smirk.

We must have lost our entire set of wrenches that trip but we managed to finish changing out the engine as we barreled through the pit gates. Tommy's hands were bleeding from bumping up against parts, I had a black eye from where Scooter dropped a crowbar on my face, and Scooter had a fat lip from where my hand slipped off a bolt and smacked him in the mouth, *after* he dropped the crowbar.

To this day, I hold my ground that that was an accident.

We ended up setting fast time that night but didn't do so well in the feature and finished seventh.

Later that night, another driver and friend of ours, Reece Wilcox, a tall southern driver out of Memphis, came walking up to our trailer holding up our wrenches. "Can you believe some asshole was throwing wrenches on the freeway?" Scooter and I exchanged a smile. "His loss. Got me an entire set by the time I reached Olympia," Reece shrugged and walked off with my wrenches.

Aside from scrambling to another track each week, I also had to deal with other racers and their attraction toward my best friend and sister. It never failed, no matter what track we were at, the men flocked to the girls. Alley was attractive—you could say that, with big tits, long legs and blonde hair, Spencer's type. Not mine.

And, Emma, well she's my little sister but she had the cute thing down and men loved that shit, I guess. But what was harder than seeing men pick up on my little sister was seeing them flirt with Sway. Maybe I didn't know how I felt about Sway or the reasons why I was attracted to her but I was; seeing other men and, more specifically, other racers swarming her in the pits was not something I enjoyed. Avoided actually and I did a lot of walking away during conversations just to avoid it.

Unfortunately, there were times when I couldn't walk away, like in Williams Grove in late October that year. It wasn't long after Sway's eighteenth birthday, I'd placed third in the feature so I was slightly annoyed just by that and the fact that we needed to be in Lernerville later in the week had me thinking we should have left by now but no, everyone was standing around bullshitting and drinking. This happened after every race so I shouldn't have been so surprised. Besides Spencer and Alley, none of us were twenty-one, but that never stopped us from throwing back the beers after a race.

Parker Dunn, one of the biggest trash talkers in USAC, was another Silver Crown racer who'd I began to get to know based on the fact we were competing on the same series and I'd grown to develop a racing relationship with him, the kind where we showed each other respect on the track. That ended later that night when he crossed the line. The "Sway line" I'd built around myself and others.

"Hey," Parker sat down next to me on the back of my tailgate after brushing off the dirt. Still suited in his uniform I could smell the mixture of methanol and mud. "Is Sway like your girlfriend or something?"

I took a slow drink of my beer, contemplating how I might answer that. It took me a few minutes and when I answered, it seemed I was trying to tell myself that same thing. “No, she’s my best friend.”

“Oh, okay. So she’s available then?” he asked looking over at her. I craned my neck forward to look over at her. She was standing beside Spencer drinking a beer, giggling at Tommy. Her hair was blowing with the subtle wind, her cheeks flushed from the cool crisp fall air. Wearing a black Bowman Oil hooded sweatshirt, she hugged herself to keep warm.

“No, she’s not *available*.”

“You said you weren’t dating,” his expression bewildered by my sharp threatening tone.

“Yeah,” I jumped down from the tailgate and leaned against it resting my weight on my arms. “She’s not my girlfriend but that doesn’t mean she’s available. I’m sure as shit not okay with her seeing you.”

“Why?” he glared my direction but looked back over at Sway.

“Because you’re a racer—nothing means anything to you but the next race.” I stood straighter.

He let out a dark laugh while raising his beer to his lips and then laughed again shaking his head. “I never said I wanted to date her. I’m just looking for a little fun. You stick around her so I’m assuming she’s a good time.”

It’s no surprise to anyone who knows me that I had a short fuse. I knocked the beer from his hand and punched him square in the mouth before he finished the words “good time.”

Like I said, our friendship ended that night.

Walking back to the hauler, Sway caught up with me and pulled me aside.

“What’s wrong with you? I heard you punched Dunn?”

“I did,” was my only answer. My eyes focused on her lips.

“Why?”

This was another time, I reacted without using my brain, leaning forward to kiss her forehead.

“Because,” I mumbled avoiding her questioning glance. I couldn’t even look her in the eyes. "You deserve better than him and all he wanted was a one night thing." I told her placing another kiss against her forehead before walking back toward my car.

That night, laying in the hotel I watched Sway sleep again. We could only afford one room so Alley and Spencer were in one bed while Sway and Emma slept in the other—I slept on the couch next to the bed.

I knew I had feelings for Sway but, for the life of me, I couldn't decipher what they meant to me. I wanted her but did it go beyond that?

Her body was amazing. I've always found Sway attractive but now, as she matured, *Jesus Christ*. There wasn't a man alive who wouldn't wish she was in his bed every night, including me.

The following weekend in Lernerville, Dunn and I still weren't on speaking terms. It wasn't uncommon for pit lizards to be hanging around our pit these days and the more races I ran, the more it occurred. It seemed there was at least a few hanging around at all times.

Before our heat races, one brave girl made her way through the crowd gathered around while we made some adjustments to my car.

Sway was scraping tires off to the side of the trailer with a handheld grinder but I could see her out of the corner of my eye from my spot on the ground under the car.

"Are you Jameson Riley?" Beside me, I could see Sway roll her eyes.

Squinting into the bright sun, I made out her silhouette, tall, curvy, sexy, I guess. It'd been a while since I'd had sex, so naturally I looked.

What man wouldn't?

Tommy, being Tommy, made his way over before I could say anything.

"Hey, there, what brings you over here?"

The girl laughed, twirling her hair on her fingertip. Rolling my eyes at Tommy and his flirting antics, I continued to change out my shocks. You'd think him and his orange hair wouldn't catch the attention of girls, but he could. I think they were all stunned at the bright hair or maybe felt bad for him.

"I'm Lindsey," she chimed, "I was hoping to meet Jameson." She crouched down beside me. Out of the corner of my eye, I examined her long tanned legs. Her jean shorts appeared painted on and her shirt looked like it belonged on a toddler, *still*, I couldn't avert my eyes. I imagined how her legs would look wrapped around my waist or thrown over my shoulders.

Shit. Stop it, you idiot.

Sway snorted and threw the grinder down beside her, walking away.

I sighed running my hand through my hair. I had no idea what was wrong with Sway these days, but lately, she'd become exceptionally annoyed at the pit lizards.

To be fair, they were annoying.

"Did you want an autograph or something?"

I didn't have time for this.

"Well ..." Lindsey bit down on her lip. "I was hoping for something a little more *personal.*"

I knew what she wanted, as did Tommy who let out a low whistle. I'd moved from under my car and leaned up against the right rear tire glaring in Tommy's direction.

Lindsey being the standard pit lizard you'd find in the pits before a race, took no time at all to straddle my lap and whisper in my ear while slipping her number inside the front of my racing suit. "Come find me after the race, darling."

"Lindsey is it?" she nodded as I pulled her to stand up. "I'm sure you're a nice girl but I have to be in Grand Rapids tomorrow night. I don't have time."

I turned away so she didn't try again. I prided myself that I was starting to get the hang of this rejecting thing. With time, maybe I could ignore myself, myself being the asshole who couldn't stop thinking about his best friend being naked.

Lindsey left with Tommy after that, not sure where to and could care less. Since he and his girlfriend broke up, he and his orange hair were having a good time on the road.

After finishing up the adjustments on the car, Scooter and I walked the track like I usually did, checking the surface. For the most part, he was mostly quiet and understood that I was thinking. I liked to check the ruts and the coloring of the track. I knew if it was darkening, I would need to make air pressure and spring adjustments.

Kicking clay around, I glanced over at the pit bleachers to see Sway and Dunn talking.

Scooter laughed when I glared in their direction. It was becoming pretty evident that I was protective of Sway and *everyone*, I mean *everyone*, mistook this as me having romantic feelings toward her. It wasn't that. I wanted her with someone who deserved her. None of these assholes did.

"Careful there, you don't want to confuse the pit lizards," Scooter remarked on our way back to the pits.

"Shut up," I shot back defensively throwing my helmet at him.

The race couldn't have gone any worse. My car was horrible and didn't improve one bit throughout the seventy-five lap main event. I took my frustrations out on Dunn in front of me and, with one lap to go, I bumped him a little too hard and sent him into the marbles; he lost control and flipped his car a few times on the backstretch. I did not feel this was entirely my fault. He was the one who lost control, right?

After roughing up Dunn on the track, Sway came to find me.

"You're being an asshole!" she told me while I opened my second beer.

I heard this a lot so it really didn't mean anything any longer. It was just a fucking word.

Toward the end of October, the schedule for USAC was clear until the Perris Auto Week the first week in November. This left us running sprint cars and late models at local tracks whenever we found one. I was tired having run four nights a week for the past four months but I also knew I needed seat time in anything.

Emma had heard from a group of guys about a sprint car invitational taking place at a track outside of Republic, Washington, called Eagle Racetrack. It is a 3/8-mile dirt track out in the middle of nowhere.

After getting lost for a good hour we almost turned around when we spotted a track on the side of the mountain. It was *literally* on the side of the mountain. There were no signs for the track at all. You came around the bend in the road and there it was.

It appeared they decided while logging trees, "Hey, let's build a track."

And, so they did.

I'd never seen something like this before. It was crazy.

There were no bleachers, just rusty metal pieced together. The flag stand was about eight pieces of plywood strung together in odd directions and the track, well, it looked as though they mowed through the brush to create something resembling a track and then added clay.

Did I mention there were no guardrails, just trees?

I wasn't positive this would end well.

After getting registered, Tommy and I walked the track with Ryder, Justin, and Cody. The dirt was dry, nearly sand, combined with rocks, maybe even boulders and there was a fucking ditch about two feet wide on the backstretch.

I was not impressed.

Dallas, an official I assumed by his black shirt that read, "Official" across the chest, walked up to us. He was an old worn out man with teeth just as worn.

We made small talk for a moment before he commented on my previous wins.

I'd never met anyone quite like Dallas and that was apparent when he said, "I hear you're good," in my direction, his toothless smile caused Spencer to take a step back and Sway to lean into my shoulder.

I didn't answer right away and then he was off in the other direction.

"Where'd he go to school?" Sway whispered when he strolled away. "West Virginia?"

"Nah, I don't think they have schools where he came from," I replied.

Somewhere between the hillbilly announcer singing the national anthem and the eighty-year-old trophy girl making ogle eyes at me, I was beginning to understand why it was invitation only.

Emma refused to get out of the truck and spent the remainder of the night in there with the window up and doors locked.

They had no setup for the night and it seemed like they were flying by the seat of their pants when Alley stepped in and asked if she could help them.

This got the night moving along because I couldn't wait to get the fuck out of here.

"Nice trailer," Tommy snorted in the direction of a homemade trailer pulling into what they called the pits. This was just another field of ditches and boulders.

Walking up to me with a basket of fries, Tommy laughed. I glanced over my shoulder after stealing a few. It looked like something out of *Sanford and Son* out here.

Not knowing what else to do, we made our way over to the pit bleachers.

Sway dropped down beside us to watch the modified heat races.

After glaring in Tommy's direction, she kicked her feet up on the wooden step in front of her. Sighing, she took a long look behind us at the pits.

"This is insane," she finally said turning back around to look over at me. "Did you see that ditch on the back stretch? You could bury a body out there." She glared at Tommy again.

They still weren't seeing eye-to-eye after the staple incident.

I followed her gaze across the pits. Between the homemade haulers, roughed up drivers, and junky cars, it was apparent we were smack dab in the middle of *Deliverance*.

"No, shit," I muttered scraping my hand across the makeshift bleachers. A rusty nail snagged my index finger, tearing the skin open. "You had a tetanus shot lately?"

Sway nodded and looked down at my finger pricked with blood. "Have you?"

We sat up there for another twenty minutes as Dallas attempted to water the track with buckets.

"Where are you going?" I asked when Sway stood.

"To get beer. I'll be fine." She sighed when I stood beside her. "I don't need a chaperone."

"Oh, yes, you do," I challenged. "There are some ... questionable people around here."

"All right fine," she motioned for me to turn around. "You're carrying me then."

After getting a beer for Sway, I was tempted to take one for myself but I never drank prior to a race, so tonight wouldn't be any different regardless of my sanity to get out there on the track.

Ryder and I decided to take some hot laps prior to qualifying. Once on the track, I was convinced this was a horrible idea and was ready to pack up and leave.

Not only was there a ditch on the backstretch but some dumb fucker decided to put a knoll out there in front of it like it was some Supercross race.

That jump launched you a good two feet off the ground before you hit turn three. Being airborne in a sprint car was not something I enjoyed because it usually means I'm wrecking.

I was okay with the pebbles smacking my visor but when Ryder kicked up a few bowling ball-sized rocks that his right rear unearthed, I began to wonder if I would die here tonight.

After ten laps, I had enough of the whoops and decided to park my car.

Since we arrived, Justin, Ryder, and I had attracted most everyone in the pits to come check out our cars. Judging by the appearance of their cars, I was sure they'd never seen any as nice as ours.

Two older men, Holden and Kenny, had migrated over to us and asked if they could pit for us.

Sway thought this would be entertaining, so we agreed.

"Aren't you supposed to swarm over here and change my tire?" I teased Holden when I pulled up to my hauler after the hot laps.

"Boy, you'd been watchin' too much NASCAR," Holden laughed. "We old boys ain't move that fast. Christ, Kenny could break a hip!"

Holden walked away laughing. Kenny stood beside me smiling as he had the entire afternoon. Kenny was just that happy. Why wouldn't he be? He had all his teeth in a town most didn't. It's like he was royalty or something.

Sway walked past us toward the concession, my eyes followed her until Kenny chuckled beside me.

"Oh, I get it," he said spitting into his beer. "That your girl?"

"No, it's not like that." I said, and then looked down to see spit on my shoe where he'd missed his cup. I almost gagged. I hated anything on my skin and spit on my shoe seemed to be something else that made me want to burn them.

"Yeah, but you wish."

I smiled despite my urge to remove my shoes.

Out of nowhere, he slapped the side of my head.

"Watch your speed out there, when there's a cloud of smoke, stick to your line." It was as though he was giving me the *Days of Thunder* speech.

I laughed gesturing to my car. "You wanna drive?"

"Fuck no," he said, "those guys look crazy."

They were crazy, that was noticeable when the heat races came around and they combined classes. Putting a group of sprint cars on a track with hobby stocks was something similar to running a bicycle next to a Formula One car.

During the feature, I passed a road grader on the backstretch—an actual road grader. The worst part, they never threw the caution. Even after a flock of chickens came onto turn two and sat there, still no caution flag.

It soon became a game between Justin and me to see how many chickens we could hit when we slid into the corners.

I have to say it was by far the worst track I'd ever been to, but it was also some of the most entertaining racing I'd ever done.

Ryder came up to me after the feature, if you could call it the feature, that he won. Something about the chickens in turn two made me think it wasn't a real race.

I plucked some feathers from my helmet. He laughed pulling some from his.

"Once you get used to the bump, it's kind of fun."

I laughed. "Yeah, sure."

Now that we weren't out there in that madness, yeah, it could be considered fun.

Holden and Kenny were a good time that night. Old men were always entertaining to me and, despite their age, they knew how to have a good time.

Sway and Tommy convinced Kenny that he should ask this girl out that was hanging around our pit. I knew what she was looking for but I wasn't in the mood tonight. That's a lie, I was but I didn't feel the need to be with anyone other than Sway. She was sitting on my lap when Kenny walked up to me looking a little humiliated.

"I saw that going differently in my head," he said sitting down beside me on a tire.

"Not like you planned, huh?"

"Not at all," he let out a nervous chuckle.

"Come on, Kenny, let's show you a good time." I said, throwing my arm around him and tossing him and Sway another beer. "Nothing ever goes the way you plan with women."

Dallas turned out to be quite the party animal, as did Kenny and Holden.

This town may have had one strange setup for a track but they all seemed to know how to have a good time. The coolest part was, they didn't make us leave after the race, you could camp in the pits.

I was fairly shitfaced by the time I made it to our tents to sleep that night and saw Holden fall over in front of his more than once.

"What happened to you?" I asked Holden who was now laying on his back in the gravel.

"Hell, I don't know." He examined his shoes before standing up. "I adjusted my feet and fell down."

"Come on, old timer, let's get some sleep."

"Who you callin' old timer, son?" he slurred brushing dirt from his overalls.

He passed out within minutes of hitting his sleeping bag.

When the chickens from turn two woke us up at four that morning with only two hours sleep, we decided to make our way down to California for the final week of USAC racing.

We ended up choosing to stop off at a hotel to get some sleep but we had to find the hotel first. It seemed getting here wasn't half the battle, finding our way back to the hotel was.

"What are you doing? I just want to get to the hotel," I told Sway when she pulled over alongside the road in a questionable mobile home park. She was driving my truck because Alley and Spencer were fighting in the back seat.

Above their bickering, she yelled, "I have to pee."

"Where are you going to go pee at? That person's house?" I gestured the mobile home with a blue tarp on their roof and a sign on the door that said trespassers will be executed.

"Fuck you. I have to pee."

"Fuck me?"

"Yes ... fuck you," she nodded and then ran for the woods to pee.

Concerned for her safety, I followed her.

She was pulling up her pants when I found her. "Don't run off in the woods like that."

"Oh, stop being so protective," she said itching her arm. "I'm fine by the way."

"Why are you itching and did you step in your pee?" I asked helping her over a log as we made our way back to the truck.

"I don't know ... my arm itches. I don't think I stepped in my pee, why?"

"You're not getting inside my truck with pee on your shoes." I stated stopping short of the truck.

"Well, how am I going to know if I stepped in it? It's wet out there." She reached for the handle. "What's the matter with you?"

"Take your shoes off."

"No, I won't," she huffed. "Get in the goddamn truck, Jameson."

We were all tired by that point but the thought of pee in my truck was not all right with me.

"Take off your shoes and throw them in the back."

"Fuck you, Jameson!" she yelled and jumped inside.

Eventually I got in but I was still angry that she didn't care enough to take her shoes off.

"That was rude." I slammed my door shut wishing I didn't have a suspended driver's license.

"*Really*," she drew out putting the keys in the ignition. "We have been sleeping in this truck for months. Alley and Spencer have fucked in that back seat more times than I can count and you're worried about pee on my shoe?"

My head spun around toward Spencer in the backseat who was suddenly not so vocal arguing with Alley any longer.

"Are you fucking kidding me?" I lost it.

One thing was certain and that was that I would be selling this truck when we got back to civilization.

They all got a good laugh out of it. When we got to the hotel, I made them all sleep in the damn truck while I enjoyed the freedom of the hotel room all to myself for them being assholes.

I was in one of those moods where nothing was going to make me happy. I just wanted to be left alone. I was tired, and not only tired, but I wanted to sleep in my own bed and not have to get up in the morning. I also wanted a vacation away from my brother and sister. I was literally ready to kill Spencer and Emma.

By the time Perris Auto week rolled around, I was in my last week of the USAC title chase. I was thankful when the week flew by. I finished third the first night and then won the other two of the three-day event.

We wouldn't know who won the Triple Crown until after the final USAC sprint race in Hanford the following week but I was hopeful. With those two wins in both the midget and sprint races I slid into the lead with just an eight point lead. Justin was behind me with six hundred and seventy nine points with Ryder right behind him with six hundred and seventy eight points.

It was the closest Triple Crown battle USAC had ever seen and I was right in the middle of it. Even though I wanted to win badly I enjoyed the points being as close as they were. It meant that I was battling with guys who could compete with me. If it had been an all-out wash where no one stood a chance much like the past championships I'd won at the tracks on the West coast, it wouldn't mean as much to win.

Now that I had competition, when I won, I knew it was because of my talent not because I had the cars with money. You see, in the divisions like USAC and NASCAR, the cars are all similar and the drivers racing in them had money. When you go to local tracks, there is a huge difference between cars because of lack of money. When you start racing in the divisions with money, you see what you're made of and how other talent stacks up.

I snuck off to World Finals for the World of Outlaws in Charlotte prior to the race in Hanford. One more weekend in sprint cars was exactly what I needed.

Sway, Alley, Emma, and Tommy stayed in California with my mom while Justin, Ryder, and I flew back to North Carolina to race. It was fun to hang out with my dad and friends that weekend but I rarely got to see him besides the few times during the drivers' meeting and the pill draw for the trophy dashes.

I enjoyed hanging out with Justin and Ryder that weekend too even though we were so close in the championship points together. We had become good friends this season and I hadn't realized how refreshing that was. Sway was different from my guy friends. They were fun to bullshit with and talk trash about other drivers and setups whereas Sway was *mentally* what I needed.

It took me until the third night to realize why I felt so abnormal these last few days. Sway wasn't there.

Our relationship lately was still the same though, after that night where I attacked the poor girl in my hauler, I had left her alone.

I stopped with the innocent touching and kissing and whatever else my dick decided it wanted to do because nothing about it was fucking innocent. I couldn't take any more chances. That night prior to the race, I had been moments away from ripping our clothes off and fucking her against the wall in my hauler. She didn't deserve that and I knew her well enough to know if she thought that's what I wanted or needed, she would have let me. I wouldn't have been any different than that douche Dylan Grady.

How could I have even risked that?

I was beyond upset with myself after that night but it didn't change anything for her. She was still Sway. Still the same caring, witty and supportive Sway. No matter what I did to fuck things up, she just blew it off and continued to be my roll cage.

I'll never understand why she did it but, again, I was glad she did.

My dad ended up winning his twelfth championship that weekend. I caught up with him after the trophy presentation.

"Another one, huh?" I motioned to his trophy. "Do you even have room for that?"

He glanced down at it smiling.

"You know as well as I do, it's not about the trophy."

I nodded looking down at my feet. He slung his arm around my shoulder as we walked back to the haulers.

"Let's go get that Triple Crown."

"Sounds good to me," I told him with a grin.

The following Wednesday was the last point race of the season and marked the end of the USAC schedule. After this race at Giant Chevrolet Speedway, we would know the winner.

Even though this was the last race, my nightly routine was pretty simple and hadn't changed much besides maybe a few interviews on my thoughts about the title chase.

We were all at the track by two that day. The race was under the lights, for the effect, I could only assume.

Our entire family was there and many of my brother's friends had shown up along with a few of mine. The pressure to win was there but I also wanted to win badly to show everyone that I had done it.

Part of me, and this was a very small fraction, wanted Chelsea there to see it. After her harsh remarks, I wanted to say, "See, I told you I would make it."

Sway and I walked up to the pit entrance together with my arm thrown over her shoulder. I handed over my credentials which consisted of my suspended driver's license, my USAC license, and my insurance card. I also had to sign the liability waiver and list all the crewmembers we had with us that night.

Two people I thought I'd never see again showed up, Kenny and Holden, from the dreadful race in Republic.

I laughed when they walked up behind us.

"Do you got room on that crew of yours?" Kenny asked.

I smiled, as did Sway who reached up to hug the old roughed up boys from Republic.

"Sure," I motioned for them to come with us.

When Tommy saw help coming, he was all smiles. He was another one who could use a break.

These days we were hauling around a grill to make our own food so my mom and Sway began cooking burgers and hot dogs for everyone. I was so worked up over this race and it being the end of the most grueling season that I was hardly myself.

I barely spoke to anyone. I stayed away from Sway, and the two women who threw themselves at me when I walked toward the bathrooms probably thought I was the world's biggest asshole when I told them to get away from me. I just wasn't in the mood. I wasn't in the mood for anything, only for this to be over with.

After we ate, the pit steward came around and had us draw pills to see what group we ran with for the hot laps.

When hot laps were underway, it was a battle with adjustments trying to prepare the car for the race.

That night we were in a USAC sprint car, which was non-winged. The setups were completely different because once you take away that wing all your down-force is gone. You struggle to find grip anywhere you can which means an entirely different spring and shock setup as well as stagger and air pressure adjustments.

I made an appearance in the hospitality tent for Bowman Oil and Sound Logistics, a sponsor I had recently picked up that manufactures exhaust systems.

Between those two sponsors and Bucky, I was able to run the remainder of the USAC season with a full sponsorship that helped considerably since I'd torn up more sprint cars this year than I cared to admit.

Time trials started after that and Sway handed me a bottle of water before I got inside the car but took off in another direction when a girl came up and asked for my autograph.

She was polite, so I said yes, but I couldn't help but wonder why Sway was reacting the way she was. These last two months she disappeared instantly when another woman would come near me.

Time trials set the field for the feature events. There was still last chance qualifiers in the sense that if you placed in the top two of your feature you could advance to the next. Tonight they had 3-Feature events. If you were the top two in the C-Feature, you advanced to the B-Feature. The A-Feature was fielded by the top nineteen qualifiers with four transfer spots available. The top four from the B-Feature started in the rear of the A-Feature. Each track was different but this was how most of them operated.

Dad caught me before the main when I was lined up on the front stretch. He ran out there and stuck his head inside the car. "You got this kid. Don't think, drive!" he yelled over the idling engine.

I only nodded, there was no way he'd hear me even if I did say anything.

I wouldn't say I was nervous but I was tense. The entire season came down to one night.

It had come down to forty laps. Anything could happen in those forty laps. Tires shred, engines blow, drivers misjudge and it's the luck of the draw.

With Ryder and Justin voraciously behind me, I needed to focus so, once again, while inside the confines of the cramped cockpit, I was one with the car.

Giant Speedway is a 3/8-mile clay oval and by the main that night, the surface was glazed over, slick and full of ruts.

It was a night Jimi would say, "Stand up and drive."

I did.

Ryder was all over me. I wasn't sure if maybe he was sizing me up or if he was actually struggling to pass. He took a look at passing me each lap but that's all he ever got, just a look. I led the entire feature. I wasn't sure where Justin finished so I had no idea if I won the title until I pulled into my pit and saw my family jumping up and down.

Sway was the first, always the first, to congratulate me. She leaned inside of the car before I was able to pull myself out and kissed me. I froze since my *entire family* was watching but she pulled away and I realized it was her excitement for me.

"I knew you would do it!"

"Thanks, honey," I said, hoisting myself from the seat to stand through the top roll bars. Everyone was screaming and throwing beer and champagne at me. It wasn't just the thrill of the victory that night it was finally being able to take a breath. There was an end in sight.

Ryder had become one of the best drivers in the USAC divisions that year. To beat him at tracks like Eldora and Knoxville and then to come back and beat him when track conditions couldn't have been any worse; that was something I was proud of. I gave those Beasts from the East a run for their money this season and proved to them that a kid from the Northwest could pull it off.

I may have been considered Jimi Riley's son but, that night, I was known as Jameson Riley, the eighteen-year-old kid that just won the USAC Triple Crown.

I stayed at that track celebrating with my family, friends and fans until the lights were turned off. Right after the race, I started signing autographs before loading the truck. This was something I learned from Jimi.

You rarely got him to sign anything for you during a race night, but afterward that was about the fans who had just devoted their entire evening to watching him race. So did I … I stayed until I signed everything they wanted because, without them, I wouldn't be racing at these levels because there wouldn't be these levels of racing without them coming out and watching.

After standing there for three hours signing for people, the last kid said what pretty much summed up the season for me and made me understand, once again, *why* I risk it all.

He couldn't have been much older than ten, maybe eleven. He was all smiles as he handed me a program to sign. I asked his name, he said it was Jake. I'd seen him before but I couldn't place him but then I'd seen a lot of kids these days. Just as he was about to leave with his autograph he stopped and smiled back at me pushing his golden blonde curls away from his face.

"Jameson?" he asked politely.

"Yeah?"

"Do you think maybe I could get a picture of you and me?" his voice was soft and timid.

"Of course, buddy."

Sway took our picture and I gave him my address and told him I expected a copy of it when he got it developed.

He eagerly agreed and then said, "I can't wait to hang it up in my room!" he ran off to his mother after that when his dad approached me.

Right then I realized why I recognized him. It was Shey Evans' grandson.

Shey's son-in-law, Greg, laughed leaning into my shoulder. "All my kid talks about is this Jameson Riley kid who is supposedly his hero."

I smiled placing the cap back on the black Sharpie I was holding.

"Is that so ...?"

"It is," Sean put his hand on my back. "He started racing quarter midgets this last year and tells everyone he's going to be like Jameson Riley someday."

I risked everything to become Jameson Riley and that night I did. Now was the time to cast who I would become as a racer. People in the racing community were starting to see me as me.

I will say *starting* to because the following morning when I picked up the newspaper it was packed with articles saying:

Riley's kid making a name for himself

Jimi Riley's son snags USAC Triple Crown title.

I had some work to do but still, I won the title.

It's what I set out to do this season and I did. Next season I'd work on making these reporters aware that I had my own name.

Displacement – A measure of an engine's size. It's the difference between the volume contained in the cylinders when the pistons are at the bottom of the stroke and the volume that remains when the pistons are at the top of the stroke.

I had one of those mornings where I didn't want to move let alone wake up. But when I thought about the articles I wanted to read, I shot up with a renewed sense of motivation.

I found the daily newspaper. Smiling, I looked over the article a few times, my finger tracing over the title that read:

> **Kid from the West Coast outsmarts the Beasts from the East**
>
> Jameson Riley left home a few days after graduation to make the next race in the USAC Division. Having been competing since the season opener in March, he'd made all the races and managed to graduate high school. Don't expect his dad to let him drive the team hauler to the races any longer but this kid proved he could battle all season with those fire-breathing beasts from the East.
>
> We caught up with Jameson after the Silver Cup in

Lernerville. When asked about his goals for this season he replied with, "Well, of course, we want that Triple Crown." Some USAC drivers spend their entire lives trying to win a championship in all three of the USAC divisions, only two other drivers have ever done it at this point, so what made the son of legendary World of Outlaw driver, Jimi Riley, think he had what it takes. "I've always had too much confidence," Riley said after Summer Nationals in Williams Grove. "But I know what I want and well ... I spend every chance I can in a race car preparing myself. I'm ready."

And that he was. Jameson struggled in the early part of the season with engine troubles, and pushing a USAC official didn't help his standings but he prevailed and won events like Oil City Cup, Knoxville Nationals, and still came back to pull off wins in the USAC midget, sprint and silver crown divisions. He's a dirt track prodigy from the passive Northwest but his talent hasn't gone unnoticed where the heart of open wheel racing resides. Bucky Miers, USAC owner and World of Outlaw driver, saw his talent back when he raced quarter midgets. "You know I was there when that kid first sat in a quarter-midget and I remember telling Jimi that kid of his would give him a run for his money someday." Bucky said. "Now look at him. All I do is provide a car and that kid drives the wheels off it. There is nothing he can't drive. I can give him a fifth place car and he'll bring home a victory in it. That's just Jameson."

We asked Jameson what his plans were for the winter, you have to remember, he not only competed for the Triple Crown and won it by less than ten points over Justin West, he competed in numerous World of Outlaw events, and various winged-sprints and dirt late models, surely the kid needed a rest, right?

"Nah, I got Turkey Night planned and then it's back to racing in February." Riley told us in victory lane at Giant

Speedway.

So what's up for the new eighteen-year-old Triple Crown Champion?

"Another Triple Crown?"

Riley laughs. "I don't know, maybe. West was tough competition."

I read it again. I couldn't stop. All that hard work led him to the title he so desperately wanted and I was there to witness it.

We got into town late last night; Jimi flew us home on a private jet because God knows all of us wanted to get home. I personally couldn't wait to sleep in my own bed. Not that I minded sleeping next to Jameson every night because, let's be real, I did. I missed my bed though. I had a good bed, comfortable. I was also excited not to be riding around in a car.

I planned my morning out, decided to go for a run as soon as I got up, the road trip did nothing for my ass.

Taking a fist full of it in the mirror, I admired my tan. I looked good, with a few extra pounds.

Charlie was finally up when I bound down the stairs. He smiled, I smiled and then I lunged for him wrapping my arms tightly around him. We had talked every few days or so but I hadn't seen him since the morning I left in June; it was now a week before Thanksgiving.

"You've grown up!" he said with wide eyes.

"Is that your way of saying I got fat." I questioned arching an eyebrow at him.

"No, Sway, it wasn't," he moved to sit down at the kitchen table pushing a plate of cookies toward me I was sure he didn't make. "What're your plans today?"

"Nothing much," I sat down beside him toying with a cookie before taking a bite of one. I then thought about my run, spit the cookie out on the plate and said, "I will be going for a run today."

Charlie chuckled. "You free for dinner tonight?" he picked up the paper, thumbing to the sports section to read the article about

Jameson.

"I don't have any plans per se, you?"

"Just thinking that maybe we could go to dinner together."

I looked down at the paper in front, shocked to see the photograph they used. It was the one of me kissing him after the race. My brow furrowed as I examined it, scrutinizing it carefully for any sign he might have felt something. He was still inside the car and I was strained inside his wingless sprint, my chest pressed against the side. He had taken his helmet off, his hair was a mess, eyes closed and, to my surprise, he was leaning into the kiss, one gloved hand touching the side of my face. *Hmmm.*

"I see you had fun this summer," Charlie remarked.

I slapped at his shoulder jolting him. "It wasn't like that."

"Have you thought about college?"

"Yes, dad," I sighed standing. "I'm going for a run before I need to roll myself out the door."

He grabbed my shirt before I got two steps away. "You're plans then?"

"Oh, yeah, dinner ... hmmm," I evaded. "Sounds good,"

"Though I'm happy we're going to dinner, I was referring to college."

"Yes, dad, I start online classes after winter quarter." My plan was for taking online courses because I thought for sure Emma or Alley would kill Jameson if left alone with him on the road. I seemed to be the only one who could tolerate his bullshit.

Charlie let me be after I promised I would be taking online classes so I continued on with my run. Jameson called asking where I was which then resulted in us going for a run together.

We ran in comfortable silence, both of us listening to our music, conversation wasn't needed. After the five mile run, I thought for sure I was going to die and collapsed in the street. I moved when I thought I would actually die when a car came by and then stumbled into the grass where Jameson fell next to me.

"Holly shit, I'm out of shape," he panted fumbling with the hem of his t-shirt.

He lifted his shirt to wipe sweat from his face. I watched the muscles in his honed physique as they flexed with each breath.

I was becoming morbidly obsessed with him.

I felt like every other pit lizard out there but I knew there was more to my love for him. I didn't see him as this idolized figure, I saw him as the boy I grew up with who, over the span of our summer together, and I discovered that I loved him.

Jameson sighed when his breathing returned to normal and sat up wrapping his arms around his knees to stretch. "What are you doing tonight?" he asked looking back at me; still sprawled out in the grass.

"Charlie and I are going to dinner."

"Oh, yeah," he leaned back on his elbows beside me. "Let's go have lunch then."

"I could eat."

And so we went to eat. That's how simple it was with us. No questions, no awkward moments, just two friends. Sure, I was feeling something for him that I associated with love but it wasn't awkward like you'd think it would be. I think he got that from Nancy. I felt at ease around him.

My alarm clock blared loudly in my ear as my head was right next to it.

Sweet love of sleep, why did I ever purchase that thing?

I whacked my arm in the general direction I thought it would be; it fell to the floor, but continued making that obnoxious sound. I had to hang off the side of the bed to reach it but wasn't successful so I yanked hard on the cord and ripped the motherfucker out of the wall.

That wasn't enough for my little temper tantrum so I chucked it across the room and it shattered against the wall. My first thought was, holy shit, what a piece of shit was it that it shattered on impact, but judging by the dent in the drywall, I may have thrown it a little too hard.

I rolled over on my back throwing my arms over my eyes, willing myself to go back to sleep. Alley assured me that didn't happen when she threatened to send Spencer in my room if I missed my flight.

After showering and getting dressed, I let her in my room. I knew she meant business by the way her glasses were pushed up on her narrow nose, her yellow notepad in hand.

"Your flight leaves at nine tomorrow from SeaTac. Justin, Tyler and Ryder will meet you at gate C. From there, you guys will pick up the rental car and head to the track," Alley flipped her notepad over. "The track is located twenty-five minutes from Los Angeles in the San Gabriel Valley."

I nodded and shoved a few t-shirts in my bag. "When do I come back?"

"Your flight leaves on Friday morning."

I was attending the Turkey Night Grand Prix at Toyota Speedway, once again, in Irwindale, California.

So far, I've been there four years in a row and had yet to win it. I wanted that win. My dad has won the event eight times. All eight times he's gone. I was both happy and depressed to see he wasn't going. Instead, he was in Australia racing sprint cars and wouldn't be back until the Chili Bowl.

Turkey Night was an annual national race held on Thanksgiving Day. The first one was held in 1934 so it was a tradition. The only years they hadn't held it at various tracks in southern California was during the war years. It was more than a tradition to racing though. Families and racers showed up and camped out. The fans cooked Thanksgiving Dinner and served it to the racers, mechanics and team members on these large picnic tables.

The greatest midget racers around the world attended this event each year so, to me, it was a chance to see how I stacked up against the competition. I knew I'd gotten better over the last year; that was evident when I watched highlights from this past summer. Now was a chance to test it out.

I wanted drivers like Justin West, Tyler Sprague, and Ryder Christiansen there. I wanted them there because, to me, they were the best USAC racers out there. If I won against them and the other midget racers, that meant something.

I needed a break from my family and I didn't feel an ounce of sadness when Emma and Spencer stayed home.

Spencer, who asked Alley to marry him during an argument, was now planning a wedding. Those two did not need to be married but who was I to judge? I know they told me the date of the wedding but I silently hoped I had *other* plans. Attending a wedding was not something I wanted to do. It didn't appeal to me.

Glancing around my room to make sure I didn't forget anything, I reached for my cell phone. There was a message from Sway telling me good luck. I asked her to come with me but she said she needed to spend some time with Charlie and with the race being on Thanksgiving, she didn't want to leave him. I couldn't blame her.

While I played puppet to sponsors this last season racing four nights a week, the rest of our team, Sway included, was as exhausted from the temper tantrums, mood swings, and whatever else I subjected the poor bastards to. I can't even begin to tell you how many times I heard the phrase: "You're an asshole."

So I welcomed traveling alone.

I was racing Bucky's midget that Bowman Oil, Sound Logistics and my new sponsor Skinner Welding, was sponsoring for me.

Bucky lined up a crew. It was a good setup and all I needed to do was show up and drive.

I got to keep sixty percent of whatever I won. That seemed good to me but, then again, it was never about the money. I didn't do any of this for the money; I did it for myself. I wanted to know I was the best and races like Turkey Night or The Chili Bowl confirmed that. Sadly, I wasn't making it to the Chili Bowl this year. I've been numerous times with my dad but had yet to race it. That was my next goal.

Mom cried when I left because she wanted me there for

Thanksgiving. She knew exactly why I was doing it though and ended up fixing Thanksgiving dinner earlier in the week for me.

The race was on Thanksgiving, so I left that Wednesday morning which put me in California that afternoon.

I met the guys where I was supposed to, an hour late. I was never timely while traveling through an airport. I was lucky security hadn't detained me after I told a flight attendant that she could suck my dick because I wasn't checking my bag.

I had a real problem with all their damn restrictions. I barely had anything in that bag and yet she wanted me to check it, I don't think so. I don't know if I scared her by telling her to suck my dick or if she was tempted but, regardless, she didn't call security and left me alone for the remainder of the flight.

"It's about fucking time!" Justin grumbled hoisting himself from the metalschairs they were sitting on. "What took you so long?"

I shrugged and gave them a blank expression. I didn't think I was that late until they informed me I was an hour late. I blamed the flight attendant.

We went to dinner that night as none of us were old enough for a bar yet so that left us at an Applebee's.

"I have to ask," Tyler began smiling and I knew what he was going to ask. It was the same question everyone asked, "What's with you and Sway?"

I dug the heel of my palms into my eyes and sighed heavily with my arms resting against the table. The rest of the guys chuckled. "Fuck, I don't know."

"Are you together or is it just like friends or something with benefits?"

"What?"

"Oh, well, I saw you two ... I don't remember when but you two were drunk and well I thought ..." his voice trailed off when I groaned.

"It's not like that with us, we haven't ... it's not like that."

"My God!" Tyler nearly shouted causing a few kids to turn and look toward us. "What is wrong with you, why haven't you? She's fucking hot!"

"Do you mind?" a woman's voice demanded beside us. "There are children present." Those fucking snot-nosed brats beside us were hardly kids and judging by the appearance of their parents, I highly doubted they were subjected to proper language.

We all nodded but you couldn't expect a group of guys like us to behave, let alone keep our voices down or censor our language.

I glared sharply at Tyler. "If you want to keep your good looks you won't ever say that again."

Tyler laughed at my threat.

"But you want it to be?" Justin continued, still laughing at me.

Why they found this funny was lost on me.

"I don't know what I want anymore," I grumbled picking at my fries.

"Didn't you fuck that Erin chick?" Tyler questioned taking a large bite of his hamburger.

The woman shushed us again. Ryder started laughing at my expression of pure disgust that her snot-nose kid sneezed on my goddamn arm.

I dumped my entire glass of water over my arm to wash off the rheum.

"Who in the fuck is Erin?" Once again, the woman shushed us so I turned around in my seat to face her. "Fuck you, sit somewhere else if this bothers you." I turned toward Tyler. "Who's Erin?"

"That chick from Banks,"

I racked my brain trying to remember who Erin was but, then again, I never knew any of their names. I didn't care to. If I recalled correctly, Erin was the trophy girl the night my engine blew and we used the one out of that guy's Mustang.

"Oh, yeah ... I guess so," I finally answered.

Justin let out another laugh and leaned back in his chair stretching his arms over his head. "You either did or didn't," his voice was muffled from his yawning. "It ain't that complicated."

"What is wrong with you guys?" I barked. "I'm not talking about this with you."

I was never one to share personal details and I wasn't about to start now. I didn't do the whole kiss and tell thing, Spencer used to and I saw how many times that backfired on him throughout the years but, most of all, I was private about that sort of thing.

"Hey, we gotta get the dirt somewhere," Tyler said. "None of us are gettin' any and you seem to have the largest following. Must be the eyes."

"Yeah, it's the eyes," Ryder commented in a voice I was sure would be considered gay.

This surprised me for a number of reasons, not that Ryder could make his voice sound that feminine but that they didn't sleep around. I thought for sure Tyler and Ryder would be. I also knew I was the last person Ryder would talk about this with after I found out that he took my sister's virginity this last summer.

Justin was head over heels for that Ami girl, so I didn't feel I could connect with any of them.

"I'm sure you two have had your fair share," I said.

"Nah, I have a girl," Ryder said in a normal manly voice again, well, normal for his pint-sized being. "And, no, it's not your sister," He added.

Tyler never answered but I saw him leave with a few at times so I knew damn well he wasn't perfect.

Thankfully, the conversations changed to racing because I'd had enough questioning into my relationship with Sway. I couldn't answer the questions because I myself had no idea what our relationship was.

Texts messages were something fairly new now and I got ones from Sway, mom, Emma, dad, Spencer, and even Tommy wishing me good luck the night of the race.

They all made me smile but Sway's hit home when I read it.

Thinking of you right now. I have no doubt in my mind you'll win tonight.

I felt an unfamiliar ache when she wrote the words "*thinking of you.*" I hoped like hell she was and then that scared me. I was all sorts of a mess during the drivers' meeting but calmed down when I was around the boys.

The format for the race was a little different; they ran both midgets and sprints that night with a 98-lap midget main event.

I ended up qualifying sixth, Justin got fast time while Tyler got fourth and Ryder ended up tenth.

When the green flag dropped for the main, I was on a mission feinting my way to the lead.

Justin had pulled away to a good lead around lap thirty-five when I caught him. He seemed to be using up his tires because I passed him with ease. That wasn't normal for him. Justin started strong and stayed strong. I should have known he wouldn't stay back there for long and, with ten laps to go, him and Tyler were all over me.

I held my own but with one lap to go, Tyler, who came out of nowhere, passed us both like we were sitting still.

I can't say I wasn't pissed because I was. I wanted to win Turkey Night just as bad as the next guy but to have a guy like Tyler, who struggled each weekend to make it to these races for lack of sponsorship, win was fine with me.

I was proud of him. He deserved it.

I ended up second with Justin third. Ryder blew a tire halfway through and then pegged the wall so he finished near the rear somewhere.

Despite all this, we were all celebrating with Tyler that night and eating turkey dinner. We put our own envy aside and showed respect and goodwill for the seventeen-year-old kid from Birmingham, Alabama.

We all had a lot of respect for each other going back to our days racing quarter midgets. I think we all developed a real appreciation for our talents.

The hardest part about wanting to win so badly was that it would mean beating another guy, in this case a friend of mine, who deserved that same win just as bad. He got it that night.

I've said this before but a good showing at the Chili Bowl Midget

Nationals or Turkey Night can make a huge difference in a racer's career. It can mean leaving with sponsorship or looking for a seat over the winter.

Tyler left there with a full-time ride from Ron Walker, one of the biggest, most respected owners in USAC. So, even though I held some bitterness that I didn't win Turkey Night, it was rewarding to see a guy like Tyler Sprague pull it off.

Redlining – The maximum engine speed at which the internal combustion engine or traction motor and its components are designed to operate without causing damage to the components themselves or other parts of the engine.

I was surprised at how quickly my winter filled up. I thought for sure I'd get bored at some point but never had the chance. I managed to go play around one weekend at Crystal Mountain with Spencer and Tommy on a pair of snowmobiles, but other than that, I hung around the house and caught up on sleep for a good couple of weeks. Before I knew it, Christmas was there and then soon I was heading east again.

The World of Outlaws started their season in February and then the USAC divisions opened soon after that.

I planned to make every race I could. I needed to be prepared and prepared meant racing anything I could.

I still hadn't decided on what cars I wanted to run professionally. There were so many options I moved from one division to the next testing my ability in each one.

My brother, like the dumbass I always knew him to be, was planning a wedding. I had nothing against marriage. I didn't think my brother was the marrying type.

When he was in high school, I was positive he slept with the entire female population and now he was supposedly settling down? I highly doubted that. He and Alley had been together for a few years now but still, it didn't seem like something he would do. I guess maybe the reservations I held for it had something to do with myself as I couldn't see tying myself to someone or something other than racing.

Spencer was different though and he loved Alley. That was evident and he never showed any signs of regret.

They got married on January 2, 1999. It was the perfect date for Spencer because he couldn't forget the date since it was the day after his twenty-second birthday and it was one-two.

At least we knew he could count that high.

Luckily, since I stayed so busy, I hadn't seen anyone from high school, which was fine by me. I didn't like any of those assholes anyway except for Tommy and Sway.

On the day of the wedding I walked over to Sway's house to pick her up. She was my date and I silently hoped she was wearing the same tutu from prom. I smiled to myself thinking of her dancing around in it that night in the tree house.

The cool crisp winter air blew across my face, burning. It had snowed a few nights ago leaving a few patches on the frozen grass along with traces of ice along the sidewalks. Keeping my eyes focused on the pavement so I didn't slip, I realized I had walked past her house and had to back track. When I got there, the front door was open and I could hear her and Charlie talking in the living room.

"I expect you to take the classes like we discussed, Sway. You can't follow that boy around forever," Charlie reproached. "He's using you."

I stepped down off the porch and sat down on the steps resting my elbows on my knees.

Was I using her?

Well, *yes*, I was but I didn't think it was using. I needed her.

After about five minutes of sitting there, Sway walked out wearing a short black dress with matching heels.

Instantly, I averted my eyes when all I saw were her long lean legs tempting me.

It was going to be a long fucking night.

"How long have you been here?"

"Long enough," I mumbled.

"You heard?"

"Yeah,"

She sighed sitting beside me, shivered and scooted closer.

"I'm sorry ... *Jesus,* it's cold."

"Do you think I'm using you?"

She answered immediately, her voice sure. "No. Not at all. I go because *I* want to."

I only nodded and she shivered again.

"You should put a coat on or something."

"I would but I don't want to go back inside."

I knew exactly why she didn't want to go back inside so I slipped out of my jacket and draped it over her shoulders.

"We should get going. I can't look at your legs much longer without my self-control wavering," I admitted.

Sway laughed and I smiled. I'd do anything to hear that giggle. "Let's go to a wedding."

I found Spencer once we arrived and gave him my speech. "Are you sure about this?"

I wasn't much of a best man so luckily he had chosen someone else for that duty. But I did feel it was my place as a brother to offer some words. Good or bad, I offered them.

"Yeah, why wouldn't I be?"

"You used to be a slut."

Spencer shrugged and stared back at me analyzing my expression.

"People change." His voice seemed to hold some warning but, for the life of me, I couldn't figure out what the hell he was talking about.

It might have had something to do with the fact that I was working on a 6-pack of Coors Light but that's beside the point.

"How did you know she was the one?"

Spencer dropped down beside me on the couch as we waited for the wedding to begin.

He was a nervous groom. I was the drunken groomsman and we were quite the pair.

"I'm not sure how I knew ... she puts up with my shit, and, for the first time, I wanted someone," he intoned. "I want her, *always*."

I listened to him. I couldn't say much. I'd never felt the way he did. He loved someone and while I had feelings for Sway, I didn't know what love even meant to me or if I loved anything besides racing.

"Jameson," Spencer turned to me removing the beer from my hands. "There will come a point when racing isn't everything to you. Someday, you'll understand the way you feel about her."

I'm sure my expression was slightly alarmed that he implied Sway. "It's not like that with us. We're just friends."

Spencer laughed shaking his head and then stood. "Come on, bro, let's get me hitched!"

The wedding was simple. Alley planned everything perfectly with the help of Emma. Spencer didn't have to do anything, which was a good fucking thing because you couldn't expect him to do much of anything at a wedding besides be there and say, "I do."

Sway and Emma were Alley's bridesmaids. I spent more time staring at Sway in her dress than listening to what the preacher said because she looked absolutely beautiful. It wasn't fair to Alley to have someone like Sway standing next to her, that's for sure.

I started to get antsy standing up there when the words were finally spoken, "Spencer James Riley, do you take this woman to be your wife?"

To my surprise, his response was a tad emotional, "Yes."

"Do you, Allison Nicole Dailey, take this man to be your husband?"

She said yes, they kissed, everyone cheered and the reception was underway, so was I with the open bar.

I don't know why I felt I needed to drink, I just did. My dad noticed around my fifth beer while I glared in Cooper's direction as he danced with Sway.

That was another thing I couldn't understand. Why was I so jealous over this? When someone else besides me touched her, I got a sick feeling in the pit of my stomach and a tight pain in my chest.

"What are you doing over here?" he asked over the blaring music. "Why aren't you tearing it up out there on the dance floor with your girl? I know you got moves kid."

"My girl?"

"Sway ... she's your girl," he slurred.

Judging by his appearance, I wasn't sure I wanted his advice tonight. He had just flew in from Australia this morning so I gathered he was jet lagged but he looked as though he'd had too much whiskey.

"She's not my girl, Dad," I snapped cracking open another beer.

No, she wasn't my girl. I had no claim to her but, for some reason, I wanted to. I wanted to be the one out there holding her.

Dad snatched the beer away. "You're not of age, give that to me."

"Since when have you ever worried about me drinking? If I remember correctly, you gave me my first beer."

"Yeah, well I'm clearly not a good role model." He held up his glass and tilted his head at Sway. "You've learned nothing when it comes to treating women with respect."

That pissed me off. My eyes that had once focused on Sway shot to his.

"What the fuck is that supposed to mean?"

There was a double meaning behind his words and both meanings pissed me off, probably because it was true.

"You know all these tracks you go to and fuck around at?" he arched his eyebrow at me setting my beer down on the table in front of us. I watched as Cooper pulled Sway closer for a slow dance.

"What are you talking about?"

"You dumbass ... *those* women, *those* trophy girls ... yeah, well, when I come around they want to know why my son hasn't called."

"And you say?"

"He's an asshole."

"Hmmm," I reached for the beer again, this time he let me have it. "At least you're not lying."

Jimi stood and cracked his neck to one side.

"Go rescue her from him. There's something not right about Cooper," he motioned toward Sway.

Cooper's hands were dangerously low and it made my stomach drop.

I could be that guy right now if I pulled my head out of my ass. She did deserve better. I *was* an asshole.

I watched for a while before retreating. They seemed to be having fun and when he bent down to kiss her, I hated the jealous feeling raging through me, so I left. My brother's wedding was the last place I needed to cause a scene.

I hadn't seen Jameson for most of the reception but, when I did, I was surprised at his rigid posture and defiant stare in my direction.

He came toward me but instead of coming where we were all gathered dancing, he bypassed us all and headed for the bar. I tried to grab him but he shook me off and reached over the bar taking the bottle of Jack Daniels and left out the back entrance.

It didn't take long to find him. He was leaning next to the wall, his jacket thrown over his shoulder and the white sleeves of his dress shirt rolled up to his elbows.

"I should have told you he'd be here."

"Don't apologize. You did nothing wrong," he sighed with closed eyes taking a drink straight from the bottle and then sliding down the wall to sit on the cold pavement.

I contemplated sitting next to him but decided against it in this dress and the cold ground.

"What's the matter?"

"Nothing," he answered.

"Is this about what Charlie said?"

"No."

"Cooper?"

"No."

"You're lying."

"Yeah, well, I'm an asshole so I guess maybe I'm a liar, too."

"You don't always have to be an asshole. And being a liar is up to you but that's not us."

He simply grunted in reply and kicked his legs out to lean further back against the wall.

This was my fault. I shouldn't have agreed to dance with Cooper but, then again, I couldn't figure out *why* that was even a big deal.

Was he jealous? Nah, that couldn't be it. I thought Jameson wasn't the jealous type.

"So it's not Charlie, it's not Cooper ... is it me?"

He threw his arms up in the air in frustration.

"I'm ... I'm ... It's nothing!" he snapped causing me to jump. "Drop it."

We sat in silence for a few minutes before he sighed with a growl and pulled his knees up.

"I'm sorry," he sighed, seeming even more annoyed. "I didn't mean to snap at you. I'm frustrated with a lot of things right now. It's not you though."

I shrugged. I'd been on the receiving end of his temper tantrums long enough to know it wasn't me. I should have been pissed but, then again, I didn't take it personally. He meant absolutely nothing by it.

I never did figure out where all the moodiness came from but within a few hours and half the bottle of Jack Daniels, we found ourselves back on the dance floor, together this time. Jameson could barely stand, let alone dance, so he spent most of the time with me holding him up.

I don't know why I let him take his frustrations out on me but if I had to guess these days, it was because to me that's what friends were for. If he couldn't show frustration to me, who could he show it to? To me, that's the best friend I could ever ask for. He was one I could vent to and he understood. He was one who never asked questions and was simply there because they wanted to be. That was us.

As winter passed, I found myself in Barberville Florida, for the sprint car DIRTcar Nationals and then it was onto Ocala, Florida, for the USAC Sprint season opener in February with the rest of my team including Sway.

Judging by the conversation I'd heard from Charlie, Sway wouldn't be traveling as much and by mid-summer, she'd missed an entire month of racing including the Knoxville Nationals and the Kings Royal which were two sprint car events she loved to attend.

It wasn't the same without her. I found myself turning to other women in the hopes that they provided a blanket for the pain but it did nothing; it only made me feel worse and guilty but I still turned to them. And it was easy.

I didn't even have to try. When the race was over, they were all over me. They knew what they wanted and I just wanted relief. They never asked questions and never expected anything from me. It was almost like a silent agreement and it worked well with my lifestyle.

My season started out shitty, got shittier, and then ended shitty. It was, by far, the worst season I'd ever run but I took comfort in knowing all the frontrunners struggled, too. I ended up third in the Silver crown division, we struggled constantly with the asphalt tracks and when half the races are on asphalt—it did nothing for our points.

I did better in the midgets and ended up second in points but the sprint cars I placed fifth. I was not pleased with that at all. I was pissed actually.

I still raced in everything I could and won quite a bit but it wasn't enough. It seemed that besides the asphalt tracks we struggled on the dry-slick as well. By winter, we did some serious re-structuring and even switched manufacturers of a few parts.

Something wasn't right and I didn't feel that my driving ability had dropped off because I could still compete at the same level in the Outlaw sprints, late models and the occasional modified.

Top five finishes in all three divisions wasn't bad but I was a perfectionist and hated losing.

Justin and Tyler felt the same way, so on the way back from Turkey Night, that I lost once again, this time to Justin, we vented.

"I can't believe this fucking season!" I griped. "I've never raced this horribly."

"I feel your pain, man," Tyler said. "I think I destroyed ten cars this season and a few concrete walls."

"Yeah, well," Justin began tossing his bag in the overhead compartment on the plane we were boarding. "I got more fines than both you put together."

"Tsk, tsk, tsk, Justin," I taunted. "You should have learned pushing a USAC official."

"Yeah, like you?" he countered sitting down next to me.

He may have beaten me in fines but that was only because I harassed them in ways I didn't get caught. It seemed that I spent more time defending my actions on the track than I did racing, but when you're having luck like our team was and sponsors began breathing down your neck, you tend to get a little fired up at times. Those who didn't understand that clearly didn't understand the pressures put upon us.

"You are so full of shit, Riley," Justin pushed my shoulder. "My foot slipped off the throttle, I swear!" he mimicked in a deep voice he tried to push off as mine.

My voice was hardly deep, crackly at times, but not deep.

"I don't sound like that. I still maintain my foot slipped."

"Can I get you boys anything to drink?" a flight attendant asked us politely.

"Beers ... keep 'em coming honey," Justin teased with her.

We all ordered non-alcoholic drinks because she checked our damn IDs.

I leaned back and relaxed, needing the alone time. It didn't stop me from checking my phone once more, hoping to see a text or voicemail from Sway and she didn't disappoint.

There's always next year buddy. I have a beer waiting for you.

I smiled and sent a text before the plane departed.

Thanks. See you soon.

I couldn't wait to see Sway. The last time I saw her was toward the end of October and I missed her.

She was finishing finals for her freshman year at Western. I wasn't sure I could take another three years like this one. If her not being with me had an impact on the way my racing would be affected without her, then I was fucked. I knew she couldn't continue to travel and go to school and something had to give this season, for both of us.

When I got home that night from seeing Jameson and the rest of the Riley family, Charlie was waiting up.

By the grim expression on his face, I knew what was coming.

"You need to get your head out of your ass, Sway, if you're going to do this, finish it. If not, follow him around but I guarantee you he won't see you for who you are," his voice continued to rise with each word. "I didn't raise a pit lizard!"

I didn't know what to say to that, what could I say?

I was acting and behaving like a pit lizard. When he called, I came running. I blew off finals, I stood up friends, anything if he needed me.

Something had to give and I knew what it was ... me. I couldn't be in two places at once and it wasn't fair to Jameson for me to promise to be there and then not show. He didn't deserve that and I couldn't handle the guilt any longer.

I loved him but yet I couldn't tell him. I couldn't tell him simply because I knew how he felt. I was a distraction to him and he needed to focus. Last season was a prime example.

I watched highlights from the races I wasn't at and heard about the temper tantrums and the girls. This wasn't my best friend but that somehow had something to do with me. There were times that I thought maybe he might have some feelings but then he'd pull away. I don't think Jameson knew what he wanted, besides racing.

Alley told me he checked his phone more than anything, called non-stop, and when I was there, he finally focused.

That meant something, right?

Some could view this as him having feelings but I knew Jameson well enough to know that wasn't the case. He depended on me because I was the one person who could keep him at ease. But I also had my dad to think about.

He wanted me to take over at Grays Harbor eventually as he had no one else to do it and I couldn't let him down.

Charlie had worked so hard for so long to build Grays Harbor into the facility it was and I couldn't let him throw all that away. That track meant more to us than we could ever really express. When he was broken, racing put him back together, that track put him together. I couldn't let him down so I made the decision to focus on school. I wasn't sure how the hell I was going to make it away from my family for so long but I tried to be a big girl about it, *tried*. It didn't work out so well when I saw Jameson the night before I left to go to Bellingham for winter quarter.

"When did she tell you that?" I demanded of Spencer.

We were standing inside the sprint car shop in Elma and I set the torsion bar down. I was far too unstable to be holding something capable of destroying anything. I had been in here all morning avoiding my family and everyone else.

"She told Alley and I overheard," Spencer sat down on a rear tire crossing his arms over his chest. "It was too hard for her last season ... you can't expect her to travel with us forever. Like you said, she's not your girlfriend."

"What exactly did she say?"

"Just that she's leaving for Bellingham. In order to graduate in three years she has to finish up there. Her online classes weren't working out real well."

I knew this was going to happen but it pissed me off to no end that she didn't tell me first. I thought we were best friends and now I have to find out from my fucking brother that when I leave in a few weeks she's not coming with me?

I spent the rest of the day out there afraid to be around anyone but myself.

Sway came over that night and one look at her flushed distraught appearance and I couldn't stay mad.

We sat in silence on my bed for a while before I sighed. I had to get it over with and it had been eating at me all day.

"Spencer said you aren't coming," I mumbled, my stomach knotted at the thought. I was surprised I got the words out.

"That fucking brat," she said shaking her head defeated.

"So, it's true?"

"No ... I mean, yes, it's true. I can't go with you guys but I wanted to tell you myself not have that ape tell you."

Hanging my head my eyes dropped to my hands.

"When do you leave for Bellingham?"

"Tomorrow."

Nodding, I reached for her and pulled her into a tight hug and moved to lay down on my bed holding her. I nearly cried. I could feel the tears sting my eyes but I held my own, barely. My self-control was wavering when she burst into tears and clung to my sweatshirt.

"I'm sorry, I just ..."

I silenced her cries with my lips for a quick kiss and pulled away before I gave in and kissed her the way I wanted to, did the things I wanted to. "Don't apologize."

"I just ... I want to be there with you guys. You guys are my family and now I'm traveling to Bellingham alone ... I don't even know anyone up there," she wailed.

"It's all right, honey. I can come see you when I can. I'll fly out there or something," I reassured her. "I think maybe July might be fairly open so I'll skip a few races."

"No," she shook her head. "You can't do that. You made this decision to race and I will not settle for you doing this half-assed. You want to be the best, you have to work hard."

I knew that but the thought of her alone up there was killing me.

We eventually stopped talking and fell asleep like that on my bed. I held her the entire night hoping that offered a sense of comfort for her. I knew then that she didn't want to leave and not come with me but it was, once again, Sway choosing someone else's needs over her own. I was furious with Charlie that he was making her go to college. What if she didn't want to work for him? He never gave her an option and I hated that. At least with me, I asked her if she wanted to come. I may have thrown a fit when she didn't but I still asked. Charlie told her what she'd be doing and assumed that's what she wanted.

When it was time to say goodbye, she was an emotional basket case and, like everything else, I held it in, afraid that if I allowed myself to feel, it would break me.

"It takes a tough person to do what you do ... don't second-guess yourself," Sway choked over her tears.

"I won't," I mumbled.

I had yet to look into her eyes. My own were fixated on my hands fumbling with the hole in my jeans as I sat on the porch.

"Just don't forget that. Remember why you're doing this."

I nodded pulling her into a tight hug. I said nothing else but when I got home that afternoon, I sent her a text.

See you in Eldora.

The next time we would get to see each other was three months away. I had a feeling this wasn't going to work and when the season opener for the USAC sprint cars opened in Ocala the following week and I wrecked, it was confirmed.

It didn't help that a new driver, Brad Wheeler, tangled with me every lap and then finally clipped my right rear sending me flying into the catch fence.

I was not happy.

When USAC suspended me for two races, I lost it at the hotel room that night.

I destroyed everything in that hotel room. I couldn't stop.

The thought that Sway wasn't there any longer was maddening to me and being suspended was the cake topper. I couldn't control myself. I even went so far as punching my own brother when he got in the way of that Wheeler fucker and me earlier in the night.

An hour later, I sat there curled up on the floor of the shower, my knuckles bleeding. I was almost positive a few bones were broken in my hand but, then again, I couldn't feel the pain. I could only feel the constant ache thinking of her alone at college without me but worst of all, me without her.

That night while the water washed away the debris from my engine failure, I contemplated not racing anymore. I did. For the first time in my career, I thought maybe this wasn't for me.

In the morning, when I was testing in Lernerville with a broken hand, I realized why I could never quit racing.

Comparing Sway to an engine, she's the oil and what holds me together and keeps me running smoothly but racing makes up my engine. It's the pistons, the bearings, the values and the headers.

Without racing, there would be nothing for her to lubricate and I wouldn't be a running engine. It's *all* I've ever known and *will* ever know because that was me. Even though I had been running in the red for years, my engine had finally blown.

I knew the first step to a rebuild of an engine failure.

Now was the time to tear it apart and figure out where the mechanical failure had gone wrong in the first place and then rebuild it. I needed to drain the coolant, disconnect all the hoses and start from scratch.

Dirt Tracking – Driving hard into a corner on a paved track causing the rear end to swing out wide as if on a dirt surface.

Discovering why an engine failed isn't always an easy process. And, sometimes, it's unexpected. One minute you're riding around the track, passing cars and gaining positions, and then the next thing you know all that power is gone, and it just blows.

No warning, no shaking, just blows.

I knew why my engine failed.

I was poorly lubricated, overheated daily, had too much heat and pressure, and my bearings were misaligned.

I had no choice now but to disassemble, clean, inspect and rebuild.

"Everything I'm doing is for a reason. This is what I wanted."

I told myself that daily.

No matter how many times I told myself that, I still wondered what would be different if I didn't let Sway leave.

Not that I could have stopped her had I told her I felt something; that I didn't understand if that something was more.

Would that have stopped the engine failure?

Probably not.

Regardless, something had to give. I'd been running in the red too long.

Sway was always there. If I called in the middle of the night needing reassurance, she was there no matter what. Even though she wasn't physically with me, she stood by me through it all. Despite being crabby and irritable most of the time, she was there talking me through it. She knew to leave me alone when I needed solitude and supported me when no one else did.

We talked often. She flew out to see me whenever she could and I even made the occasional trip to Bellingham. Sure, I made use of it by racing up at Skagit but I got to see Sway and that was the real reason.

During my 2000 season, I needed all the seat time I could get as my season was a string of shoddy performances in the USAC divisions. I was hanging strong with the World of Outlaws and even contemplated running their season full-time next year with a car from my dad.

It had been a while since I had last seen Sway as she had been concentrating on finals and my schedule had been tight, so I sat alone in the hauler prior to the opening night of Las Vegas Nationals for the World of Outlaws and talked to her on the phone.

"Everyone knows you around here. They keep asking me if I know you!" Sway chimed. She seemed in good spirits today after her finals. It was now the middle of April and soon she'd be on spring break and I couldn't wait for spring break.

"And, you say?"

"I say, nah, I don't know him. I hear he's an asshole though," she laughed.

"That's what they all say," I laughed. Leaning down to pick up the shock on the floor of the hauler, I continued our conversation. "So, when do I get to see your smiling face again. I miss you."

"Um ... well, my finals are finished now so I was thinking by the time you are in Eldora I could come and see you."

We had planned on her coming to Eldora eventually for the Kings Royal in July but May sounded a whole hell of a lot better to me.

My mood improved immensely.

"That would be good. I could use some Sway time."

"I could use some Jameson time," she sighed contently. "No one gets me here. They all look at me like I'm crazy."

"You are crazy."

"I know but, jeez ... they don't have to look at me weird all the time."

"Who looks at you weird?"

"Other girls."

"They're jealous because you're so hot."

"Thanks," she replied sarcastically and then laughed.

Spencer opened the door to the hauler and stuck his head inside. "You're up for hot laps."

I nodded and then yanked the door closed.

"Hey, Sway, I gotta go ... call you after the race?"

"Yeah, sure, good luck tonight."

"Thanks," I said, before bolting out the door.

I made fast time, no surprise there but I didn't think people noticed until I got back to the pits, my grin ratted me out when a pregnant Alley came waddling up to me with a clip board.

"Must have talked with Sway."

My grin widened and thankfully I hadn't pulled off my helmet and could disguise it.

I still hadn't figured out what had gone wrong with my mechanical failure but I had a good idea of where to look. Sway.

Something was changing within our friendship but instead of trying to locate it, I overlooked it. Now wasn't the time. She had the college thing going and I was still undecided as to where I wanted my racing career to go. So, it was what is was ... friends who talked almost daily, texted like high school girls and kissed when they saw each other. To the outside world, it looked like we were dating on our own schedules but it wasn't that. I just could never control myself around her and ended up attacking the poor girl.

I ended up winning the feature that night and felt good about my chances for next season; after battling my dad all night long, I beat him by a mere three inches.

If you think about it, slowly, I was rebuilding my engine and was trying to ensure it wasn't just a rev motor because it needed to be one to last.

I also needed to work on my concentration. I wasn't focused as I've always been so I was working on that, too.

Sway came out to see me during her spring break when we were racing in Kansas City at Lakeside Speedway. She was originally going to come for Eldora but she ended up needing to stay and finish a few classes.

After that trip to Kansas, I swore I'd never return to that fucking city. Eventually I did but never during tornado season.

The day started normally as I picked Sway up from the airport and we went to the track after eating some breakfast. I admit that I did kiss her and it was as gratifying as it had always been.

When we got to the track, the weather started changing and the sky started talking.

Ryder and Justin were both racing with us this weekend. Sometime after we ran our hot laps and before the heat races began, Ryder came up to me.

"Those skies are rumbling, man."

I looked up from the tires I was scraping mud from into distant fields. Through a dark skyline, you could see thunderclouds rumbling and lightning flickering.

"Yeah, they're talking that's for sure."

The race was scheduled to start sometime after three that afternoon but the weather, being spring in the Midwest, was sketchy. We sat around most of the morning wondering if they'd even get the race in until the announcer came on and said they were cancelling it.

We packed up and pulled onto Highway 5 toward Wolcott when I noticed the sky turning colors off to the east of us. Having been around some crazy weather at times in the Midwest, I chalked this up to a thunderstorm rolling though. Oh, was I wrong.

It wasn't until the hail started and cars began to turn around and travel the opposite direction from us that I realized something might not be right.

Spencer, being Spencer, was driving blaring his new Britney Spears CD.

Sway was just as alarmed as me but because of Spencer's singing voice and not the weather. Alley, being pregnant and extremely exhausted, was sleeping.

I could still see Ryder's hauler in front of us and knew Emma was with him and Tommy.

No one else seemed to be alarmed. I thought maybe I was overreacting. I was so wrong. The shit was about to hit the fan.

While merging onto Hutton Road, I realized this shit was flying. Looking off to the West, the sky had turned a pea soup color and the hail was coming down so hard that you couldn't see a foot in front of the car.

Spencer turned the stereo down. "Shit, look at that hail!"

Ryder pulled over before merging onto the Interstate and got out to run back to our truck with Tommy and Emma following close behind. So now we had seven people piled into the truck with Tommy sitting on my lap.

I was not amused.

"What are you guys doing?" I was more specifically asking Tommy this question, but not directly.

Everyone looked skeptically at each other before answering.

"We thought it was safer in here ..." Tommy answered.

None of these assholes seemed particularly sharp at the moment.

I couldn't understand the reasoning behind them thinking they were safer in here and I was not impressed that Tommy felt the need to sit on *my* lap, but was cut off by a loud siren blaring. It sounded like a bullhorn but kept going, and going.

Everyone panicked so I tried to take control. Taking control in my mind was getting Tommy off my lap and assessing the situation outside, without seven people yelling their own theories as to what was happening.

"What's that noise?" I asked when Spencer and I got out of the truck, everyone else stayed inside, scared I imagined.

"What noise?" he asked covering his ears.

Calmly, not at all like I wanted to, I removed his hands from his ears, "That noise."

"I don't know!" he yelled. "I can't hear anything over that siren."

"What is it?" I thought I was being clear.

"What is what?"

"The fucking siren!" I screamed. "That's the noise I'm referring to!"

"Oh, that. Hell, I think it's ..." we looked up to see everyone, aside from Alley, running full speed in our direction.

Being nine months pregnant, Alley was in no shape to be running.

"It's a tornado siren, you dumb shits!" Sway yelled as she ran past us. She was practically carrying Alley until she stopped to look back at us.

Spencer, being the fucking idiot I always knew him to be, stopped to take pictures.

"Are you fucking serious?" Sway asked looking back at me in mock horror.

"Just run toward the underpass, follow Ryder!" I yelled over the steering winds picking up and the golf ball hail attacking us. She stood there. "Run!" she finally did so I turned to go get Spencer.

"Come on!" I reached for his sweatshirt. I'd never been properly educated on Tornado 101 but I was certain he was not standing in a safe zone.

His response, "Dude, look at that funnel!" he was animated as he said this, or it could have been my imagination, or shock.

What funnel? I thought to myself.

Like I said, I had no tornado training.

Until now, I hadn't looked around and before I could, I was hurled into a field. At least it appeared to be a field. I was somewhat disoriented so I could have been in Iowa now and wouldn't have known the difference.

The good thing was, when I was hurled, I landed fairly close to the others so I scurried under the overpass with the rest of the guys while Spencer stumbled over holding the side of his head.

As the winds got stronger and the howling became louder, and louder, I honestly thought we may die under a freeway overpass. The wind and noise around us became deafening and so did Spencer's screams.

"Oh, my God, this can't be happening," Sway muttered pushing herself further up the concrete banking we were on.

"Well, it is," I leaned into her, blocking any of the shit flying around us from hitting her.

You couldn't see past a few feet with all the dust and debris.

"You know what? Fuck you, this is your fault," Sway insinuated, scowling but cuddling into my embrace. I could feel her entire body shaking with fear, which only made me pull her closer.

"Hardly," I mumbled against her shoulder. It was kind of my fault, not really ... okay, it was my fault but I refused to take the entire blame for it. I wanted to race at Lakeside Speedway but I hardly thought the weather was my fault.

I was scared. I'll admit that but that was another thing I refused to admit out loud in this natural disaster we seemed to be having.

Alley was crying hysterically, so was Spencer but not in a normal way. Sway looked pissed and Ryder and Emma were practically on top of each other, screaming. I laughed at the sight of my barely five-foot sister clinging to Ryder who was also, barely five feet. Together they almost looked like a normal sized person.

It's amazing the thoughts that go through your head when you think you're going to die. I was livid I wouldn't make it to the Chili Bowl this year, that's all I cared about. I was also upset that I wouldn't be able to eat dinner because if I was going to die, I wanted to die on a full stomach. I began to wonder if that was why people who were about to be executed got to pick their last meal. It made sense to me now.

When the violent shaking and winds began to diminish, Sway went to get up. Again, I knew nothing about tornados but I was sure it wasn't safe yet.

"That is a horrible idea," I told her. "I'm alarmed you'd even try that."

Just as I said that, a car blew past us, in the air, I might add, where Sway almost walked out.

Her wide eyes focused on mine.

"See," I motioned to the car with my head and then pulled her back in my arms.

Afraid to move, we stayed under there for a good twenty minutes before anyone tried to move again.

Without collecting my thoughts on what occurred, I asked, "Do you think Burger King will be open?" It was apparent I was in shock.

Sway's wide eyes met mine again, "Yeah, their sign says they are." She motioned toward the Burger King sign lying about fifty feet away.

"That was not at all like the movie *Twister*," was the only coherent thing said by Ryder.

Emma was running off pure adrenaline and jumped out of the underpass like popcorn popping to see the wreckage behind us.

"Your enthusiasm is disturbing," I told her. "We almost died, if you forgot."

She said nothing, just hopped away.

It's exhausting being around her sometimes not to mention the fact that we did almost die and I was in no mood for anything cheery. I needed a nap and food.

Devastation was all around us. Cars, houses, people, animals ... you name it ... it was in the rubble left in the aftermath. I had no idea what to make of all of it. Everything these people knew in this city was destroyed. Homes they lived in were now relocated. Cars they once drove were in another county ... it was crazy.

"Where's Tommy?" Sway asked suddenly.

I spun around, "I thought he was under there with us?"

"Obviously not."

Just as we began to panic, Tommy came walking up holding a cat in his arms. His hair looked like he let a four-year-old little girl style it with pudding and dirt, his clothes not much more than a few pieces of fabric remaining.

"That was … a little much," he said, and then sat down in the grass, sighing contently as though he was relieved. I could only imagine. He glanced down at the cat in his arms, purring. "I have no idea how a cat got in my arms but she won't leave now."

We had no choice but to laugh at all this, or cry. We chose to laugh and, to this day, we still get a chuckle out of Tommy and that goddamn cat.

After my brush with death in Kansas, my season began to pick up and I saw hope and the end to the season in the near future. It helped that Sway spent an entire two weeks with me after that.

I was determined not to let what happened before happen again. I questioned my ability and I shouldn't have. I knew I was good. I don't mean to sound conceited or be an asshole, but if I could go out and beat my dad of all people at tracks like Eldora and Knoxville where he's broken records time and time again, that said something about my ability as a driver. There were times when I had an ill handling car but pushed it as far as it could go just to finish.

I was slowly climbing back up in the points.

If someone told me "You can't" I would say watch me motherfucker. I didn't like the word can't. I would have done about anything to prove them wrong.

We were at Williams Grove for the Morgan Cup Challenge that weekend racing a winged sprint car. I was having a decent night and had qualified second but I had a feeling my night was about to get worse when Alley came up without my helmet.

"I lost your helmet. Wear this one," and she tossed a silver one my direction.

I'm not superstitious but I have had the same *Troy Lee* helmet for the last few years. I wanted *that* helmet.

"What do you mean you lost my helmet?" I glared at Alley.

She glared right back.

Being nine months pregnant and a week overdue, I shouldn't be yelling but if you've ever tried to run at a track like Williams Grove without tear-offs, you were fucked.

"That's exactly what I mean!" she shouted at me and waddled away.

"I don't understand her at times," Tommy said shaking his head.

"It's Alley, she's a bitch. I stopped trying to figure her out a long time ago. She's beyond any normal sense of comprehension," I groaned looking at my spare helmet. "What the fuck am I going to do ... I don't have any tear-offs for this one!"

"Sucks to be you," Alley yelled back over her shoulder and flipped me off.

They all blamed me for that stupid tornado still. It was not my fault. I couldn't control the weather.

The night was horrible in and out of the car. Ever try muscling around an 800 horsepower sprint car and keep your vision clear at the same time?

It ain't easy. I ended up with a fifth place finish and was surprised with it. Tracks like Williams Grove were difficult to find a good exit on the corners subsequently causing your car to slide up the track. I must have pegged the outside wall a half a dozen times in the feature but I finished.

I got another surprise when I headed back to the hauler to find my sister-in-law, in labor, in my hauler. If you thought I was picky about urine being in my truck, well, I was no more excited about whatever it was that was about to come out inside there.

All the safety vehicles were surrounding my pit and my first thought was who did my brother get in a fight with but when I saw Alley laying down, I knew she was in labor. Never in my wildest dreams did I suspect that she would have that baby inside there though.

I don't know who screamed louder, Alley from pain, Spencer from fear, or me, from total disgust at the mess it made in there.

"That was disgusting," I finally said when they wheeled Alley and the new baby away.

"That was beautiful," Emma said through her hysterical tears.

"I'm with Jameson," said Justin who stopped by my pit to make sure I wasn't in another fight. "That was disgusting."

I couldn't step foot inside my hauler after that. All I saw was the blood and obscene amounts of whatever the fuck that was that came out of her. I'd never seen a baby born and now that I just had, even though the paramedics were mostly in the way, the mess it left behind assured me that I didn't care to see what made that.

Spencer headed to the hospital with Alley while Tommy and I cleaned up. Well, Tommy did, I gagged most of the time and then ended up putting the hauler up for sale after that. It was damaged now.

I called Sway later that night and let her know Alley finally had the baby. I had yet to see him but Spencer called and told me he was perfect and healthy. Mom and Dad were on the next flight from Mooresville to Mechanicsburg where we were. Sway wanted to come but couldn't because of school. I felt bad for her and she cried because she couldn't come.

These were the times that bothered her the most. We were her family and a new addition, Lane Anthony Riley, was added and she wasn't there. I got to see Lane later that night and he was adorable. He looked similar to Spencer when he was a baby but with Alley's blonde hair, nose and eyes.

The following weekend when we were in Concord, North Carolina, Justin and I took Spencer out for drinks to celebrate his new fatherhood. Well, Spencer drank. We stole his drinks when the bartender wasn't looking.

I don't remember much about what happened that night but when I woke up on the beach naked, I was concerned.

This wasn't the ideal situation for a number of reasons. I didn't know where I was and I didn't care for the beach for the obvious reason of sand being on my skin and, oh, yeah, I happened to be naked.

It couldn't have looked any worse.

I went to get up to bolt for cover, though I had no idea where I was going to run too and tripped over Justin and a girl, who was also naked.

I'll admit I looked away from Justin but the girl, she was worth taking a double take at.

It wasn't Ami and I had a feeling he wasn't going to be happy about it when he realized that something may have happened between them as they looked awfully cozy.

I soon found my clothes a few hundred feet away and then finally, Spencer, curled up with a bottle of rum. At least he had clothes on.

I left all of them on the beach. I had to get the sand off my skin and then figure out what in the hell time it was. I had to be in Lake Odessa by four that afternoon so now was not the time to stall. We weren't far from a life guard station so I got washed off, spotted the rental car in the distance and then found the guys again.

"I'm so screwed," Justin looked remorseful. "What the fuck happened last night?"

"Are you serious?" I groaned rubbing the back of my head. "I have no idea where we are let alone what happened."

"We're at the beach," Spencer grunted walking up with a limp.

We both laughed and then stopped when we realized how badly it hurt our heads. "We need to get going," I told them and washed the last of the sand.

The girl on the beach confirmed what we didn't want to hear. Though Spencer and I had stayed away from her, Justin did not.

We never did figure out how we all got on the beach but that was the last of our worries when we realized that one, our friend was freaking out that he cheated on his girlfriend and didn't remember and two, we had to be in Lake Odessa by four. It was seven in the morning and it's a twelve hour drive to get to Lake Odessa from Concord.

We were fucked.

Our sprint cars were already there since I was driving for Bucky and Justin was driving for Ron Walker by that time but we still had to get there.

That left us with one option ... calling my dad for a favor. He arranged for a private jet to come get us and we arrived in Lake Odessa with an hour to spare. Jimi didn't let us get away free. He made us pay for the gas in the jet which wasn't cheap.

We decided we wouldn't be drinking alone any time soon after that. Keeping one of the girls around us at all times was pretty much a necessity.

I felt for Justin. He didn't want to sleep with that girl but his judgment was lapsed and he made a bad decision. He did the right thing in telling Ami though.

Her reaction was to be expected and she did break up with him. I thought Justin felt relieved that he told her the truth but by that point they had broken up. Being away from each other was taking a toll on their relationship already and that seemed to be the final straw.

Ami had graduated college and had gotten a job in Los Angeles, which meant they pretty much never saw each other unless she was able to fly out to see him at a race.

"I would take you out drinking to relieve the pain ... but we both know how that ended last time."

"I don't want relief. I want to forget altogether," he grunted kicking his legs out in front of him as he sat in a folding chair next to his hauler. "How could I have been so stupid? I loved her, Jameson. I loved her more than anything and I threw all that away in one night."

After wrecking each other in the Lake Odessa race that night, Justin and I sat in his pit after. Spencer and Tommy strolled up and tossed us a couple of beers and then Ryder, Cody and Tyler found us. The best comfort we could provide for a fellow heartbroken racer was talk racing, and that's what we did.

I thought about Sway a lot that night. This was exactly why I kept Sway at a distance ... it was because I was afraid of something like this happening to us.

We had women pushed upon us out here after races and at bars. They knew who we were and tested our self-control. If I was with Sway physically, which was appealing to me, what happens if I had a lapse in judgment like Justin did? I couldn't hurt her like that, ever. Besides, I had no idea if she even felt that way. Sure our friendship worked and when I touched and kissed her she responded but so did I when other women touched me. That didn't mean I had feelings for them, it just meant I was attracted physically to them.

There was a fine line and I wasn't ready to cross it yet.

By the time July had rolled around, we settled into a routine with the new addition to our traveling team, Lane. It was tough for Alley to still travel so she stayed in Mooresville with my mom for about a month and then started again.

Lane was a sport and loved the sound of the cars. My sprint car revving lulled him to sleep on more than one occasion. It was cool having him around and I took pride in knowing that his first smile was a product of me. I was laughing at something Ryder did while holding Lane for Alley and he smiled when I laughed. Like I said, Lane was pretty cool and not at all what I thought he was going to be like, until he puked on me.

I was not okay with that.

By August, Sway was on summer break and traveled around with us again which meant I was back to normal and aggressive on the track. Not that I wasn't when she was around but I fought harder for position at times and didn't take shit from anyone. I wouldn't say that was because of Sway, by any means, but I seemed to find myself when she was with me and remembered why I was racing in the first place.

I was still racing with the USAC divisions but I was making every Outlaw race I could and running roughshod through it.

I wasn't known for being nice on the track, I knew that, as did the handful of other drivers I'd raced with all these years. I was ornery, surly and would call anyone out on their bullshit passes or unjustified hits. I also wasn't afraid to back it up, if needed. So far this year, I had brawled with track owners and officials over rules, shoved photographers, and sparred with a few hometown favorites. I had a temper. What can I say?

But, most of all, I wasn't about to be pushed around. I didn't risk everything to be just an average driver. I risked it all to be the best and that's what I was becoming, temper or not.

That temper got me in my fair share of wrecks that summer as well, most of which I walked away from but there were a few I either crawled or stumbled away from.

At Eldora in the middle of September while racing a Silver Crown car, I took a few flips on the back stretch coming out of turn two and landed on the guardrail upside down. I felt that one.

When they flipped me back over I was able to get out. It was apparent after a few steps that I was going to need to get checked out. I could barely put one foot in front of the other. I waved to the crowd when they started cheering but that's about all I was able to do. Once inside the infield care center they had set up, I collapsed.

My knees were sore and bruised from the impact; all the blood vessels in my face had broken and my arms and legs had so many bruises on them you'd think someone beat me with a baseball bat.

I was a mess.

I ended up spending the night in the hospital with a broken rib and a concussion on top of all that bruising.

I called Sway from the hospital that night to tell her what happened. I hoped they hadn't announced it on the news or anything. She freaked out and told me she was skipping classes for a week to come see me but I wouldn't let her. She needed to finish college so I could have my friend back.

I knew where the failure went wrong. It was a combination of everything and to rebuild I had to do it right. Right meant focusing on what was important, racing, and Sway focusing on what was important for her, school. Later we could figure out where we stood. I hoped.

That season it seemed I wasn't the only one doing rough driving. Justin and Tyler were making themselves known as well for being hotheads. Justin punched a USAC official after a race in Lernerville and Tyler sent a kid to the hospital when the kid pushed him.

You don't push the *Beasts from the East* and walk away. There was a reason they were called the "Fire Breathing Beasts from the East," even I knew that.

The veteran drivers weren't pleased with us and they had every right not to be but I *understood* them. Here these kids were coming into the divisions they had once been winning in and now, all of a sudden, they weren't winning, the kids were.

Jimi found humor in it and joked that he was going to retire but other drivers, they just thought we were a bunch of arrogant little shits.

I understood why veteran drivers raced us the way they did. No one realizes the pressures put upon these guys to race, but to win. And the longer they go without a win, the harder it is for them that these kids are winning. I knew why they raced us the way they were and respected them for that.

I knew they made this sport what it is today and they deserved respect in my mind so that's how I raced them. I raced them as if they were all my dad and I'd never rough up my own Dad on the track for the simple fact that I feared him out there. If there was one driver who could fool you, it was Jimi Riley.

Sway took another break in October for Thanksgiving and Christmas so this meant she was there for the last few races of the season.

Having Sway back around also meant the women I usually found myself giving into, didn't exist. I had all eyes on Sway these days and that scared the shit out of me after what happened to Justin and Ami. It didn't stop us from kissing and touching but I kept it innocent as did she.

She seemed different, hesitant even. I wondered if she found someone at times but then again I thought she'd tell me. Tommy kept tabs on her and said she only hung out with girls at school that he could see. Tommy also took a break but was finishing his degree in engineering. He wanted to continue working on my cars but also felt he needed to get the education to back it up. It made me feel better to know that Tommy was there with her and was ensuring the scum bags stayed away.

When she was here with me on the road, it was like she never left. We were back to our usual selves, flirting, touching, and teasing each other. That's what I enjoyed most about her company. I could be myself for one, but it was just easy. Even after months of separation, it was as though we'd never been apart.

Slowly my engine was rebuilt and now was time for maintaining it. Proper maintenance was essential. What maintains the life of your engine?

Proper maintenance and lubrication. It took me a long time to discover the cause to the failure, an entire racing season to be exact but it was me.

I let it happen and damn sure wasn't about to let it happen again.

Tether – A braided Kevlar double strap that is bolted to the wheel on one end of the chassis as well as on the other end which keeps the wheel attached to the chassis in case of an accident.

With a handful of races remaining in the 2000 season, we found ourselves in Williams Grove toward the end of October racing with the Outlaws before we finished out our USAC season the following week in California.

Here's what you have to remember. You can't expect a group of guys like us to just relax when we weren't racing USAC because that wasn't us. If anything, racing was our relaxation.

That left us racing sprint cars in Williams Grove.

Ryder, Justin, Tyler, and I were running in the top five in all three USAC divisions. Some thought we should be racing anything other than USAC but again, we just wanted to race.

Ryder had been running up high on the cushion all night, and at tracks like Williams Grove that meant trouble.

"You better watch that," Dad told Ryder after his heat race. "That wall bites."

Ryder laughed and went about his way. None of us really thought anything about what Jimi had said.

Halfway through the feature Justin and I were up front battling with my dad when we saw the lights flash yellow and then immediately red. This usually meant someone crashed badly or something was wrong with the track.

They stopped us coming out of turn three. When you're inside those cars cramped in small quarters, it seemed like hours waiting but when they landed a helicopter in the infield, I knew it was serious.

I had no idea who was injured or how badly. The outlaws don't have radios so we couldn't ask.

Sometime after about forty-five minutes, they had us make pace laps and then I saw the car being hauled away. It was the number two of Ryder Christensen. I groaned to myself knowing he was badly injured. I hated to see him get hurt but, as I said, none of us did things half-assed.

That night at Williams Grove, the wall bit back hard and Ryder saw that.

From the time I was old enough to know better, I knew the dangers of racing. I was also too caught up in racing to be scared when I was inside the car. I'd seen first-hand the gnarly wrecks my dad endured and I'd had my fair share over the years as well, but that night in Williams Grove scared me.

I knew Ryder well from our times racing in the quarter midgets together and now with racing USAC, he was my friend, and seeing him airlifted away was not something I took lightly.

I wasn't naïve. I knew we could get killed doing this and I'd seen it before and I was sure I'd see it again.

Spencer, Justin and I drove up to the hospital in Pittsburgh that night to check on Ryder while everyone else went back to Mooresville. They had him listed in critical condition but they said he'd be all right. Broken ribs, concussion, broken arm, broken leg, broken pelvis and broken back was bound to keep him out of racing for a while.

Dad and Bucky met us at the hospital as well to check on him and, for the first time, I talked to my dad about the dangers of racing. It's not that I didn't know how badly we could get hurt, but between racers it's not something you talked about, it just wasn't.

I think that night shook Jimi a little as well because Ryder and I were around the same age.

He saw me walking down the hall with Justin and reached for me, pulling me into a hug. I didn't pull away, I stood there, part of me shocked that he was hugging me but also relieved that he was all right. That could have been him and that could have been me. It could have be any of us.

"How's Ryder?" he finally asked pulling away.

"Pretty banged up but he's stable. His dad is back there with him now."

"Who'd he wreck with?"

Bucky cleared his throat beside us, his demeanor shaken. "He and Tyler were in a close battle for fifth and Ryder came around the outside just as Tyler's left rear tire blew."

I shook my head remembering my crash a month earlier when I destroyed the catch fence and myself doing that same thing. All of us loved the high side but it's dangerous up there at times. It's fast and sometimes too fast for conditions, but in Ryder's case it was just bad timing. It wasn't his fault and it wasn't Tyler's. It was the dangers of racing.

Dad and I flew back to Mooresville that night. They had bought a house there to make things easier on traveling; being able to sleep in our own beds at times was a nice change from sleeping in hotels and along the highway.

"Are you okay?" Dad asked when we drove from the airport to the house. I was in the middle of sending Sway a text to let her know I was on my way back to the Mooresville and was relieved to know she was there, too.

"Yeah, I'm fine." I slipped my phone inside my jacket. "I feel bad for Ryder. And Tyler."

Tyler felt horrible afterward and left without saying anything to anyone. When Dad and I left the hospital, Tyler was still sitting outside the ICU waiting for Ryder to come around.

"I know," he agreed shaking his head. "I hate to see that sort of thing but when you race as long as I have ... it happens ... too often. I haven't seen a wreck like that since O'Neil's kid."

We didn't say much else after that, just rode in comfortable silence.

When we got home, it was around three in the morning but I wanted to see Sway. She was in the guest room so I snuck inside there. To my surprise she was awake, pacing the room.

"Are you all right?" I whispered watching her pace. She was only dressed in one of my t-shirts and her panties.

I prayed she was wearing a bra and then I silently hoped she wasn't. I was so fucked.

I almost turned around and left but she didn't let me before she was in my arms, hugging me tightly.

"I'm so glad you're okay," she wailed.

"Sway ... shhh honey." I stroked her head as she cried. "You knew I didn't wreck."

"I know but I was ... worried," she sniffled into my neck. I could feel her ragged heartbeat against my chest, her tears wetting my neck. "Seeing that helicopter ... the crash ..."

I held onto her tightly, trying to comfort her in any way I could. That's when I moved to sit down on the bed and she straddled my lap. *That* position did nothing for my self-control.

My breathing hitched, as did hers, and I may have even groaned when she made contact with a very eager part of me. One second she was crying and the next we were moving away from each other.

"Sorry," I muttered pushing myself off the bed.

Sway's legs fell from my waist and she let go, sitting back on the bed and then curling her legs up.

"It's okay. I forgot I wasn't wearing any pants."

"You should put some on."

She glanced around the room, found her sweatpants and thankfully pulled them back on.

"Thanks," I whispered before sitting back down on the bed beside her.

She looked at me for a long moment before chewing on her bottom lip. "Do you ... um ... okay, I'm going to be a total girl right now," she sighed in defeat. "Can you um ... hold me?"

I had to laugh at her expression, so I did, and then she punched me in the shoulder. "Christ ... if you want me to hold you ... don't physically hurt me."

"I'm sorry, get over here," she patted the bed.

"One condition,"

"What would that be?" she rolled her eyes.

"One, you keep those goddamn sweatpants on, and two..." I paused and laid down next to her. My hand came up and touched her cheek softly before leaning in. "You let me kiss you."

She never answered, just leaned in and pressed her lips softly to mine. I wanted to remember the feeling, see if the same electric all-consuming feeling shot through me when our lips touched.

It did. The kissing only lasted a minute, maybe less before I pulled away and tucked her head gently against my chest. I don't know why I tested myself so much with her. I didn't want to, but as soon as I was around her lately all I wanted to do was be closer, kiss her more and never be away from her. That scared the shit out of me.

Over the years, I've met my fair share of cocky drivers, myself included. You needed a certain amount of confidence to go out and do what we do but there was a fine line to walk there. Too much in one direction and it's never good.

I'm not saying I was a saint, because really there were times where I didn't like myself.

Here's the thing though, I would never go out there and intentionally wreck someone. Unless they asked for it.

While running the last night of the World Finals for the World of Outlaw series at the Dirt Track at Charlotte in Concord, North Carolina, I ran into a driver I'd heard a lot about these days, Darrin Torres.

He just started in the NASCAR Cup series this last year. He thought he was hot shit whereas I had my own theories having seen him race before. Most of the Cup drivers who started out in open wheel racing reverted to it in the off-season or on Saturday nights when they weren't racing so I wasn't surprised to see him there.

Dad was there since he was an Outlaw driver, but what caught me off guard was the conversation before my heat race.

"Listen, Jameson, be careful out there." The intensity in his voice was enough to make me look up from strapping on my belts.

Everyone was still a little shook up with what happened to Ryder, so I wasn't all that surprised but we'd talked about this already. I knew the dangers but I didn't suspect this had anything to do with Darrin.

"Darrin isn't someone you can trust out there," his eyes focused on the track, and then back to me. "Hold your line but if he pushes, back off."

I scowled. I never gave my line up. Why would he even suggest that? He wouldn't lift if it were him, why should I?

"It's not worth it." He muttered tucking his helmet under his arm. "I've seen too many guys wrecked by him.

I nodded and slid down into the narrow cockpit when he walked away, not completely understanding what he meant.

Sway and Emma came by with Lane prior to the race and said hello. I got a baby high-five from Lane. He was seven months old now and got more adorable every day. Sway hugged me and gave me a kiss on the cheek for good luck and Emma, naturally, kicked me in the shin.

In the feature, Darrin and I lined up in row four, beside each other, with me on the outside.

Dad was right about Darrin. He was reckless on the track but I was faster, stronger and outsmarted him, taking every line he chose and pushed him up the track. I knew my abilities on tracks like Charlotte. He wasn't even in the same league as me, and judging by his movements inside the car, he wasn't adjusting well to the difference in handling from the Cup cars.

He was on my ass mercilessly though but I was satisfied he was using his tires up trying to catch me.

I ended up taking second. My car was no match for Justin's and Darrin came in seventh.

All good, right?

Not exactly.

After the race during the cool down lap, he shot around and clipped my rear tire.

I think I've said this before but what happens when you clip the rear tires on these beasts? That's right. Over you go.

It was a cheap-ass hit. It was deliberate and I lost my temper.

I jumped down off the wrecker tossing my helmet and gloves in the same motion once we were back in the pits. Rage roared through me. Fuck being calm and reasonable. That was gone.

"What the fuck was that?" I snarled at him, getting in his face.

I didn't give him a chance to answer. No way was I letting him get away with that shit. Punches were quickly thrown and I struggled furiously against crewmembers and officials fighting to separate us.

I was too caught up in my rage to listen to the officials. I lunged against the restraining hands but they had me pretty well contained. That's when I noticed he'd gotten a hit in on me and I was bleeding.

I growled doubling my efforts to get at him when my dad yelled. "Jameson! That's enough!"

Getting light headed, I realized it was enough when the officials pulled Darrin away from me; either that or we were going to kill each other out here.

Stomping my way toward my pit I realized the blood was now pouring out. I had no idea he even got in a hit to do that damage but I was hardly paying attention.

Head wounds bleed like a bitch and I had enough sense to know this one needed stitches. I stormed back to the hauler with Tommy, Sway and Spencer following. Everyone who knows me knows my temper is legendary and I proved it that night. It took me a good four hours and six stitches above my eye before I calmed down.

It was all over the papers the next morning that Jimi Riley's son tried to teach the NASCAR Winston Cup series Rookie of the Year a thing or two about retaliation.

I'd like to say that was our last run-in with each other but it wasn't. Far from that.

That night was the end of the racing season and, once again, I was thankful. Not only for a break but my head was pounding and I had a feeling it would be for a while. I'd taken some hits this season. I was becoming used to double vision these days and, after a while, it seemed normal.

I was heading to Turkey Night in a few weeks but this also left a little time for a vacation and then, for the first time in my racing career, I was finally racing in the Chili Bowl in January. Schedules lined up with an open seat in Bucky's midget car. I couldn't wait.

Ryder was still in the hospital in Pittsburgh, so before flying home to Elma I decided to make a detour to see him. Justin came along with me and we spent most of the night there recapping the last few races for him.

He was doing better, still not up and walking around but the doctors assured him *eventually* he'd be able to get back into a race car if he wanted. He was young, just a year younger than I was, so it meant he'd heal faster than veteran drivers.

Justin flew home to Bloomington and I flew back to Elma later that night. It felt good to be home but I was so amped about Turkey Night and the Chili Bowl I couldn't wait for January to roll around.

Dad decided not to race in Australia this year and forced us all to go on a vacation for Christmas. With some persuasion, I convinced Sway to come with us. Charlie was also going to come but cancelled at the last minute because he said he wasn't feeling well.

On the way to Vail, Colorado, where we'd be spending Christmas, I decided it was time to tell Sway about the Chili Bowl. So far, the only people who knew I was going were dad and Bucky.

"Sway, I have something to tell you," Jameson said, suddenly on the flight to Vail.

What, that you love me?

You wish, Sway.

"Yeah?" I flipped my magazine closed and looked over at him, ignoring my internal stupidity.

"I'm going to the Chili Bowl this year," he smirked.

"What?" I nearly fell out of the chair. "Are fucking serious?"

"Calm down."

"No, I won't calm down! You've been saying this for years! Oh, my God, this is so exciting. When do you leave?"

I'll admit, my enthusiasm for this was even alarming to even me but you have to understand, every year he plans to go and schedules cross or he can't get a car together in time.

The Chili Bowl, Turkey Night, The Hut Hundred ... The Night before the 500 ... those were the races that got you noticed and into full-time rides. This was huge for his career to be able to go. As it was, he was racing Bucky's car and had a part-time sponsorship with Bowman Oil and a handful of other sponsors, but he funded his winged sprint car and that seemed to be what he *wanted* to run. If he had a good showing at an event like that, it could mean leaving there with sponsorship. Jameson *needed* this.

He laughed at my enthusiasm. "If you would calm down for a minute I would tell you."

"I can't believe this!" I launched myself into his lap. "Does Jimi know?"

"Yeah, hey ... listen ... I wanted to know if you would come with me?" he smirked again.

"Come with you? To the Chili Bowl ... like in Tulsa?"

He nodded. "Yeah, I'll be there for a week ... I thought it would be a good break for you and I would like you to come with me."

"Like to Tulsa?" I repeated.

"Yes, Sway," he sighed. "Am I not explaining myself very well?"

"No, it's just ... you took me off guard."

"So, that's a yes?"

I was silent for a few minutes and I had no idea what to say.

Of course, I would go with him. I would have skipped school in a heartbeat but thank goodness my classes hadn't started yet.

The Chili Bowl was only three weeks away and I almost thought I showed more enthusiasm for it than Jameson did that week we were in Vail.

It was fun being around the Riley family again, all of them. When I was with them, I felt as though I never left.

Jameson and I spent most of the time playing in the snow and trying to snowboard. This was one sport Jameson hadn't mastered and neither had I. After that, the majority of the trip was spent in the hot tub nursing our sore bodies.

I had never laughed so much, ate so much, and been, well, as horny as I was.

Everything Jameson did turned me on. He breathed and I wanted to jump on top of him. He laughed and I wanted to hump his leg, he smiled and I nearly died. But it wasn't just that I was horny. Everything he did was endearing. He looked at me, I fell deeper. He kissed me, I melted.

I never thought anything of the kissing because ever since Jameson and I were little, we kissed. When we saw each other after a long departure, we kissed. When we got drunk, we kissed.

It never escalated to anything of substance because he always stopped. I wouldn't have stopped. Most girls would have gotten mixed emotions but I knew Jameson well enough to know that it wasn't that he had romantic feelings but that he was just horny. I didn't care. Should have, but didn't. I would take anything he was willing to offer, that's how truly pathetic I was.

By Christmas, I was wondering how in the hell I was going to make it another week and then be in Tulsa with him.

We spent New Year's Eve together and watched Lane while Alley and Spencer did God knows what behind closed doors. Lane was a hoot and definitely part of the Riley family. He thought his uncle Jameson was pretty cool, in turn, Jameson thought he was pretty cool.

I could see a lot of Spencer in Lane. The kid loved to laugh whereas Jameson was serious and had a contemplative nature. I wondered what a baby Jameson would be like, preferably mixed with my genes.

Have you lost your mind? I asked myself.

He doesn't feel that way about you and you're already envisioning your babies with him.

Crazy person.

"He's cute, isn't he?" Jameson said watching Lane sleep on his chest.

"Yeah," I smiled adjusting his blanket so it covered his chubby little arms. "Hard to believe your brother of all people could make something that cute."

"Do you want kids?" Jameson asked yawning.

I thought about it for a moment. I was imagining our babies.

"Yeah, I think someday I would."

Jameson didn't say anything and smiled.

"What about you?" I asked trying to remain sneaky. Jameson had leaned back on the couch so I sat down beside him and Lane.

"I don't know. I guess maybe someday but not any time soon," he chuckled softly and adjusted Lane on his chest. "I barely have time to sleep these days let alone take care of a kid."

He was right. Usually when I heard from him, it was in the middle of the night. He didn't have time for even himself these days and if he wanted this as a profession, it wouldn't end.

After New Year's we all headed back to Elma and then it was off to Tulsa. I had to be back in school the week after so it was nice to get such a long break away from everything.

Tommy, Spencer, Jameson, Jimi, and I headed to Tulsa on Tuesday with the racing starting on Wednesday. The main event was being held on Saturday night.

The Chili Bowl Midget Nationals is the biggest midget car racing event and some even refer to it as the Super Bowl of midget racing. It's held in an indoor facility in Tulsa, Oklahoma, that can hold 15,000 fans. It's one of the only races where you'll see around two-hundred and fifty drivers from the USAC divisions, NASCAR, World of Outlaws, and all the best open-wheel drivers in one facility all competing for only twenty-four positions. It's some of the best midget racing you'll ever see. Being an indoor facility, they never have to fight weather conditions and the track is never subjected to too much rain and wind that would ordinarily dry it out. They keep the quarter-mile clay track tacky and perfect, just the way the boys like it.

The format is different from any other race. The first day is practice, and then from there it's five hours a night of racing with a fifty-lap feature event on the last night. Each night they have heat races, dashes and twenty-five lap features to make it to the last night to be one of the twenty-four cars that fielded the A-feature.

The way it worked this year was we arrived on Tuesday, practice sessions were held Wednesday, and then on Thursday racing started. Each night there would be twelve heat races with starting positions determined by a pill draw, then two B-features and the A-feature. Points were accumulated for finishing positions plus passing points. The optimum objective would be to start last and finish first. This would allow you to gain the most points, but with the competition at the Chili Bowl, no one ever accomplished this unless you were Jameson and Justin.

The goal was to advance each night until you made it to the A-feature on Saturday night.

Thursday's practice session went good and Jameson's car was fast. Bucky had provided him a crew and the midget to race. Tommy and Spencer helped but they weren't obligated to assist. It had to be nice for everyone to just show up and race and not have to worry about fixing the car when it broke.

Justin was there this year as well driving Bucky's other car so Jameson and Justin were teammates.

Justin and Jameson raced well together. They both had their strong points. Justin had a rap for getting fast starts and staying strong, whereas Jameson would lag back and come on strong in the end. Both techniques worked well but this provided Jameson with more points and moved him up faster. Justin won more heats but Jameson gained more points.

On Friday, the night before the A-feature, Jameson and I walked through the pits with Justin. They were stopped every few feet but eventually we made our destination, Bobby Cole's pit.

Jameson admired Bobby for what he'd done in the USAC divisions as he was the only driver who had won the Triple Crown.

Bobby was a rookie this year in the NASCAR Winston Cup series and hadn't been to the Chili Bowl in years.

I wasn't surprised to see a crowd around him, but Jameson was surprised when Bobby knew who he was as did another Cup driver Tate Harris.

"Hey, Jameson," Bobby said conversationally when we walked up. Jameson threw his arm around my shoulder and shook Bobby's hand with the other. "Glad to see you made it this year."

Jameson smiled. "Yeah, finally lined up this year."

"Who ya drivin' for?"

"Bucky."

"You smoked me last night in that heat race," Bobby grinned.

"Must be the car," Jameson teased with another smirk.

"Or the driver," Bobby hedged. "Have you met Tate Harris?"

Jameson shook his head and looked over his shoulder to see Tate making his way through the crowd. He bumped Jameson's shoulder when he walked through and back at us.

"So you're the kid who's won the Night before the 500 three times now."

"That would be me," Jameson said and leaned into me slightly. I tucked my hand into his back pocket.

Oh, jeez ... now I'm touching his ass. God help me.

Jameson didn't seem to mind and never attempted to move so I kept it there. His arm never moved from my shoulders either.

"I've tried to win that for the last six years."

"Yeah, and I've tried to win Turkey Night for the last six."

They all continued to tease each other about their wins that never came. It was nice to see Jameson mingling with guys around his age. He grew up around the legends in the Outlaw series but he never mixed with the USAC guys. Sure, he was friends with Justin, Ryder, and Tyler, but other than them he rarely even spoke to any of them. He seemed to be at ease around Bobby and Tate. It was nice to see.

One thing was for sure, there were a lot of people who disliked Jameson as well. When you have two-hundred-and-fifty drivers from all over the world and from different divisions, they all had different racing styles. Some didn't like that Jameson would lag on restarts or his tetchy personality but you either loved Jameson or hated him.

I honestly believed that if you hated him, you didn't understand him. He was the type of person who you had to understand and to see the real him in order to like him. He only let a few people see him for who he was.

Watching him that night, I couldn't help but admire who he was becoming.

"Racing gods ... please, help me!" Jimi groaned carrying a rear shock to his midget.

"I think that's supposed to be on the car," Jameson jutted. "And, in one piece."

"No, shit," he tossed the shock at our feet. "You guys got a spare?" he asked Bobby and his mechanic who were standing next to him.

Without question, Bobby handed over a spare shock.

That's the thing with racing. On the track you fight for every position, every point but I guarantee you that if someone wrecks or breaks something, you'll have ten guys waiting at your pit to get you back out there.

I wasn't surprised to see him here being as this was the Midwest, but Grandpa Casten, Jimi's dad, walked up holding his flask and motioned behind him.

"Hey, Jay, those girls over there are screaming your name."

I don't know if I need to point this out, but given the chance, Casten would do anything to embarrass you, much like Spencer.

"Grandpa ..." Jameson shook his head in embarrassment.

We weren't expecting to see old Grandpa Casten here but I was pleasantly surprised. He was always good for a few laughs and loved to make fun of others, this is why I loved him. The only problem was that old Casten had a way of enlisting me into his army. This meant I somehow ended up wondering how in the hell I got myself into a situation when the outlook couldn't have looked any worse. The old bastard got me arrested once when I went to a Nine Inch Nails concert with him a few years back. I'll spare you the details but I was arrested and wasn't happy about it.

"Hey, that one's got a set of lungs," he elbowed Jameson. "That could be a good time right there."

Jameson leaned into my ear. "Kill me now, please," he begged me.

I giggled. "Nah, this is entertaining."

Jameson stayed and talked with Tate for a while so I walked back to his pit with Casten and Tommy.

"What's with you and my grandson?" Casten asked conversationally, his eyes glued to the woman's ass in front of us.

"Who are you talking to?"

"You. I was talking about you. Now settle the fuck down," he grumbled taking a pull from his flask. "It was only a question."

"I don't know?" was the nonsense that left my mouth in the form of a question.

What the fuck is wrong with me today?

I started to panic and, thankfully, he lost interest when the Red Bull girls caught his eye.

Later that night we all planned to go to dinner since Grandpa

Casten made the special trip out here.

When I told Jameson what we were doing his response was, "I don't like the sounds of that."

"You wouldn't," Casten grumbled at him.

Grandpa Casten was hardly suitable for public. The Nine Inch Nails concert was a prime example of that.

"Do you want to sit with him?" I asked Jameson motioning to Spencer and Casten in the backseat of the Suburban Jimi rented.

Jameson gave me a glare. "No, I can't sit back there with them. I might strangle them."

Spencer perked up and nudged grandpa. "I can't understand why he wouldn't trust us."

Grandpa snorted. "It's like he has no faith in family. Dumb shit."

Jameson looked at them and then back to me. "Do you see what I mean?"

The days flew by and before we knew it Saturday had arrived and the field was set for the A-feature. Twenty-four cars had fought for a place on the grid.

Tyler had missed the lock-in by one position when he finished fourth in the B-feature. I felt bad for him when he threw his helmet against the side of the transporter and punched the wall. These poor guys had battled for days, and then to not make the main by one position, he had every right to be angry.

It was a rugged field for the main with all good drivers but Jameson had the confidence in him. Not once throughout the week had his optimism wavered. I watched him closely thinking at any moment he'd lose it and show some sort of nervousness but he never did.

Jameson started eighth in the main lined up behind Jimi and Bobby Cole. Levi was on his outside with Alex Reed right behind him. I bite off all my nails thinking of the last time he and Reed tangled but I hoped Jameson kept his head.

Prior to the feature, he pulled me in for a kiss, telling me I was his good luck charm.

I couldn't turn him down even if I wanted to.

After that Tyler, Spencer, Tommy and I made our way to the pit bleachers to watch when Tommy nudged my shoulder as we walked. "You know, some would think you two were dating by the way you act."

Spencer chuckled, as did Tyler, but I wasn't laughing.

"Shut up, fire crotch!"

"I'm just sayin'," he dodged my swing for him and then leaned in to whisper in my ear. "He'll come around."

I choked on my own spit. Tommy had to pat my back as we took a seat.

"You have no idea what you're talking about. It's not like that," I managed to say between coughs.

Tyler and Spencer looked over at me as I continued to choke.

Announcing the drivers for the feature got underway and thankfully no more talk about Jameson and I was mentioned. I knew people had their assumptions.

To the outside eye, we couldn't have appeared any stranger. Here we were best friends, but we touched and kissed all the time. Who wouldn't think we were together, but the thing was it never escalated. Besides the time in the sleeping bag when we woke up without shirts on, we kept it innocent.

That's not to say these days I didn't want things to escalate, because boy did I. But that wasn't us. We were friends. At least this is what I told myself.

For never being at the Chili Bowl before, Jameson received quite the uproar when his name was announced.

When the green flag dropped I was ready to start biting Tommy's nails if he would have let me. I was crushing his hand that I was holding in an attempt not to have a nervous breakdown with the insane battle between him and Alex Reed for sixth halfway through the race.

Jameson had pulled his usual lagging back until half way and then became like a different driver. The caution came out soon after that for Jimi when he tagged the wall after his right rear blew.

Reed slipped coming out of four on lap thirty-one, Jameson passed him on the bottom for fifth. He went high for a few laps and came up on the Cup drivers fighting for fourth and they caught up with the lapped cars. Jameson seized the opportunity and rallied by both Cole and Harris on the high side and was reeling in Justin and Levi, the kid from Australia, with six laps to go.

He passed Levi with little effort and I honestly believed that if anyone was going to stop Jameson that night, it was Justin West.

Justin was strong but so was Jameson. He couldn't pull away and slowly, Jameson began taking his line. One slip by either of them and the third place of Bobby Cole would be ready. They raced each other clean but they also never lifted. They both wanted the win just as bad.

Every time Justin came off three, his car would sputter. After two laps Jameson knew the exact moment his car did that and passed him on the inside. One thing about Jameson was he never passed on the inside, I don't know why, he just didn't. It wasn't his style.

Jimi had pulled his car to the infield and sat on the roll cage watching, by now with one lap to go he was standing on it waving his arms in the air. He was one proud dad.

Grandpa Casten, who appeared out of nowhere, leaned into my shoulder. "He looks like a fucking idiot out there."

I assumed he was referring to Jimi, at least I hoped he did, because Jameson looked far from an idiot. Every move was smooth and controlled.

Justin didn't give up though, stayed right on his outside but when they came out of four, Justin's tire hit the cushion on the outside. And, once again, Jameson was on it and pushed past him enough to get his front tires over the finish line before Justin.

Jameson won the Chili Bowl Midget Nationals by less than a foot.

The crowd was in an uproar around me but I sat there staring at him as he spun his midget around in front of turn three where we were all sitting.

Leaving his helmet on, he pulled himself from the car, stood through the top roll bars and pumped his fists in the air while Jimi ran over to him, as did Justin. They all knew how much a win like this meant to Jameson.

The sports announcers swarmed over to them after that and Jameson was still showing an extreme amount of excitement for his win, as was Spencer and Tommy beside me ... Grandpa Casten ... well, he was too busy watching the Red Bull girls at the other end of the bleachers to care.

"Jimi," the announcer tried to push his microphone in his face but he and Jameson were still hugging. It was sweet to see them so happy together. "Jimi," he tried again. Finally, Jimi turned toward the announcer. "Did you give him advice?"

Jimi laughed.

"If he wants it, I give it," he looked at Jameson tucked under his arm. "There's not much I can tell him he doesn't already know though. He's been around racing since he was born. He knew what he was doing tonight," Jimi looked around and motioned to the track. "Obviously."

"Jameson," the announcer turned the microphone toward him. Jameson wiped sweat from his face before nodding for him to continue. "How close was Justin to winning or did you have it all along?"

"He's was pretty damn close! I didn't think I had it until I saw his struggle coming out of three and saw my opening."

"How does it feel to win your first Chili Bowl?"

"I don't know. Ask me tomorrow when I've calmed down," he laughed. "Right now, I'm just in shock!"

Victory lane was a mad house and I could barely see Jameson once we arrived. There were other drivers, reporters, crewmembers, sponsors, car manufacturers ... there were people everywhere.

Being a little over five feet tall, I couldn't get close enough to see him when Tommy picked me up and carried me toward Jameson.

"I'm following orders," he grunted and hoisted me over his

shoulder.

I wasn't amused.

He set me down in front of Jameson and then before I could move Jameson wrapped his sweaty arms of steel around me and pulled me tight against him chest.

"Can you believe this?" his voice was breathless and incredibly sexy.

"You did great out there," I replied pulling back to look at him, his eyes focused on my lips for a second before looking into my eyes.

"I ..." he sighed letting the words go. I felt like he wanted to say something, I *wanted* to say something but we didn't.

After a moment, he tipped his head in Tate's direction.

"He wants to introduce me to someone."

I wasn't surprised. Tate had big-time sponsors in the Cup series and had been watching Jameson's every move this week.

Without a doubt, Jameson had rocked the Chili Bowl Midget Nationals. He was like a possessed man on the track racing with consummate skill and showing his immense talent and intelligence for racing.

He was making a name for himself and everyone was seeing that. They were seeing him as Jameson Riley.

Catch Can – A small can with a spout that is used to collect the over-spill or run-off from the fuel overflow port when a race car is fueled up during a pit stop.

Coming off my Chili Bowl Midget National win, I was in pretty good spirits. I had won against 250 of the best midget racers in the world. Even better news, I was introduced to one of the leading shock manufacturing sponsors in racing, Simplex Shocks and Springs. They sponsored guys like Tate Harris, Adam Parson, and Langley O'Neil. The list was endless, and now I had a chance at landing them as a sponsor.

If this was a relationship, we were in the friend stage. There was a possibility of more, but it wasn't for sure. I still had to prove myself worthy of a prestigious sponsorship.

Well into my '01 season, I was running like a mule. Half way through the new agreement with Bowman Oil and Bucky, I began to feel the pressure. It was a different track, different city, every day. I'd been on the road for the last seven weeks straight and looking at the schedule in front of me, I was sure I wouldn't see home any time soon. I didn't do anything besides race, in anything I could. I was running another full season of USAC sprints and midgets along with the World of Outlaws in one of my dad's cars.

Usually when I got any free time, I'd sneak up to Bellingham and see Sway but these days that was just a far-fetched dream. I hadn't seen free time in months.

After Indianapolis, I was on my way to Lernerville for an Outlaw race and then it was off to Milwaukee. Judging by my schedule, it was going to be much longer before I saw Sway again.

That night I stopped off at a diner outside of Sarver to grab some dinner before my flight to Milwaukee. Sitting in the back of the restaurant in an open booth, I began looking over the menu, my phone ringing non-stop. The waitress noticed and said, "Your phone is ringing."

"It's always ringing," I mumbled checking the number to make sure it wasn't Sway.

It wasn't, it was Bucky. He was probably calling to ask why I'd missed the flight to Knoxville last week. These days I was traveling alone. Spencer and Alley came to the majority of the races, as did Emma, but with the new contract I had for USAC, everything was funded. All I did was show up, drive and collect my sixty percent.

With the World of Outlaw team with my dad, Spencer helped work on the car, Alley did all my scheduling and public relations that I wasn't allowed to do, and Emma was there to annoy me, at least that was my theory. I'm sure she had an actual title but you couldn't prove that by me.

I checked my message from Bucky, sure enough, he wasn't pleased about the flight.

I was constantly missing the flights he booked for me. If I was being honest with you, I really did think ten minutes was plenty of time to navigate my way through the airport. I failed to realize there would be other people slowing down the process.

"Say," the waitress began leaning against the table. She was attractive and I'd be in denial if I didn't say so but I was trying to get away from the meaningless sexual encounters. For the last three months, I'd managed to stay away from all women. "You're Jimi Riley's son ... Jameson, aren't you?"

I didn't look up but answered. "Yeah, I guess I am."

"Wow, I saw your dad in here a couple months ago." I glanced up at her to see her smiling as if she'd won the lottery. "He's really nice."

I only nodded and handed the menu back to her. "I'll take the bacon and eggs, scrambled," was my response.

She smiled again and went about her job. While texting Sway, I noticed the waitress watching me carefully.

Eventually she made her way back to my table as I was leaving, wearing her street clothes.

"So Jameson, you got plans for the rest of the evening?"

I drew in a deep breath, glancing down at my phone to check the time. "I was just leaving. I have to catch a flight in a few hours."

"Well, you could crash at my place for a little while, it's late and I know you'd probably like to relax."

I had a feeling she did this sort of thing a lot and I could tell by the twinkle in her eyes what type of *relaxing* she had in mind and yet I didn't stop her or myself.

I knew these women I'd been with recently wanted nothing from me and as I was letting myself out of her apartment a few hours later, she summed things up when I overheard her on her cell phone.

"You wouldn't believe who was in my bed!" she said to her friend I assumed.

"No ... Jameson Riley as in the USAC Sprint Car driver ... yeah, the one who won the Triple Crown a couple years ago ... *I know* ... I can't believe it either."

The door slammed behind me.

I managed to catch my plane to Milwaukee on time. Spencer met me at the airport and told me about his time at home. Sway had been there for the weekend visiting Charlie so he and Alley had lunch with her. This put me in a bad mood the remainder of the flight.

The pain of not having Sway here was becoming unbearable. If I knew anything, it was that the pain wouldn't go away unless you healed the wound causing the pain. Start from the source right, but what was the source? I knew the source but refused to look for it, just like the blow engine. I seemed to be mastering avoidance and the ability to patch the hole. Sooner or later, just like the engine, I would run out of patches.

A few days after my twenty-first birthday that year, my dad asked me to meet him in Charlotte, so I did. I showed up at Lowe's International Speedway not exactly sure what I should be expecting.

For a few years now, Jimi had been contemplating starting a race team. Having already owned an Outlaw team for about four years now, he looked into a USAC team like Bucky had but the big teams were in NASCAR these days.

Why?

NASCAR had the ultimate exposure. How many people outside of the Midwest know what USAC is or even the World of Outlaws?

Not many. But nearly every red-blooded American citizen knew what NASCAR was, and sponsors wanted exposure so where do you think they dumped most of their money?

NASCAR.

It was early when I got there, probably around seven in the morning and I wasn't sure if I was tired or hallucinating when I saw a stock car parked beside him on pit lane.

Harry Sampson, a mechanic/engine specialist I'd heard a lot about these days, was leaning against the side of the car.

You have to keep in mind at that point, I had no idea why I was asked to come to Charlotte. Other than the dirt late models I'd driven in the past, I'd never been in a stock car on asphalt and now I was staring at one with Harry Sampson beside it.

"What's all this?" I motioned to the car and then toward Harry, who was still staring at me.

"Well," Jimi took a drink of his coffee. I highly doubted it was straight coffee by the way. "I need to know if you can even drive this thing first," he gestured with a tip of his head at the car.

Believe it or not, five minutes later, I was strapping myself into a stock car.

I would like to say I wasn't nervous, but I was. What if I couldn't drive it?

Sure, I could *drive* it but could I push these cars like I did with sprints. I felt at ease muscling around sprints but stock cars, I wasn't so sure.

"You know how to operate this, right?" Harry asked tugging on my belts.

I didn't answer and gave him a blank expression.

"Great," Harry muttered to himself. "Listen up, then. These beasts are much simpler than those sprint cars you're used to. Aside from the direct drive transmission in sprints these are just like any other car with a manual transmission."

I smiled, firing up the engine and easily shifting into first gear.

"Kidding," I told him, laughing.

You could literally see the anxiety drain from his face. "Jesus, I nearly had a fucking heart attack, kid."

Sprint cars were different in the sense that sprint cars were simple to me. These stock cars had switches, knobs, tacks, roll bars—they had shit everywhere. When you looked inside of a sprint car, all you saw was a bar to engage the coupler, steering box, fuel pump, power steering pump, and inside of the torch tube was the driveline. Then you had the steering wheel and a seat. That's it.

Getting them running is similar. Cup cars, you flick a switch.

Being direct drive, sprint cars have no clutch, transmission or starter. There's a coupler that connects the drive shaft to the rear end but the engine has to be shut off before you can engage it. Once you engage the coupler, the car is pushed with a truck to get it started.

Then to shut the sprint car off, you have to disengage the coupler, turn off the fuel valve and run it out of fuel.

Sprint cars are complicated to some, but there's no other car like them with the unique design and setups. They were half the weight and size of the car I was in, but the same amount of horsepower. It would take some getting used to.

I took it for a spin, made something like twenty-five laps and then brought it back in.

Harry smiled. "Looks like you knew what you were doing."

Dad laughed beside him but didn't say anything.

We left after that and my dad indicated he was thinking of starting a NASCAR Busch team first and then he'd look at the Winston Cup series. We never talked about me being the driver but I had a feeling that's what he was hinting at when he had me testing out that stock car.

I wasn't sure what to make out of all of it, so before heading to Terre Haute that night I called the one person I always called when I needed advice, Sway.

As luck would have it these days, she wasn't home.

That night in Terre Haute was horrible when a lifter broke in my sprint car and, to make matters worse, I left with the first woman who asked.

That wasn't the worst part though, the next night was. Terre Haute was running a double feature and I should have known better than to take a girl back to the hotel with me.

She caught up with me the next night and I had some explaining to do, which is why I preferred to never see these women again. I didn't like explaining myself.

I tried not to on all accounts because really, what would I say?

"I'm an asshole with extreme commitment issues, oh, and by the way, I'm falling for my best friend and refuse to admit it so that's why I was with you last night."

That's not exactly what women want to hear, could be wrong, but I was almost certain that wouldn't go over well.

"Hey, you," she smiled while I loaded my bag to catch my flight to Tri-State Speedway where I was meeting up with Spencer and Tommy. "Where did you go last night?" I gave her a blank stare so she continued. "I thought you would have stayed last night."

"Oh, uh," I mumbled, I looked down at my cell phone that was ringing, *again*. I silently wondered if it ever stopped. "I don't do that sort of thing," I finally said.

"Sleep?"

"No, stay with women," I slipped my phone inside my jeans and adjusted my bag on my shoulder.

"Oh ... I see ... *wow* ... okay." Her eyes focused on mine before darting to her feet, ashamed.

Damn it.

This was one more reason why I preferred never to see these women again. I couldn't stand to see the hurt in their eyes. I knew I was being a jackass. I didn't need to see it to know, so I avoided it as though it wasn't happening.

"Listen, it wasn't you. I just ... well, I'm not in town more than a day and, to be fair ..." I shrugged. "I left."

"I get it," she was quiet for a while before I saw a tear slip down her cheek. "You don't even know my name."

Great. Now I was giving innocent women a complex and making them cry. This was not a list I wanted to be on.

I leaned in and kissed her cheek. "You were wonderful. I ... I can't stay, Lindsey."

"I understand," she choked with a smile that I knew her name and started crying all over again. Because of me.

I hated this. Trying to be an asshole wasn't working out for me.

For a while, pretending as though I didn't care but that I was a cold-hearted prick worked, but I never wanted to hurt anyone.

I don't think I ever felt like a bigger piece of shit as I did right then.

Finally, in August, I was able to see Sway again. We were heading to Knoxville Nationals in Iowa and my excitement was almost unbearable for even me. To tell you how much excitement I showed for this, I was friendly to my sister and offered to buy her lunch on the way to the airport.

And don't think she didn't notice this change in behavior, because she did and questioned me endlessly on why I was nice today as opposed to my usual.

I hadn't seen Sway since right after the Chili Bowl and that was seven months ago. Of course, I'd show excitement.

I made Emma stay in the car while I picked her up. I was in a hurry and had no intention of dealing with airport parking garages. Also, if you hadn't picked this up by now, I didn't like Emma for obvious reasons and had no desire to stroll around an airport with her. I'd buy her lunch but strolling the airport, nope, not a chance.

I found Sway about fifteen minutes later at the baggage claim. She had the paper in her hands with a picture of me covering the front page holding a trophy from Indiana Speed Week.

"I hear he's an asshole," I whispered with my lips next to her ear.

She jerked forward as if this stunned her, spun around and jumped into my arms.

My heart was pounding as was hers. I could feel it thumping against my chest. She smelled like I always remembered, coconut and vanilla. I closed my eyes and buried my face in her hair.

She clung to me, her arms wrapped tightly around my neck, her legs around my waist. It probably looked rather inappropriate but I wasn't at a point that I gave a shit. All I wanted to do was hold her.

"Jesus Christ, I've missed you," she whispered and hugged me tighter.

A chuckle escaped me but I didn't say anything, just held her.

"Could you two move? I need to get to my bag," a male voice asked politely.

Without saying a word, I stepped back against the glass windows facing the parking garages in between the baggage claim and the ticket booths. After another few seconds, Sway came back to reality and let go of me.

I don't know why I did what I did next, probably just to fucking torture myself but I leaned in and kissed her lips, slowly, and then pulled away to run my fingers over where I kissed. "You're just as beautiful as I remembered."

Sway smiled and then let out that giggle I'd missed so much.

"Well, you're just as handsome as I remember." Her eyes raked down my body. "Christ almighty, why hasn't someone snatched you up by now?"

My eyes narrowed, she usually didn't say things like that unless she had been drinking. "Have you been drinking?"

She smirked and clicked her tongue. "I may have convinced a flight attendant that I was twenty-one."

"She believed you?"

"I'm very persuasive."

"I don't doubt that," I laughed pulling her against my side to get back to the car. "Now come on, Emma is waiting for us."

That week with Sway was unreal. It was as though we'd never been apart. I honestly believed that's why I enjoyed being around her so often and missed her so much when she was gone. I never had to explain myself. If I didn't call, she understood. If I was tired and didn't want to do anything, she understood. I was relieved to hear she was taking the summer off from school this year and would be traveling around with us for the next few weeks.

But like anything these days, I never had any time to spend with her. It's not like I needed to entertain her, but I wanted to spend time with her and, surprisingly, not at a racetrack.

I did take her to dinner once, and though this could be considered a date by some, she never questioned it and neither did I. It was us, like we've always been, no questions.

Right before she left to go home for school, we celebrated her twenty-first birthday. I gave her a little something to remember me by, my lips on her ass. I might add, I had a matching pair on mine.

After Sway left, I once again looked at filling the void I refused to admit was there. And where do you think I turned?

The more I won, the more the pit lizards slithered their way toward my pit after the races. It didn't matter if I raced Outlaws or USAC, they were always there. Not that I didn't already know this, but they only wanted one thing, the thrill of sleeping with the driver.

I meant nothing to them but if I was being honest with you, they didn't mean anything to me either and never would. I never knew their names and once I was finished, they left. I never held them, barely kissed them and usually never attempted to get them off. If they did when I did, well then more power to them, but I never focused on it. I was an asshole through and through. I was appalled at myself during that time in my life. My mother certainly didn't raise me to treat women that way, but that's exactly how I was treating them. Something had to give.

Alley and Emma were not happy. Every time I left with a girl, I got a lecture the next day about God knows what. I never listened.

Near the end of the 2001 season, I started to look at where I *wanted* to be. Not just with Sway but with racing. I felt a strong sense of attachment to dirt track racing and always would. My heart may have been leaning toward sprint cars but my head led to NASCAR.

On the East Coast, the Carolina area in particular, believed that all the best raced in NASCAR but I raced enough in various divisions to know that there are great drivers in all forms of racing. Just look at Jimi or those grassroots drivers banging it out at the weekly races in Grays Harbor.

I don't think all the best are in NASCAR. But it did catch my attention. I wanted to be the best and most thought the best were there. For me, it wasn't about that. It was more of about the uncharted territory.

When I began weighing my options after my conversations with my dad, Bucky and Tate, I looked at all aspects of the sport.

NASCAR drivers made the most money but I wasn't in it for money. In my eyes, if you choose to race for money, you were doing it for the wrong reason in the first place.

So I looked at what made me happy. Sure, I could continue racing sprint cars and probably end up competing against my dad for the title but there was something drawing me toward stock cars.

I could make my own name for myself.

When you're touted as the next legendary sprint car driver to someone whose mystique alone was intimidating, you tend to get lost and wonder who you are.

This had me thinking those stock cars could be pretty cool.

At the end of the 2001 season, I once again made it to the Turkey Night, broke a driveline and ended up not finishing the race, which sucked. Sway was taking winter courses that year so I decided to head to Australia for a month and check out their season with my dad.

That's when he hit me with his plans one night at dinner with my uncle Randy.

My uncle Randy was only remotely approachable when he was drinking, but otherwise he's a cold-hearted prick who's been divorced eight times. You'd think he'd get the point by now that he wasn't meant to be married but no, still doesn't understand. If this gives you any idea about why his marriages fail, it might have to do with the fact that his newest girlfriend is only a month older than me ... I hear she's mature for her age.

Like any other senseless jackass, he drives around in a Jaguar. That has asshole written all over it if you ask me.

His son, my cousin I guess you'd classify him, Rex, was a dirty fucking liar and I couldn't stand the son of a bitch. The few times I'd been in the same room with him usually resulted in a fistfight. If you think that's bad, you should see when he mingles with Spencer.

So there we were having dinner in Sydney one evening when in walks my uncle, his new girlfriend, and his asshole son.

I groaned when I saw them approaching the table, to which my dad slammed his foot into my shin rather hard.

"Why is he here?"

"Don't be a jerk ... it's business."

They approached the table, Rex and I glared at each other. I gave him nine stitches above his left eyebrow the last time we saw each other, judging by his glare, he hadn't forgotten that.

I stood and shook hands with my uncle, thought I'd be polite since I hadn't seen him in a few years. His girlfriend smiled at me. I offered a small smile but she had whore written all over her so I steered clear. My thoughts of her being a whore were confirmed when she leaned in to hug me and slipped her number in my jeans.

Conversations soon got underway and I ordered beer after beer to keep from punching my cousin when he said, "How's that girl ... what's her name?" he drummed his index finger against his forehead for a second before winking. "Sway ... how's Sway these days?"

This was the exact reason he received nine stitches above his goddamn eye in the first place. He knew how to set me off. My jaw clenched as my grip on my beer did as well. "She's fine."

Rex thought for sure Sway had a thing for him but I knew better. Sway couldn't stand him.

"Jameson," Randy interrupted our glaring. "So, Jimi and I were thinking of starting a race team, as you know. A NASCAR Busch team to be exact and then we'll look at the cup side." He shifted in his seat to lean forward, looking directly at me. "Would you drive the car?"

I didn't say anything at first, just stared back at him before darting my eyes to my dad, who smiled. I didn't particularly want to go into business with my uncle Randy, given his cold-hearted prick tendencies, but I also knew dad couldn't do this on his own and fund an Outlaw team at the same time.

Currently, I was driving his car on the Outlaw series with him driving for his team ... he had a lot on his plate and now being a team owner of a Busch team, he'd need help.

"That depends," I smiled wickedly at Rex and then my uncle. "When would we move to cup?"

I had no problem racing the Busch series but I also knew for myself, I wouldn't be happy unless I was behind the wheel of a Cup car. Looking at a Winston Cup car and a Busch car side-by-side, you probably wouldn't be able to tell the difference between the two but there were differences.

For one, the wheelbase is shorter by five inches on a Busch car. This changes things like down force, aerodynamics, handling, gearing, and even driving style. They also run a smaller carburetor and weren't as fast.

Now knowing me, what do you think I would want to drive?

"Probably the following season," Dad said.

This would mean being under the reins of my dad and my uncle but this also meant a chance at my own name. No matter how hard I tried, open wheel guys knew me as Jimi Riley's son.

NASCAR, they knew me all right, but they knew me as Jameson Riley.

"Yeah," I finally said. "Who's sponsoring us?"

I knew dad had been in contact with Simplex, as was I, but I wasn't sure exactly what they had planned.

"Simplex offered full sponsorship for next season."

I think there comes a point in your life when you realize that everything is falling into place, that dream you've dreamed about, you know the dream you thought was so far-fetched, isn't anymore, it's looking at you in the face.

What did I say in that moment?

Stupidity.

"Are you sure you want me driving the car?"

Rex laughed. "That's what I said."

"Shut up, asshole!" I snapped glaring at him. "You're still racing super stocks."

"At least I race on asphalt. You can't race on anything but dirt."

"Really? Half the fucking USAC races are on asphalt smartass," I chuckled sarcastically. "But you wouldn't know that because you've never raced anywhere but Havasu."

"Boys!" Dad barked. "Jameson, we want you in the car because you have the most diversity. You're the only driver I know who can jump into any open seat and be competitive. That's not something you learn. And to be competitive in NASCAR, we need that. We need a driver who can just get in and drive, so that's you."

I always knew my dad had confidence in me but I'd never heard him say something like that before. I haven't met a parent who didn't believe in their kids and tell them, but with Jimi, he didn't just say things to make you feel better. When he spoke, he spoke the truth and meant every word of it.

Later that night, after a confrontation with Rex in the parking lot, I was back in my hotel wishing I could call Sway. With the time difference in the states, it was near four in the morning and I doubted she'd be real happy if I woke her up so I simply sent her a text telling her I missed her. I know, pretty pathetic, but I did. I hadn't seen her in three months now and, well, I did miss her.

No matter how much time you spend avoiding something, eventually it will rear its ugly face and force you to make a decision.

I still hadn't.

I knew something had changed in regards to my feelings for her. There was no denying it any more. No one made me feel the way she did. I think I started to understand the difference when she was no longer around every day.

For so long it was just there, taunting me. It's like trying to find the remote to the television. You know it's there, you're searching everywhere for it, overturning everything to find that goddamn remote you know is there somewhere but can't quite find. Then you find it in the same spot you looked for it ten minutes ago, but didn't see the first time. You see it because you got to the point you were so frustrated that you gave up. You throw yourself down on the couch, refusing to get up to turn on the television without the remote to find that you're now sitting on it. It was there all along but because you were looking so hard for it, you looked right over it. You found it because you were no longer looking.

Just like the remote, I stopped looking at what she meant to me and ignored it all together. Then, when I least expected it, I felt it. I couldn't tell you if I loved her because I don't think I knew the meaning of love. I've seen it in my parents and my brother, but did I feel for Sway that way?

So while I found the remote, the batteries were still missing.

Turn In – As a car reaches a corner, this is the moment in which a driver begins to turn the wheel.

"What is this?" I asked examining the documents set in front of me.

I was sitting in a large conference room in downtown Charlotte with my dad, my uncle Randy, and Alley going over the sponsorship for our new team, Riley Simplex Racing.

"It's your prohibited activities," Melissa Childers, Simplex's representative stated.

I was silent.

They can't be serious … no sprint cars? I must be reading this wrong.

Melissa continued. "You can't do things like skiing, motorcycles, or … any other form of racing outside of the car we sponsor."

"I can't drive sprint cars?"

Marcus Harding, the President of Simplex Springs and Shocks, and Melissa, exchanged a glance. I think they knew I was moments away from walking out.

"It's the only way for us to protect you and us," Melissa added. I understood but I wasn't about to agree to something like that. Sprint cars are where I came from.

I went to stand when my dad glared and cleared his throat.

"Can we have a few days to think about it? Racing sprint cars is not something I'm *willing* to give up," I gritted, moving my leg away from him. I had a feeling his was about to kick me any minute.

Marcus seemed to contemplate what I just said but before I made it to the door, he spoke again. "I think we can work with you on that one." I turned around to look at him. "You have to understand where we are coming from Jameson," he paused, his eyes focusing on me. "We are offering up a large amount of money here for you to race. If, by chance, you are injured, well, we don't get the exposure we are paying for. We expect you to take that into consideration."

I went to speak but was silenced by my uncle Randy. "I think Jameson would just like the opportunity to still race sprint cars on occasion and, I assure you," he shot me a warning glance, "he *will* be careful."

"Careful?" I thought to myself. Was I careful in a sprint car?

Not really.

In some ways, I signed my life away that morning as a puppet for Simplex and my dad. It felt different from the times with Bowman Oil and Bucky. For one, this was bigger, millions of dollars to be exact, and they weren't just paying for me to run a limited USAC schedule. I'd be running a full season in the Busch Grand National series next year. It was different. I still felt like a puppet but I'd like to think I grew up a little in the last four years and realized that this dream of mine wasn't possible without playing by their rules to an extent.

I had only been back from Australia for about three weeks. It was mid-January and I had missed the Chili Bowl. I wasn't thrilled by that but I had more important things to deal with now, like the testing of our Busch Grand National car.

I walked inside my dad's race shop in Mooresville. It was freezing that morning, I felt like my eyes were even frozen. An involuntary shiver ran through me when I stepped out of my truck and walked toward the shop. My eyes focused on the sign above the door that said: ***Staff Only***.

Chuckling to myself that I was an employee of my dad's now, I opened the door to the shop.

I'd been in this shop countless times but there were new additions. Amongst the sprint cars, chassis were lined up in rows, engines lined up in front of them. Racks of metal tubing hung on the walls beside axles, front clips, shocks, springs ... basically, anything to build a car from the ground up.

Harry met me at the door with Tony Eldon, the tire specialist who I met last night.

Tony smiled, "You've met Harry, right?"

"Yeah," I reached out and shook Harry's hand again. "We met a while back and then again this morning at the meeting." Dad had put together a breakfast this morning to get the team together. Right now, we were all just pieced together and in the development stages, but slowly the Riley Racing team was being formed.

"Great, you guys will be working together today. We need to get everything setup for these engines and what feels right for you," Tony smiled at Harry, patting his back. "Harry here can't drive in a straight line to save his life but he could build an engine in the dark with a screw driver and a pair of pliers."

I chuckled and leaned back against the wall. "So, we're testing tomorrow at Homestead?"

"That's the plan," Harry told me with his own smile.

Harry Sampson was the one to show me my way around a stock car, besides Tate. Tate Harris had become a vital part of all this, he got Simplex for us and, well, he was there when I had questions.

Harry was similar to Hitler but he had his own form of punishment for me. He'd send me to the hauler when he felt I was out of line. This had me spending most of my time inside that damn hauler.

I came from open wheel racing so I knew jack shit about how to handle the cars and Harry, well he had these strict rules that he felt I needed to abide by in order to learn them. Like listening to him.

Not being one to follow the rules all that often, I tested him. Often.

It took me a while to get the hang of the cars so Harry had me running laps during the week to get seat time. The only problem was, he wanted me to run lap times that were the exact same each lap. I wasn't real sure why but Harry scared the shit out of me so I never asked why.

At Daytona, my curiosity got the best of me and I tested out the speed despite what Harry wanted me to do.

After I got my adrenaline rush, Harry signaled to come in.

And when I say signaled, he held up a sign written in black Sharpie on a piece of cardboard that said: "What the fuck was that?"

That's when I knew I was in trouble.

I pulled onto pit lane to have him standing there looking down at me with his trusty red stopwatch in his hand.

He leaned into the cockpit, motioning toward the time on the stopwatch with a particular sour edge to his flip. "What was that, boy?"

"I ... just wanted to test it out," I cringed internally thinking he was going to castrate me for doing this.

His eyes narrowed, looking over the car and then me again. "That's not what I told you to do. Go sit in the hauler."

I spent the remainder of the test session in that hauler.

Harry may have been a cranky old bastard, but he was the perfect bastard for me to learn from. He came from dirt track racing so we understood each other. We spoke the same language.

Once Kyle Wade, my crew chief, came on board, it was easier and the team dynamics were built from there. I liked Kyle and respected him. He was honest and you never wondered where you stood with him. If he didn't like you, you knew it. Kind of like me.

Kyle also let me out of the reins a little more than Harry. We ran testing at Texas, Loudon, and Phoenix wide open. They let me get as comfortable with the car as I wanted. I bet he never said anything to Harry. If he knew, I'd still be in the hauler right now.

As the new team formed that winter, my spotter, Aiden Gomez, came on board. I liked Aiden from the moment I met him and the more we worked together, the more I realized he was just as insane as the rest of us, which worked out well for everyone.

We traveled around pretty much all of January testing and then it was off to Daytona for my first race.

I wanted Sway there badly but she was wrapped up in her classes with finals nearing and I was far too busy to sneak off to Bellingham to see her. I even went so far as having her text me a picture of her. It depressed me even more.

So, there I was testing stock cars, making sponsor appearances, press releases, commercials, meet and greets, oh, and occasionally I had time to sleep, but not much.

My dad was just as busy and for being the owner of this new team, you'd think we would get to see each other, but nope, the only people I saw on a regular basis these days were Kyle and Alley. Sounds ironic, but these days, a NASCAR driver needed a publicist. She also acted as our team manager and told us where we needed to be and when. Having to boss around Spencer and Lane, she had the right amount of training for the job.

Come February, I was at my first Busch Grand National race in Daytona.

The first fifty laps were good, not much activity but I was cruising around toward the rear of the field getting a feel for everything.

Aiden came on the radio a few laps later, "Cautions out, car slowing down low in turn four."

"How's it feel, bud?" Kyle asked.

"Um ... I can't ... turn in as well into two and three but I can go high when I want in three and four."

"All right so we can make air pressure adjustments and take a round out of the right rear. That could help."

I nodded. Then I realized that he couldn't see me and I needed to vocalize this, "Copy?" this was meant to be a statement but came out more of a question.

The only series I ran in prior to this that permitted the use of radios was the Silver Crown series but we only talked about cautions, not about setups or how my car was handling. NASCAR seemed to have its own language and I evidently did not know it.

For instance, loose in a sprint car was where you were comfortable. Loose in a stock car was not an experience you enjoy, particularly when you're going two hundred miles an hour next to a concrete wall.

So we agreed on what was going to take place during the caution, it was time for the pit stop.

Yeah, right. "You want me to do what?" That was my first reaction.

Until now, I'd never had to make a real pit stop. Sure, I'd limped my car back to the pits with damaged midgets and sprints but to pull smoothly down pit road and squeeze into a pit stall surrounded by other cars was nerve racking. Not to mention, this shit was time sensitive!

"So, I'm supposed to fit in there with forty-two other cars speeding past me?" I asked. I'll admit my voice was slightly alarmed.

"That's the idea," Kyle chuckled. He was eating this shit up.

I ended up spinning myself leaving pit road and the race didn't go any better when I inadvertently caused a fifteen-car pileup.

I tried to make light of my mishaps by rattling off responses like, "Did you see that guy? He came out of nowhere."

Kyle laughed. "Yeah, that black number nine is out of control."

It was all in good fun and learning, but I had to admit I was frustrated that I was struggling.

After my first disastrous race where I ended up spinning myself on pit road, we did practice runs at the shop where I'd roll in, the crew did their jobs, and I'd roll out. Sooner or later, *much later*, we had it down, or I should say I had it down because clearly I was the one with the issues.

Now I just had to figure out how to do this with actual cars instead of orange cones.

When I raced sprints and midgets, I didn't have to worry about much other than finding my line. I adjusted everything with either throttle control or the wing. Now I had a pit crew to do this. Only problem was I needed to explain what I needed them to do and nodding and shaking my head at them wasn't working well.

In sprint cars, if you told me the car was pushing, you're driving it in too hard. In stock cars, that's entirely different. It can mean a number of different things from tire pressure, wedge, camber ... the list goes on-and-on.

I got schooled my first few races on how little I actually knew about stock cars. It was embarrassing.

But like any division I raced in, it was all about experience: logging laps. So that's what I did. My experience was critical in all this. Every point counted, every turn, every pit stop. The difference between winning and losing is so small and it was easy to take for granted.

Carbon Fiber – Carbon fiber is lighter than aluminum, stronger than steel and expensive material. It's used to construct chassis or modern open-wheeled cars.

Come April, I had won my second career Busch Grand National win at Chicagoland Speedway. So far, I'd won two races. My family wasn't at any of them besides Spencer who was working on my pit crew as the jack man.

It felt different from winning in sprint cars or even the USAC divisions. I wasn't sure what the change was but it just felt different. It might have something to do with the fact that this was different. Sway wasn't around and, well, this was bigger. Even though I wasn't racing in the Cup series yet, this was a NASCAR division and had all the same impediments.

I was still in bed around ten that morning, contemplating whether or not I would roll over and go back to sleep. My phone vibrating assured me that that wasn't going to happen but I was pleasantly surprised to see Tommy's name appear on the screen.

We made small talk a little while before he finally asked, "How have you been?"

I knew he was asking more on a personal level. I never flaunted the fact that I slept around and kept it as discreet as I could but still,

Tommy knew and he knew why I did it without even telling him.

"Can't complain," I paused and I think he knew right then what I wanted to ask. Tommy had been giving me updates on Sway for a while now. I had to know she was okay and she would only tell me so much.

"She's fine, Jameson." I could sense he wanted to say something but he didn't. So I did.

"Has she ..." I could feel the unnerving tension burning in my gut. I hated to even think about it, let alone imagine it. I had no right to even know, or have a say in where she went or who she chose to hang out with but I still felt the pain.

"Abby and I took her to Skagit the other night. They had the I-5 Dirt Late Models there."

"And how did that go?"

"Good, she got drunk with Abby and, well ... you know," He didn't want to say it any more than I wanted to hear it. Tommy knew me well.

"So she ..." I had to sit down. "Did she go home with someone?"

"Jameson," he paused again and then let out a whoosh of air. "Are you sure you want to torture yourself like this? I know you feel something for her or you wouldn't be asking."

"I don't know what I feel ..." I paused. "Did she though? Did she go home with someone?"

"Not that I should tell you ... but, yes." He finally said, and the pain, once again, shook me to my core. My hands were shaking, my stomach was in knots and my breathing was ragged. I was a mess.

Fucking embarrassing one girl, the only girl, could make me feel like this.

"Why don't you tell her?"

"I can't, Tommy," I sighed deeply. "I can't."

Tommy knew me well enough to know that if he pushed, he'd regret it, so we went on to talk about his plans after graduation. While Sway had another year, Tommy was graduating in a few weeks.

"So what are your plans?"

"Well, I was thinking I'd see if Jimi needs any help … or you."

"Oh, yeah? I was thinking of starting my own sprint car team and, well, I'd like you as the mechanic."

"Really?" I don't know why, but he honestly sounded shocked by this. Tommy was an excellent mechanic and knew sprint car setups better than most in the business.

"I want the best."

"You barely have time to sleep," he laughed, pointing out the obvious. "How are you going to run a sprint car team as well?"

"I have no clue but I can't stop what made me all together, you know? I can't walk away from it." I wasn't sure if I was making any sense but he seemed to understand.

"No, I get it." And he did.

Tommy, Sway, my family … they understood why I did this. They understood why I risked everything, including my sanity, to follow this dream. I honestly believed they understood this better than I did at times. I didn't have time to run a sprint car team but every time I was back at the local dirt tracks, I missed it. It was as if running the sprint car team could keep me in check with reality.

Later that morning, after looking over my schedule for the next week, I sat down on the bed in my hotel room to call Sway. It was the middle of June and I saw an opening this week for three days before I had to be in Vegas for the Busch race and then it was off to Rockingham.

She answered on the second ring. "Well, hey there, superstar!"

"How's my girl doing?"

My girl? You fucking idiot.

I didn't give her time to catch on before I asked another question. "How's school?"

"Boring … it's not the same as being at the races," Sway said. "I made it out to Skagit the other night with Tommy."

"Really … anyone good out there?" I knew she went, I heard from Tommy but I didn't feel the need to tell her I knew she had been with someone.

"No one like you," she assured me.

Silently, I was hoping that had a much deeper meaning than implied, and by the tone of her voice, it wasn't a total off the wall assessment.

I was silent for a moment before sighing. "I really want to see you, honey."

I admit, I wasn't exactly saying the right lines in this conversation but really, could I have sounded any more pathetic? And, to think, we'd only been on the phone less than five minutes ... it was still early. Who knows what other insanity I can knock off with before the end of it.

Suddenly, she was about as silent as I had just been. "Are you there?"

"Yeah," she said, softly. "I want to see you, too."

Why was this so fucking hard? Why couldn't I tell her how I felt or the confusion I was feeling?

Oh, yeah, because you're the master of avoidance and if by some slim far off chance she felt the same way, it would scare the shit out of you.

I cleared my throat before talking. "Can I come see you in Bellingham before I head to Vegas?"

"Oh, my God, really?" her voice filled with enthusiasm and had me laughing.

"Jesus, you act as though I just offered up a million dollars."

"Well," her voice lowered to an incredibly sexy tone. "At this point, I'd pay a million dollars to see you."

"I think that goes for both of us," I laughed and leaned back on the bed. I was suddenly aware of the prominent erection straining against my jeans at the tone of her voice. "So, I will book a flight here in a few minutes. Can you pick me up in Seattle tonight?"

"Tonight!" she screeched.

"Well, yeah, I said I only had a few days."

"I thought you meant like in a couple weeks."

"If you don't want me to—"

"No!" she cut me off. "I mean, yes, I want you to come."

I groaned and she sighed dramatically.

"Jesus Christ, you fucking pervert! I want you to come see me, not *come*."

"Sorry," I muttered with a chuckle. "So I will text you with the time my flight gets in there."

"Sounds good, see you tonight," she said before hanging up. I hurried and bought my ticket, told Alley where I was going and then headed for the airport, after some bleeding of the valves. That was essential if I was going to be around Sway for a few days.

Once I got to Bellingham, we found ourselves back to our usual ways.

"Is this where we've reached the point of no return?" Sway asked outside the apartment complex we stood in front of dressed in our usual, all black, breaking and entering gear.

"I'm pretty sure we passed that when we got out of the car."

"Good point," she acknowledged with a nod and then pulled her hood over her head. I kissed the top of her head.

"Remember what that asshole did."

Sway began nodding her head as the she was preparing for battle, tossing her head from side to side and bouncing on the balls of her feet while shaking her arms at her sides. I chuckled watching her display and then she clapped her hands together. "Let's do this!"

"Listen," I put my hands on her shoulders and grinned. "Control yourself. We can't afford to get caught doing this."

She nodded but her enthusiasm soon vanished when we approached the door to his apartment.

Tommy came running up behind us holding a paint ball gun as though it was a rifle.

"Where did that come from?" Sway asked with excited eyes. She had a thing for paint ball guns.

"Oh, please. I used to live in Elma. Of course, I would have a paint ball gun," he remarked.

"You don't have to be so rude!" Sway punched his shoulder.

Tommy pushed her back. My hand jetted out to stop him. "Push her again and you'll regret it," I warned him.

"That's right," Sway taunted behind me.

It took me a while but I got them focused enough to complete the task at hand. "Are you sure it was this apartment."

Sway shot me an alarmed expression. "Well, fuck ... now I'm not sure ... it was dark."

"Fuck it," I took a deep breath, braced my hands on the doorframe and kicked as hard as I could. Much to my surprise, the door came crashing down.

Sway, Tommy and I stood there looking at each other, amazed I was able to kick it down, when Sway giggled and then stopped abruptly and gazed at me with a completely blank expression before saying. "I don't think it's his apartment."

Twelve doors later, we still hadn't found his apartment and I was positive this was not a good thing. My legs were sore, Sway was sweating profusely and Tommy had shot up everything with that damn paint ball gun. We had to get out of there before the police came because surely someone had to have noticed the breaking of doors by now. Also, I don't know if I need to point this out, but some of the doors we broke down, people were home.

Sway and I hid behind a group of trees when we heard police cars and what was Tommy doing?

He was loading his damn paint ball gun—in plain view.

I decided by myself that since I broke down the doors, it was up to Sway to get him. I leaned back in the grass panting. I did break down twelve apartment doors. I was exhausted. "Go get him."

"Do I have to?"

"Yes," I kept my expression grave and not friendly. "At some point everyone must take one for the team. Guess whose turn it is?"

"Mine?"

"Yes, now go," I swatted her ass when she stood brushing the grass from her jeans.

This had bad idea written all over it but so did this entire mission. My paranoid thoughts were confirmed moments later when the police swerved into the parking lot, shining their lights on Sway and Tommy, holding a paint ball gun, dressed in all black.

It couldn't have looked much worse than that.

There has been a few times in my life when I thought, "Well, that should have gone differently." Now wasn't any different. We should have thought this through a little more.

Sway wasn't impressed and had me cornered as they questioned Tommy about the paint ball gun, at this point, they didn't know it was us who broke down all those doors. "Listen, you got me into this mess," she not-so-calmly replied shoving my chest. "Get me out of it!"

This was going to take some persuasion on my part, highly analytical persuasion skills. Just as I was about to explain to the cops that we were only searching for the guy who keyed the red dragon, a crazed tenant, who we broke down their door, showed up pointing fingers.

"They broke down my door for no reason!" she yelled in the officer's face.

"You have no proof of that," was my genius response. I did, in fact, have cuts all over my hands and splintered chunks of wood covering my jeans. Couldn't have been more obvious.

There all three of us were in the cop car with Sway on my lap because she refused to sit next to Tommy. She blamed him for this, which was fine by me because it was my fault, my idea at least.

Being inside the cop car was another story. Sway wouldn't stop moving around on my lap. It didn't take long before she noticed the reaction it was causing.

"Are you ... is that your ...?" She had the most adorable blush spreading across her cheeks.

"In my defense ... you're wiggling around in my lap."

Sway giggled. "Should I ... I mean," she cleared her throat. "I should get off."

I grinned. "You're welcome to," I implied lasciviously winking at her, "but if you stay, I might."

Apparently that was the funniest thing she'd ever heard because she started laughing hysterically to the point where I have to hold her up. Tommy grumbled next to us. He was more upset that the cop now how his paint ball gun.

Once they had our IDs and ran background checks, I'm sure they saw Sway and I already had B&Es on our records and also theft but they were distracted by me. Like I said, before racing in a NASCAR series, I was becoming someone people recognized by the name.

So here the officer came, smiling. "You're Jameson Riley, like the driver of the number nine car?"

"Yeah," I moved Sway off my lap. She giggled again when I had to adjust myself. "Are we free to go?"

His smile grew when his partner approached the car. I was all about getting out of this mess without jail time. I didn't think my dad or Simplex would appreciate me being arrested when I was supposed to be in Vegas tomorrow.

This went on for a few minutes, the officers asking me questions completely unrelated to the crimes we committed. I was fine with that as long as we weren't arrested but I also began to think we'd be here most of the night by the way they were talking.

How all this was relevant to our situation was not lost by me.

They were both a bunch of weirdos but I had a real problem with the short-haired blonde officer who kept eyeing Sway.

"Are we free to go?" I finally asked leaning against the side of the car.

"Yes, but it appears you may need to pay for those doors you broke." The blonde officer said to me.

"I'll pay for 'em." I said. "It was a misunderstanding."

"I'm sure," he remarked with a sour edge.

I'm sure he was thinking I was trying to use the fact that his partner was star stuck by me but that was beside the point. I had to be in Vegas tomorrow, I couldn't be arrested right now. I should have thought of this earlier in the day when we planned this escapade but I was too caught up in paying back this asshole who keyed Sway's truck almost daily. I didn't think of the consequences, which was usual for me and Sway, she did everything on a whim and looked at the consequences later. Tommy, well in his defense, he had orange hair, we shouldn't expect much decision making from him, in general.

In the end, I handed my credit card over to the apartment maintenance manager. Tommy's paint ball gun was confiscated and Sway found the dude who keyed her truck, keying her truck again.

Let's say he won't be keying any more cars in the near future.

"That was awesome," Sway said once we were back in the truck. Only having two seats, she made Tommy sit in the bed. By the time we reached our destination in downtown Bellevue, a nightclub by the name of Vertigo, Tommy's hair looked much like the time we got caught in the tornado.

Abby, Tommy's girlfriend met us there and thought his new orange hairdo was pretty awesome. I liked Abby, she was good for Tommy and, let's face it, he and his orange hair needed someone special.

We spent the remainder of the night dancing and drinking. Sway and I got a little frisky and I was having a hard time keeping my hands to myself. I pretty much lost most control I was wavering with when she downed her last beer and dragged me out on the dance floor. Let's just say our hands were places they probably shouldn't have been and we spent a good part of the night making out in her truck.

And then I puked for three hours in the parking lot.

I hated being hung over. Most of all, I hated being dehydrated when I had a race the next day.

Racing sprint cars, it wasn't as bad because your feature event wasn't longer than fifty laps. I think your body worked harder to control the car in a sprint car but stock cars were just as physically demanding but, also, mentally demanding because you had to constantly think strategy. Now instead of making fifty laps I was making three hundred.

Leaving Sway in Bellingham was hard. We had so much fun together it was difficult to leave. I was so close to giving in at the bar that last night, I honestly think if I wouldn't have gotten so drunk, I might have acted on what I was feeling that night but, no, I got scared and downed as much alcohol as I could and left myself a mess.

"I thought for sure that you two were gonna ..." Tommy said as we headed for baggage claim.

"Yeah ..." I hung my head. "I almost did. I wanted to."

"So why—" he started and I groaned.

"Stop talking, Tommy."

Tommy came to Las Vegas with me and then he was off to Mooresville to see my dad about the sprint car team. I told him he could either work on the Busch team or sprint cars and he chose sprint cars. I couldn't blame him. That's essentially where I wanted to be, too. Don't get me wrong, I enjoyed racing these stock cars but you have to understand that's where I came from, it was in my blood.

We landed in Vegas, Aiden met us there and we drove to Las Vegas Motor Speedway where I was met with yet another girl I despised these days, a reporter for FOX Sports, Ashley Conner. She reminded me of Chelsea but with black hair. As you can probably guess, I slept with her one night after my first Busch series win in Nashville back in February. I'd avoided her ever since because, really, I did this all the time.

She caught me when I entered the paddock looking for Spencer and Kyle.

"Why haven't you called?" she asked keeping step with me.

I didn't look her direction just stared straight ahead. "I didn't know I was supposed to."

"Well, we slept together," she said this like it meant something. "I thought you'd at least call."

"I don't know what you expected this to be?" I motioned between us. I'd seen her around the track; she slept with most of the drivers so I couldn't understand what would make me any different.

"Not this ... you led me on and now this ..." she threw her arms up.

I hung my head walking. It was the same shit all the time and you'd think I'd learn by now. "What do you want Ashley? What do you want from *me*?"

"You."

"No," I shook my head. "You don't really."

"Yes, I do."

I stopped walking and turned toward her.

"No, you don't." I tried to convey the warning I was giving her but I could see she wasn't buying it.

"You have a girlfriend?"

"I don't do girlfriends."

"So, what is it then?"

"It's nothing."

She sighed dramatically and shifted her weight to one foot. Her black hair blew across her face until she tucked it behind her ear. I looked into her blue eyes, watching as she finally grasped what I was saying.

"Don't act like it meant anything to you either," I chuckled despite my annoyance with the situation. Spencer appeared at the corner of the hauler watching us from about twenty feet away. "The next weekend in California I saw you all over Mason."

I may not have cared about these girls but I was well aware of the fact that they were usually with another driver by the following weekend. They were not about to make me feel like shit when they were using me for the exact same reasons.

I started to walk away when she gave me that blank expression. When I approached the hauler Spencer laughed and tossed a bottle of water at me, his head tilted toward Ashley who was still standing where I left her.

"Making the rounds?"

"Fuck you," was my only response as I tossed my bag on the

ground.

You would think by now I would have learned to stay away from these women but you also have to understand that the need was there and so were they. It was wrong but it went hand in hand. Everywhere I went, women hounded me and, sooner or later, I crumbled and gave in. Now I had to pay the consequences. Ever since I won my first race in Nashville, it was worse than ever.

Before practice started, I was waiting for Kyle and the car chief, Mason Bryant, to finish up the notes from last week's testing here. They entered the data and then calculated a setup that would work for practice. We usually liked to practice in race trim, change a few small adjustments for qualifying and then revert to race trim for happy hour. After the cars were inspected prior to the race no more changes could be made so you had to be pleased by that point.

While I waited beside the car, my phone buzzed.

Are you still alive?

I laughed. ***Yes.***

Good.

Good?

Yes. Just good.

Hmmm. Good.

Good luck?

Yes. Good luck is needed. My head still hurts.

Yeah well so do my legs.

How so? I kicked down the doors. Not you.

Dancing.

Mmmm. Forgot about the dancing.

I'm hurt.

I didn't forget about the body shots.

Good?

Kyle nudged me when he walked past. "Practice time, lover boy. Put that shit away."

Gotta go.

Bye.

It took me a few laps to get focused but I did. The car was setup the way I liked it so we didn't make that many laps. I didn't get a chance to talk to Sway again that night with all of the meet and greets Simplex had me doing and then, before I knew it, Saturday was here and it was time for the race.

So far, I'd won two races in the Busch series and was well on the way to my third when another driver, Dave Lutz, got into the side of me and took us both out. Ordinarily I would have been upset with this but I had such a pounding headache and he didn't mean to wreck me. Dave was a nice guy and would never intentionally wreck someone just to advance in position.

Marcus caught up with me after the race and suggested that my team and I head over to Caesars Palace after the team meeting where Simplex was throwing an after party.

Having nothing else to do that night, we decided to make an appearance. Much to our surprise, they didn't serve beer, only wine and champagne. That was not impressive to me or Aiden and Spencer. This was even worse news for Simplex because, as it turns out, wine doesn't agree with Aiden.

Three bottles later, yes, three bottles of red wine later, we were all three annihilated. I was in no condition to be drinking anymore that night but when you're twenty-one and have a brother like Spencer, he convinces you that drinking is a good idea.

Aiden could barely speak, let alone stand, in one spot without swaying.

Spencer, once again, smelled blood and thought now was a good time to embarrass the poor country boy.

"I bet you can't chug that entire bottle of wine," he prodded Aiden.

Too late, before Spencer even got the words out Aiden had half the bottle gone.

If you've never chugged a bottle of wine, I don't suggest it, it's not enjoyable.

Poor Aiden.

By the end of the night, Aiden somehow lost his shirt, shoes and socks and walked back to the hotel half-naked.

I wasn't any better when I thought I could table dive and ended up with three stitches above my left eye when a glass bowl broke against my head in the process.

Two pain pills later, a night with the nurse who stitched me up, I was curled up on the floor of my hotel room puking my guts out ... for the second time in a week, and swore I would never ever drink again.

The nurse, who I have no idea what her name was, came to check on me before she slipped out of my hotel room.

"Who's Sway?" she asked examining my face while she threw her lipstick in her bag.

"Huh?" I asked not even bothering to lift my head again, I knew it would hurt too badly.

"Umm ... Sway. Is she your girlfriend or something?"

"Did she call?" I couldn't understand why she'd be asking about Sway. I never mentioned her to anyone but family.

"No ... it's just that when we were in bed last night you ..." she looked down at her bare feet shifting her weight from one foot to the other. "When you ... well last night, you called me Sway. More than once,"

Well, shit.

"Shouldn't you be getting to work?" I asked.

I knew I was being rude but it was none of her business who Sway was and I didn't feel like I needed to explain my situation to a complete stranger.

"Yeah ... I should," she agreed. "See you around, Jameson."

I didn't say another word to her, partly because I was in no shape to. It hurt to even blink, let alone speak.

I spent the majority of the morning in that bathroom. Later, I found out Aiden never even made it to his room but instead spent the night, naked, on a white Persian rug in the lobby of the hotel until security found him.

To this day, I haven't touched a drop of wine and neither has Aiden.

I also had some serious battery searching to do.

Something I knew had to give, it was teetering on the edge and needed to be either tipped the rest of the way, or rescued all together.

Not only did I hate sleeping around but it was evident I couldn't keep doing it. I was tired of explaining myself to them. I didn't want to be known as the driver who made his rounds with the girls.

I was here to race, not get a reputation, and judging by Ashley's comments, I felt I was heading in the wrong direction. It just seemed like I'd come to a point where I didn't know myself. This wasn't me. I wasn't this guy who slept around and treated women like shit and, most of all, lied to myself.

It was time to find the batteries.

Bladder – Located inside the tail tank, the bladder holds fuel and keeps the fuel from spilling and catching fire in case of a rear impact.

In late August after the Bristol race, I was heading out to Knoxville for the World of Outlaws Nationals.

The Busch series had a by-week the following week so schedules lined up and I jumped on the chance to get back behind the wheel of a sprint car.

After I signed with Simplex, I got the same standard question from everyone when I showed up at the local bullring dirt tracks: "What are you doing?"

What did they expect me to do?

It wasn't like I would settle for bowling in my spare time. I started racing because that's what I loved to do. Just because I'd been signed with a team and they were paying me to do what I loved, didn't mean I lost that desire to race at the bullrings.

When I asked Sway one afternoon if I should stop, she again offered her timeless advice.

"The people asking you to quit don't understand why you're doing it in the first place. It's what you do, it's all you've ever known. So you now have a job doing it. That doesn't mean you give up what relaxes you."

Everyone thought because I was now being paid to race that I had it easy but that's not the truth at all. I had stress, lots of it. I had sponsors breathing down my neck, my dad watching my every move, women hounding me and, to top it off, I was falling for my best friend. So when I'm stressed, I act like any other twenty-two-year-old, I do what relaxes me: racing.

Even though I was battling it out in the Busch series and I'd just signed with Simplex for next year in the Cup series as well, I still showed up at those bullring tracks when I could, for one simple reason, okay, well two, I loved to race and get more seat time. I brought my helmet wherever I went. You race your best when you're prepared and ready.

I was.

Being back around sprint cars was exactly what I needed. Tyler, Ryder, and Justin were out there. It was the first time I'd seen Ryder racing since his accident. You could tell he still had some setbacks and walked with a limp but he did good.

We hugged when I saw him.

"Look at you big man!" Ryder said, with a bright smile sweeping his golden brown hair from his eyes. "NASCAR driver now, huh?"

"Yeah, so they say."

"They say? I saw you've won a few races."

"It's just luck," I shrugged. "How are you feeling these days?"

"Oh, you know ... good. I walk with a limp but other than that, back to normal."

Justin pushed against him as we walked toward the pit bleachers for the drivers' meeting. "It's good to see you back out here, kid."

"Who you talking to?" Ryder asked looking between Justin and me.

"Both of you actually," he said as we filed into the bleachers together. I noticed my dad walking toward us now with Bucky and Shey. "I'm lonely out here these days."

"Hey!" Tyler punched his shoulder.

"I'm just sayin' ... we all used to race together. This kid goes and gets hurt and this one ..." he gestured to me with a nod. "Goes and gets himself a NASCAR gig." Justin threw his arm around Tyler. "It's just you and me Ty."

Jimi walked up right about then as we were all laughing.

"Hey, Jameson, some girl is looking for you," he waggled his eyebrows.

"Who?" I glanced down at my cell phone that vibrated. Sway sent me a text.

Good luck tonight.

"Uh ... I think she said her name was Nikki or Natalie ... or something like that. I don't know," he sat down next to Ryder. "How ya' feeling?"

"Pretty good," Ryder nodded. "These assholes like to make fun of my limp but, yeah ... I'm feeling good."

"I walk with a limp, too." Dad replied.

"That's cause you're old," I added sending a text to Sway.

I need the luck. Thanks.

It felt good racing sprints again and I was pleased to see I was able to pull off another win. It was nice to know I hadn't lost the ability to race open wheel but it was a gratifying feeling knowing I could battle it out in the Busch series each week and then jump back into open wheel and compete.

I ended up dodging whoever that Nikki or Natalie pit lizard was and, for good measure, I left as soon as the hauler was loaded so I didn't have a chance at meeting up with her. This was happening way too often.

After what transpired with the nurse in Las Vegas, I swore off women.

I was being paid to race, not fuck around.

I saw the way other drivers were looking at me and I didn't want to be that guy. So I focused on what I did best, racing. If I wanted to run with those Cup guys next year and compete for a title, I'd need to up my game. No more of this getting a feel for things and, if I won, even better. This needed be something where I let Simplex, my dad, and my uncle, know that I was the right driver for this team.

We spoke habitually about the plans for next season. It was decided around May that we would move to the Winston Cup Series and add another car to the team.

In August, dad and Randy approached Bobby Cole as his contract with Durham Motorsports was ending. Having Bobby as a teammate was exactly what I needed. He was a patient, methodical driver and, let's face it, I wasn't. It would be good for someone like me to learn from Bobby.

Every time I opened the paper, Jameson was in it these days. It made me feel closer in a way, seeing him everywhere but it also held a sense of yearning, I missed him.

I opened my laptop, searching the latest articles on him. The article on him in *PEOPLE* magazine was posted so I clicked on the link waiting for the article to load.

I smiled to myself like a goon when I saw the picture they used. Jameson was in the most form-fitting, tailored, black suit I had ever seen as it clung to his hard body. He was standing tall, against the side of his Busch car, with his arms crossed. On the other side of him was one of his sprint cars.

Though his appearance looked a little different, his eyes were the same.

There was a fire behind him that I adored. I played with the ends of my hair as I read the short biography under the picture.

MOST ELIGIBLE BACHELOR

Jameson Anthony Riley

Age: 22 **Birthday:** June 22, 1980

Hometown: Elma, Washington

Current Residence: Mooresville, North Carolina

Jameson Riley comes from the inert Northwest where

you wouldn't expect dirt track racing. But it was there this brooding prodigy made his mark. Now he's tearing it up in the NASCAR Busch Grand National Series and breaking hearts along the way. His World of Outlaw Champion father, Jimi Riley, and mother Nancy, have raised two boys and a daughter but Jameson seems to be the only one making his name in the racing community. As an aggressive, up-and-coming driver, the youngest Riley brother has already been said to be the new James Dean with piercing green eyes that can mesmerize any pit lizard.

"You know, most guys will tell you they like a girl who has a certain amount of confidence. For me, I like both. I love a confident girl who will come up and talk to me but I also find the shy ones enduring and adorable at times," Riley told PEOPLE.

While Riley isn't planning on settling down in the near future, with a thirty-six week schedule, he hardly has time but he doesn't kiss and tell as he puts it. "I can be a gentleman when needed and I don't talk about things like that. I'm private."

Most women from 15-35 know who Jameson Riley is these days and would quite literally kill for a chance to run away with the hothead, preferably inside his car. Jameson laughed with a slight flush to his cheeks. Looks like this one might be shy too ladies.

Shy?

I don't think so. They clearly don't know him well.

Since I couldn't sleep, I spent my time on the internet reading about his races.

Raise your hand if you are a pit lizard stalker.

Despite talking to myself, I did raise my hand in the middle of the library.

Sitting back against the large leather chairs in the library at the school, I once again read the article I pulled up on the internet about his last race in Knoxville.

"Why are you smiling like a fool?"

I swear I jumped out of my skin hearing her voice. "What are you doing here?" I scrambled to close my laptop.

"Came to see you," Emma remarked handing me an iced mocha. She held another securely to her lips as though she was drinking crack. "They don't have these on the East Coast."

"Is Jameson with you?"

She laughed and sunk down in the chair next to me kicking her tiny bird legs up on the table. "No, he's racing in Darlington tonight." Her brow furrowed at me. "I would think you would know that though."

"I do, I do. I just thought ... I don't know." I wasn't even making sense to myself right now.

"You thought he'd come see you?"

"Hoped, I guess."

"He wants too ... believe me when I say, he *wants* to." She reached over and gave me shoulder a reassuring squeeze.

"What's that supposed to mean?"

"It means what it means. He's a moody asshole when you're gone and he's constantly staring at his schedule trying to find openings," she said, lamely. "You don't know how often he asks Alley if he has any free time."

"Really?"

"Yes. Now let's go to Bellevue."

"I have class in an hour. I can't."

"Oh, please." She stood straightening out her summer dress and reaching for her lotion in her suitcase of a bag she carried around. "I'm only here for two days, let's go do something."

Emma shot me a sidelong glance before lathering her legs with lotion.

"Just because you come to town doesn't mean I can blow off class for you."

"Oh, yes it does, hooker," she finished polishing herself. "Now, let's go."

Emma was about as good at persuasion as Jameson so in the end, I went shopping.

Emma talked endlessly about Aiden, Jameson's spotter, who I had yet to meet. She had never talked about another guy since high school so it didn't bother me that much.

Aiden, who was from Alabama, sounded like he was nice.

Those two days with Emma were incredibly strenuous and I was thankful when she left. Emma was only tolerable in small doses and two days was plenty.

Also, she redecorated my dorm. I spent a good week trying to find my underwear.

After my Economical Projections class and Emma's departure that night, I called Jameson.

It was nice to hear his voice and a relief. He was stressed about racing and I was stressed with school. We both needed to laugh. I could always count on him for that.

He spoke briefly about his engine specialist, Harry, and how he had spent most of the afternoon in the hauler for not paying attention to his temps in practice. Harry sounded like a nice guy but the way Jameson described him made it even funnier.

Jameson sighed. "I'm jealous Emma got to see you and I didn't."

"I would have preferred to see you over Em."

He laughed and I could hear the faint rumbling of engines in the background followed by Spencer's booming voice.

"Do you have any plans for Christmas?" I asked Jameson as I took a bite of my left over pizza.

"Who knows? I have to look at my schedule but I think that entire week I'm in Los Angeles filming a commercial and then I fly to Tulsa the following week."

"It sounds like you'll be all alone."

"I could come see you maybe," he suggested.

"I'd like that ... but I'll be here in school."

"I could. Only for a day and leave for Tulsa."

"No, that'd be worse," I said, pretty much dejected. "If you stay for one day, then I'll be sad when you leave."

"And that's a bad thing?"

"Well, no, but everyone will recognize you." I was going for anything I could think of at that point.

"So?"

"Do you realize how crazed some of these people are? They love you. You're like their hometown hero or something."

Other students were constantly asking me if I knew Jameson once they found out I was from Elma.

"What is your point?"

"I just, everyone talks about you here and if you come up here, we won't get to spend any time together. Even if you are here for one day ... things have changed Jameson. You're a star; you can't go anywhere you like anymore. Besides, my class on Retail Merchandising starts that week and I need to get together with Blake to go over our assignments."

Jameson stopped tapping his pen he'd been hitting against the table I assumed, whatever it was that he was obsessively clicking, he stopped.

"Blake? Who's Blake?"

"You know, Blake." I stammered. "I've told you about him."

I frantically raked my brain to remember if I'd told him who Blake was, not that he was important.

"Um, no ... I know each man's name that has come out of your mouth and not once have I heard Blake."

"Oh, well, Blake is just ... a friend," I shrunk back into my bed not knowing what else to say. "We have a few classes together."

"A friend? I don't think so. What the hell does that mean?" Jameson demanded.

"A friend, not like you but he's just a guy here that I've had a few classes with."

"So, he's your sex buddy?"

"What?"

"How long?" Jameson growled.

"Are you for real?" I asked. "Why does it even matter? What were we originally talking about?"

"I don't remember. You distracted me. I'm more concerned with this Blake guy. How long have you been fucking him?"

"Jesus Christ, Jameson, what the hell? I haven't slept with him, not that it's any of your business anyway. You don't see me questioning who your pit lizards are these days."

"That's hardly relevant."

"Okay, so what's the problem?"

"I don't like this guy. Does Charlie know about him?"

"No," I sighed.

I knew him well enough to know that he wasn't jealous, but he and Spencer, hell, even Tommy, felt the need to dictate who I hung around with. I wouldn't be surprised if Jameson pulled background checks on everyone I went to school with.

It was actually cute and funny to see him this way.

"You're being irrational."

"No, I'm not," he defended. "And now, I'm definitely coming to Bellingham to meet this Blake guy."

"You stay away from Bellingham, Jameson!" I snapped. "You have to go race."

"You can't tell me what to do. I'm buying a ticket," Jameson said with a hint of finality.

"No, you're not."

"I need to meet this boy of yours."

"He's not my boy!" I stressed. This was getting out of hand.

"Whatever," Jameson huffed like a child.

"You're being irrational."

"I'm mad."

Jameson was being petty and angry with me for the rest of the phone call, groaning about how I kept things from him and how could he trust me.

I could only roll my eyes at him. I didn't think it was that big of a deal.

By the time we ended the phone call, he was in a better mood but was threatening to kill Blake.

I finally came to the conclusion that I wouldn't be surprised if he showed up in Bellingham but it was comforting to know that he really didn't have the time.

For Blake's safety, I warned him to avoid Jameson just in case he showed up unannounced.

This wasn't supposed to happen this way. I wasn't supposed to feel anything for her besides friends. That didn't bother me as much as the fact that I fell so seamlessly that I hadn't even realized it.

Now I was ready to fly to Bellingham to meet this Blake jerk. Hearing her acknowledge the fact that she knew I slept around, was even worse. I'm sure she didn't hear it over the phone line, but I gasped when she said it out loud.

I thought I had been discreet, but I wasn't. It wasn't hard to figure out. People knew when I'd disappear and wouldn't see me for hours. I hated myself for it.

Mostly, I hated the image that it had created of me to her. I never wanted Sway to think of me as someone like Dylan Grady when, in all actuality, I was behaving just like he had. It was repulsive and was just one more reminder that she deserved so much better than someone like me. What kind of relationship could I even provide for her?

Sitting on the couch in my underwear on the only free morning I had for the next two months as I headed into the last few races of the season, I drank whiskey from the bottle as I watched the sun rise over the track Spencer and I built in the backyard of my parent's Mooresville home.

I thought about calling Sway, but didn't. Taking another drink of whiskey, I thought about why I felt like this in the first place. What bothered me most was why she had this control over me.

But that was Sway. She did things to me emotionally.

I think that's what made this so hard for me and actually made me angry.

I was supposed to be a hardcore racer who only thought about the next race but now, my best friend was slowly captivating my every thought. She was becoming an obsession.

"Stop being a pussy," running my hand over my eyes, I set the bottle down in front of me.

It wasn't even the fact that I felt something more. Something in me had changed. It had been for years and it was making me want to spend time more time with her.

So what did that make me? More than a friend, right? Boyfriend?

I cringed at the word.

Boyfriend was more than I was willing to deal with right then. I wasn't in any position to offer her the things that came along with that title. The only problem was that I didn't want her to be out there with some other guy.

She was mine.

The harder I tried to deny it, the more she pulled me in.

What Sway and I had couldn't even be defined. I thought about her constantly.

We spent time together, we kissed on occasion and we messed around. I took her out to dinner and I held her hand.

What did the word boyfriend mean anyway?

If it meant that, I was fucked.

When the front door opened, I jumped at the sound.

"Jameson ..." I heard my mom's voice, "We're home."

"Mom? Jesus, you scared the shit out of me!" I yelled back trying to calm myself down.

"Watch your language, asshole," Dad said, grinning as he made his way inside. "Put some clothes on, boy." He hit the back of my head with his hand.

"We need to go over your fan club!" Mom said, with wide excited eyes. I groaned.

Dad chuckled. "And, *we* need to go over your contract for next season." He held a thick manila envelope in the air and then tossed it on the table with a thud.

Awesome. I thought to myself.

Here I was debating with myself all morning and now more were joining the party.

"What fan club?" I asked apprehensively.

"Yours," Mom said opening her laptop on the table in the dining room. "You got fans, sweetheart. Those fans need to be able to get in touch with you."

"No, they don't. I don't want to get in touch with them."

"Yes, you do. You wouldn't be racing if it wasn't for them."

"That's not entirely true," I groaned until dad kicked me again.

"Go put some clothes on." His eyebrow arched at the bottle of whiskey I was holding. "Give me that."

Mom glared at the bottle. "Jameson, sweetie ... it's a little early for that, don't you think?"

"Not if I'm spending the day going over a fan club for stalkers."

"They're not stalkers. They love you."

"Stalkers," I mumbled again. I threw myself down next to her in a wooden chair. My head slumped against the table.

Dad hit my shoulders. "Go put some damn clothes on. I'm not about to have you sitting around here naked. It's weird."

So much for trying to decipher my feelings.

The afternoon was spent setting up my fan club website and signing my life away to Simplex and my dad. It was exhausting so I took a nap afterward.

The season was flying by and, before I knew it, we were in Homestead and the Winston Cup career was promising when I won my fourteenth race there in Florida. I finished out my rookie season in the Busch series with a second place finish in the points and won the Rookie of the Year award.

Not bad.

As the leaves turned burgundy and began to fall, the nights got colder and, before I knew it, winter was here.

I thought maybe I would be able to take a quick breather but time was not something I was in control of any longer. Right after Homestead, I was off to Turkey Night, which I finally won. Then the Chili Bowl followed by testing of the new Cup car.

Before testing started, I had a chance to get together with Justin after the Chili Bowl, which was welcomed. It was good to see him. I hadn't seen him since Knoxville and I forgot how much fun we had hanging out.

"How've you been?" I asked taking a drink of my beer and then leaned back in my seat.

He shrugged. "Can't complain. I lost my ride in USAC though."

"Really?" this shocked me. "What happened?"

"Sponsors—they ran out of money, *apparently*?"

"So what's your plan for next year?"

I've known Justin since I was eight years old. He's raced every season since then just like me.

"I haven't given much thought to it yet," he construed taking a drink from his beer. "I could use a break but, then again, come February, I'll probably be pulling my hair out at home with my parents," he smiled. "I hear you moved up to the big leagues?"

A small chuckle escaped me when he said *big leagues.*

"Yeah, we start testing the Cup car at Fontana in about two weeks." When I told him my plans for next year, that's when an idea came to me. "I've got a car running in the Outlaw series this next year, too," I smiled. "You wanna drive it for me?"

"You can't find a driver?"

"Nah, I think I just did."

And that was that. I didn't need to worry. Justin was one of the best. Even though I would be racing Cup cars, I wasn't about to get away from dirt all together so I started a sprint car team in the World of Outlaws. I knew eventually I wanted two cars running in it but I started with one.

I got a chance to talk to Sway later that night. It was right before I flew back out to Charlotte to meet with Melissa to go over the merchandise contract.

Sway congratulated me on the win at Turkey Night.

Being the possessive jackass I'd become, I responded with, "Let's see Blake do that."

Despite my jealousy, she giggled. "Here we go again."

"I'm just kidding," I offered though I wasn't. "How are you?"

"Eh, pretty good." I could hear a twinge of sadness in her voice. "Looking forward to school being over with. You know," she paused for a moment. "I never liked high school. I don't know what made me think I'd like college."

"I don't know how you do it."

"I have it easy compared to you."

"Nah, I love what I do. All the other shit just comes with it but when I'm in the car ... I don't even think about all the other obligations."

I wasn't lying when I said I didn't think about it. When I was behind the wheel, nothing mattered. I was in my happy place so to speak.

I had to catch a flight to Charlotte so that ended our conversation early but I promised to call her soon. A day didn't go by when I didn't hear her voice. As stupid as it sounds, it was vital for me to keep going.

I'd like to say I was strong without Sway, but I'd be lying. Everyone noticed, it was hard not to. I was never the same when she wasn't around and as much as I tried to hide my feelings, I know they saw it.

One afternoon in January, before I left for Florida for testing and Speedweek, I was changing gears and other parts on one of my sprint cars before Justin came to pick it up. I wanted everything done a certain way and didn't trust anyone else to do it besides Tommy and, alas, he was home in Elma for the holidays so this left me doing it.

I had been at it awhile and my head was pounding in my ears, my vision was blurred so I decided I needed a break.

When I glanced at myself in the mirror, there was no doubt I was in need of a break.

I'm sure everyone knew why, but I tried to convince everyone that I was fine. To be honest, I was getting sick. I could feel it. I was trying so hard to be everything I could and prove to everyone that I could do this, that I was forgetting about myself.

Most of the time I was lucky if I got five hours of sleep a night. I knew come February, this wasn't going to cut it and I knew something needed to change. I had to get my shit together.

Splashing my face with water, I reached in my bag on the floor and grabbed two pain pills, taking them back dry.

When I got back in the shop, Dad was there knocking on the door, glaring.

"Let me in, asshole." He had his hands shoved in the pockets of his jeans, shaking. "It's cold out here."

The beginning of January had brought a rush of frozen air and snow that stuck this time.

"I thought you were in Sydney."

"I had some things to take care of," he walked around the sprint car. "Gears?"

"Yeah, coupler, too," I sat back against the rear tires. I tried to sneak the bottle of Jack Daniels under the car so that he wouldn't see it but, of course, he saw.

"Drinking again?" He sat across from me on a set of tires, leaning to one side.

"A little," I shrugged.

"You know what I mean," he picked up a screwdriver from the floor and began twirling it easily in his fingers.

"I was thirsty."

"Then drink water, dumbass."

"I needed something ... *stronger*."

He sighed through his nose.

I rolled my eyes. "Jesus, Dad, is that why you came?"

"Jameson ... you need to stop drinking so much."

"You're one to talk. You named me after whiskey."

He didn't say anything just sighed heavily and shook his head. "How can you drive the way you do and drink this much?"

"I don't drink on race days. I never have. And it's not like I have a problem for Christ sakes, just taking the edge off."

He sighed again and ran a hand through his black hair. "I need you to be focused. I have a lot riding on this new deal with Simplex and, well, I can't have you drinking all the time or popping pills every day."

"All right," I groaned, "I know."

"Do you though? Do you even understand what this all means? I came to see how you were doing. You look awful." He gave me a disappointed look before standing and glancing down at me. "I know you miss her and that you love her ..." I was about to interrupt him when he shook his head. "Don't lie to me, Jameson ... I can see what you clearly can't. Just don't fuck this up," was his request.

No one knew what was going on with me and Sway. Hell, I didn't even know.

How could I tell them something I didn't know?

I think they distinguished from my drinking and mood swings, but I didn't feel like talking about it, so no one brought it up. I never like people prying into my personal life. And, if they did, I'd throw a fit. If anyone mentioned her name, I'm sure they saw the pained expression flash across my face, so eventually they gave up fearing my reaction.

I knew I needed to lay off the drinking. NASCAR required a physical and prohibited drinking when you're at the track and had strict guidelines on prescription drugs. I'm sure they knew most race car drivers took pain relievers with the way they are tossed around in the cars but they sure didn't allow addictions.

I hated the feeling of being hung over. Welcomed the numbness I felt, but the hangovers, I could go without those. So it surprised me that I'd been drinking so much lately.

I never made it back to Elma that winter. With my parents having the house in North Carolina now, we didn't make it back there as much. I got tired of living with my family real fast, so that winter I purchased a few acres of land in Mooresville and started building my own home.

Mostly, it was living with Emma that I despised. Spencer and Alley had moved into their own house not far from my parents but I saw Spencer and Alley so much it was as though we all lived together. Lane was a hoot and I enjoyed corrupting him for future retaliation against Spencer. Being two now, he had quite the personality.

Sway was trying to finish her classes so she stayed in Bellingham that winter, but to be fair, I didn't have a chance to see her either. Since that weekend I flew out to Bellingham, I hadn't seen her. Naturally, we spoke nearly every day but I hadn't seen her smiling face in months.

I will say it gave me a chance to think, well, that's a lie, I never had time to think. Since the last time I saw her, it was a different track, different city every week and even though it was the off-season right now, I still didn't have time.

The last few races of the season turned into a media showdown into my personal life to which I was not impressed. Even in Mooresville I was still dealing with the constant banter that surrounded me.

"There's Jimi Riley's kid, the Busch driver ..."

" ... Did you know he slept with that one girl ...?"

"I hear he's dating some girl from Elma ..."

I'm not sure what the lure into my personal life came from but I had a feeling Ashley had something to do with that or maybe it was that I was just in the public's gaze more. Ashley did follow me around the track mercilessly but all that did was ensure I didn't make that mistake again.

Since the nurse in Vegas, I hadn't slept with anyone and willed off women all together. I had a job to do now and that didn't entail sleeping around.

It didn't feel right. I had nothing to offer those women. Sure, they got what they wanted as did I, in a way, but every time I felt the crushing guilt that it was wrong, it was just wrong. They weren't what I wanted. I wanted Sway, in any way I could have her, and right now, that was as friends.

My dad and I were on our way to Daytona for Speedweek when he felt the need to talk to me about my temper that had been flaring lately.

"This is different this year. You need to keep your head together and stay focused."

"I know." I didn't want another speech about how I needed to keep my shit in line but I had a feeling the first time I fucked up I'd hear about it, only this time I'd hear it from him, my uncle Randy, and Simplex.

Dad pulled through the gates of Daytona International Raceway, handed his credentials over and pulled through the gates.

"I know you know, but I can't have you causing problems, you understand? No more pain killers either. If you're in pain, go to the doctor. Drinking is one thing, outside of the track only, but pain killers ... that's not something you need to be abusing. I won't have my son taking that shit."

"I know," I said, again, and reached for the handle of the door before pausing. I felt I needed to say more this time. I wanted him to know that I was ready for this and took this opportunity seriously. "I know you think I don't understand how this affects all of us, our family that is, but I do." My eyes stared straight ahead and focused on Spencer walking toward us. He rode over with Kyle and Mason to meet the rest of the pit crew dad hired. "I haven't forgotten how I got here and why this was all made possible," I told him.

I finally looked over at him—he smiled. "Let's go show these guys what Jameson Riley is made of."

That sounded good to me.

I like to think I was a renewed man and completely focused but I did have distractions. Everywhere I turned another woman was throwing herself in my direction. Other drivers were testing me and we had a new team. A new team in general is frustrating and taxing.

Most of the same crewmembers were the same but anytime you put a new team together, it takes time for everyone to adjust and amend the team dynamics.

I seemed to be the one everyone had a hard time getting used to, for good reason. I wasn't exactly the nicest guy to be around. I had a few good qualities but they were mostly overshadowed by the bad.

I was possessive of Sway, and though she wasn't mine my team, unfortunately, knew that when anyone asked about her, jealousy ran through my veins as I had the temper of a bull and little patience to go along with that. I had to be in control at all times and didn't take orders from anyone besides my mom and dad—mostly my mom.

I didn't have time to cultivate relationships or friendships and I rarely had time to sleep. Who cared if I didn't have friends? Well, I did care. I'd be lying if I said I didn't, but there was only one friend who mattered to me ... Sway.

As far as my team went, Kyle was the same. Kyle and I trusted each other and you needed that in a crew chief/driver combination, it was vital for trust to be there. When he or I made calls, I had to know he had my back and vice versa.

Aiden transferred over, as did Mason as the car chief since we no longer had a car running in the Busch series. We also added Kyle's younger brother, Gentry, as a tire carrier. Harry stayed as the engine specialist along with Tony, the tire specialist. Most of the crew was the same other than these few additions but it would be a little different.

Everything was faster paced in Cup. The pit stops had to be perfect as did my racing. So much goes into the pit stops that you don't realize how crucial they are.

For instance, when you pull down pit road, there are seven guys swarming around your idling race car all waiting to perform their piece of that 12-second stop. You have the tire carriers, front and rear, a jack man, officials, a gasman and then someone who catches the overflow.

Occasionally there is another guy standing by to clean the windshield, hand me water, or assist another crewmember, if needed.

The NASCAR official stands there to make sure you're not breaking any rules.

When you think about all that happening within twelve seconds and if one guys slips, everything is thrown off.

Talk about pressure, huh?

When testing began I met Darrin Torres again, the asshole who wrecked me a couple years ago in a USAC Silver crown. Now I'd seen Darrin at the tracks this last year. It's hard not to when you're both at the same track each weekend. Outside of the occasional glare, we didn't speak and I had no desire to befriend him anyway.

I was surprised when he approached me after testing one afternoon.

It was our last day before Speedweek started and I had a lot on my mind to begin with so I didn't need to deal with another confrontation with him.

"So, you're the badass USAC driver everyone talks about? You don't look so badass now," was his *kind* way of greeting me.

Asshole, huh?

"I've had my moments," I responded signing a few autographs as I walked toward the paddock.

"Guys like you have it easy," he followed me. "Your father funds everything for you."

Guys like me? He had no idea how much time I spent racing as a kid. How ever since I was old enough to walk, it's all I've ever wanted. The long hours, the time spent traveling, how I never had a childhood, the things I gave up ... Sway ... he had no fucking clue what it was like for me.

Fuck him.

Luck ... sure I had that on my side at times but I worked hard for everything I had. I wasn't going to let anyone tell me differently.

"Yeah, I have luck but I've worked for everything I have," I told him unemotionally walking away.

"Yeah ... right," he muttered and walked away himself.

You know that feeling you get when you know something is wrong, yeah, well, anytime I was around Darrin, I felt that unnerving feeling.

He made me nervous.

After testing, we had about two weeks back at the shop where we adjusted the car we needed in preparation for Speedweek. You would think all I would have to do is drive the car but, no, being a NASCAR driver is so much more in-depth than that. There are appearances to make, meet and greets, fan clubs obligations, autograph sessions, commercials, pictures, team meetings ... I could go on and on with this one.

Most see the glamorous side. They see the money and publicity of it all but it's draining both mentally and physically on everyone involved. Most all the drivers out there are in it to race and now, they were puppets to their sponsors whether they wanted to be or not once they were outside of the car.

Have you ever watched a driver get out of the car?

He immediately puts on his sponsor's hat and then when the camera swings to him, he takes a drink of whatever drink of choice is sponsoring him. That's advertisement and is exactly what your sponsor is seeking when they agree to provide you with the funds. We promote them and, in turn, they give us money to do what we love. Fair trade? Maybe.

I hated doing anything that wasn't racing, but when I was in the car I forgot about all that and raced. It was as though life outside of that cockpit didn't exist, and that's exactly what I loved most about racing. So, was it a fair trade? Yes, it was to me.

I'd probably stand on the corner in chicken suit waving a sign around while shaking my ass if I got to race each week. That's how badly I wanted this.

I had tested at Daytona, and I ran well there. I was comfortable with the fast speeds and drafting. I definitely was no master at the air, but I was comfortable at least.

But now, I was out there with more than just Bobby and me; try forty-two other cars pulling on and off the track.

Aiden managed to keep me calm by adding simple things like, "Remember to blend," when other drivers would merge onto the track. Seems silly that he'd have to tell me that but it helps. It helps because when you're on the track you're so focused on what's happening that you don't necessarily look to the line to see the other drivers until it's too late.

The other obstacle was getting other drivers to draft with you and drafting with them. Drafting is almost like a fine art or a formal ball as Harry told me. It's not easy when you're a rookie driver getting other drivers to dance with you but, thankfully, Bobby was there and other drivers like Tate Harris, another rookie Paul Leighty were all willing to work with me. Others like Darrin and his teammate weren't easy to work with. I didn't have a problem with his teammate, but Darrin, I couldn't stand the asshole.

I spent most of the practice sessions working with the draft and other drivers, trying to get a feel for how the race would be. I raced here in the Busch series but Cup cars held about four hundred more horsepower so, as you could see, they went faster.

I'd take about fifty laps and then come in, give my feedback to Kyle and Mason and then I was off again. Being a new team, we didn't have a lot of data to form. We just kind of winged it and hoped for some sort of break. I also had to provide feedback for them. I learned a lot in the Busch series and knew when the car was pushing and tight but I still didn't know everything, and that was hard on everyone. I would get frustrated because I couldn't drive the car like I wanted and the team was frustrated with me because I couldn't tell them what the car was doing.

If it weren't for the help of guys like Tate and Bobby who came from dirt track racing, I wouldn't know what I was talking about in these cars. But they were there for me and helped me tell Kyle and Harry what I needed from the car.

I made it through practice on Thursday and then came the Budweiser Shootout on Saturday night. It was rare for a rookie driver to be in the Shootout but I was selected as the wild card, so there I was preparing.

I never got nervous prior to a race but I did have some butterflies that night so I did what I always did when I was nervous. I called Sway before heading out to the driver introductions. I only had about an hour, I knew I needed to eat, but Sway was more important.

She answered on the first ring, as she always did. "Hey, honey," I smiled.

She sighed contently. I could hear the faint sounds of the television in the background and loud voices, one sounded like Tommy.

"I was hoping you'd call before the race."

"Did you watch my interview this morning?" I groaned. I hated doing interviews generally because I never knew what to say. If I spoke my mind, they wouldn't be happy.

"I did. It was so weird seeing you on TV."

"How have you been? How did your class go?"

"Good, I got an A so I guess it went well. Just three more months to graduation!"

"I think I'm more excited for you to graduate than you are," I told her with a chuckle.

Alley, with Lane on her hip, made her way inside the motor coach. With traveling so often these days, I purchased a Featherlite Motor coach. Most of the drivers had them and I definitely saw the advantages. You didn't have to find a hotel room and you could sleep longer on race days.

Alley pushed a plate of tacos at me so I began eating while Sway talked about her classes for a moment. After ruffling Lane's mop of wavy honey blonde hair, Alley went back outside with him.

"What are you going to do after you graduate?"

"Well, I'm sure Charlie has everything lined up for me ... he wants me to be the General Manager."

"I heard that ..." I paused, taking a drink of my water. "Is that what *you* want to do?"

"Yes, and no," she admitted. "I miss you. I miss everyone. I had lunch with your mom the other day and it just reminded me how much fun I had with everyone."

"I hope you mean me. I believe *I'm* the one you like the most."

She giggled. "Yes, I'd say I'm partial to you."

"You probably can't come out for the race, huh?"

"I'm not sure yet. I need to put some finishing touches on my Marketing Management assignment."

"I understand," I said, before I gave myself away.

This was a significant step in my racing career but I couldn't expect her to be there for everything. I wanted her to be but I couldn't expect it. She wasn't my girlfriend and I had to stop acting as though she was.

"I'll try," she offered. "But I can't promise anything."

"Well, when you graduate ... we need to get together at some point."

"We could run away together."

"That sounds nice."

"Yeah, but there would be a lot of jealous girls if you ran away with me," Sway teased with a giggle. I'd recently did a magazine interview where all they talked about was how girls wanted to run away with me. Clearly, I'd provided ammo for Sway.

"Shut up," I groaned pushing my plate away, not surprised I'd just eaten six tacos. I glanced at my phone and realized I needed to get to the pre-race activities. "I need to get to driver introductions but I needed to hear your voice for a minute."

"Just remember, you'll do fine."

"I know," I rubbed my belly. I definitely ate too much.

"I ..." Sway paused and let out a shaky breath. "I will see you soon okay?"

"Yeah, somehow ... maybe I can make it out there for graduation or something."

"I know you're busy, Jameson, but please don't forget why *tonight* ... you're racing in the Budweiser Shootout, that means something. This is what you worked for all those years."

Honestly though, it hadn't hit me how real this all was. I'm sure it would when I got inside the car but, as of yet, it hadn't. I think I was too full to feel anything else.

When I walked out to the grid for introductions, the nerves hit. Knowing I would be fine once inside the car, I wanted to rush all the pre-race activities and get on with it. I didn't like butterflies.

Having seen the fan fair I was developing throughout Speedweek I was prepared for a few cheers but I wasn't expecting to hear the crowd roar to life when I stepped on stage after Tate.

He turned around clapping himself and did this stupid bow that made me chuckle.

I waived to the crowd as they cheered louder and then I punched Tate's arm when I got closer. "Stop that."

"You have more fans than me," he gestured to the crowd.

I saw my mom and Emma jumping up and down amongst them. "Nah, just a loud family."

Races like this, guys put it all on the line and I had to rise to the occasion. I was racing with the best as I should be but I also sensed they thought the kid shouldn't be racing with them. I had to prove that I was worthy. No one thought a sprint car driver could come out and drive these stock cars competitively but I was hell bent on proving them wrong.

Chicane – A quick succession of sharp, slow turns, usually intended to reduce straightaway speeds.

"He doesn't know, does he?" I bit the last of my fingernails off. I was sure this was a bad idea ... it had to be.

Tommy laughed his loud cackling laugh that never sounded normal on him but I blamed the orange hair. You probably wouldn't sound normal either if you had hair that bright.

"No, he doesn't."

"He thinks I'm staying in school?" I looked down at my fingers, picking at the chipped nail polish that I hadn't chewed off.

"You're such a fucking weirdo. How many times do I need to explain this college girl?" he smacked my forehead and jerked my chin up. "He. Doesn't. Know!"

"All right," I huffed pushing myself from the couch we were sitting on in Starbucks at the SeaTac airport. "He doesn't ... you know, have a girlfriend you're not telling me about, does he?"

I wanted to punch myself.

Tommy chuckled and picked up our bags. He was flying out to Daytona with me and then he was off to Eldora for the start of the Outlaw season.

"He doesn't, that I know of ... but when has he ever had a girlfriend?" he looked at me like I was stupid.

I felt stupid for even asking.

"Good point. But you never know."

"He spends all his free time on the phone with you," he insinuated. "Or racing sprint cars."

"So?"

"What I mean is how would he have time for a girlfriend? He's either racing or talking to you. Obviously I'm no judge of character here because I can't keep a girlfriend more than a few months, but I'm almost certain no woman would tolerate that."

He had a good point there.

Jameson and I talked every day no matter what time of the night it was. It was almost as though we had an unspoken rule that we *had* to talk.

The entire flight I was nervous and downright jittery. I hadn't seen him since last April and I wasn't sure how to act around him. I knew once I saw him, everything would be back to normal but I was still nervous anticipating what he would think. Did he want me there? He said he did but, then again, maybe he was trying to make me feel better.

So now, there I was surprising him in Daytona. It was Tommy who convinced me to surprise him. I planned on going to Daytona but surprising him seemed like a better option or a dumb one, not sure yet.

As I said, we hadn't seen each other in nearly a year and, if I was honest with you, my feelings for him hadn't diminished. If anything, it was stronger from the separation. My tv in my dorm in Bellingham was kept on the SPEED channel or ESPN just in case I was able to catch a glimpse of him in an interview or just the mention of his name.

Our plane was delayed due to a thunderstorm rolling through Atlanta during take-off, so when we finally touched down in Daytona, the race had already began.

The Budweiser Shootout was not a race you qualified for but, in Jameson's case, he was the wild card who made it by setting the fastest lap time. The Shootout was an annual Winston Cup series invitation-only event the weekend before the Daytona 500 held on Saturday night. It generally served as the kick-off for the NASCAR portion of Speedweek. The field consisted of drivers from previous race wins who clenched automatic berths, former pole sitters who also clenched automatic berths and a wild card, Jameson.

The event was an opening 25-lap segment, followed by a 50-lap race to the finish after a ten-minute intermission. Similar to the All-Star race held at Charlotte, the race had no championship points for the winner, just a nice purse.

The field was made up of twenty-eight cars as opposed to the usual forty-three starters in a typical Cup race, with the starting line-up determined by a random draw.

To me, the racing itself was similar to what you'd see at the local bullring tracks.

With no points on the line, drivers usually went all out and created some of the most exciting racing.

By the time Tommy and I made it to the track, got our hot passes and found our way into the pits to find Alley, the second 50-lap segment was underway. I was so eager to get a glimpse of Jameson's car on the track I hardly heard anything Alley was telling us. I hadn't seen him race stock cars in person yet, only on tv.

I was literally in awe at how huge the venue was. You can't grasp how large it is until you see it in person. Under the lights, you could hear and feel the loud resonant rumble of the cars as they roared down the straightaways, vibrating right through you. The smells ... *oh, the smells.* Rich sharp biting aromas of racing fuel pooled with rubber from the heated tires on the asphalt. Once we stepped out of the car, I inhaled a deep breath, remembering everything I missed about racing and Jameson, the two fused together. Distinguishing between it all, burnt rubber and racing fuel surrounded my senses, I thought of Jameson and always would.

"Calm down," Alley grumbled as I bounced up and down once we found her.

Pit lane was busy, as to be expected. I knew enough about being at the dirt tracks to know that the pits, or in this case pit lane, was a place of business and when the guys are working on cars, that's their job and they take it seriously. To be competitive in this sport, they have to otherwise, they wouldn't be here.

Tommy shot a sideways glance at me while looking toward the pit box. I was showing an alarming amount of enthusiasm for this.

Kyle was up on the box, though I hadn't met him yet, Jameson talked about him often so I felt as though I already knew who he was.

"He's running fourth right now," Alley announced staring at her Blackberry. "He placed second in the first segment." She tucked her phone away and waved goodbye.

Being the Public Relations representative for the team, she was busy, always busy.

I don't think you could wipe the grin from my face. This was so exciting. I couldn't see much, being as short as I was so Kyle motioned for me to come on the pit box with him. You couldn't see much better from there either as the infield was never a good spot to watch a race but it was the most exciting. You get to hear all the commotion between the crewmembers. I believe that being in the infield at the races is the place to be as it gives you the full experience including hearing the strategy calls made by the crew chief and car chief.

Kyle smiled and pulled his headset away from his ear.

"I'm Kyle Wade, Jameson's crew chief, and this is Mason." I shook hands with both of them while Kyle pulled the headset back. "Hey, bud," he began in the microphone attached the headset. "Sw—"

I smacked the back of his head so hard his headset fell off his head. "Don't tell him, it's a surprise!"

I don't think Kyle knew what to do so he scrambled to adjust his headset.

"Sorry, bud, uh ... ten laps to go." He gave me a glance like I was clinically insane but smiled despite this.

I'm not sure what Jameson was saying but Kyle was lying. "Don't worry, it was nothing. I dropped the headset."

I shook my head and watched as Jameson's black number nine car flew past us on the front-stretch. Mason moved around Kyle to sit next to me. I watched as Tommy hung by the pit wall to get a better look at the cars when they came by. At tracks like Daytona, you can only see them on the front-stretch when you're watching from the grid.

"So, you're Sway?" Mason asked peeking over his clipboard.

"Yeah, and you're Mason?"

He nodded. "Jameson talks about you *a lot*." He grinned, his smile boyish. "So does Spencer and Emma."

"What can I say—I'm awesome."

Mason laughed, as did Kyle.

"He's freaking out right now." Kyle said, motioning toward his headset. "You guys might want to watch this." He gestured with a flick of his wrist at the laptop they had opened to the broadcasting station.

I glanced over at it to see Jameson drafting with Bobby only Jameson was leading.

"Holy shit!" I yelled and practically sat on Kyle's lap to get a good view of the screen. "He's leading! He's fucking leading!"

"That's what he just said."

By the looks on their faces, I couldn't have made my obsession any more obvious.

Way to give yourself away.

I wasn't sure what to make of it all. I was leading a pack of cars at Daytona International Raceway. In a race. Yeah, it wasn't the Daytona 500 but it was even better, it was a race with the best of the best, the Budweiser Shootout.

"Is this the last lap?" I asked Kyle when we crossed the start/finish line. "Please let this be the last lap!"

"Yeah."

Tate and his teammate, Austin Yale, teamed up beside Bobby and me on the inside. They had the preferred line coming out of turn two. "Inside on the line, ten cars got a run ... inside at your door ... clear."

Damn. Nearly had it.

Tate took over position but he did something I least expected him to do; he shot over in front of me on the outside instead of teaming up with Austin again. I wasn't sure what to do so I drafted with him. Bobby stayed right behind me and Austin swung in line behind him creating a four-car line coming to the green.

I had two options. Stay where I was, or try to pass. I knew Bobby would follow but I wasn't sure my car could pass Tate, he was strong. He did just pass me outside of the draft. There wasn't enough time to make a move so I stayed where I was, second place.

I grinned when I saw the checkered flag. I ran a race with the legends of stock car racing and placed second.

I'd say that's respectable.

I hated not winning, I don't know of any racer who didn't, but when you think about, what experience did I have in race trim on a track like Daytona?

None.

I'd never raced a Cup race before this, and to finish second, I shouldn't be complaining. I think the part that upset me the most was the fact that I could have won, there wasn't enough time.

Tate waved when I pulled up next to him, as did I. I'd finish second to a guy like him any day. This just goes back to my feelings about that Triple Crown Championship over Justin, you want to win so badly but you also know that means beating a guy who wants it just as badly.

When I pulled down the grid, still smiling, I removed my helmet while Spencer pulled my window net down. That's when I heard a familiar giggle. My head shot up, my eyes glancing around figuratively; no one else had that giggle.

Sway.

I'm almost certain I got out of that car quicker than I would have if it was on fire and had her secured in my arms.

"You lied to me," I breathed against her neck. "You're really here, right? Am I dreaming?"

"You're not dreaming. And I didn't lie," she giggled. "I didn't tell you the *whole* truth." She pulled back to look at me. "I was in Atlanta, getting ready to board the plane, when you called."

I still hadn't let go of her. Instead, I pulled her against my chest tighter.

"Thank you. Thank you *so much* for coming, honey."

"Did you honestly think I'd miss Daytona two years in a row, let alone," —her eyebrow arched— "your first Cup race?"

"No, but ... you're busy these days."

"I'm never too busy for you," she assured me kissing my cheek.

Dad was at my car after that so I couldn't kiss her the way I wanted to. "Good job, kid." He smiled.

"Thanks." I pulled Sway closer and tucked her under my arm. I wasn't about to let go.

She giggled. "You're wet."

"I'm sweating," her eyes focused on mine when I spoke. "It happens."

She didn't say anything for a while as she stood there beside me as I did a few post-race interviews. When the last reporter left she reached up and kissed my cheek again.

I could get used to that.

"I'm so proud of you!"

I had other plans and pulled her aside out of the public eye. We walked back to my motor coach; I kicked Spencer and Aiden out and brought Sway inside. After a few beers, I wasn't thinking, neither was she and before we knew it we were making out on the bed in the back.

She deserved so much better than this and I couldn't just have sex with her.

What would happen if I did?

All the times we'd been like this with each other, she never stopped me and that scared me. If I instigated it, she went with it. If I pulled away, so did she. After a few minutes, I was ready to ask for more, take more, and, *oh,* did I want more.

Her body moved against mine in a desperate way pulling me against her. Her soft hands swept over my shoulders and down the contours of my back. I let out a whimper pulling her hard against me. My mouth moved from its place against her neck back to her warm lips, moving frantically. Lust began drowning any rational thoughts I had about this and I was scrambling to gain control.

Her arousal was evident, as was mine but how could I take this from her?

This would change everything. The worst part about it was she was leaving in a few weeks. It wouldn't be anything more than what I had with other women and I wanted more from Sway. I didn't want a one-time thing. Did she?

No, she couldn't want that.

Unconsciously, my hand moved from her breast to the button of my jeans and she moaned arching against me. I froze, that moan made me comprehend what exactly was happening. I couldn't do this. She deserved better. She wasn't another pit lizard. This was Sway, my best friend.

I moved my hand from her waist to run through her hair lightly skimming the apple of her cheek. My gentle touch elicited a moan of pleasure from her.

It was hard to pull away. Her legs were wrapped around my waist and her hips moving against mine. I briefly contemplated giving her pleasure but I also knew I wouldn't stop. It'd been almost a year since I'd been with anyone and I was close already by her hips wiggling against mine. I also knew that seeing her pleasure, I wouldn't be able to stop myself and she was far too willing.

Miraculously, with some Herculean self-control, I managed to pull away from her.

It took me a moment to calm my need and hormones but I did and finally looked down at her. Sway's cheeks were flushed—her eyes half closed as she scrambled to sit up. “Sorry,” she mumbled running her hand through her long hair once.

I sighed heavily.

“You didn’t do anything wrong, I’m sorry. I always attack you.”

“Well, I’m not any better,” her hand rose to wipe her swollen lips, “you didn’t see me stopping you.”

“True,” I smiled.

We were both silent for a few minutes before I chuckled. No matter how hard I tried, I wanted her. It was undeniable.

“Are you tired?” I asked trying to turn the focus from my desire.

“Yeah,” she yawned.

“Come here,” I motioned for her to come closer. “You can sleep here.”

We did sleep. Surprisingly we only slept. I forgot how nice it felt to have her in my arms and the fact that she came to see me, made it so much better.

I barely had any time with all my sponsorship obligations but in the evenings I was able to hang out with Sway. The trip was so unexpected for her that she didn’t have time to get a hotel room so she stayed in the motor coach with me. I wasn’t complaining.

Tommy ended up sleeping on the couch a few nights before getting a hotel room with the rest of the team. I wasn’t the easiest person to stay with. Luckily, Sway found humor in my OCD tendencies, Tommy did not.

We hung out by the motor coach at night, usually Cal, my motor coach driver, cooked dinner for us. He was awesome. Anything you could dream of wanting to eat was stocked in the motor coach for us. Cal could throw down some wicked meals at the drop of a hat, too. For a group of guys like ours, it was appreciated.

There wasn’t a lot of privacy between the motor coaches, but it also provided a sense of camaraderie between the drivers.

Much like the team haulers, the motor coaches lined up side-by-side each other in the compound (different from the paddock where the haulers are located) which was a secured area for the drivers to stay that you had to show special passes to get in ... and you don't ever forget your pass.

Even if you are a well-known driver and dressed in a racing suit, they will not let you in without that pass. I did this once racing in the Busch series. I was not happy that I was dressed in my uniform and they still wouldn't let me in just because I forgot my pass. I ended up having Spencer go get my pass. He took his sweet ass time and then when I showed the pass to the official, he made sure he called to the NASCAR hauler to make sure it was legit.

I wasn't impressed.

The week seemed to fly by, and before I knew it it was time for the Duel 125's that Thursday night.

I did good, placed fourth, which gave me a good start for the 500 on Sunday. Now I needed to prepare myself. This was the biggest race of my career. I knew that, as did everyone else, including the media but they had this habit of reminding me all week; everyone but Sway.

She was there, constantly assuring me I could do this and offering her advice when I asked for it. Bobby and Tate were there, too, offering up any pointers they had and helping me with drafting throughout the practice sessions. Like I said before, drafting was an art.

Unlike pit road, where everything was business only, the garage area was slightly more laid back. You would often see a driver chatting with other drivers or goofing around with one another. With the Riley Racing team, there was a lot of goofing around.

"No, Spencer. That's the wrong size splitter," Aiden took the splitter from him and handed him another one.

I had never met Aiden until this week and I already loved the country boy and saw why Emma was so attracted to him. Not that I was attracted to him physically because I wasn't, I just found him completely fascinating. I never knew someone with his analytical thinking and found myself instigating it as much as Jameson and Spencer did.

The garage was filled with cars, each lined up side-by-side with their respective numbers identified above each bay. Jameson's team was making some last minute adjustments before the final practice sessions. Harry and Kyle hunched over the hood making notes on their clipboards and checking temperatures. I contemplated leaving. I couldn't handle Jameson saying the word piston stroking again, once was enough.

Tony checked air pressure readings while Shane and Josh made sure everyone had the tools they needed.

"That's not the right one," Jameson handed them the correct splitter and Aiden took it and gave Spencer the other one again. "If you do that again, I'll punch you in the face."

"According to the rules, that's the right one," Spencer pointed to the splitter on the floor next to the rear tires. "Both of you numb-nuts are wrong."

Jameson sighed and shook his head.

I kept watching them humorously from the doorway for about three more minutes before Spencer noticed me.

"There you are," he turned to face me. "Tell this asshole he is wrong."

"I'm not getting in the middle of this," I wrapped an arm around Jameson.

"Okay, get your hands off so that we can finish this." Aiden pulled us apart. "You still need to test this out."

"Save me," Jameson mouthed as Aiden pushed him to the other side of the car.

I waved and went back to the motor coach to find Emma.

Daytona was such a large venue that it was easy to get lost, as I did. Inside the race loop there was the garage area that I just came from. The restricted garage area is where all the cars are kept and worked on throughout the race weekend.

Once again, you needed a special pass to walk through that area.

NASCAR was big on passes that's for sure. Everywhere you walked someone was asking to see your pass.

I learned quickly there were three types of passes. You needed either a hot pass which took you everywhere; a cold pass that took you to the garage area and pit lane prior to the race; and then there was a one-time walk through pass that allowed you a walk through the garage area prior to the race and then you were kicked out.

This weekend I was sporting a hot pass so I was able to go everywhere. This is how I got lost.

I saw the sign for the garage area sign-in. So, basically, I went in a loop. Then I saw the NASCAR hauler. NASCAR hauled around a big red hauler that acted as the official's command post as well as sign in for the drivers. This was also the principal's office as I referred to it. If a driver was ever summoned to the NASCAR hauler to discuss his actions, this is where he went.

I spotted Tommy's orange hair when I walked past the hauler and sighed in relief. Before I could get to him, a tall raven-haired woman approached me.

"Excuse me, Miss?" she asked with a smile that I was sure I would only ever see on a Dallas Cowboys cheerleader.

"Yes," I replied and kept walking toward Tommy.

"Are you Jameson Riley's girlfriend or something?" she glanced down at the pass around my neck. "Oh, you have a paper pass."

"Paper what?" I looked down at the pass blowing with the slight breeze in the air. "And, no, I'm a friend." My eyes focused on the pass around her neck, it appeared to be a hard plastic pass with the words press across it and her picture.

"Oh, okay," she said with another smile and then walked away as if nothing happened.

Tommy spotted me and ran up to me. "Hey, I thought I lost you."

"You did."

"Who was that?" I glanced behind me and saw her walk inside the media center. "She said I was paper."

"Paper?"

"Yes, paper."

Tommy looked more confused than me at what occurred until Emma found us.

"Hey," Emma smiled. "Jameson is looking for you."

"What's paper?" we both asked Emma noticing the pass around her neck was hard plastic like a credit card.

"Oh, some passes are temporary, so they're paper. They only get you in this weekend. If you have a hard pass, like this one," she held up her own pass. "It gets you into every race. You don't have to stand at the credential sign in. You just walk right in after you show them the pass."

That made sense but why did that woman make a big deal out of it. I was only here for the weekend. Naturally, I wouldn't need a hard pass.

"Is that some sort of status thing among women?" I asked Emma as we walked back to the compound area.

"I've heard it is. Most of the drivers bring girls to the races and give them paper passes for the weekend. Some of the wives and girlfriends around here believe you're a pit lizard with a paper pass until you get the hard card. They're expensive so obviously a driver doesn't give them out to just anyone and the owners are the only people authorized to purchase them."

"So, she thinks I'm a pit lizard?"

"Pretty much," Emma replied like this was no big deal. I was less than pleased but when you think about it, I guess I was kind of a pit lizard these days. Sure, I wasn't trashy like most of them but I didn't follow Jameson around like he was the mythical idolized creature he was to me.

Pathetic.

Tommy laughed when we entered the motor coach mumbling something about me being a pit lizard. He didn't get to finish his sentence though. My fist in his stomach ensured that.

I did a little more observing into those so called "Plastic Passes" the women seem preoccupied with and found out there were two different passes as Emma indicated that either the wives or the girlfriends wore. If the woman was a permanent fixture in the driver or team's life, they got a hard plastic pass that had their name, picture and what team they were with.

I wasn't sure what that chick wanted when she asked me if I was his girlfriend, but these last few days I was constantly being asked if I was his girlfriend by the other driver's girlfriends and wives. I gave them all the same answer, "Just friends" when I wanted to say "Touch him and die."

The whole pass thing was enough but really, did everyone have to constantly ask and then stare at the paper pass around my neck? Talk about a bunch of superficial bitches.

The night before the race, Cal fixed dinner for everyone. Grandpa Casten had showed up, which made life interesting to say the least.

Jameson had been a little fidgety with everyone around, but he did well as long as I held his hand. This didn't go unnoticed by old Casten either when he elbowed Jameson in the side as we sat outside the motor coach.

"Taken the old dermal tool to the crankcase, huh?" he smiled nudging his shoulder with his elbow.

I choked on my beer, as did Jameson. "Grandpa!"

"Hey, back in my day ..." he paused for a moment and then smiled. "Hell, I don't remember what I was going to say."

"I think that's enough whiskey for one night there, dad," Jimi suggested removing the flask from his hand.

Casten grumbled for a moment but I think he knew he'd had enough. He was starting to fall asleep.

"What a de ... mal?" Lane asked looking up at Jameson who was holding him.

Jameson snickered. Alley slapped the back of Grandpa's head and

Spencer choked on his beer. Little Lane was almost three now and asked *lots* of questions. Last night, he asked Jameson why he was an asshole. Jameson had no response I might add.

"You know back in my day ..." he paused again. He did that a lot and most of the time he forgot what he was even saying when he spoke again, as you can see.

"When was that, Grandpa? Back when they still had wagons?" Spencer smiled knowing damn well this would piss him off. "Now tell me, when was it that they went to a rubber tire as opposed to wood?"

"Oh, fuck you, Spencer," he grumbled and then spilled his coffee down the front of his clothes.

"Are you nervous?" Emma asked Jameson while he fumbled with the hem of his shirt. He hadn't said much tonight and, as of yet, no one had called him an asshole.

"No," he answered adjusting Lane, who had fallen asleep on his lap. "It's just a race."

"You're lying," Spencer chuckled across from him. "It's the Daytona 500. You're probably shitting your pants right now."

"Like I said ... it's just another race," Jameson replied stretching his long legs out in front of him to lean back in the camping chair he was slouched in. "And, I'm not *shitting* my pants."

He was constantly being asked the same question these last few days. *"Was he scared?"*

I knew he wasn't. Nervous? Maybe, definitely not scared though. The thing you had to understand about Jameson was that, yeah, he would show nervousness to a point, but once inside that car, he was stalwart and fearless. Inside the confines of a race car, he was a different man. Sure, he had a few sides to him, what person didn't, but the best part about him was that he never changed. Jameson would always be Jameson. I never doubted that.

You saw it all the time when someone comes into money or makes a big career move, they change. They suddenly become this distant version of themselves that no one recognizes. With all the success that Jameson has had over the years, he never changed. I heard some say, "Well, he's not approachable either."

The thing was, he has never been approachable, so why would he be now?

Money and fame didn't change that. He'd always been that way.

Old Casten had fallen asleep by now and Tommy and Spencer were making fun of the drool coming over his beard. "That's so disgusting," Tommy laughed.

"You boys better stop messing with him," Jimi warned shaking his head. Jameson didn't get his wicked temper from just anyone. Jimi could be quick tempered at times, but Casten, he put a bull to shame, much like Jameson.

"He's asleep." Spencer defended. "He ain't gonna know."

Glancing around, I noticed an awful lot of people had gathered outside his motor coach. I don't know how some of these pit lizards managed to get into the compound area where the drivers were, but I had a feeling some of them sweet talked the officials at the gate. Anyhow, a few had made their way over to Jameson's motor coach while we continued to make fun of Casten and his drooling.

They were slutty leeches and I had no doubt they were only looking for one thing. Jameson.

One of them seemed taken by Jameson and kept moving closer to him. No one paid any mind to her, as it was usual for pit lizards to be hounding him. So there she was, about a foot from him, and I didn't want to steal her thunder or Tommy and Spencer's, so I discreetly took a seat across from them next to Jimi. Undoubtedly, I was not thinking when I did this.

Steal her thunder, you fucking idiot!

Maybe I wasn't breathing enough and the supply of oxygen was being diverted again.

Alley came by, picked up Lane from Jameson's lap and walked inside the motor coach out of the line of fire.

She didn't like all the women hanging around and I couldn't blame her. We were a bad enough influence on little Lane. I usually didn't care for these pit lizards either but I'd had a few beers by then and was contemplating how to entertain myself at Jameson's expense. This was dangerous territory by the way.

About ten minutes later, the girl noticed me and introduced herself. "I'm Sabrina," she said, extending her free hand, the other wrapped around a glass of wine.

"I'm Sway," I said, politely.

"Well, that's an interesting name."

"Yeah, I guess it is."

"How did your parents come up with that one?"

"I was named after the Rolling Stones song *Sway*."

"Oh," she smiled glancing over at Jameson like he was a piece of meat she was ready to tenderize. "Are you two ...?" she pointed back and forth between Jameson and me when he smiled.

"Oh no, no, he's my best friend. We're tight." I winked at her and pounded my fist to my chest as though I was from the hood or something.

Jimi's shoulders were shaking as he tried to control his laughter along with Spencer.

Jameson wasn't impressed.

I might have only continued this because Jimi was so entertained. It had been a while since I saw him laugh this much but, then again, I was drunk.

I could only assume I was doing this because I'd been drinking because if he demonstrated any interest in her, I would have shit my pants at how incredibly stupid this was.

Jameson turned his head in order to avoid eye contact with me, and her.

Sabrina had a confused look on her face and opened her mouth to say something when I jumped in.

"Don't worry, he doesn't have a girlfriend."

Jameson coughed loudly and stood. "Actually—"

I interrupted. "He's shy."

What is wrong with me? It's like I'm trying to get her to come on to him?

She turned to Jameson about the time Jimi excused himself, his face red from suppressing his laughter.

Tommy and Spencer were glancing in between Jameson and me probably wondering how this was going to end.

"I think being shy is adorable," Sabrina said, in his ear.

Jameson glared in my direction.

I didn't know what to do, so I winked.

Ordinarily, I wouldn't have done this but the fact that I knew he wouldn't be interested made it that much funnier to me, and everyone else ... aside from Jameson.

"I'm getting hungry," I announced standing. I was also starting to panic and ready to bolt at any moment.

Jameson shot up out of the chair.

"I'll go get you something," he said, with a venomous look on his face. "Since we're tight and all."

He came back a few minutes later and tossed a bag of chips in my lap before sitting back down in the only open chair, next to Sabrina, glaring in my direction.

"So, how did you two meet?" Sabrina scooted closer to Jameson.

I started to make something up when Jameson jumped in.

"We met when she got out of rehab," he picked up my drink and sniffed the red cup. "Goddamn it, Sway. You shouldn't be drinking!" he pointed his finger in my face. Then he shook his head, took me by the elbow, and said, "Let's get you away from the temptation."

Well, that did not turn out in my favor. Why does it always backfire on me when I'm trying to embarrass him?

Tommy, Spencer and now Emma, were laughing so hard they could barely stand.

I shrugged out of his grip. "Asshole," I muttered.

He pushed me inside his motor coach. "What the fuck was that?"

I couldn't help it; I once again panicked and started giggling. I panicked because I wanted to tell him, I was testing you to see if you'd leave with someone. Did I tell him that?

No, hell no.

He was not pleased by this and, if possible, became even angrier and left.

"It was just for fun!" I yelled after him still giggling. He flipped me off.

Nice going, asshole. You pissed him off.

After composing myself, I walked back outside the motor coach to find Jameson had left, Tommy chatting it up with Mariah, and Casten sound asleep.

I strolled around the compound looking for Jameson when I spotted him at Tate's motor coach talking with him and Tate's teammate Austin.

When I approached them, Jameson, with his arms crossed, shot me a look like "don't you even think about embarrassing me," so I didn't. I figured I'd done enough for one night.

"This is Tate Harris," he gestured toward Tate. "You guys met at the Chili Bowl, right?"

I nodded shaking hands with Tate and then turned to Austin.

"And this is Austin Yale," Jameson said. "He drives the number thirty-two car."

"Nice to meet you guys," I said, smiling. Jameson surprised me and slung his arm around my shoulder pulling me next to him when Austin made small talk with me.

The gesture didn't go unnoticed by Austin who moved on to converse with a group of girls gathered near Tate's motor coach.

So, he doesn't leave with pit lizards, he makes out with me and shows possession? Can you say confused?

Jameson and I left soon after that to walk back toward his motor coach. I could tell a lot was on his mind. My first plan to distract him backfired and in fear that his tenuous good mood would get worse, I decided to talk racing and asked him if he thought his car could win tomorrow.

"Yeah—probably," he said, disinterested. "It's fast in the draft." I thought he would say more but he shrugged his shoulders.

By the time we got back to his motor coach, Casten was on his second wind and had his flask back. I wondered how Nana kept up with the old bastard at home.

Spencer's eyes lit up when he saw us. "Natalie asked me how you were."

"Spencer, not now," Jameson groaned.

Natalie? Who's Natalie? I thought to myself, my stomach churning. Here I was, moments ago, provoking a pit lizard and now when another one is mentioned, I become terrified.

I'm such a girl that it is revolting.

"She left her phone number," Spencer snickered handing him a napkin. He crumbled it up and tossed in the garbage next to the food table without looking.

"Who's Natalie?" I asked hesitantly taking a seat. I tried to play it off like I wasn't interested but I'm sure it didn't appear that way, my face was reasonably flushed and prickly feeling. I could feel the heat radiating off myself.

"No one," Jameson replied sitting next to me, his thigh touching mine. "She's no one." When he finally glanced over at me his look of honesty had me once again questioning his intention.

"Oh, come on, Jameson," Spencer teased. "You remember her ... the freaky one from California?" all the guys started laughing as Spencer wiggled his eyebrows.

"Can we not do this right now?" Jimi took a drink of his whiskey shaking his head. "I don't think I want to hear any of this."

Nancy, Emma and Alley had left with Lane leaving me and the guys standing around.

"I agree," Jameson nodded and I could tell that he was trying not to look at me again. "Let's not talk about this right now."

"What are you doing, Grandpa?" Spencer asked when Casten slapped the back of his head.

"That's for being stupid," he remarked in disgust. "Jameson obviously doesn't want everyone to know who he's been align boring." Jameson shot out of the chair and locked the door behind him.

I'm sure by then Jameson was second-guessing my presence here.

Later, as in two hours later, he let me in because all my stuff was in there but he didn't speak to anyone the rest of the night and insisted I sleep in his bed with him.

"Aren't you mad?" I asked timidly crawling into bed with him.

"Yes, I'm mad but I'm also tired," he grumbled tweaking his pillow the way he liked it. "Now, let's sleep. I'll be mean in the morning."

"Oh, goody."

He was quiet for a moment before leaning over and pulling me against him. His hand cupped my cheek. "Don't do that to me again. I don't want those girls," his voice was drowsy, his eyes half closed. "I don't want them." He repeated and then let his eyes close, his beautiful thick lashes cast shadows over his cheeks. I ran my fingers over the rough edges of the stubble of his jaw.

So he slept and I contemplated what I had done. I don't know why I tested him like that and if he would have left with Sabrina, I would have cried. I could only presume I did this out of pure curiosity. I wanted to see if he was presented the opportunity to leave with a girl, would he take it. During our summer, he would have left with her. Now, he didn't seem to show any interest in other women. He glanced, but that was as far as he ever took it and never anything more than a quick glance.

Did this mean something?

I watched him sleep for an hour. He was on his stomach clad in a pair of black boxer briefs, his arms curled under a pillow. Every muscle in his body was sculpted to perfection and I wanted to run my tongue over every inch of the exposed skin, tasting him. I wanted to rape the poor boy for Christ sake.

Grumbling to myself, I turned the other way in fear I'd attack him. Images of our hot make out session the night I arrived replayed in my mind.

The way his body felt hovering over mine. The way his camshaft felt against me. I knew he wanted more, it was obvious but he stopped. He always pulled away, collecting himself before things advanced, which made me think he didn't want this. That might have been why

I tested him with Mariah.

That was stupid, Sway.

"I know," I told myself.

It was around four in the morning before I finally fell asleep, but even then I dreamt of all the things I wanted to do to him and all the things I wished like hell I had the nerve to tell him.

My alarm went off a four-thirty that morning, not that I wanted it to, but I wanted to get in a run before all the pre-race activities began. I knew I shouldn't run before a race, but I had to clear my head and that was the only way I knew how.

Hoisting myself up, I turned off the alarm and sat on the edge of the bed in my motor coach for a moment before getting up.

I tried to remain quiet, though Sway pissed me off last night with her little stunt, I still didn't want to wake her. It was my own fault anyway. If I would have been able to control myself more often, I wouldn't have to deal with these stalkers. Yeah, my family loved to remind me of it nowadays but it was my own fault.

Sway was curled up next to me, her hands next to her face made her almost look angelic, almost. If you knew Sway, you knew that was not possible for her. Even though she pissed me off, I couldn't *not* sleep next to her.

Being away from her for nearly a year, I had to be next to her. With the way our schedules were, what if I didn't get to see her for another year? I couldn't take a chance.

She looked so peaceful, her dark hair fanned out over my pillow. I watched for a moment her chest rising and falling with each breath. Her beauty was remarkable and had me wanting to hold her, so I left for my run.

The sun was beginning to rise over the track creating an array of light cerise across the sky. My favorite time of the day to run was at sunrise because it was the beginning of a new day, usually nothing had gone wrong yet and the possibilities were endless.

My iPod played Metallica loudly in my ears and I was able to tune everything out, tried at least. The scattered motor coaches and camp trailers in the infield passed by me in a blur as I picked up the pace of my run. I chuckled to myself as a few fans waved their hands in the air from where they were perched up on the roofs of their camp trailers. It's hard to believe people willingly got out of bed this early.

I pushed myself harder, my feet hitting the asphalt faster. I envisioned the race in my head, my lungs burning painfully from the exertion. I tried to keep my thoughts clear, but they shifted back toward last night and the hounding pit lizards. I never thought Sway would instigate them, she knew how I felt about that but, then again, her words never matched her facial expression. I saw something behind her eyes I never saw before, compunction.

Once I made one lap around the track, I headed back to my motor coach to find Sway and Cal up already making breakfast. Simplex had delivered an array of apparel to us yesterday so I wasn't surprised to see Sway wearing a black hooded sweatshirt with the logo plastered across the chest with matching sweatpants that appeared to be at least three sizes too large.

She was adorable.

"Are you in a better mood, asshole?" was Sway's way of greeting me when I walked through the door.

"Hmm," I contemplated taking a few strips of bacon, chewing slowly. "That depends," I grinned looking down at her.

"On what?" Her brow furrowed as she ate her own bacon from the plate on the counter.

"You apologize for last night. That *was not* funny."

"I thought it was funny," Cal said loading a plate for me with his egg white mixture that I loved so much and wheat toast. "Your face was priceless."

"You don't have to do all this, Cal," I chuckled as he poured some orange juice for me. "Driving my motor coach around for me is enough. You don't have to feed me, too."

"I enjoy cooking, Jameson. It's no problem. And I've seen you make toaster waffles before." His head tipped in the direction of the black smudges on the wall where I'd caught the toaster on fire last season.

Ignoring him, I turned to Sway, her mouth full of scrambled eggs. "Are you going to apologize?"

"Oh, yes," she grinned and sat up straighter. "I'm so sorry," she mocked.

Before I could tell her that the apology needed to be better, Alley was knocking on the door. "Jameson, you got a sponsorship meeting in an hour."

And so it begins.

On race days, you had a sponsorship meeting where you basically kissed their ass and told them how you were going to win the race for them. Then you usually had about an hour of signing autographs, a team meeting, more autographs, the drivers' meeting, more autographs, introductions, more autographs, and then the race.

I left after finishing breakfast to meet with Melissa at the Simplex hospitality tent. When I returned I walked toward the hauler to see Sway standing there dressed in a red dress that I wanted to rip off with my goddamn teeth. I hoped like hell she wasn't wearing that all day.

Kyle was saying something to me but I gave him a blank expression until he punched my arm.

I was distracted, that was unmistakable, but in my defense, she was revealing a lot of skin. Skin I desperately wanted my hands, mouth, and any other body part on just to feel her against me.

"I've got a new rule," Kyle leaned against the hauler crossing his arms over his burly chest. "No girls in your pit."

"Why would you do a thing like that?"

He smiled. "To keep you focused."

"That's not going to happen," I watched as Sway strode away with Emma and Alley back to the motor coach.

"She's something."

"Yeah?"

"She's all fast-talking and brusque, wouldn't want to mess with her."

"You have no idea," I rolled my eyes. "You should have seen what the little shit did to me last night."

"I heard. Spencer told me."

"Of course he did."

Kyle and I headed for the drivers' meeting after that and met dad there. Usually the only ones allowed in the meeting were the driver, crew chief and owner and, if you were late, you started at the tail end of the field.

On the way there, I hoped that I placed well in points next year. For one, I wanted to, being the single-minded guy I was and two, it's a long ass walk anywhere you went. The team haulers were lined up by the previous year's points, being a new team, guess where are hauler was parked?

Yep, last.

I listened in the drivers' meeting but lost interest. NASCAR ran their meetings more formally than your average dirt track but they were still boring to me.

Everything changed each year in NASCAR. Rules change, drivers change, sponsors change, the schedule changes. I changed. I was no longer the kid I was when I began racing. I was now a Winston Cup driver with a multi-million dollar contract backing me.

You know back when I raced USAC and Outlaws and I thought I had stress trying to become Jameson Riley. That's laughable now. I had no fucking clue what responsibility was then. I'm not sure I did now but I had constant reminders of how I could easily fuck things up. I still didn't want to be known as Jimi Riley's son and with him now being the car owner, I still got that from time to time, but it was getting better. In NASCAR, I was making my own name.

I thought about the times racing quarter midgets, telling myself that I'd be happy if I was racing full-sized midgets or mini sprints.

Once I was in those, I wanted full-sized sprint cars, and so on.

Now I was at the top of stock car racing, what did I want?

I wanted to win. I wanted to win that Rookie of the Year and I wanted to win the championship. No driver had ever won the championship in their rookie season, I wanted to.

On the way back to the hauler after the drivers' meeting, I ran into Darrin.

Apparently, I bumped him in practice and he felt the need to express his distaste for this. It went something along the lines of, "Hit me again and I show you how that wall tastes."

I never did respond to him as fans began to surround us. I learned to pick my battles with him and it wasn't worth it right then.

I'd gotten a lot of advice from other drivers on racing in the Cup series but they failed to mention what happened when you got out of the car. Suddenly reporters, fans, and, in my case, other drivers I'd pissed off at some point during the race were in my face.

I couldn't offer them much, even in interviews I never knew what to say but when other veteran drivers would approach me and ask why I came down on them or took their line, I didn't know what to say to them. I never did it on purpose but I was an aggressive driver out there. I didn't think about what happened when I got in the pits until Dad pulled me aside a few days after the Budweiser Shootout.

"Jameson, be careful," he told me offering his wisdom. "You don't want to piss off the veterans or any driver for that matter. You never know when that guy may be your boss or teammate."

That made sense to me, it did, but I also didn't want to be the driver who was pushed around. Finding a middle ground was hard but I took to guys like Bobby and Tate and watched them closely on how they dealt with it. Bobby was reserved and shied away from the media at all costs but Tate was in their face telling them what he thought about this or that.

Clearly, I was going to need to do some more observing.

During the duel 125 races, I got bumped by Doug Dunham, a veteran driver on the series and ended cutting a tire. I ended up getting my spot back but it still pissed me off that he did that, it's not like he didn't know I was there.

I had never been afraid to tell someone exactly what I thought of them but I wasn't exactly in the place to be telling a veteran driver that he had no right to bump me in the corner. Ordinarily, I had no problem with this, but with Dunham, he was a veteran driver in the sport and had a hell of a lot more clout than I did, so I bit my tongue and simply gave him a head nod after the race. I think he knew I wasn't happy about it.

When I reached the hauler prior to the team meeting Kyle was laughing at me, once again, as Sway strode past me still wearing that damn dress.

Fuck me. Believe me, I wanted her to.

Looking away, I was starting to get irritated with all his laughing at my expense and really, I was having a *hard* time. I didn't need him laughing at me.

"We've made a collective decision," he teased elbowing me. "You need to tell that girl how you feel."

"Well, let's say hypothetically, maybe, let's say probably that I feel that way ... it doesn't change anything."

"You never know," he smiled. I didn't want to be talking about this with Kyle, but over last year he had become a good friend of mine.

If I couldn't talk about this with him, who could I?

"What will it change? I don't have time for a relationship," I sighed. "Do you know when the last day was that I had time for myself?"

"But you had time for pit lizards."

"That was different."

"How so?"

"Well, for one, they don't want more. They only want sex and there was no strings attached."

"Maybe that's what Sway wants."

I had no response for him, I'd never thought about that but, then again, why would she want something like that?

Or did she? She didn't have time for a relationship either.

Well, that throws a wrench in my thinking, doesn't it?

Diffuser - The bodywork at the rear underside of the car that controls the underbody airflow as it exits the back of the car.

I couldn't stop thinking about what Kyle suggested and the thought wasn't absurd to me. What if she didn't want strings attached? What if all she wanted was what we had and nothing more?

We were friends, yes, but what if we could have something more without the complications. It was noticeable the sexual attraction was there between both of us, so why not?

I wanted to be alone with her for a few minutes before the race started but when I returned after my interview with SPEED, she was gone.

It didn't take long to find her though as she still had on the red dress.

Prior to the start of the race, Sway was sitting on the edge of the wall looking over at the steep banking of turn one.

Her eyes were closed as the slight steady Florida breeze blew through her mahogany locks that cascaded down, framing her beautiful face. It was as though she was in a trance. She gripped the concrete barrier with her fingertips and her legs dangled off the side as she slipped her flip-flops on and off.

I stared at her, my gaze locked on her as she smiled back at me. It was as if a spotlight was stuck directly on her and that's all I noticed, soft and warm, like an aura. In the raucous of the grid behind me, I could only see her; pure tranquility.

For a moment, I was held rooted to the ground as I felt the immediate draw to her. A magnetic pull drew me toward her, the feeling hot and caustic in my stomach. In a daze, I began to make my way to her, pushing through the mass of reporters.

I paused a few feet in front of her; the warm humid air blew across my face, dampening my skin. The smells of the engines and exhaust mixed with the warm moist air. The hums of racing was all around us as it always was but that's what defined us, defined me and defined her.

It's what brought us together and always brings us together. Neither of us knew a life outside of racing.

Sway tilted her head to the side, inhaling a deep breath before giving me a heavily lidded smile.

I moved closer settling down next to her throwing an arm around her. I wanted to move my mouth next to her ear and tell her how much I missed her and that she was the sexiest thing I'd ever seen, but instead I caved, flustered and simply mouthed, "Hi," when she looked over at me. She answered me with a smile. Her eyes sweeping into mine and I was lost in their beauty, swimming in the deep pools of green.

I wanted to say so much to her right then but I didn't, terrified she wouldn't want to hear it.

I don't know why it has taken me so long but I guess it took me a while to figure out what I wanted or what I wanted to say, more importantly, how to ask for it. You don't realize how important your choice of words are at times. It can either go smoothly or you can fuck it up with one wrong word. With so much weighing on that, you can see my hesitation here.

So I remained quiet and stared out at the grandstands teeming with fans.

It wasn't long before Alley found me and I was being whisked away to driver introductions while Sway went with Emma.

Yet another time where I could have said so much but didn't. With so much weighing on my words, I froze.

One of the coolest things about the morning of the race, besides having Sway around, was seeing my grandpa walk out onto the grid with me. His only comment was to poke fun at my driving suit that was plastered with logos.

"You look ridiculous," he told me laughing.

Then he took a long pull from his flask that I was sure was filled with whiskey, his drink of choice.

"It's just a driving suit, grandpa. It's designed to keep me safe."

"Son, I used to dip my britches in starch to keep from catchin' on fire ... things have advanced since my day," he sighed and smiled at me. "We didn't see the dangers of what we were doing, until it was too late."

I knew what he meant by that and that was his way of telling me to be safe. In all the years I'd known him, he'd never said anything nice to me. I wasn't sure how to react.

Much like Uncle Randy, Grandpa is only remotely approachable when he's drinking, otherwise he's a cold-hearted prick but he was also my grandpa and, like any other Riley, hotheaded.

"Well, doggoned, Jay, I knew you'd be here someday."

"Thanks, Grandpa," I signed a few autographs from some fans who approached me.

Grandpa lost interest with driver introductions and ditched me for my Nana who showed up as well. I wasn't nervous until I became aware that my entire family had shown up.

Bobby must have sensed this and nudged my shoulder standing there waiting to be introduced. "You all right, kid?"

"Yeah," I nodded looking down. "I'm fine."

Bobby had figured me out and knew when I was quiet. I didn't want to be bothered so he made small talk with Tate and Austin standing behind us in line.

I only wished the reporters knew how to figure this out, too.

All the reporters seemed to ask the same question, "Can you win?"

I don't think of it as can I win because the answer will always be yes. Obviously, I could win, I have many times. Their questions should be, "Could I win the Daytona 500?"

And even then, my answer would be yes.

Watching all the pre-race activities going on around us, I found it entertaining that my first Cup race was the Daytona 500 because it was the biggest event NASCAR has.

It's like the Super Bowl, but bigger.

Glancing around, I saw Darrin glaring in my direction. Rolling my eyes, I looked away. He still wasn't happy about my frivolous meeting with Mariah, his girlfriend.

She had approached my car about an hour ago before I found Sway. I looked away but she got right in my face and pushed her tits against my chest and said, "I'm Mariah," her hand sliding down my arm caused me to flinch back at the unwanted contact. "You should find me after the race."

"I don't think so," I had replied immediately.

"Oh, come on, Darrin will never know."

I removed her arm from my shoulder and handed the autograph back to the fan standing in front of me. "I said no," I told her sternly and walked away.

Darrin caught me before I made it too far.

"What was that about?" his tone was sharp and accusing.

"What?"

"Don't *what* me you little shit," he snapped stepping closer. "Stay away from Mariah."

"Mariah is it ...?" I arched my eyebrow gesturing toward her with a tilt of my head, "... was all over my dick back there. You should tell her to stay away from me," I snapped at him continuing to walk away.

"See you on the track, Riley," he taunted after me.

"Fuck you," was my response.

That rivalry racing USAC hadn't diminished.

Anytime you put forty-three drivers together some are going to rub you the wrong way and others become your guide. With Darrin, I guess with me implying his girl was on my dick, he wasn't going to be my guide.

Andy Crockett, another rookie driver, rode around the track with me in a Ford truck after being introduced. After a few minutes of silence, I struck up a conversation with him.

"Good luck today," I told him waving to the screaming crowd. He did the same which seemed to ignite them in some thunderous roars.

Andy was a quiet, respectable guy and he always seemed to choose his words carefully. You never saw him getting into it with other drivers, it wasn't his style.

"I'll need it with you racing," he grinned.

Andy had grown up racing stock cars so it surprised me he would think I was better, if that's what he was thinking, maybe he wasn't.

"Nah, you'll do fine."

"You say that now but ... it's different out there. You know that."

"Yeah, but I've also seen you drive. You didn't get here by accident."

He smiled. "Oh, I know that."

By now, we were back around the track and heading back to the cars before he leaned over and shook my hand. "Good luck."

I grinned. I absolutely believe that I'm insatiable, more so than most other racers but that's also how I've gotten this far in a callous sport, one that doesn't leave room for uncertainties. Most don't understand that burning need to be better but those around me, the other drivers, they did and I was surrounded by them.

After driver introductions, I headed back to my car to wait for the opening ceremonies to begin and to see Sway.

Interview after interview, reporters were constantly asking me how I was feeling, if I could win, what I did last night to prepare myself and what I ate for breakfast ... It wasn't until I walked over to get into the car that I started to grasp how big this all was. There were pre-race festivities, music, you name it, NASCAR had it and I was somewhere in the middle.

I watched Jameson closely that morning, wondering when he'd break. I couldn't believe the tout surrounding him and his team. It was unreal. The media was pegging him as a champion already anticipating him winning today.

The thing that got me was they wanted to put this mold around him, like he was some cookie-cutter driver conformed to be a certain way, the way they wanted. But that wasn't Jameson, not by a long shot. He was one of the truest, most exciting drivers around but he wasn't fit for a mold.

They compared him to the younger version of Doug Dunham, a veteran driver and I saw the similarities but, then again, Jameson was inimitable. He knew he could never please everyone so he didn't try but he could please himself, and that's exactly what he did.

I stood there next to his car leaning up against the side. I ran my fingers over the Grays Harbor Raceway sticker he had stuck on there.

"Reminds me of you," he whispered in my ear and smiled. His nose skimmed through my hair and I could have sworn he sniffed as he did so.

"It does?"

"Well, yeah, what else would it remind me of?"

"Racing," I said, shrugging.

"No, well yes it does, but I think of you when I look at it."

Alley approached us with Lane on her hip. Lane jumped into Jameson's arms. "Uncle Jay!"

I laughed. There were only two people who could get away with calling him Jay, his Grandpa (he refused to say his whole name) and Lane, who couldn't pronounce it yet.

Other than that, if you wanted him to answer you—you had better use his full name. I had always loved his name so I called him by it. I also knew how much being called Jay bothered him, so I didn't.

"Good luck—good luck!" Lane chirped bouncing in his arms and then wrapped his arms tightly around his neck for a hug. I couldn't think of a better hug than one willingly given by a child.

Jameson tickled his sides. "Thanks, buddy. Are you going to watch me?"

"Yes, yes, yes!"

He was at the stage where he repeated everything twice. I blamed this on grandpa Casten. Lane loved him and, in turn, when Lane said anything Casten, who was hard of hearing, responded with, "What?"

Now little Lane was in the habit of repeating *everything*.

"That's my little buddy," Jameson replied spinning Lane around.

Alley took Lane back as they got the announcement to get inside the cars. My heart started pounding hard, my stomach tied in knots. I never got nervous when he raced but I did now because this was so much bigger than dirt tracks and though you could easily get hurt racing sprints, these speeds were higher. That frightened me for about half a second before my mind caught up with me and I reminded myself that I couldn't think about what could go wrong. I had to trust that nothing would and know that he did this because he loved racing, that's all that mattered ... he was happy.

I kissed him on the cheek before he got inside the car. He had other plans and openly kissed me on the lips in front of everyone. I wasn't sure how to reply to it, so I kissed him back trying to guard any feelings I had from the hundreds of thousands of people watching.

Strapping myself into the car, that's when the nerves *really* hit me.

I'd never been claustrophobic before but with the panic attack I was having, it seemed like the only clinical definition that came to mind. I'll admit, I was intimidated by this race at first. If I screwed up the first time I raced full-sized sprint cars, no big deal.

Now if I screwed up at the Daytona 500 that was *different*.

It was Sway's words that calmed me, as always.

She leaned inside the car, her grin wide. "Just remember, it's just like any other race."

Anyone could have said that to me and I'd still be freaking out, but because it came from my best friend, my counterpoint, it meant everything. It wasn't just any race though. I kept telling people it was, but it wasn't.

It was bigger than those races like the Chili Bowl or Turkey Night. It was the Daytona 500.

Kyle did exactly what a crew chief should do, he kept me steady. Before I fired up the engine, he leaned in and said, "Just treat today like another practice session. That's all this is."

That was exactly the right thing to say to me. It reminded me of all the training I had and all the test sessions we did. The important thing was to remain focused and smooth.

"You guys copy?" I tapped into our radio frequency.

"Yep, we gotcha bud," Kyle said. "Fire it up."

"Aiden, you copy?" I adjusted my helmet and flicked the ignition switch, pulling my visor down. I usually ran tinted tear-offs on my helmet to aide in the changing of the sun by the end of the race. Now I didn't have to worry about mud on my helmet but visibility could be as harsh with the sun here at Daytona.

"So you're coming up on pit lane. Check your speed," Kyle said. "That will tell us your pit road speed."

"Where's the line? I don't see it."

I peered to the left, with the limited visibility I had, I tried to find my pit and the line for pit road. These were things I wanted to find before I was speeding down pit road in attempt to make it on and off quickly and without spinning myself.

"How can it be more obvious?" Aiden laughed. "Spencer is standing on the wall."

I glanced toward the wall to see Spencer waving his arms over his large egg-shaped head. "Pace car is at pit road speed."

I checked my RPMs. "Four thousand second gear."

"Let's have a good race boys," Jimi said. "It's a long day, stay *focused.*"

"Lights are out, comin' to the green," Aiden announced and my mouth was suddenly dry and that panic attack feeling had returned.

My entire body seemed to be jittery and uncontrollable, I couldn't understand the feelings I was having so I took a few deep breaths, pulled on my belts once more and gripped the steering wheel. I was lined up fourth in the second row behind Tate on the outside. Guess who was beside me?

Yep, Darrin, in the number *fourteen.*

"Watch you're shift," Kyle said. "Harris lags back on the restarts, you saw that in the Duels."

The problem with lagging back on tracks like Daytona was that you have forty-two other drivers setting pace by your car when you're the leader. When you lag back, so do they. Sure, those first few cars see what you're doing but the back half can't. It's an easy way to get smashed into from behind on the restarts. The last thing you want to do is get bumped when you're trying to get up to speed and miss a shift or something similar, or worse, hit the car in front of you and smash in the nose. Aerodynamics were everything at Daytona, mess that up and you can pretty much forget your chances at the front. Not only will you not be able to cut a hole in the air needed to draft but you won't be able to draft with anyone else. You need to be able to get right on them, the nose of your car pushed against their bumper so if you're car is torn up, the contact will be harder to reach and maintain.

So there I was trying to anticipate Tate's jump on the line. I shifted into third when we came out of three.

Aiden came on the radio. "Keep coming, flag's in his hand. Keep coming ... keep coming ..." Tate did what I expected, lagging back but I had it timed and came off the line as strong, if not stronger. "Green!"

"Inside on the line, even with you," Aiden guided me into the first turn.

This went on for a few laps; Darrin remained on my inside while I worked with Tate on the outside. His car was stronger than Bobby's though so we were able to keep in front of them. Once the green flag had dropped, the nerves left and I felt like the same fixated single-minded guy I always was on the track. I led a little and did exactly what Kyle had told me to do; I stayed focused and smooth. As with any temper sensitive track, conditions began to change after about a hundred laps and the adjustments we made didn't help.

"Can you see the air?" Kyle joked at one point.

"I can barely see the fucking gauges," I mumbled, "let alone air."

That got a chuckle out of both Aiden and Kyle.

I was trying desperately to hang on to my vibrating race car. I was fine in the draft but once I would get in front my car slid all over the place. It was apparent I wasn't going to be leading this race. No matter what we changed, the car wouldn't tighten up and there is no scarier feeling on a track than when you reach speeds near two hundred and your car's loose.

It never got better but I managed to hang onto it and pull through with a third place finish. Again, I wanted to win but it goes back to forty-two other guys wanted a win as well.

During the cool-down lap, Kyle picked then to provoke me. "What's the matter, couldn't hang onto it?"

"Obviously I did hang onto it," I snapped. "I finished, didn't I?"

"Well, yeah, but third ... I thought for sure you could win."

"If you keep talking, I'm pretty sure I'm going to kick your ass when the race is over."

"You're all talk."

"Really? You're gonna test me, huh?"

"Let's see what you got, Riley," Kyle teased laughing.

I wasted no time at all in climbing out of that car to kick his ass. I failed to realize that Kyle was the size of a black bear so my chances of victory were slim.

The media got a kick out of the wrestling match, as did the rest of our team. It's not like two guys pushing and shoving each other in the pits wouldn't go unnoticed in a sport that thrived on temper tantrums from drivers but this was all in good fun.

In the end, we laughed and he responded with, "I knew you had your hands full out there." He slapped the back of my head and then bounced on the balls of his feet like a boxer then ruffled my hair. "You're an awesome wheel man."

After our childish wrestling, the rest of the team congratulated me as did Sway.

Reporters were standing by but I didn't care at that point. I wrapped my sweaty exhausted arms around her, pulling her against my chest tightly.

"You stink," she giggled but made no attempt to pull away.

"I just raced hours in a car that was well over a hundred degrees inside."

"You still stink ... but I never said it bothered me."

"In that case ..." I grinned wickedly wiping my face against hers. I could feel the wetness on my face when I got out of the car so I knew damn well that was now all over her.

"Jerk face," she snapped pulling away from me. I let go this time.

"Jerk face?" I chuckled brushing a towel over my neck.

"Yes, I said jerk face."

It was hard to respond after that as the media was wanting their interviews from the rookie driver who placed third in his first Cup race.

I gave them what they wanted, interviews, one cookie-cutter interview after the next. Finishing in the top three meant another round of press known as the Contenders Conference. This was a press conference held for the media to ask questions of the driver, crew chief and car owner, as though the interviews after the race weren't enough. If you haven't noticed by now, I did not like interviews.

After the race, most of the team had flown back to the shop to get ready for California next week.

My family decided to go to dinner together since it was rare that we were all in the same city at the same time. We ended up going to an Italian restaurant in Daytona Beach by the name of The Cellar restaurant.

A few of the other drivers told us it was good and usually wasn't crawling with pit lizards as were most of the bars in the area.

When my Grandpa decided to tell stories about me learning to be potty trained, I wasn't impressed. This is exactly why I did not enjoy my family.

I was not laughing, not even a little when the subject turned toward an obsessed fan who asked if I'd sign her inner thigh. Ordinarily, I would have said, "Sure, why not," but something about my mother and Nana sitting at the table struck me as not the time or place for that sort of thing.

And don't think Spencer didn't notice because he did, laughing like the idiot I always knew him to be.

There are a few things I've learned about Jameson over the years.

He never sits still, and I mean that. Even while sleeping he's constantly moving. Sleeping next to him is similar to sleeping with an overactive toddler.

He is always thinking of racing. He can be having an in-depth conversation with someone about politics (not likely, but you never know) and that boy is thinking of racing in some form, I guarantee it.

And, lastly, if there is a lastly, his phone was always ringing.

His phone rang twenty-six times during the two-hour dinner we had with his family. Not once did he answer it, but the fact that he couldn't actually have a meal without someone wanting something was evidence that this lifestyle was trying.

I could tell it bothered him when his Nana was speaking and she could hear the vibrating of his phone. He finally got to the point that he simply turned it off.

It was nice being around his family again and they did nothing but make me feel like one of them. I will say that his Nana made me feel a little strange when she caught me in the bathroom and said,

"Oh sugar, when are you going to marry that handsome grandson of mine?"

"Spencer is married already, Nana," I told her squeezing her.

I had a problem with squeezing elderly people. They were so damn adorable to me that I squeezed them. And they were fragile. I should be more careful.

Nana pulled back, her pretty-blue eyes glazed over. "My dear, I'm speaking of Jameson."

I knew that. I was buying my time, thinking of a lie I could tell her.

"Uh ... I ... shit," was about all I could articulate at that moment as Emma barged into the bathroom.

She started fussing with Nana's curls, so I made my getaway.

When I got back to the table, Jameson was ready to go. I think he was exhausted for one and Casten was on his fifth whiskey. To save himself the brunt of embarrassment, we left.

Cal drove the motor coach to Rockingham and Jameson was tired so all of us just ended up getting a hotel room for the night in Daytona Beach. I had to fly out in the morning so this was my last night with him. Thoughts of raping the poor boy came back when we ended up in bed together.

With Emma, Alley, Spencer, and Aiden in the room, I wasn't able to. Not that I would have. I'm pretty chicken shit when it came to this but the idea was still there.

I think he had some of the same ideas because when the lights went out, his rough calloused hands explored, as did mine, and we ended up kissing again and doing some more touching. The thought wasn't lost on me that we were both extremely horny and needing relief.

But with each other, that was dangerous.

Our friendship was intense and to cross a line like that whether there were feelings involved or not, was dangerous. Jameson never showed anything but sexual attraction toward me though and it didn't appear emotional.

His hands moved quietly, his kisses were soft and tender and before I knew it, I was crying and he knew it.

In a gesture attempting to comfort me, he dragged me against his chest. I could still smell the lasting hints of the race on his skin, mixing with the salt from tears. My body shook in silent sobs as he held me tightly. We never spoke but we also never let go all night. Regardless of my crying for no apparent reason, I never felt more tranquil as I did with him.

Being with him this week made me realize how much I missed him.

I missed the warmth of his body against mine at night. I missed the smell of him, methanol and dirt. I missed watching him race in person and the exciting thrill I got seeing him take the checkered flag or doing a burnout. I missed the smell of the car after a race. The way *he* smelled when he finished a race and would pull me into a hug before he showered, albeit covered in sweat, I didn't mind.

I missed being in the pits, wondering where he was and then he appeared out of nowhere to put his arm around me, the warm feeling I got, feeling like I belonged to him.

Nothing was the same without him.

I missed my life.

But mostly, I missed *him*. I missed my life with him. It had been nearly a year since we last saw each other. A year since I'd felt the impossible strength of his arms wrapping around me and the way his warm touch felt against my skin and that's why I was crying.

Now that I was finally here, surrounded by him, I didn't want to let him go again.

I knew why Jameson wanted me around. I was like a security blanket for him as he was for me. We knew each other and that was comforting.

The next morning, it was hard to say goodbye.

"You sure you want to leave?" he asked in a voice mixed with annoyance and uncertainty.

The only reaction I had was to nod and look at the pavement because I couldn't speak. I couldn't look at him either. If I did, and I saw the sadness, I wouldn't leave and I needed to.

He took the first step forward so I followed and wrapped my arms around him, fisting his shirt in my fist. "Promise me something, Jameson?" I whispered against his shoulder and he nodded his head. I slowly pulled away from him, and without trying to hide the tears falling from my face, I finally looked up at him. "Promise me you won't change."

"I will always be who I am right now, Sway," he whispered leaning in again.

He pulled me into another hug and I let myself get lost in him. His scent, the way his concrete arms felt around me, and the way his heart sounded with my head pressed to his chest.

"Thank you," he whispered against the top of my head.

I pulled away from him. "For what?"

He put both his hands on my face and looked down at me. "I couldn't have done any of this without you."

I wanted to cry, worse than I already was.

After a brief hesitation, I smiled and shook my head. "You did this yourself."

"No, you did. I race the car but you are what has kept me focused on what I wanted."

"Well, then, I believe I should be getting half your salary then," I teased.

"Now you're getting greedy," he laughed shoving his hands in his pockets. "Will you call me when you get to Seattle?"

"Yes," my voice was shaky again. I knew I needed to leave but my feet wouldn't move.

I think he sensed I couldn't do it on my own so he walked me to the car, but before he let go he paused and stared at me for a long moment, his voice cracked when he spoke. "I ... I will miss you, honey."

I started crying again.

Eventually I did make it on the plane and home but it took a lot of convincing from Emma, who flew back with me. It was Jameson's orders, or punishment, depending on how you looked at it.

JAMESON

For ten years I wondered why this girl owned me the way she did. When I thought of myself, I thought of Sway and always would. The night before she left, I held her as she cried and I realized exactly what I'd been denying for ten years. I loved her.

There was so much I could have said when she left the next morning. But I was too blinded by the loud thumping in my heart, the pain of letting go, to say it. This girl owned me, owned my thoughts. I drove myself insane thinking about her but still, I couldn't fucking say it.

I knew she was leaving, I knew she wouldn't stay but what scared me even more were the words that were on the tip of my tongue when I kissed her goodbye ... I love you.

I wanted to say it. For the first time in my life, I wanted to tell someone I loved them, and she was my best friend. I didn't love her as a best friend either, no, it was so much more than that.

It was the kind of love that you felt in your bones; deep blinding love.

I'd be lying if I said I was okay, I wasn't okay with this. I was far from being okay.

If I asked her to stay would she? And if she did, then what? Could I handle it if she felt the same way?

No, I probably couldn't because I could not offer her what she needed. I wasn't in the position to.

Then I thought back to what Kyle said. That maybe she didn't want the relationship, maybe she wanted the benefits. If my siblings hadn't been in the hotel room last night, I'd have been tempted to ask her for more but they squashed that idea. But then again, I wasn't ready to ask for what I wanted in fear she'd agree.

With the pressure put upon drivers now, we had little time for personal relationships.

Sure, other drivers were married and had girlfriends but they also traveled with them and were able to maintain a sense of normalcy that we wouldn't have. I wasn't in the position to offer her that and with the track she wasn't in the position to give that up.

So where would that leave us?

I had no answers and didn't have time to think of answers the day she left. I wasn't even able to drive her to the airport because I had to leave her at the hotel that morning to catch a flight to Charlotte.

By Tuesday, I was like a zombie and had a day to myself before heading to Rockingham for the next race. At home, I had time to think or beat myself up, whatever way you want to look at it.

I heard my alarm going off that morning, knowing I had a team meeting to be at but I ignored it, hoping the awful buzzing would stop.

The sun coming in through my window hurt. Rubbing the grit from my eyes, I cracked my neck, relieving the pinching as my neck painfully throbbed.

I sat up slowly realizing that my phone was also ringing and I reached over to get it.

"Hello," my voice was groggy.

"Where are you?" Alley demanded.

"Huh?" I looked at the clock. It was nearly six in the morning. "In bed. Where the fuck else would I be?"

"Jameson, you are supposed to be at the shop this morning."

"Oh, I don't think I'll make it," I shook my head, still trying to wake up.

"Yes, you will! Spencer is coming to get you."

Before I could tell her no, she hung up on me. I scrambled to focus but I couldn't.

I couldn't think or see straight. Probably because they only thing on my mind was Sway and the tears in her eyes when she left.

"Damn it," I hit my head on the floor. "Why does it have to be this way?"

I got up from the floor and into the shower. Still, all I could think about was Sway.

I managed to make it to the team meeting an hour late, but I made it. Dad wasn't too excited about me being late. After a few choice words, well yelling, he told me if I was late again he'd be taking it out of my pay.

I had the rest of the evening free and did what I always did to get my mind sedated ... I drank.

Three hours later, I was sitting at the bar in my parent's kitchen drowning my sorrows in a country song. I felt like a country song and then started to wonder who would sing it.

Staring through a whiskey glass, I saw the reflection of my brother walking back toward his room carrying Alley in his arms. I didn't even bother to look up, just grabbed a bottle off the table and popped a couple of pills.

Squinting at the bottle I attempted to read the label. It was probably wise to know what the fuck I took with whiskey.

Vicodin. *Nice.*

I need pain relief and lots of it.

Avoiding my thoughts, I turned the bottle around and read off the side effects out-loud. "Blurred vision ... I'm okay with that. Difficulty breathing ... already had that. Dizziness, drowsiness, mood changes ... *hell*, how is that any different from my usual personality?" I asked myself.

No one answered, so I answered myself. "It's not any different," I continued reading, "Severe allergic reaction may occur." I squinted at the bottle.

Allergic reaction meant itching. That did not sound okay with me. "Anxiety, fear, unusual tiredness."

This shit wasn't going to make me feel any better so I turned the bottle of whiskey around to see if it had side effects ... none listed.

I gladly accepted the side effects though, anything was better than what I was feeling right now.

Emma pushed me off the chair when she walked into the kitchen. I didn't bother to get up but tripped her as she walked by.

"You brought this upon yourself, asshole."

"Get out," I rubbed my forehead.

"No, I live here, too." She sat down to annoy me some more. "Why are you so mopey?"

"Get out!" I yelled and then calmed myself a little. My dad would skin me if he heard me yelling at Emma like that and I was sure he was somewhere within the huge house. "Please, leave me alone."

I think Emma knew me well enough to know when harassing me wasn't a good idea and now was one of them.

I stared at my phone, wanting to call Sway, wanting to hear her voice.

Would she want me? Would she love me in the ways I loved her?

After the entire bottle was empty and I was searching the liquor cabinet for more, in walked Spencer.

He looked at me contemplatively, I think. I did just drink a fifth of whiskey, he could be flipping me off for all I know.

"You know," he began and I groaned.

Why can't people leave me be?

"You can't expect her to know how you feel if you don't tell her."

"I thought you were leaving for Rockingham tonight?" I growled slamming the cupboard door closed when I couldn't find any more alcohol.

He shrugged taking a seat at the breakfast island. "No, I'm going with you and I'm hungry."

I found another bottle of whiskey stashed above the fridge, pulled it out and dropped down next to him. "Here."

"I said hungry," he looked at the bottle of Vicodin. "Combining alcohol and narcotics, huh?"

"Fuck you."

"I don't get you." He shook his head and took both my bottles away from me. "You fuck around for years avoiding what you feel for her. Then," he emphasized this by throwing his hand in the air. "You finally pull your head out of your ass and realize you love her but you let her leave again."

I slammed my fist down on the granite not wanting to hear the truth but then I gave up. My head fell forward. I'd barely admitted this to myself, why would I want to hear someone else say it?

"You told me, too." I pointed out trying to emphasize he aided in my sleeping around.

"I didn't think you'd listen!"

"Fuck you, Spencer," I ripped both bottles from his hands and stumbled to my room.

I couldn't feel much of anything within an hour so I guess the intended use worked.

I knew I loved her, took me long enough to discover that but how could I actually have her?

I could cut the strings and let her go, let her have the life she deserved with a man who could provide her that.

It was a good idea except it didn't give me her and it was impossible for me because letting go was not an option.

What else was I going to do, tell her how I felt?

Nope. That would be far too easy but the hardest part would be hearing she didn't feel the same. It also goes back to finding the right words to say. I usually never faltered for words, but with her, when everything depended on those words, I couldn't form them.

The next morning Tommy stopped by, he was going to Rockingham with us and then back to Elma for a few weeks. I wasn't in the best mood, I did drink a little, okay a lot, but that wasn't why. I still had no clue what I should do. I was sick of feeling like this.

For a guy who had been so vigilant on one mission for so long, I was thrown a curve ball with this newfound discovery that me, Jameson Riley, loved someone. That *someone* wasn't just anyone either, she was my best friend.

"Did you change out the coil springs in Justin's car for the torsion bars?"

"Yeah, I changed the gears, too."

Tommy tried to get me to talk but I remained silent most of the morning as we loaded the sprint cars for Greg West, the driver of the transporter for my sprint car team. Once that was finished, we had about four hours before we had to leave. The nice thing about the next race being in North Carolina was that we didn't need to fly.

"You know," Tommy began, kicking my leg as I slumped on the couch in the race shop. "I'm tired of you being so stubborn."

"I'll be sure to drop your comment in the I-don't-give-a-fuck pile later."

"That's harsh."

"It was meant to be harsh."

He dropped down beside me on the couch. "I'd offer you a beer but I think you had enough to drink last night."

I was silent so he kept talking. Tommy never knew when to shut up. "Did you talk to her last night?"

I shook my head. "I fucked up, Tommy. I don't know how to fix this."

"Let's go fishing."

"What? Why? I don't fish." How this had anything to do with my problem was what I wanted to know.

Tommy jumped up from the couch. "Well, when my dad said he fucked up with my mom, we went fishing so he could think.

Not understanding his logic, we went fishing until we had to leave.

Tommy being Tommy didn't allow me to think, he talked the entire time.

"If you don't stop talking, I will throw you out of this fucking boat."

"I'm just saying."

"Saying what? You're not making any sense and I thought I was supposed to be thinking."

"We are."

"No, you're talking. I'm listening. Well, not really." I dangled my fishing pole in the water but I had yet to catch anything and doubted I would. I knew nothing about fishing. Honestly, the sport seemed boring to me. To fish you needed patience, something I didn't have.

"Well, then think ... I shouldn't have to tell you to think."

"Stop talking."

I did think a little but it confused me more. I had no idea how to tell her what changed in me and I wanted more from her. Could I ask for more but still remain friends with her?

I wanted to know that if I couldn't have her in all the ways I wanted, that I could at least have her in some way, the only way I thought she wanted me, and that was physically. It would be ideal. We wouldn't have to worry about all the hassles of a relationship that neither of us had time for.

Grid – The starting order of cars, as determined by qualifying position. The cars line up on pit road prior to the race in qualifying order; this is referred to as the grid.

In racing, I honestly believe there comes a point in your career where everything changes. People stop seeing you for you and start seeing a NASCAR driver. From that point on, nothing is the same and everything you thought you knew about fame, was nothing at all.

That was the feeling I got when I arrived in Rockingham, North Carolina.

And I will say that was also the point when I stopped and thought is this what I wanted?

The answer was absolutely. I had no doubt I wanted this. I wanted to be the best racer I could be and I was on my way to that. I could see the light.

I still had no idea what I wanted out of my personal life but all signs pointed to Sway in some form or another. Telling her would be the hard part and wasn't something I could do over the phone. When we spoke on the phone, I never led her to believe anything had changed. This wasn't something you tell someone over the phone or in a text. What would it say, "Oh, and by the way, I love you more than anything. Can we have sex and remain friends because I'm a dumbass and can only offer you that?"

Yeah, I wasn't about to say that over the phone.

So instead, I focused on what was important, my career. It wasn't hard to do either, everywhere I looked, someone was pulling me in a different direction.

That week was my second start in a Cup race and I loved the track. Rockingham Raceway is a one-mile oval track with twenty-two degree banking in turns one and two and twenty-five degree banking in turns three and four.

Back in January, we tested for two days here so I knew a little about what to expect but testing is different than a race.

I qualified for the pole and set fast time in both practice sessions. In happy hour, I raced in race-trim and wasn't surprised that the car was awesome. I could drive in hard and the car wouldn't slip.

By the time race day arrived, I couldn't wait for the race but I was a little apprehensive that Doug Dunham was starting on the outside of me.

The pressure put upon drivers to win is tremendous and I knew Doug was feeling that. The longer they go without a win, the more rattled they become with shoddy performances and it reflected in their driving. Usually where a driver would say, "Nah, that's just not worth it," when trying to make a hole where there isn't one, Doug made them.

I was confident in the power with my beast that once the green flag dropped, my car was up to the challenge.

You always hear people talk about their first Cup career win. They remember everything about the win to when pit stops were to who they passed and years later, can recount them just the same as they did that day.

I can't say the same. I was all over the map emotionally in that race. I fought Doug hard to pass him and then Andy Crockett was up in the mix for a while as was Tate and Bobby but, like I said, that car was awesome.

By the time there was ten laps to go I had a two-second lead over

Tate and was feeling like I was about to win my first race.

When the checkered flag waved and I did win, I was silent. I didn't know what to say. I had won my first Winston Cup race, on my second start. Fortunately, for me, I was in the car with a helmet over my face so no one could see the emotion I was feeling.

Not only was there a point when you realize nothing will ever be the same, but there is also a point when you think to yourself, "I can do this."

You know you're different.

Every professional anything whether you are a race car driver, basketball player, football player ... you realize at some point in your life that you're different and have something more to offer.

I always knew I could do it and that I had talent when it came to racing, but after Rockingham it became real because not only had I moved from one series to the next but I'd won in different divisions now.

All doubts I had about this being what I was meant to do, vanished with that win. Here I was a dirt track racer from the Northwest and I won a NASCAR Winston Cup race, on my second race. I knew I was different.

I had an understanding for the way things worked with a win and the post-race activities from the Busch series. It was fairly similar with Cup.

By the time I left the track and was able to grab some food, I was exhausted and not up for any company. Alas, Spencer, Aiden and Tommy went with me. I was okay with that but I wasn't okay with Spencer's behavior that night.

I wasn't paying attention to what was going on around me as I was busy texting Sway.

I read her last one before looking up. ***I'm so proud of you!***

Aiden nudged my shoulder. "It was nice meeting Sway last week," his blush said it all.

Sway and Aiden met in Daytona and Sway's way of introducing herself to him was asking if his carpet matched the drapes. Aiden had this rich golden blonde hair that you would think belonged on Malibu Barbie, not a country boy from Alabama. Sway also asked Tommy this when she first met him as well. Although back then, we were only thirteen when we met Tommy, it sounded funny coming from a thirteen-year-old girl, but that was Sway. She could make any man blush if needed. It's an acquired skill and she had it mastered.

Smiling, I took interest in the commotion at the table. As you know, Spencer was into playing practical jokes on *everyone*. As usual, I was his target this time.

My newfound fame, was also that target. I don't know how many times we'd walk into a restaurant and we'd be quietly enjoying our meals when my model citizen of a brother would stand up in his chair and shout: "Hey, look, it's Jameson Riley!"

I just won a race that most of these bystanders had watched. This wasn't the ideal situation for a number of reasons. I didn't joy the herding fans, I hated attention, and I was fucking hungry. Leave it to Spencer to ruin my evening.

"Spencer," I seethed. "You better run for your motherfucking life!"

This did nothing to Spencer, who relished in finding new and innovative ways to annoy me.

After Rockingham, I swear the pit lizards multiplied by the thousands. I'll never understand why pit lizards went to the fanatical extreme ways they did, but I'll tell you something else, I was not okay with it.

It never failed. I'd walk out of my motor coach and they'd be waiting. How they got into the private compound where the drivers stayed was an entirely different issue I'd be talking to NASCAR about. They card me every time but these girls get free roam because they have tits?

I don't think so.

And it wasn't just in the compound that I found these fans hounding me. The garage area was just as bad.

What irritated me to no end were the people who would get mad when I wouldn't sign something for them when passing through the garage area.

In my defense, would you stop to sign something when you were at work?

Probably not.

When I'm in the garage, walking to my hauler or working on my car, I'm working. My mind is focused on what I'm doing, not on the fans.

Getting an autograph out of *any* of these drivers in the garage area is slim and depended solely on their moods. We're working and most forget that.

On my bad days, if a fan wanted an autograph, I wasn't doing it. They barely got so much as a glance in their direction.

If I was having a good day, they might get a head nod, but still, I was in the garage working on my race car. I wasn't there for them. And I rarely would sign anything in the garage area.

I'm not there to be their Hollywood star.

To show you the extent these fans would go, one even broke into my motor coach.

After the race in Las Vegas, I entered my motor coach wanting to relax but no, there was a girl inside.

"What the fuck are you doing in here?" I snapped, slamming the door hoping to startle her.

The girl spun on her heel with excited blue eyes, my harsh tone did nothing.

"It's really you!" she squealed and launched herself in my direction. She was insane and that's putting it lightly. I ended up calling the police just to get her to leave and even then she wouldn't budge.

The police laughed at me, actually laughed that I couldn't get this girl to leave my motor coach. I was terrified and, if possible, even more disgusted at their lack of concern.

This happened to me more times than I could count but what was unacceptable to me and had me calling the police, was the fact that she felt the need to explore, in my underwear drawer.

"Oh, Jameson, I'm like your *biggest* fan!" she kept telling me while I yelled at the cops to get her to leave. I didn't want her to be my biggest fan because frankly, this sounded odd and certainly couldn't be good at the way she implied "biggest."

When she finally left with a police escort Spencer had his laughs, as did the rest of my team. Fucking assholes.

I was completely fine until some grinning son of a bitch of a police officer said, "Do you feel violated?"

He was mocking me but I rose above their childlike maturity to this serious criminal offense and refused to comment.

For one, I wasn't about to give my asshole teammates *any* ammunition, and two, I was too tired to put any energy into this.

Instead, I turned on my heel and went back in my motor couch, locking the door. I had a feeling this would be happening a lot and was not excited about that.

I called Sway that night before we left to go back to Mooresville and then it was off to Atlanta, a track I absolutely loved.

I still hadn't led her to believe I loved her. I wanted to tell her every time I spoke to her but I couldn't.

Another thing that came with winning was rivalry with other drivers. You don't notice it until you are suddenly competition for them. Competition for guys like Darrin.

The rivalry with Darrin Torres seemed to escalate with each race.

By Las Vegas, he'd spun me on pit road for no apparent reason other than just being a dick. Being new to the series, I didn't want any enemies, so I let it slide.

When Atlanta rolled around the following week and he did it again, I wasn't as quick to let it slide. As a matter of fact, I was hot after that, partly because my car was smashed and the other was that I hit Bobby in the process.

There was nothing I hated more than ruining an unsuspecting driver's day. And, more importantly, my teammate's day.

After I tagged Darrin's bumper, he knew I was pissed. As did the media and NASCAR. I was tired of his shit of spinning me on pit road and those cheap shots he'd been taking at me lately.

After the race, when I pulled up beside him, he had some hand gestures and I had a few words.

Everyone kept asking us why we hated each other so much but you have to remember our days go all the way back to when we raced in the USAC series.

It didn't matter what way you looked at it, we weren't friends and we were never going to be.

This left me having some words with him after that Atlanta race.

Once I was standing in front of him, I had no idea what I wanted to say, only that I was pissed. Unfortunately, before I could tell him exactly what I thought of him, the NASCAR officials were separating us.

I wasn't going to give up though. He needed to know I wasn't one of those guys he could push around.

It just so happened that our motor coaches had parked right next to each other so that's when the real fun began.

Again, he got right in my face and I hated confrontation. Sounds ridiculous coming from a guy like me, I know, but you also have to understand I only wanted to race. All this other shit, I could do without in a heartbeat.

"You need to watch where you're going," he told me, after a string of profanities I could barely keep up with. "You drive like an asshole out there." He was also animated while doing this and he looked as though he was an air traffic controller.

Just to ensure I got my point across, I said. "Fuck you!" and intended on leaving it at that.

I felt the need to make my point since he made his when he spun me on pit road, twice.

Once again, NASCAR separated us and I left after that before I got myself in hot water with my dad.

I decided to leave it alone that night and left without saying anything more.

The races seemed to be flying by and every week it was a new track, different city but the same bullshit with Darrin.

Most of the tracks I'd either raced on in the various USAC Divisions or Nationwide Series, but a few like Bristol and Martinsville I'd never been to so that was entertaining to watch, but when you add someone constantly seeking out trouble with you, it makes it difficult to keep track of the bigger picture. The bigger picture being that this was my job now.

Once the series rolled around to Darlington in March, our rivalry didn't end and he took us both out in the first few laps when he cut down on me going into turn one.

We managed to piece the car back together only to blow a left rear tire with thirty laps to go.

The following weekend in Bristol, he slammed me into the wall on a restart. Well, I had enough and bumped him entering turn three.

It wasn't my fault he couldn't correct it, right?

If only NASCAR saw it that way.

Later, as I expected, he came into my hauler. Where I come from, the bullring tracks, you enter someone's hauler after the race and that meant one thing: You were looking for trouble.

Neither of us acted as we should have, but he did throw the first punch.

The thing about a fight at the track was that NASCAR race was officials were all around. We only got a few punches thrown before they intervened.

After that altercation, the nickname, “Rowdy Riley” was born.

Not that I disagreed that I was “rowdy” but I came to realize that NASCAR fans, and reporters were different from the fans at the bullring tracks. They remembered everything.

Every interview I did from that point on, they asked about the rivalry with Darrin, trying to keep it in everyone’s thoughts.

I wasn’t exactly thrilled with the media and their lack of concern for my privacy so when the FOX Sports reporter asked me after the last ten reporters asked the same thing, I took my frustrations out on him when I slapped his recorder out of his hand and then kicked it under the hauler for good measure. If they wanted Rowdy Riley, they had him.

“You know exactly what happened,” I yelled over my shoulder in response. “Watch the goddamn tapes!”

It wasn’t exactly what I should have said but I was pissed and I said what I felt.

This wasn’t the first time Darrin and I tangled with each other, surely it wouldn’t be the last. But for reporters to constantly instigate it, that was crossing the line.

My dad, as the owner, wasn’t pleased with this relationship I’d formed with Darrin.

“You can’t keep this up,” he would tell me. “I can’t keep compromising with NASCAR and Simplex.” His voice would rise to nearly a shout and then he’d calm down. “I’m a new owner Jameson. A new owner with no clout and you are not helping me.”

I backed off Darrin after that. I didn’t intend to cause problems for my dad. He had enough. He didn’t need his asshole of a son causing more.

I liked to think I backed off completely but still, like any red-blooded, twenty-two-year-old male, I had my moments.

“Jameson, you need to realize that this is not about talent. Yeah, you’ve got that but it’s not *just* about talent,” my dad told me over dinner after the race in Martinsville. “If you want to be a champion,” he tapped his index finger to the side of his head. "It's up here. This sport is just as equally challenging mentally."

I nodded. I didn't exactly want to argue with anyone at that point.

He continued. "There's a fine line between aggressive and overly aggressive. Too much one way and you'll find yourself in the wall ... *or* in the NASCAR hauler in your case."

Again, I nodded.

"Have you talked with Sway lately?" he asked picking almonds from his salad and tossing them on my plate.

"Yeah, before we left the track after I met with Gordon."

Gordon Reynolds, the Director of Competition, was the warden for NASCAR. If you got in trouble, you saw him.

"And, she said?"

"Nothing really," I shrugged. "She saw the fight on ESPN and wanted to make sure I was all right." I took a bite of my hamburger.

"Are you?"

"Yeah," I straightened my posture chewing slowly. "Why wouldn't I be?"

"You're different when she's not here."

"How so?"

"You're just different, almost like you're running on seven cylinders."

"I feel like I'm running on seven."

"Is the pressure getting to you?"

"Yes and no." Even though I knew how I felt about Sway now, I wasn't ready to tell anyone. "I guess I wasn't prepared for how political and commercialized everything is."

"Kind of makes racing the weekly races appealing, huh?"

I smiled taking a drink of my iced tea in front of me. Pouring ketchup on my plate, I began to dip my French fries in them. "You don't see how demanding the sport is until you're in the middle of it."

"You don't have to do it. You know that right?"

"I do know that ... but it's what I want. Even if it comes with all this and more ... I still wouldn't change anything."

"You know Simplex said they may be interested in sponsoring your outlaw car. Justin is doing good. Little shit beat me the other night."

"He is doing good," I agreed. "So is Tyler. I was thinking—" My phone buzzed just then causing me to jump backward. Jimi laughed when my drink spilled on me. It was Charlie calling me, which was strange. He never called these days.

Worried something was wrong with Sway, I rushed through the rest of dinner and called him in private.

"Charlie?" he answered on the first ring.

"Jameson?" his voice sounded tired and worn, similar to the way I felt.

"Yeah, it's me."

He was silent for a moment before speaking. "I need to speak with you, in person."

I was on the phone with Wes, the pilot of our private jet, to arrange a flight immediately. Charlie wouldn't ask me to come unless it was important.

Tear offs – A plastic cellophane strip attached to the visor of helmets designed to improve vision when racing on dirt.

The afternoon light streamed in through the windows of their living room, the rays of light reflecting off the glass in front of me as I sat there in their living room and though it was familiar to me, it was different. It was different because I wasn't with Sway and different because Charlie needed me. Hell bent on keeping me away from Sway for the last few years, now he wanted me to take over ownership of his track, which would mean always being around Sway.

"Why do you want me to take over?" I asked.

I couldn't understand why he would offer up something like this. Grays Harbor Raceway meant everything to him. He turned a struggling track into a thriving business that drew hefty crowds each week.

Charlie was only forty-one so how could he possibly be thinking of retirement? My next thought was why me? Why not Jimi or, hell, even Mark, who ultimately contributed too much of the track's success. Either man would be better, so again, why me?

He hesitated for a moment, selecting his words carefully.

"I have brain cancer," he paused as his eyes met mine. "They're treating it aggressively but ... it's cancer. Metastatic brain cancer and there's not a lot of hope right now."

I felt the blood drain from my face as my heart pounded desperately, pumping the blood toward my heart.

He wasn't serious, was he?

After a moment of nerve-wracking silence and hyperventilation, I choked out, "Cancer ..."

My mind raced to process everything he said. I thought of Sway's mom and the way it affected her and now this? How could one person be subjected to so much and how much more would she be asked to endure?

"Are you sure?"

"Yes," he said and added one request that was deeply important to him. "Don't tell Sway."

"When are you going to tell her?"

"I'm not ..." —he sighed hanging his head— "She doesn't need this ..."

"She needs to know!" I demanded jumping to my feet. For the first time in my life, I wanted to punch him. For a minute, I hated him with everything I had.

Then the blinding anger subsided and I thought about what he meant to me, and the fact that he was dying. His affliction was evident in his shattered features. I could tell it wasn't that he didn't *want* to tell her and for a minute, I understood him completely because by not telling her, he was doing unerringly what I was doing.

Here was a man standing before me who had aided in my career. If he hadn't allowed me to race sprints before I was sixteen, I would have never gotten the experience I did. How could I hate him for helping me so much and for protecting her in the same ways I was? Though we were both fighting two entirely different battles, I think we understood each other more that day than ever before.

"I know you love her in your own way." He was standing by the door as I was leaving. "Just don't hurt her, please."

I didn't answer, not because I didn't want to but it didn't strike me as a question, it was more of a demand.

Charlie said he would wait until he found out more from the doctors before transferring the title but the outlook was not promising. I left there with only one thing on my mind, Sway.

I looked down at my phone, my fingers traced over the numbers. What would I even say to her? I couldn't tell her, not when he specifically asked me not to.

I had to see her though. There was no other option.

Unsure as to whether or not my schedule would allow me to, I called Alley. "When do I have to be in Talladega?"

"Tomorrow afternoon by four," she told me sounding annoyed. "You don't have time to go off and play, Jameson."

"Goddamn it, Alley, I didn't ask for your fucking advice!" I shouted. "I asked you what time I needed to be there." I was tired of everyone acting like they knew what was best or that they felt the need to control me. "I'll be there by four."

"If you're not, I'm not making excuses for you this time."

"I never asked you to," I hung up after that and called Wes.

He answered after a few rings. "Hey kid, where are you?"

"Well, I'm in Olympia now. Can you take me to Bellingham tonight?"

"I thought I was taking you to Dega?"

"You are but I need to make a stop for the night."

"No problem," he replied without hesitation. "I'll see you in two hours."

I thought a lot waiting for Wes.

What would I say to her? I couldn't tell her about Charlie and telling her how I felt seemed just as hard. It goes back to that thing I couldn't get over, with so much weighing on my words, how do you know what to say and how to say it?

It was Tuesday night and I was doing what I usually did, studying for my Wednesday marketing class. I had a final next week that I wasn't prepared for. I couldn't wait for graduation, for one. I hated being by myself and I hated school, but mostly I was all alone and that's what was depressing.

I thought of Jameson a lot. I watched every race faithfully and cried like a goddamn fool when he won and I wasn't there. Every interview was taped and every newspaper article was clipped and stored in a box under my bed. I was damn near a stalker and it was disturbing even to me. But I loved him. It took me a while to understand *why* I loved him; it was gradual but surging.

I loved him more than I ever thought possible and with it came a world of passion, confusion, intensity, desire, jealousy, heartache, and comfort. I wanted to tell him how I felt, make him see that we would could be great together but he didn't need that right now. He needed to focus on his career and I'd be another distraction he didn't need.

"Ugh," I groaned and once again opened my internet browser to read the latest news on him. NASCAR's website had a picture of him holding Darrin by his racing suit, both still clad in their helmets in what appeared to be a heated conversation. I hadn't read this article so I opened it.

Tempers flared in Texas

Around lap 72 of the Samsung Mobile 500 race, Jameson Riley, driver of the No. 9 Ford Simplex and Darrin Torres, driver of the No. 14 Wyle Products Chevy got into each other setting off a chain reaction followed by a red flag. That wasn't the only red on the track as these two got out of their cars and were involved in a major shoving match that resulted in Riley nearly taking a swing until NASCAR got involved.

> When asked by a television broadcaster what was said Riley replied with, "I wanted to see what his problem was. He seems to have a problem with me *every* week. I'm sick of it." Torres later said that if the incident was his fault he would take responsibility and apologize but he felt it wasn't. "It wasn't my fault," Torres told ESPN after the altercation, "I have little respect for that kid. He comes in here and acts like his daddy is going to bail him out of everything. He's got talent, sure, but his aggressive disregard out there gets him nowhere." Both team owners said the incident was unfortunate but refused to discuss it any further as they have appealed the fines handed down from NASCAR.

Engrossed in my own personal Jameson daze, I nearly pissed myself when my phone began vibrating on my desk beside me. I noticed Jameson's picture pop up on the screen so, of course, I nearly broke my neck trying to get to it in time. The line was static and muffled with a loud humming.

"What's that noise? Where are you?" I yelled attempting to talk over the noise.

"In an airplane," Jameson yelled back over the humming, "will you pick me up at the airport?"

"What airport?"

"The one in Bellingham,"

"There's an airport in Bellingham?"

"There better be. That's where the plane is heading," he laughed. "I can only stay for one night."

I was silent. Was he serious? Why would he fly all the way here for one night?

"Are you going to come get me or shall I call a cab?" he pressed impatiently.

"Yeah ..." I cleared my throat. "I'll come get you."

We hung up and I panicked. I had no idea where the airport was and why in the world he was flying here for one night? Google had quickly become my guide for navigating but I was left with my paranoid thoughts and Google had nothing to offer me on that one.

I printed out directions from the internet and then headed out except there was one problem with this, two really. First, I am navigationally challenged beyond belief. I once got lost going to Jameson's house when we were kids. I might add that he lived down the street.

So then you add the weather, yeah, I was having a hard time. I shouldn't have been surprised living in Washington, guess what the weather was doing this fine spring evening?

Raining.

And not just any kind of rain, it was the kind that you couldn't see a foot in front of your car or, in my case, the red dragon. Also, I didn't have windshield wipers.

So there the red dragon and me were, trying to find the Bellingham International Airport that wasn't much bigger than a landing strip you'd see in Playboy. Oh, and it was pouring. I might have said this already but this added to the confusion because I was almost certain I was night blind. I needed all the assistance I could get at night.

It didn't help that my mind was more focused on what Jameson wanted flying all the way out here for one night. Was something wrong with him or someone in his family? Something had to be wrong. He wouldn't come out here for no reason, would he?

I tried calling him a few times to tell him I was lost but as luck would have it, I had no cell reception. Staring at the screen it flashed "No Service" and I snapped.

"You stupid piece of shit with no service!"

It then sprung up with the message "Call Failed" again.

Tossing the phone in the seat, I continued to navigate. I think most of my frustration was fear of why was he was coming here?

I could understand maybe if it had been a while since we'd seen each other, but as it was I saw him not more than a month ago.

When I finally found the airport, much later than I should have, Jameson was laying on a bench outside of the closed airport asleep.

He looked adorable.

I felt like an asshole having gotten lost so many times. I'm sure it didn't help that I was speeding to try and get here and I missed a few turns due to poor handling and visibility as a result.

When Jameson awoke, no longer adorable, he was not amused with my tardiness and replied with, "Nice of you to hurry."

I also wasn't amused because in order to navigate accurately the last leg of my adventure, I ended up sticking my head out the window. I now looked similar to a drowned rat or cat.

"Get up lazy ass," I kicked him.

"Get up? I just spent the last two hours waiting for *your ass*," he finally looked at my hair. "What the fuck happened to you?"

"I don't have windshield wipers. I got lost and I had no cell reception." I shrugged swiping a few wet strands out of my face while one stuck to my cheek. "It's your fault. Now let's go get some ice cream."

He smirked. "I could use some ice cream right about now."

So we ate ice cream at Dairy Queen and then headed back to my apartment I was renting off campus this year.

When we walked in, Jameson looked around before slumping on the couch and kicking his feet up on the coffee table, well not really. My coffee table was two sprint car tires holding up a piece of sheet metal.

"This place is a shithole, Sway." His eyes focused on the table. "Nice table by the way."

I raised an eyebrow at him. "Well ... not everyone makes millions."

"Neither do I," he replied defensively.

"Fairly damn close and I know you're lying when you add on what you make with the sprint car team and all those foam fingers."

He shook his head drinking his chocolate milkshake. "I haven't made shit off that sprint car team. All the profit goes back into the team right now. Although, those foam fingers may be my retirement someday."

I was about to ask him how his sprint car team was going until my perverted neighbors began making noise.

Those assholes made me so jealous lately that I had to invest in a vibrator. I'm no audiologist or anything like that, but a quick assessment told me those were sex noises ... sex noises that were not coming from me.

With the way our apartments were laid out, you could see into their dining room from my bedroom. Not once had they been in the dining room but there was always a first in the heat of the moment I guess.

So there Jameson and I were, on my bed watching Sports Center when I sat up to grab the remote, catching a glimpse of my porn star neighbors. "Holy shit, they're doing it on the table."

Jameson sat up.

"Who is?" his eyes frantically searched for what I was pointing at.

He hadn't shown that much enthusiasm since the time when we were fourteen and he had found a porno in the VCR of his parent's living room, compliments of Spencer.

"My neighbors," I giggled with a snort. "Right there pile driving her on the table."

He burst out laughing and moved by my window for a better view. To be fair, we *both* watched.

"This feels wrong," I said, watching closely.

When he pulled back and lowered his head, I cringed. I didn't want to watch this out of plain jealousy.

"He's doing it all wrong," Jameson sighed rolling his eyes. "Jesus man, save some of your fucking dignity."

I wanted to ask him how often he'd done that to know that this guy was doing it all wrong but I didn't. I felt my entire body burst into flames when my perverted brain imagined Jameson doing *that*, to me.

"He clearly has no idea how to properly debur a crankcase."

"I can't believe we're watching this."

"It's like live porn," he pulled back from the window to look at me with an accusing smirk. "Is this what you do all day? You naughty girl, you."

"No, this is the first time I've watched this."

"Yeah," he shook his head, "sure it is."

When the girl arched her back into him, I thought maybe this was too much. "We shouldn't be watching this."

"We can't stop now. That's like not finishing a race, it's not an option."

When they finally finished, Jameson fell back against the floor and slowly turned his head to me and winked.

"Did that turn you on pervert?" I giggled at his flushed appearance. I would be lying if I said I wasn't turned on. It *was* like watching live porn.

To my utter surprise, he laughed.

"I'll admit, I was, but here's the thing, Sway," he motioned with two fingers for me to lean in closer, so I did. Then he whispered in my ear, low and seductively. "I would pay money to watch you come apart like that."

I think I let out a noise that was near a squeak but closer to a snort, either way, it sounded like something a baby pig would make and not at all sexy.

Was I trying to be sexy?

Jameson chuckled and fell back against the floor again, his rusty hair standing out against the black rug.

Looking down at him propped up on one of his elbows, my breath caught in my throat, thankfully, I didn't choke this time. The desire and want was obvious in both our eyes as he looked up at me.

Without thinking, I leaned forward and pressed my lips to his.

Jameson's response was hesitant but he moved his lips against mine alluring, soft and patient.

I pulled back immediately thinking I'd made a mistake but he surprised me when he crashed his lips back to mine with a sudden urgency and need. The kiss was explosive but remained soft. I moved my hands up his chest to the back of his neck pulling him closer. He pushed his body closer in return, a muffled groan escaped him and he rolled us both over so he was on top of me.

I moaned as his hips moved against mine and for a moment, we were lost until he froze.

"Shit, I'm sorry," his voice marred by his heavy breathing as his eyes fell closed and he sighed. "I shouldn't have done that."

"It's okay." I was panting just as hard. "We always seem to end up this way at some point."

"Does it bother you?" he whispered moving to sit up on the floor, his back rested against the foot of my bed. I watched as he not so discreetly adjusted himself.

"No, it doesn't bother me at all."

He nodded before he stood reaching for my hand.

"Let's go watch a movie before I do something stupid." His eyes raked over my body before he sighed shaking his head. "You are too beautiful for your own good."

I felt my cheeks flush as I let out a nervous giggle-snort. I was becoming good at these embarrassing noises.

"Why do you say things like *that* to me?"

"Because it's true," he told me without hesitation. "You are very beautiful and incredibly sexy. You should know that."

Leaning forward, I kissed him again. Falling to the floor again, any willpower I had was non-existent tonight when he said things like that. No one had ever told me I was sexy before, aside from him. Once again, he ended up between my legs. This time I pulled away when I thought of why he was here.

"Sorry, that was my fault."

Still lying on the floor, his head fell back when he groaned.

"You're killing me, Sway," he muttered with a light chuckle.

"Sorry."

"Don't be. I only said that because every time I'm around you, I think about you naked." He winked with a cocky nod.

Was he flirting with me?

Conscious of my tension, he laughed. "Let's get up."

So we moved to the bed, he attacked me once more and when his hands made their way to my breasts, he pulled away again only this time he set pillows in between us.

"Apparently we need barriers tonight." Trying to catch my breath, he kissed me again, his lips exultant. He moved his mouth to whisper in my ear, his breathing as ragged as mine. "Stay on your side, honey."

I giggled despite my embarrassment that we couldn't keep our hands to ourselves.

Continuing to watch Sports Center, I blurted out. "What made you fly across the country for a night?"

His head turned on the pillow, his thick eyelashes fluttered closed a few times before he gave me a soft smile. "I missed you, that's all." He turned back toward the television. "Sometimes I need to remember home."

"There's more to it than that, isn't there?"

"It's not important."

Not important? How could it not be important?

"I'm home?" I pointed at myself awkwardly. I'm not so sure it was presented as a question, or even a statement.

"Yes," he smiled.

His eyes focused on the picture on my nightstand of us when we were around fourteen in Mexico on the beach.

How was I home? Oh, geez, I was so confused.

Why did he say things like this? Why was he so cryptic in everything he did or said to me? Could it be that he was as confused about where our relationship had gone as I was?

Jameson has always reminded me of a sprint car set-up. They can be some of the most temper-sensitive cars out there when it comes to weight distribution, just like Jameson.

Take the suspension for example. You can either have a coil spring/shock combination, torsion bars, or a combination of both.

A coil spring system is used to store energy and subsequently release the energy to absorb the shock or maintain a force between contracting surfaces. When you think about it, Jameson and I used each other as coil springs to absorb anything that happened in our lives. For that, I held him to different standards. Anything else in my life, I was precipitately impulsive. When it came to Jameson and telling him how I felt for him, I couldn't form the words.

When he fell asleep on my bed, I watched him like the stalker I was. I couldn't stop staring at him, entranced by his beauty. My stupid girly brain imagined that he was here because he wanted me in all the ways I wanted him. Could it be that he got the same energized rush when he saw me as I did with him? Could it be that when we kissed, he felt the same crushing zeal?

I wasn't really a stalker, was I?

I mean he is my best friend, that's not a stalker, right? I didn't know what the difference would be. It all felt the same and now that the term was defined, I figured I should look into therapy.

And then I wondered how I would present this to a therapist?

"Hello, I'm stalking my best friend. Do you think you can help me? I'm afraid that if he doesn't love me back, I might resort to further stalking and, with my arrest record, I'd be going to prison for the three strikes and you're out deal."

Yeah, that doesn't sound dumb at all.

My phone buzzing woke me up that morning. I noticed the way we were laying and smiled. We ended up cuddling sometime throughout the night. Thankfully, we were still fully clothed.

The sun had risen, but the rain had yet to slow. The metal roofs of the cars outside pinged as the rain drops fell. I remembered the sound well, having lived in Washington where the cloud cover and rain were unrelenting.

I watched her sleep through the mirror over her dresser, the morning light providing the right amount of luminosity. Her features softened from sleep were almost seraphic. I wanted to stop time right then and never move from this place with her securely in my arms, away from any harm the world would cause her. Since hearing from Charlie, I alternated between confusion, anger, fear and sadness.

Please let her be okay with this.

The problem was, she wouldn't be okay. He was dying. The only biological family she had left was dying. I couldn't think through this. I couldn't find a way for it to be okay, she wouldn't be okay. I could only hope I would be there for her when she needed me.

Watching her that morning it was easy to see the change in me. For the longest time, it was so hard to see what was right in front of me, *her*. But now, it was so simple, so unmistakably obvious.

Just like tear offs on a visor, you don't realize how obscured your vision is at the time, until you tear away that cellophane, and suddenly you can see and you're wondering how the hell you made it through the last few laps like that. It was as though hearing Charlie tell me he was dying, cleared away any doubt I had that I was meant to be with Sway. In some way I was and I saw it so clearly now.

Sway, who'd been sound asleep until now, stirred in front of me. She was snuggled with her back against my chest, my arm draped over her waist resting against her stomach.

I should move. I thought to myself. *I really should move. This was intimate, right?*

And then she sighed.

"Jameson?" she spoke sleepy, "Are we sporking?"

Laughing, I had to spit some of her hair out of my mouth to reply. "It's called spooning, Sway."

"Spooning is a dumb word. So we're forking?" she turned her head around to glance back at me.

I groaned. The woman was killing me.

"Nope—I'd have noticed if we were forking, for sure."

A ray of sunshine broke through, shining on her face. *God, she was so beautiful.*

"I wish you were still traveling with us," I told her kissing her forehead. "I miss you."

She smiled. "I do, too."

I hated that I couldn't tell her, I wanted to. She deserved to know how drastically her life would change. I also knew I couldn't offer anything. I would do nothing but complicate the situation if she were with me all the time. Nothing would change by telling her.

My phone buzzing again ended anything I wanted to say to her in that moment. Wes called to remind me to be at the airport in a few hours so I decided to shower.

After I took a shower, I walked out into her living room to see Sway curled up on the couch, next to Tommy, who was eating cereal from a bowl in his lap. He was pointing to the television screen, thumb on the remote's pause button, wearing a look of deep concentration. He looked much like a scholar extemporizing upon his area of passionate interest. Sway was watching the screen, equally fascinated.

"You see, you need lots of assembly lube. Eventually you can—"

"What are you watching?" I was praying they weren't watching porn after watching her neighbors last night.

Tommy shrugged, eyes glued to the screen. "A video prepping the camshaft for insertion," he said. "I'm giving her a rudimentary education."

He can't be serious.

Sway's eyes focused on mine, squinting.

Running my hand through my damp hair, I motioned for the door with a tilt of my head. "I need to get going." There was no way I could watch *that*, with Sway here.

She jumped to her feet dumping Tommy's bowl on him.

"I'll drive you," she turned to Tommy. "Clean that up, fire crotch!"

As we walked to her truck, I saw a guy walking toward us who, by his grin, appeared to know her.

I said the first thing that came to mind.

"So ... Blake, how is he?"

I don't know why I asked that. I wasn't sure if this dude was him and what would I have done if she said, *"Oh yeah, we're getting married. Let me introduce you."*

Not that she would have but I clearly was not thinking.

Did I want to hear this?

No.

Did I want to meet the guy?

Without a doubt.

She looked wary, and slightly embarrassed, her eyes glancing between me and him. "You suck."

"I think he's waiting for you," I motioned with my head as he leaned against her truck.

"You stay here. I'll be right back." I did as she said. I didn't need to beat the living shit out of some college kid just because I wasn't man enough to tell her how I felt.

When he hugged her, relief washed over me. She looked uncomfortable by his advance.

The guy, Blake I knew for sure now, left as Sway motioned for me to come over. "That was nothing."

I rolled my eyes. "Well, now that we have that all cleared-up ..."

She laughed softly, the tension visibly easing from her shoulders.

"You know, you can have other friends. I'm not *that* selfish," I lied.

I hated to think that another guy was getting attention from her. I didn't care if it was a simple smile. I wanted all those smiles and sweet gestures. I wanted to hear every giggle, see every roll of her beautiful eyes and hear every adorable sneeze she made.

Good lord, when did I turn into such a girl?

Sway smiled, eyes focused somewhere around her shoes.

"I know."

We kept walking, her eyes trained on the ground, expression lost in thought. I was lost in my own thoughts, glad to have them to myself. She would undoubtedly be more than a little freaked if she could hear them. My brain was currently screaming obscenities at my heart, who was in turn telling my brain to keep the fucking noise down while it contemplated whether Sway would feel anything for me, ever.

That's not what concerned me the most. It was what I would do if she did feel more. It was easy to see we could be more without even trying but how we both dealt with that was what was causing the uncertain trepidation.

"Oh shit, I forgot my keys. I'll be right back," Sway said turning to run back to her apartment.

I watched her skipping through the rain, bouncing in every puddle as though she was a child. How could someone not love this woman? I thought to myself, smiling.

I waited by the truck glancing at my phone, trying to ignore my brain. Wiping the screen a few times as a steady rivulet flow of rain fell. I breathed in deep, remembering why I loved this state so much. The smells of my childhood were all around me and reminded me of my attachment to Sway, and why I attributed so much of what I've done in my career to her. Everything about my childhood goes back to her. She has been with me through it all. Whenever it rained, no matter where I was at and whether or not she was with me, I thought of her.

"So you're Jameson Riley?" a voice, from behind, asked.

I didn't recognize it so I glanced over my right shoulder to see Blake standing there, his arms crossed over his chest. Standing within feet of him, I noticed now that he wasn't a large guy by any means. A few inches shorter than me with dusty blonde hair, his eyes focused on mine.

I paid no mind to him and looked down at my phone.

"Last time I checked," I mumbled keeping my gaze on my phone.

I didn't *want* to know anything about this Blake guy in fear I'd have more to contemplate. I also didn't *want* to like him.

"So you're like what ... her boyfriend?" he asked stepping closer to me.

I smiled despite what I was thinking.

"No. We're friends," he gave the impression this was the answer he was looking for, so I panicked and blurted out, "Though I wouldn't say she's available."

Blake nodded.

"I never thought she was. It's pretty obvious she's taken," he said and then walked away.

No matter how hard my heart wanted to let go and allow myself *not* to be in love with her, I couldn't. I wished there was a way, but at the time, there wasn't a way, she was and always would be like a security blanket. I couldn't let go. I didn't want to either. Just because I depended so much on her wasn't necessarily wrong. It wasn't healthy but it was vital for me. Opening up to the idea she could feel the same way, it both petrified and excited me.

Just as I allowed myself to dream, I thought of Charlie and what his sickness would undoubtedly mean for us. We couldn't be together for the simple fact that we didn't have time. She was needed in Elma and me, well, I was a puppet with more obligations than most twenty-two year olds could even imagine having.

The entire drive back to the airport that morning Jameson didn't say a word and stared out the window watching the rain.

The wind had picked up today and each time a strong gust rocked the truck from side-to-side, I watched as his body seemed to tense.

"Are you okay?" I asked entering the parking lot of the airport.

He shrugged instead of answering.

I don't know what he wanted to say but it seemed like he just couldn't form the words. When he finally did speak, I wished he hadn't.

"Your graduation falls on the night of the All-Star race," he spoke soft and slow, looking directly in my eyes. There was a long pause before he spoke again. "I'm sorry." Once again, his eyes stayed connected with mine.

Although most people never bothered to, if you looked close enough, everything about him shone through his eyes. They saw what they wanted to but I never did. There was fire, fear, a hint of torment and possibly a look of being lost?

I couldn't tell.

Tears flooded my eyes and spilled over and a whimpering gasp escaped me as I tried to force myself to gain control and not look like a lovesick fool in front of him.

Was it graduation that meant so much?

No, it wasn't.

It had nothing to do with graduation. It was the fact that he had obligations, obligations I was no longer a part of. Part of me, the irrational pit lizard, wanted to tell him how much I loved him and that I would wait for him to see that we could be perfect for each other but she was quickly ruled out by the logical lucid Sway who recognized that Jameson didn't need this. He didn't need irrational clingy Sway. He needed judiciously stable Sway, if she still existed.

"Did I ... upset you?" His words were so unsure, so hesitant, that I wanted to lie to him.

I closed my eyes preparing for the conversation and attempting to redeem myself from the mini nervous breakdown I seemed to be having.

"No, you didn't upset me," I told him as we sat in the parking lot of the airport. "I just wish you could be there."

"I wish I could, too. You know that it's hard for me, right? I ... don't like being away from you." His eyes were careful, the way they were when he was hiding something.

When I didn't say anything, he continued, his lips pursed as he nodded once and hung his head. "You don't think it's hard for me?" he muttered shrewdly.

"I guess I feel like you have this life now—a life that I'm not a part of."

I turned my body to face him when he didn't speak, surprised by the pained expression he wore.

"You are a part of everything I do. You're more than just a best friend to me Sway. You're a part of me whether you want to be or not, it's just who I've become."

I smiled as a tear slid down my check. He always knew exactly what to say to make me feel better. The words were there, I wanted to speak them, tell him how much I loved him ... but chariness routed me. I couldn't form the words. For someone who was determined to live each day to its fullest, I was becoming really good at charlatanry.

There was a droning silence with Jameson's phone vibrating obsessively before he leaned over and kissed my check.

"I have to go, honey," he pulled back, his hand rose to my cheek as he thumb ran over my lower lip. "Take care of yourself."

I nodded, unable to choke out anything else and he once again opened his mouth as though he was going to speak and then sighed. He took a deep breath and then pulled away. This time he didn't look back, he reached for his bag and left.

Watching him walk away, I remembered my most important question, why he was here in the first place. He never said but it seemed so urgent and unplanned. I sent him a text.

Wait! You never told me why you came all this way.

I watched him closely as he trudged toward the plane, his back was turned to me but I saw him reach inside his jacket for his phone.

The loud thumping of my heartbeat drowned out the roaring of the jet's engine.

Jameson stopped going up the steps of the plane, to glance back at me, wearing the same expression he wore in the truck ... sadness ... confliction ... I couldn't place it.

I got out and continued to walk to the plane, the rain blurred my vision of him but I could tell he was still standing there.

Dropping his bag at his feet, he jogged to meet me halfway. I kept it together, crying that is, and wrapped my arms around his neck tightly. He pulled me snug against his chest, his strong arms wound around me, pressing his face against my neck.

His lips brushed across my skin as he spoke softly.

"I needed to see you. I needed to know ... needed to remember what's real." The low resonance of his voice sent shivers down my spine.

Have you ever thought about when your life is changing paths? Do you see it happening or do you feel it? Whether the change is somatic or not, you feel it some way. It can be something someone says to you, or something they do.

In this case, it was the words spoken.

I *would* forever be what's real to him. I needed to make him see I *was* real. I wasn't just a pit lizard, I was *his* pit lizard. Never wanting to be a distraction, I failed to understand that it was never the distraction he didn't need, it was the opposite actually, and he needed a coil spring system. He needed someone who was simplistically indulgent to what he really was. I needed to see past the imperfections and see him for who he was, perfect. In racing terms, I needed to remove the hood pins and see what he was running under the hood to understand the intricacy of him.

From the time we were eleven, that's all I've ever saw. I saw the gritty pessimistic man who saw the world the way he wanted, one left turn at a time. I saw him for who was, who he wasn't, and who he wanted to be.

Torsion Bars – Torsion bars are the most common type of suspension used on sprint cars. Used on all four corners of a sprint car, they provide the link between the chassis and track surface.

Just the same as a torsion bar, you can only go one direction for so long before something gives.

That was me and suddenly I was being asked to twist the wrong direction.

I never thought Sway would feel the same way, prayed she didn't feel the same way. The way she trembled from my touch, leaned into my kiss, sighed when I held her, she felt the same as I. That scared me. It was never that I didn't *want* her. It was that I didn't *want* her to love me.

I kept my promise to Charlie. I didn't say anything and, if I was being honest, I couldn't have told Sway he was dying anyway. That's something he needs to say. I can't even tell the girl I love her let alone tell her something as life altering as that.

If that were my dad, I would want him to tell me. Lost in thoughts of Charlie, Sway and torsion bars, Wes came over the speaker to tell me we'd be descending into the Talladega Municipal Airport soon.

When I turned my cell phone back on I noticed a new text message from Sway.

Call me when you land. Good luck at practice.

My stomach churned thinking of her. The cold claw grabbed my insides again and again as I tried to reason with myself, telling me she wasn't mine. She never was mine. She never would be mine with the lifestyle I had. What could I possibly offer her besides complicated?

It's not my place to get all stomach-achy over her.

I spent the entire plane ride home telling myself I was fine, and I was. I was trying to relate my life to a sprint car setup, the only thing that made sense to me.

By the time I reached Talladega that afternoon, I decided I couldn't wait any longer. Every time I saw her, I wanted more. One kiss left me wanting more, one touch always turned into more. Since Kyle noticed the sexual attraction between us, I thought about it constantly. Maybe she did want to have sex with me. Even the other night when we were on her floor, she didn't stop me, I did. Believe me, I wanted to continue but it felt wrong. It felt like I was just there for that. I didn't want her to think I flew in to fuck her and then leave. Not that we ever had before but it felt too much like that's what it could be construed as.

I didn't give much thought to my decision. I only knew I wanted more from her. The only reasonable option was to let it happen naturally. I knew we had a sexual attraction and I saw the way she watched me as well as the way she responded to my touch but I also wasn't sure it went beyond that. She couldn't have *those* feelings for me because I'm an asshole. She loved me, that much was obvious, but relationship love, that's different. I knew well that physical and emotional love was entirely different.

No woman in their right mind could stand me. Look at the women in my life now. Emma called me an asshole daily, Alley thought I needed anger management, and my mom, well, she thought I was perfect but she didn't count.

So who could stand me? I could hardly stand myself sometimes.

But, since we had the sexual attraction, if that's what it was, maybe someday she would want more. Maybe someday there could be a place for us. What's the harm in starting with physical love first?

I called her before practice began to let her know I made it to Talladega. She seemed down, and to be fair, I sounded the same with the goblin running rampant in my gut.

I could hear commotion in the background and wondered who was with her, hopeful it was not Blake.

"Who's there?"

"Tommy," she sighed frustrated. "He's eating all my food."

We got on the topic of some of my recent interviews when she called bullshit on me. I denied the fact that I was nicknamed "Rowdy Riley" now.

"It's on Wikipedia, Jameson," she said with absolute solemnity, "therefore, it's valid."

I rolled my eyes, not ever wanting to open the whole, "truth about Wikipedia" discussion again. "Don't believe everything you read, Sway."

"So they don't call you *Rowdy Riley* at the track?"

"No, they do. I don't want you believing everything they write about me. Not all of it's true." I wanted her to understand how the media had the ability to pad the truth with their own beliefs.

After meeting with Melissa to go over a few sponsor obligations for the weekend, I was able to relax for a few hours. Bobby stopped by my motor coach and we chatted for a few minutes before he left for dinner with his girlfriend.

After that I decided to take a shower. Being back in the southeastern humidity, I smelled.

Once inside the small bathroom, I leaned against the shower wall. The aches and stresses of the day clustered in my shoulders, my tight muscles relaxing as the hot jets of water pounded against my back. I stared as the water flowed off my shoulders and down the silver drain. The black granite glistened.

My thoughts went back to Sway and how much I missed her. Every time I saw her, she lifted the weight the world was putting upon me and she made spring adjustments at the right times.

The shell I put around myself cracked every time I saw her, breaking away piece by piece. Images of her laying under me on her floor flooded my brain as my breathing accelerated; she was so captivatingly beautiful. I meant it when I told her I'd pay money to see her come apart. It had been a fantasy of mine for as long as I could remember.

I had an interview in less than an hour so when my groin began stirring I turned the water off. I didn't have time for that right now, even though I wanted to. It'd been at least a week since I had any attention down there and though I needed the relief, I didn't have time.

The interview was held in the infield media center with one of the track promoters. The same series of questions usually flowed, but tonight he asked one that caught me off guard.

"If you could pick one person who has influenced your career both emotionally and for opportunity, who would it be?"

I hesitated for a moment running my hand through my hair. Looking at Emma and Alley standing alongside reporters, I felt one person missing. Sway.

I couldn't say it's one person because it wasn't just one person. It can't be in a sport like this.

"I can't say just one person has helped me," I told him. "My Dad has given me so much emotional and financial support. My mom believes I can do *nothing* wrong." I chuckled lightly when a few women in the audience cheered. "My brother is there each week helping on the car, he's the jack man for our team. My sister runs my fan club because, heaven knows, I wouldn't be able to. My sister in-law keeps me out of trouble, and then I have my best friend, Sway, who without her, you wouldn't want to know me. We've been friends since I was eleven. She keeps me in line."

"Fame hasn't lost that?"

"No. Never. She's what keeps me grounded. If there is ever a time when she thinks I need a reality check, she lets me know," I said, with a laugh.

"Would you say they are a big part of your operation?"

"Yes. Very much so. Ever since I started racing, family has always been there."

I could feel the interview getting more and more personal and my theory was confirmed when he asked his next question.

"Now I hear you're single?"

Shifting uncomfortably, I heard the women screaming from behind me, eager for my response.

"I, uh ... I've never been one to date. I am single ... but I *don't* have time for dating. All I do is race. If I'm not here at the track, I'm at a local dirt track."

"That's what I hear. Tell us about your sprint car team you started this year."

And just like that, I avoided the personal questions.

They didn't need to know that I was madly in love with my best friend and that I compared my life to a sprint car setup or that Charlie was dying. That was *my* life and, to be fair, these fans didn't want to hear that shit. They wanted hear about the fights. They wanted to hear I was a bachelor and that I slept around. That's what they wanted. They wanted a story. The problem with that was, *that* wasn't me.

I would always be a dirt track racer from Washington—that much would never change. I would never settle for less than I knew was possible and would always love Sway. Even if we were never allowed to be together, she showed me who I was, who I wasn't, and who I wanted to be.

The race in Talladega, Alabama, was, for one, close to Aiden's hometown, and two the largest track on the schedule. While I enjoyed Talladega, it didn't like me.

Last season while racing the Busch race, I got caught up in the

"Big One" and ended up being transported to the hospital with a few broken ribs, a sprained ankle and a minor concussion.

I wasn't exactly excited to come back to the track. Sure, I wanted redemption but some even believe the track is cursed.

One morning prior to the 1974 Cup race, drivers came out to find cut brake lines and sand in their gas tanks. Others believed it used to be an old Indian burial ground and claimed the track itself had been cursed. I tended to believe this as well considering my recent luck there. I wasn't exactly excited.

Aiden was and he wouldn't shut the fuck up.

I managed to qualify fourth but ended up clipping the wall in happy hour. Forced to go to a back-up car, I had no idea how it was going to handle. It was the same car we ran at Daytona so I hoped the set-up would be close enough to at least get a decent finish.

Turns out, it was. My only problem was all the traffic I had to get through. Bobby and me were in a pack about midway through the race when he had an opening and didn't take it. I nailed him in the bumper when he checked up, causing him to get squirrelly coming out of turn four and damage the front of my car.

When you're driving two hundred miles an hour inches next to another car, it's not the time to second guess your line. Bobby was for whatever reason.

I ended up with a twelfth place finish which was not too bad considering when I looped back down pit lane after the race, Kyle noticed my right side tires were both riding on cords.

Sway called as we were leaving the track on our way toward Aiden's house. I spent more time watching the interactions between Aiden and Emma. Something was different with them.

"Are you even listening to me?"

Surveying the two of them, I snorted. "Yeah, I'm listening."

"Really ... what did I just say?"

"I ... uh ... um ... something ..."

"See, pay attention!"

"All right, I'm paying attention now."

Sway went on to tell me about her class. She finished early and was now heading home to see Charlie. I felt my heart begin to pound and my palms were sweating thinking maybe he was going to tell her tonight. I knew Charlie well enough by now that he wouldn't, but the notions were still there.

It took us about three hours but Aiden, Emma, Spencer, Alley, Lane and me all made our way to Aiden's home outside of Talladega. Aiden was from a small town called Pinckard Alabama, population 667.

Meeting Aiden's dad explained a lot about Aiden. I understood why Aiden had an ulcer and wasn't surprised to see his dad was just as analytical as he was, maybe even more so if that were possible. I was hardly *good* company the rest of the evening and felt somewhat remorseful when Aiden's dad was telling me how to cook a raccoon in his thick southern accent and I paid more attention to my phone than him.

Emma caught me after dinner outside the bathroom and tore my phone out of my hand.

"Show some respect, Jameson. His parents are old-fashioned country folks who don't even own a cell phone and here you are ... Adam praises your skills ... checking your cell phone. It's *rude*."

"I should ask you the same question," I clipped reproachfully, my eyes watched hers carefully, "What's with you and Aiden?"

She smacked my shoulder, pushing me against the wall.

"Don't turn your shit on me," and then walked back inside the kitchen to Aiden's mom.

I hung my head knowing it was rude. Turning my phone on vibrate, I stuck it inside my jacket and never touched it again that night. Adam, Aiden's dad, was hilarious.

We ended up sneaking out back to his garage to find he had a pair of riding lawnmowers he and Aiden used to race when they were younger. With a few adjustments, Spencer, Aiden and I were tearing up their lawn.

Despite my earlier behavior toward his family, I couldn't remember the last time I had that much fun *without* Sway.

I thought of her, and every time I turned around I was thinking of something I couldn't wait to tell her. I learned a lot about Aiden that night. Even though he was crazy, I understood him a little more.

His dad, Adam Gomez, was a farmer who was born and raised in the small town. His mom, April, was probably the sweetest woman, besides my mother, who ever existed. I liked them all.

I always wondered how Aiden got involved in racing but I understood after seeing those lawnmowers. He also had a cousin who raced late models out at Montgomery Speedway, a half-mile asphalt track, so that's where Aiden found his calling. He had a remarkable sense of direction but couldn't decide where he *wanted* to go.

Much like me on the track, he understood racing and the dynamics, and was essentially worry-free at the track.

We stayed the night there with the Gomez family and then went back to Mooresville the next morning. When we arrived home, it was racing life as usual. Team meetings, sponsorship commitments, testing ... same thing it was each week.

You don't think about it when you're running yourself ragged until something breaks. Mine was that my torsion bars had been twisting in the wrong direction for so long, fractures were occurring.

For four years now, I'd been denying that I was in love with Sway and now that I saw and felt it. I didn't know what to do. I tried stagger changes, shocks, weight jacking ... I tried it all, terrified to admit I couldn't change this feeling. This wasn't black or white, day or night, good or evil, there was no answer. What scared me more than loving her was not knowing what to do with that love and how to tell her. And, more importantly, what she would do with *my* love.

Bear Bond – A very strong adhesive used to patch a damaged race car.

"Are you alive?" Ryder asked peering over the side.

It took me a minute figure out what went wrong and if I was alive. Eventually I caught my breath enough to answer him. My head rested against the dirt as I looked up at the sky. Trying to recall what went wrong when I blipped the throttle before the jump. No, that wasn't the problem. The problem was when I thought that *me*, the kid who raced cars, not dirt bikes, could kick his leg off the bike behind him like he was dismounting. Most Supercross stars have problems with this trick. Why I thought I could do it was clearly a prime example of my stubborn pluckiness. The plan was to land smoothly back on the ground but it didn't shake down that way, nope, my leg got stuck.

"I think I am," I huffed throwing my leg over the bike again. "I think we should make the jump bigger." Ryder's eyes widened with each word. "That way, you can just jump *this* part," I gestured toward the gaping hole in the ground.

The screaming of a two-stroke engine charged from behind and we both turned to see Tyler and Justin side-by-side heading for the jump I demolished with my non-existent Nac-Nac skills. The Nac-Nac was a trick where you kicked your leg over to one side in mid-air and then returning your foot to the foot pegs before landing.

It wasn't easy and I demonstrated.

Tyler saw me standing next to my bike while Justin, he did not. So while Tyler slowed his speed and trailed off, Justin pinned it.

Take a couple sprint car guys and throw them on dirt bikes. Never a good thing.

Justin misjudged the jump and did the unintentional Nac-Nac I had done, only he stayed on the bike and even as it slid down the twenty-foot embankment he stayed on it.

Ryder and I stood at the top of the hill watching Justin try and pull his bike back up. Did we offer to help?

No, hell no. We made fun of him.

I had just purchased this property a few weeks back and construction of a quarter-mile dirt track and riding trails took place almost immediately. I don't think it was necessarily the addition of the track or the dirt bikes that was dangerous but more the way we rode them. I was never the type of guy to do anything half-assed, nor were my friends.

While we all may have had obligations we should have been doing that day instead, we made time to be twenty-two-year-old kids that day.

As I've said before, when we're stressed, we did what any normal person would do, we did what relaxed us.

That was dirt bikes today.

When the world wasn't scrutinizing our every move, the engines cooled, the unforgiving sun faded and we were left with a spark of time to be ourselves.

We spent a greater part of the morning tearing those trails up and then the rest of the evening nursing our wounds throwing back a few beers. It was great to see all of them again. I hadn't realized how much I missed hanging out with my USAC buddies.

Money was rolling in from the wins and merchandise sales so I decided to buy a few things. Usually sponsors were throwing merchandise my direction so I never had to buy clothes again if I didn't want to and cars? I had plenty of those. Anything Ford made, I had my choice of.

Besides my Ford F250 I had been driving since I was sixteen, I hadn't purchased anything for myself besides race car parts.

After I poured a large sum of the money into the sprint car team, I bought some toys ... a Yamaha YZ250, four of them actually, a 2003 Mastercraft X-30 wakeboarding boat, three Yamaha Raptor quads, and then some property to play on.

Ford was nice enough to provide me a brand new Ford 4-door F350 so I definitely had the *power* to tow these toys.

I ended up purchasing a large piece of land not far from my parents but far enough that I could get away when needed. It felt good to have something of my own for once.

Do you want to know my first thought as I walked around the land after signing the papers?

Sway.

I thought of what it would be like to have her here with me, sharing a home. Brief and fleeting, the thoughts didn't last long knowing she would never be with me like *that*. Now with Charlie sick, any intentions I may have had, were now gone. It wouldn't be right to ask for more, so I thought.

While the boys ran up the road for more beer that night after riding, I wandered around the property, watching the moon slowly rising. The orange and pink shades from the sun blended with the darker hues of the night as the moon appeared.

I wanted to feel Sway against my side in that moment. I wanted to hear her soft giggle, look into her green eyes and tell her everything I feared, everything I wanted, and everything I couldn't. The gravel and dirt crunched beneath my feet, the wet, fresh cut grass smell surged throughout the air circling with the night's cool air and the lasting traces of racing fuel from the dirt bikes imbued everything together.

I spent the greater part of the night out there wandering around.

With fifteen acres, there was a lot of land to see. Changing rapidly from trees to an open clear-cut meadow, the land was versatile and allowed me to make more trails and even a bigger dirt track if I wanted.

Eventually I started a fire and waited for the boys to get back. I was sure they'd figure out where I was with the glow.

The orange flames from fire flickered against the beer bottle in my hand. When a piece of wood dropped it sent a burst light throughout the air, the white ash dusted my black fleece. Though it was summer, the breeze had a chill to it. I shuddered drawing my arms to my chest for warmth.

The fire reminded me of the night, in high school, when I went up to Dayton Peak with Sway, the same night I gave into Chelsea.

If I had my way, I'd take that night back. Hell, I would have never started anything with that whore. I heard from Tommy not too long ago that she was hanging around the dirt tracks again, even asking about me. She was out of her mind if she thought I'd ever talk to her again. Trifling thoughts of Chelsea subsided when my mind focused steadily on Sway, wondering what she was doing right now.

I heard Justin before I saw him, cursing as he tripped over a log. "Oh, goddamn it."

"Careful there," I chuckled taking a drink of my beer. "I need you in that car next week."

"You should have thought of that before you put that track in," he mused. "I think I broke my finger."

The flashlight he was holding swept back and forth watching the ground trying to guide him through the darkness at the fire. He shined it in my eyes when he got within a foot of me, blinding me.

"Jerk," it took a few minutes for my eyes to adjust. "Where's Tyler?"

Ryder had already left to catch a flight to Ohio.

"He's coming. I made him carry the beer." He glanced down at his hand, rubbing along his palm. "I really do think I broke my finger." He held his hand up to the fire; his index finger bent the opposite way between his knuckle and joint.

"Appears that way ... can you race?"

"Hell, I've raced with a broken arm, this ain't gonna stop me." Justin took a sharp intake of breath before gripping the finger tightly and then jerking it into back into place. He fell over, moaning in pain.

"Pussy,"

"Oh, fuck you," he groaned kicking my leg. "This is your fault."

"How so?" I stepped away from him so he couldn't kick me again.

"You said, and I quote, 'Let's build a dirt bike track,' really though," he paused laughing, "what the fuck were you thinking?"

"I never said I was thinking at the time. It was supposed to be fun."

Justin had this *way* of turning a conversation quicker than a sprint car flips, always had. You'd be talking about one thing and then he'd get a thought, next thing you knew, you were talking about the weather. In this case, the conversation turned against me.

"What's with you and Sway these days?"

"What do you mean?"

"I saw her in Skagit last year. She seemed different. And *you*, you're not the same when she's gone either."

"How was she different?"

Justin thought for a second before tipping his head to the side. "When she's with you, she's carefree and happy. The night I saw her, she didn't appear happy, not sad. Just different."

I nodded but didn't say anything, the fire cracked catching my attention.

"You're different, too."

I shrugged indifferently. I wasn't in the mood to "Dr. Phil" my feelings. I had enough problems trying to decipher my feelings and I didn't need more thoughts.

"All I'm saying is, if you love her, tell her."

Once again, I nodded in agreement but said nothing.

When Tyler came back with the beer, we forgot all about feelings and broken fingers.

In the morning, it was race life as usual. Justin and Tyler headed to Ohio and I flew to Virginia.

The next race on the schedule was Martinsville. It is a half-mile paved asphalt straightaway with concrete corners. It's one of the oddest shaped tracks resembling a paperclip with almost twelve-degree turns. Racing the track can be tricky because you have to slow down so much in the flat narrow turns and then accelerate.

I raced here in the Busch series last year, so I had a feel for it, but it wasn't exactly my best race.

Never good at navigating pit lane, Martinsville was even trickier with the way the pits wrapped around both straightaways. It made pitting interesting and wasn't really my favorite track because of that.

All that aside, I managed to snag a third place finish when Kyle made the right call on fuel mileage and stayed out when everyone else pitted.

The following week was Fontana and the temptation to stop and see Sway was there but time wasn't. I had to fly out directly after the race for Richmond and she was taking finals with graduation approaching fast.

Once again, my car had a mind of its own in Fontana. I was just along for the ride.

Safety at these tracks has improved light years as to what it was even five years ago.

With seventy laps to go, I was leading. When I went into turn one, everything was fine. By the time I was in turn two, everything was not fine. I had cut a tire and was heading straight for the concrete wall.

I'll never forget the first time I hit a SAFER (Steel and Foam Energy Reduction) barrier as opposed to a concrete wall I had been used to hitting. I'd like to kiss the gifted motherfucker who designed those pillow soft walls. When you looked up and saw your car heading for those concrete walls, you thought, "Well, shit, I hope we brought enough Bear Bond and hammers."

Now when you hit a SAFER barrier you think, "I hope I make it back around before the pace car."

And usually you did.

Those walls don't stop the damage from being done but they do lessen the amount.

So there I was limping my car back to pit lane so the guys could salvage what was left of it and try to at least stay on the lead lap and finish. Like I've said, every *single* point counts when you're in it for the championship.

The first priority during a pit stop like this was to get four new tires on the car. Then they work on the metal, you'd be amazed how much damage not only that wall can do but a flat tire. From my view inside the car, it looked like a biker brawl with hammers, bats, and crowbars beating all over my car.

I must have pitted every ten laps after that for tires, Bear Bond, sheet metal patches, checking the toe, more Bear Bond, oh, and more Bear Bond. I also want to point out that when using Bear Bond, which is essentially extremely strong tape, do not get it stuck to you.

My catch can man, found this out the hard way when he got it stuck on his leg as he tried to adhere a piece of it to my bumper. I nearly took his leg with me when I took off after that pit stop.

As much as I hated this part of racing and the pitting every few laps, it was part of the game. Every driver wads one up at one time or another. I tend to think it was the car more than me. That stupid car had a mind of its own, and by the end of the race I struggled just to finish thirty-first and eight laps down. I wanted to set the car on fire after that.

On the way back to the hauler some smartass member of the press said, "It's not that bad kid, smile."

Did he honestly understand what he was saying to me?

Sure, I lived a good lifestyle but what he didn't realize and never would take the time to, was that was not me.

I would never be satisfied with anything less than a win. It had absolutely nothing to do with the lifestyle I had. It had to do with the fact that this was me, being the best I could. So if I had a shitty race, I wasn't going to smile as I let myself down.

I called Sway on the way to the airport after the race. She was in good spirits which helped.

Though the conversation was quick, it was needed. I tried to picture her face, wanting to burn the image into my brain, never forgetting how perfect she was, the delicate twist of her mouth when she smiled, or the way her eyes sparkled at the mention of ice cream.

After Fontana, we flew back to Virginia for the Richmond race, which is a three-quarter mile, "D" shaped asphalt oval.

Most of my excitement for Richmond came from the fact that it was a night race, under the lights. There's nothing better than a night race on a short track to me, it always brings me back to where I started, which made me think of Sway.

Heading into the Richmond race, I was running third in points despite the horrible finish at Fontana and hopeful to gain some ground on Tate and Darrin who were ahead of me. Darrin didn't make this easy.

Prior to the race that night, he ran into me on pit lane when I was talking with Aiden.

"Why can't Tommy spot for you tonight?" Aiden asked distraughtly.

"I don't see what the big deal is," I reached inside my car for my ear buds. "You spot for me every week." I wasn't understanding his vagueness as to *why* he didn't want to spot tonight. "Besides, Tommy is in Grand Rapids tonight."

"Well," Aiden began shoving his hands deep in his pockets. "Have you ever been on *that* tower in a night race?"

"Not that I can remember. Usually I'm in the car."

He let out a nervous laugh. "Exactly ... you have no idea how many bugs are up there."

"Bugs?"

“Yes, *bugs*. Lots of them,”

“Close your mouth.”

Although I refused to step foot on the tower, I knew about the cicada in Richmond and to say they had a problem was an understatement. It was nearly a plague with those noisy obtrusive insects.

“It’s not that simple,” Aidan argued. “How do suppose I spot for you with my mouth closed?”

“Really, Aiden, this shouldn’t be that hard,” I pointed to Jeb, Bobby’s spotter. “He wears a ski mask on night races. You do the same.”

Aiden seemed satisfied with that answer but still tried to pay Ethan, the kid who drove the hauler from race-to-race, a thousand dollars to spot for me. Ethan declined the offer.

Apparently, the bugs were *that* bad at Richmond.

With any luck, Aiden would focus on the race instead of the bugs. You rely on your spotter heavily at tracks like Richmond where things happen and reaction time needs to be instant. Spotters not only act as your guide, with poor visibility due to all the safety devices in place, you can only see the car directly in front of you. That’s where the spotter comes in. Trust is essential, if I didn’t trust Aiden completely, he wouldn’t be spotting for me.

I have to be able to say, “Is there room?” and if he says, “Clear high,” he better be right.

If not, I just pushed someone up the track, possibly wrecked them and maybe a few others.

How do you think I would feel about that? Shitty. Not only do I take all the heat for that, but our team has to salvage a wadded up car all because Aiden misjudged the car beside me. Like I said, trust.

After introductions and Aiden’s rant, I was getting ready to get inside the car when Darrin walked past.

There was more than enough room in between Spencer and me for him to maneuver past us, but, no, he ran into my right shoulder knocking me forward against my car. My arms instinctively braced myself against the door.

The media was hovering so I kept my response short.

"My nephew is more mature than you."

Darrin simply snorted and kept walking toward his car.

My car was what some in the garage called as "hooked-up" and running anywhere. Just the same as dirt racing, every track has its own unique characteristics and changed throughout the night.

Despite that, my car ran anywhere I put it. I could run up high to pass and then shoot down low on the inside if needed the next lap.

What wasn't working for me was an asshole in a yellow number fourteen car with a chip on his fucking shoulder.

The race was pretty much the same cheap ass hits, all of which NASCAR seemed to turn their head the other direction. If I made those hits against the "golden boy," you had better believe they would have parked me.

When I took over the lead around lap one-twenty, I had a feeling it wasn't the last time I'd see him that night. When I say that *most* drivers love a night race, so do their tempers because not only do we love the night races, we all want to win them.

Tempers flare, drivers make rash impulsive moves, and shit gets heated even more than the temperature of the track. We don't become malleable like tires. We get rigid and obdurately focused on the win.

Just like any other Saturday night race under the lights at your local bullring track, tempers ignite.

"You want to get a drink with me?" Blake asked after class.

I have never been on a *real* date before nor have I ever gone out with guy—aside from Jameson.

Sure, I ventured to prom with Cooper but other than that, nope.

"I don't know," glancing down at my shoes, I avoided eye contact with him as I continued to walk toward my truck. Once through the large metal doors and into the spring night air, I inhaled. "I have a test tomorrow," I let out the breath I inhaled.

“So do I, any more excuses you want to use?” his head tipped making an effort to capture my attention. “Just have a drink with me. That’s all I’m asking.”

Letting go of my pathetic dithering, we went to a local bar up the street that many of the local college students flocked to on Saturday nights. Being a sports bar, racing was on.

And not just any race, the Subway 400 Winston Cup race that Jameson had the pole for. Usually I’d be in my apartment cuddled up watching by myself, but no, I was out here, at a bar, with another guy.

Bring on the anxiety.

Not that I had any need to feel this way, but I felt dirty being out with someone other than Jameson when I felt so strongly for him.

The night went relatively smoothly for the most part but when a couple guys at the bar started knocking Jameson, who was leading the race with twenty laps to go and aggressively holding onto it, I accidently-on-purposely spilled their pitcher of beer when I walked past them. Happy they were now drenched in Blue Moon, I made my way back to Blake and his friend Neil.

I didn’t like Neil, not even a little bit. For one, he couldn’t say one decent remark about Jameson and two, he had enormous eyebrows that made me think he had live caterpillars on his forehead, and they were going to eat me every time he spoke.

On top of the snide observations of Jameson’s racing skills, he had the nerve to revile Elma.

That was my snapping point and like fuel meeting spark, I ignited.

“Listen, asshole,” I began reproachfully pointing my finger at his caterpillars. “I don’t give a shit who you think the best NASCAR driver is,” I air quoted, “but you talking shit about Jameson and my home town ... I’m going to rip those caterpillars off your face before they become butterflies!”

Neil’s expression was something similar to Tina Turner when Ike first hit her, shock and then indignant.

“Jameson is her friend,” Blake whispered toward Neil with a derisory edge, his eyes dancing around the bar, avoiding mine. In spite of his mocking tone, he couldn't look me in the fucking eye.

Neil snorted taking a slow drawn out drink of his beer.

"I'm sure," setting his beer on the bar, he finally looked over at me, disparagingly. "Everyone thinks they're his friend now that he has money."

Immediately, I was protective.

"I've known him since I was eleven, jerk face,"

The group of people beside us cheered and clapped, their eyes engrossed on the five televisions spread over the walls of the bar, all of them broadcasting the Richmond race, with Jameson leading. There were about five laps remaining, with him and Darrin all over each other.

"He's not going to win," Neil mumbled.

"Yes, he will," I finished the last of my beer and slammed the glass on the bar. I wanted it to make a loud noise to show how annoyed I was but with all the screaming, it didn't make a sound.

With one lap to go, Jameson and Darrin were side-by-side coming out of four when Darrin bumped him. I know Jameson's dexterity, I know that ordinarily this would not have caused him to wreck, but he did.

The crowd went hysterical booing and some cheering. It was insane.

This wasn't good, I sensed.

I stood there staring at the screen in disbelief, anger rising within me creating airlessness. My first thought was to be pissed at this douche Neil for knocking my boy, listen to me, *boy*. I sound like I'm a fourteen-year-old.

My second thought as I watched Jameson hoist himself on the window ledge was commiseration as he was about to do something stupid.

The camera shot to him while he sat there on the edge of his window, his head hunched forward resting against the roof. Though his helmet was still on, I knew exactly what he was feeling. Particularly when his fist slammed down on the roof a few times before he threw his legs over the side, making his way toward the infield, his helmet still on.

As I said many times, I knew Jameson *very well*, better than I knew myself. Times like this he took the hardest because he was not only disappointed in himself but he felt as though he was letting his entire team down. Now it didn't consist of a few men, Riley Racing had about seventy-five people working for them on the two teams. All of them felt it when Jameson didn't finish.

To give you an example of this, take Harry, the engine builder for both teams. So he spends around sixty hours a week working on the engines for the team. How do you think he feels when the engine blows? Not good.

Not only does Jameson not finish the race, but he has sponsors looking at him as to why he couldn't finish the race. Jimi and Randy want to know why the engine failed and here Harry is wondering what the hell went wrong. Was it something he did? Was it the way Jameson was running the car? Was it an adjustment the crew made? It's a mystery, nonetheless, but my point is not just one individual is affected if the car doesn't finish well. They're a *team* and they feel it like a *team*.

Knowing all that, I knew the weight that was on him each week. Every point is critical as every race is critical.

By now, Jameson had made his way to the pits and a news broadcaster was pushing a microphone in his face as he walked stalked to his hauler.

"Jameson?" the reporter struggled to gain his attention as he kept walking, "Can you tell us what happened out there? It looked as though he just came down on you."

"I'm not real sure," Jameson said edgily.

He had sunglasses on by that point so I couldn't see his eyes to tell if he was upset or not. Who was I kidding, he was most certainly upset.

Jameson finally spoke but kept walking. "We had a run on him coming out of four but I couldn't tell how close he was ... next thing

I knew ... I was in the wall," his voice sounded wrong, it didn't even sound like him. The fact that his sunglasses were on frustrated me even more in that moment, I needed to see his eyes to know for sure he was okay.

Alley pushed him inside his hauler, which was probably wise.

I stopped listening after that, I didn't want to hear them bashing Jameson so I turned to drinking. Before I knew it, Blake was holding me up as we walked outside. College kids lined the streets, partying as usual.

Knowing Tommy was in town, I sent him a text to see if he could pick me up as we made our way through the young boisterous crowd.

I was in no shape to be driving and I wasn't about to leave with Blake.

Blake had other ideas when he followed me toward my truck, his arm slung around my shoulders.

"Don't Blake, I need to get home."

I caught a glimpse of his eyes, covetously glowing. But they were the wrong color. I wanted those grass green, intensely jaded eyes. Instead I saw Blake's muddy hazel eyes.

"You're such a tease," he groaned pushing me against my truck, his breath oppressively heavy against my skin, it felt wrong, very wrong.

Everything felt different, the hands weren't the same and the smell wasn't the same. Nothing was. Where there were soft hands, I wanted to feel the familiar calloused hands I knew so well. The smell of his *Obsession* was overbearing where Jameson never needed cologne and I worshiped the heady pungent traces of racing on him.

"I said no," I pushed against Blake again.

My hands trembled against his dark shirt and I wasn't sure how far he was going to push the issue. Not only was I impaired by alcohol but Blake had at least a hundred pounds on me.

"And I say, yes," his mouth attacked my neck with sloppy overbearing kisses.

Blake must not know me well because those who really *know* me know that when I say no, I fucking mean it.

My knee came up hastily between his legs. Any erection he may have had was now gone. “I said no!”

“Wow,” a voice behind me laughed through Blake’s howling. “And to think I thought I was going to have to fight him off you.”

I spun around letting Blake collapse to the ground to see Tommy standing there with a grin. I’d never been so happy to see that orange head in my entire life. I could fend for myself, sure, but emotionally, I was rattled a little.

Back at my apartment, a couple beers to calm my nerves, Tommy and I spent the rest of the evening talking while he tried to convince me to tell Jameson what happened with Blake.

“Why should I?”

“He’s your best friend. You tell him everything.”

“He doesn’t need my drama along with his own, Tommy.” I tossed a bag of chips at him and another beer. “Just leave it alone.”

“If you say so, but if he finds out from someone other than you,” he shook his head. “I hope I’m not there to see it.”

“He’s not *that* bad.”

Tommy quirked an imperceptive look in my direction, “Let me tell you something ... do you remember that race out in Terre Haute in 2000 when you disappeared.”

“I didn’t disappear!” dropping down beside him on the couch in my apartment—I took his beer from him. “I went to the bathroom.”

“Whatever, you were gone for like two hours and no one could find you.”

“I was constipated. What’s your point?”

“My point is ... he is protective of you. If he thought for one second you were in danger in any way, he’d destroy everything and anyone to get to you. Did you know that he refused to start the feature that night until you were found?”

“He’s not *that* bad.”

“You’re in denial. He is *that* bad, when it comes to you.”

“Why do you keep saying that? We’re friends, nothing more.”

"The sooner you two realize that you're way more than friends, the better off we all will be," Tommy laughed. "He's one moody motherfucker when you're not there."

"Do you think he wants more?"

Tommy paused and glanced at me out of the corner of his eye, then looked away. "It's not my place to say."

"Nice," I retorted rolling my eyes.

"I don't know if you have noticed this before but Jameson scares the shit out of me. No way in hell I'm telling you what he tells me."

"Get out."

"What—why?" His expression was similar to a child's when they find out there is no Santa Claus and your parents lied to you.

"Because."

"No, I have nowhere to sleep tonight."

"Fine, sleep on the couch—share with Mr. Jangles."

"Mr … who?"

"Jangles," I finished for him. "He's my cat."

Tommy glanced down at the overly large ball of fluff at his feet and then back at me with a wary expression. "Are you sure that's a cat."

"What else would he be? A shark?"

"Or a cow," Tommy balked. "I mean, Jesus Christ Sway, he's fucking huge. Did he have a twin or something and eat it?"

"That's enough, fire crotch. You don't see him making fun of your *orange* hair."

That effectively ended our argument. He was sensitive about his orange hair. When we were young, he once tried to die it brown only to have it fall out and, if possible, it was an even brighter shade of orange now.

I spent a good twenty minutes on the toilet texting Jameson. It was the only peaceful room I had without Tommy.

Are you okay?

It was around one in the morning, I hoped he had made it from the track by now and was on his way home.

It took him a few minutes but he responded.

Yeah, I'm fine. Just frustrated.

I know. Sorry.

Don't apologize.

Call me tomorrow.

I have shit to do all day. I'll call you sometime after seven, my time.

Sleep well. I wasn't sure what else to say. I didn't want to go emotional on him through texting.

He never responded so I set my phone down on my nightstand while I brushed my teeth.

Just as I was getting into bed, Tommy yelled for me to come out into the living room. Thinking he was going to complain about Mr. Jangles, I took my sweet ass time.

When I eventually walked back into the living room, I realized this time he wasn't fucking with me, his concerned expression told me he wasn't done with our *previous* conversation, before he bashed Mr. Jangles non-existent metabolism.

Throwing myself into the chair beside the couch, I sighed. "What?"

"We're friends, right?"

"Yeah,"

"So are you and Jameson."

"Yeah?"

I wasn't following this conversation real well but it might have had something to do with it being three in the morning.

"Me and you don't kiss, we don't touch, and we don't spend the night texting each other like teenager girls but ... you and him do. That right there should tell you the answer to your question."

Did I mean more to him than his best friend?

I couldn't sleep after that so I laid in my bed trying to force myself to sleep but it didn't work.

My phone buzzed causing me to jump, my head smacked against my headboard. Glancing down, I noticed Jameson had responded to my text message.

You too honey. Talk to you tomorrow. Thanks for being there for me.

Did he feel more than friend status?

Whatever he felt, I couldn't change the feelings I had. So unfamiliar, they felt like someone else's thoughts, surging tides engulfing me in the memory of him.

Running Light – This refers to a car that is running light on fuel. Most teams qualify with a light load to achieve the maximum speed from their cars.

In between the Richmond race and the Winston Open, I had a bi-week. I thought maybe I'd be able to fly out to see Sway before her graduation and make up for not being there, but no, my conscious took over.

The night after the Pontiac Excitement 400 in Richmond, I was heading to Charlotte for an interview followed by various appearances at a few dealerships and then an appearance for Simplex.

After Tuesday, the rest of the week and the weekend was opening up nicely. Feeling jaunty that I might have some time for myself, I checked my Blackberry. Shaking my head, I wasn't surprised to see around forty emails, fifteen text messages and a dozen voicemails. Most of them I knew Alley would take care of so I skimmed through a few emails from her letting me know my schedule for the next week. Thursday through Sunday looked open.

Scrolling through the text messages, I noticed a couple from Sway asking me why Tommy didn't have stuff to do. Without unspoken words, he kept track of her. Not that I thought she needed to be checked up on, I just wanted to ensure she was safe. Tommy did that when he could.

So there I was, getting ready to call Wes when I listened to my voicemails. A few were from my mom, wanting to know if I could attend a charity event for the Children's Hospital in Nashville next week. The one that caught my attention was from Justin.

"Hey, Jameson ... it's Justin. I wanted to let you know that Ron Walker was killed last night at Williams Grove. I don't know how it happened but they cancelled the Outlaw race for next weekend to run a memorial race there. You might think about coming."

Well, shit, there goes my free weekend.

The next voicemail was from dad.

"Call me when you get this. I mean it Jameson, you better call me when you get up. This is important."

And then one from Emma.

"Hey, asshole. Call me. Like right now. Where are you anyway? You better call or I will just keep calling."

Time for myself?

Yeah, that ended when I decided to race for a living.

I called dad first knowing damn well if I didn't he'd take it out of my paycheck somehow. "Hey," I said, nonchalantly when he picked up. Throwing a few shirts in a bag, I walked into my bathroom to pack a few toiletries knowing that either way I looked at it I wouldn't be home this weekend.

"It's noon, why the fuck were you still sleeping?"

Holding the phone with my ear and shoulder, I snorted. "I didn't get home until four." I replied on the defense. "That's why."

"*Oh*, well Ron Walker was killed last night at Williams Grove," his voice was rough and drawn out like he hadn't slept.

I knew he and Tyler were racing there the other night so I assumed they both saw the accident, if it was an accident.

"What happened?"

"There were a few late models on the track and Ron was out there taking photos when one lost control. Both cars hit the tractor tire he was sitting on."

As much as it sucked, this wasn't the first time this had happened.

It's dangerous being out there in the infield when a car is on the track.

"USAC and the Outlaws cancelled Friday and Saturday night races for a memorial race at Williams Grove. Can you make it? Alley said you were free this weekend."

Do I make the responsible decision here and show respect for a long-time friend of my dad's, and a track promoter who had a hand in my career?

Ron Walker was not only a well-respected USAC team owner of around ten cars that ran in the different divisions but he acted as a track promoter for not only the USAC divisions but the World of Outlaws and various sprint tours. So, do I show my respect for him *or* do I blow it off and go see Sway?

"I, uh ... can I think about it for a few minutes?"

"Do whatever you want, Jameson," he clipped and hung up.

Way to make me feel like an asshole, dad.

Was it so *wrong* to want some time to myself? And was it wrong the time I wanted, I wanted it to be with Sway?

I felt like I was about to combust if I didn't get a chance to process everything that had been happening lately.

What happens when you put high-energy fuel (this being me) into a small enclosed space and ignite it? An incredible amount of energy is released is what happens. That energy can be used as the core to your engine. And, it seemed, like my life these days, combined energy with air and the explosion took on another meaning.

I must have sat on the edge of my bed for an hour staring at my phone, pleading with it to make the decision for me.

Racing or Sway?

Another hour passed and I thought of Charlie. What if this was him, would I be there for a memorial race?

In a heartbeat.

I made the decision and I went racing.

I talked to Sway later that night and though she hid it well, I sensed the sadness when I told her I wanted to come see her, *but* couldn't.

"Don't feel bad, Jameson," she told me after I apologized again.

"I would be upset with you if you came here instead of going to that race."

"You would?"

"Yes, I would. Ron helped you get to where you are now. Pay respect where respect is due."

She had a point, she always did. "How would I ever survive without you?"

"Oh, you wouldn't," she teased. "I'm pretty sure you would combust without me."

"You're probably right," I chuckled at the irony that I was comparing myself to the engines combustion and, here she was, thinking I would combust without her. In reality, I would have already if it wasn't for her.

I called Emma back after that. Knowing me well she and Alley already had the plane lined up, which meant I left tomorrow afternoon for Pennsylvania.

"Ron Walker paved the way for many fresh faces we see today in some of the premier divisions. He had the ability to see talent where most would turn their heads but Ron gave them a chance at greatness." Mark Derkin's, track owner of Williams Grove, voice carried throughout the stands and infield prior to the memorial feature.

Standing there beside my fellow racers, fixed gazes on the flag stand where Mark stood, remembering an adherent man who changed the lives of many of us. An eerie silence fell over the mass of fans and drivers, until Justin sneezed beside me.

A few of us chuckled when he apologized.

I'd never faced death before. My uncle Lane died when I was young but I had vague memories of him. Since then, I had yet to see if first-hand. Even now, with Ron, this wasn't first-hand and though I knew him, I didn't know him on a personal level. I knew he had a daughter, Jessica who raced sprint cars but, other than that, nothing.

I couldn't have even told you how old he was.

Jessica was standing a few feet from me, watchful of everyone, taking it in. Blinking slowly, her shoulder length black hair swept across her face shielding her tears. This had to be hard for her, losing her dad. Instantly I thought of Sway, flashes of her doing the same when Charlie died, only alone.

Racing never stopped, ever. But when someone within the racing community died, that's when our sport shined. Jessica wasn't alone today. At Williams Grove, on your average weekly race, you'll see about forty cars competing for a spot in the main.

That night there were one hundred and sixty cars that showed up to pay respect for Ron Walker.

Sway wouldn't have the sentry of the racing community. I knew that when Charlie did die, hundreds of racers would flock to Grays Harbor to show their respect just as we were doing tonight, but who would be there for Sway. Who would *really* be there for her? Could it be me?

Not likely with a ten month schedule followed by two months of testing in the off-season, racing never stopped. It's a twenty-four hour a day job, 365 days out of the year.

Before the feature, Jessica made a slow pace lap in honor of him then the twenty-seven car field merged in before creating a 4-wide salute. Usually a feature only had twenty-three sprint cars but twenty-seven was the number of years Ron had been involved in race promoting, so we ran twenty-seven cars.

You'd think being a memorial race, no points, no money, just laid back racing, we would have simply raced and took it easy.

No, hell no. We are all stubbornly aggressive but guess who won?

Jessica Walker.

A number of us could have taken that win at the end but we all knew what that win would mean to a girl like Jessica having lost her father. It would have meant everything, and it did.

She approached me after the race while Justin, my dad, Ryder and I threw back a few beers. I only met her a few times before, so when she hugged me, I was a little taken aback.

"Thanks for coming. I know you have a busy schedule but my dad was proud of you and you guys," she gestured to Ryder and Justin as well. "Thanks."

I smiled kindly returning the hug.

"You're welcome," pulling back to look at her, blue gray watery eyes focused on mine. "I'm sorry about your dad."

Not sure what else to say, I left with those words, walking toward the haulers to load up the cars. Justin nudged my shoulder.

"Given any thought to adding another driver?"

For the past few months I'd be humming it over with Justin and my dad about adding another car to my sprint car team in the World of Outlaws. Not that I needed my dad's approval to add another car to my team, but I looked to him for any business endeavor I made.

"I have," I told him.

"Who's the new wheelman?"

"Either Ryder or Tyler. Though I think Ryder's contract with Donco won't allow him to race Outlaws while he's racing in the USAC divisions."

"It won't. We talked about it last week."

By now we made it back to the hauler where Tommy was already loading the cars with the help of Spencer and Aiden. Not that I would have ever asked them to, but as soon as my team found out I was racing here for Ron, they dropped all their vacation plans for the weekend and followed me. Goes back to the tight knit racing community thing I talked about. They'd do anything for you, anytime.

Loading up the last few tools and tires, I watched Tyler sign a few autographs as he strode toward us. With the humidity resiliently suffocating, his racing suit was pulled down to his waist, revealing his bare chest.

Even being around midnight by now, it was still at least ninety degrees outside and a hundred percent humidity. I was moments away from taking my own shirt off.

"Are you auditioning for *Chip and Dales* later?" Ryder teased walking past him.

Tyler chuckled and continued signing. He was becoming a popular driver admired and talented, among the dirt world and exactly who I wanted racing my other car.

Not that I wouldn't have chosen Ryder. No doubt he had the skill but unlike Tyler and Justin, Ryder preferred USAC. Since he returned to racing after the accident in Williams Grove, he enjoyed the ability to run all three divisions each season and his full-ride sponsor in all of them, Donco, allowed him to do that.

Tyler, on the other hand, was running a limited USAC schedule and any Outlaw race he could make with the help of Ron Walker. Now that Ron had passed away, Walker Racing was an unknown.

When negotiating business, my black or white personality worked well. Nothing like the cagey personality I displayed with Sway, I knew what I wanted professionally and had no problem asking for it.

"Will you drive my other car on the Outlaw tour next week?"

"Next week?" Tyler asked perplexed. "You already have another one built?"

"Yeah, it's ready to go. CST dropped the engine off last week. Tommy got everything ready."

My Grandpa Casten and CST Engines, still one of the largest manufactures of 410-sprint car engines, provided all the engines for my team.

"Sure, why not. Don't think I'm doing this for free though," he added with a smile.

Tyler wasn't a large guy, at barely five-foot-nine, and I was able to knock him to the ground with one shove.

"Sixty percent of your winnings—travel's paid for."

"Now we're talking." Tyler nodded hoisting himself from the dirt. He brushed rocks and a few leaves from his legs before smiling again. "Are you serious?"

"Have you ever known me to joke about racing?"

"Nope,"

"There's your answer." I squeezed his shoulder. "You and Justin fly out Tuesday for Grand Rapids."

Later that night, after flying home to Mooresville, it was around two in the morning when I finally reached my room. Fully clothed, I threw myself on my bed, yearning for sleep I knew wouldn't come. Racing always left me rather amped.

Vacillating between not calling and calling, I opted to text her. My thoughts had been centered on her all night and I couldn't sleep without the connection.

To my amazement, she texted me back.

How was the race?

Instead of texting her, I called. With the harsh blinding edicts of everything around me, she was like a balm, providing a refuge. As much as I didn't want to admit it, to get through the day, I needed her. For someone who was so blatantly focused to make his own path in the world, I was sure reliant on her.

"Are you all right, Jameson?" I knew right then she was looking for the honest answer, not the standard, "*Yeah, I'm fine,*" I gave to everyone else.

"I just ... I don't know, honey. I don't know what's wrong with me these days."

"You're in a stressful position," she said mellifluously. "It's understandable."

Closing my eyes, I listened to her voice, tranquilly soothing. "Are you ready for graduation?"

She laughed, a smile tugged at the corners of my mouth. "It couldn't come soon enough. I hate these assholes here."

"Who's an asshole?"

"Don't get mad."

"You know me better than that," I warned. "*Never* start a conversation with don't get mad."

"Fine, I won't tell you then."

"Don't do that," I snapped.

"Blake kissed me," she blurted out. "I kicked him in the balls and Tommy rescued me."

You could have heard a pin drop. My voice, failed. My throat felt like someone had dumped sand down it. Gasping for air, I replied with, "What?" at the same time.

"I, uh—"

"I heard you the first time."

"Oh, you said—"

"Nope, heard you," coughing, I tried to relieve the dry sensation rolling up my throat.

We were both silent for a moment, me concentrating on breathing, her with hesitation in fear I was going to snap. Finally she stuttered out. "Jameson?"

"I'm here," my answer was quick. "Just thinking,"

"About?"

"Killing Blake,"

"That's a little harsh. I already kicked him."

"It's not good enough." My voice was even again, surprisingly controlled.

"You focus on your career ... not unwanted kisses."

"Unwanted?"

"Yes, unwanted. I never had feelings for Blake."

"Good?"

"Yes, good. I don't want you kissing guys."

For the love of God! What the fuck? Do I say something else?

"I don't want to be kissing *other* guys," she offered. And don't think I didn't catch the "other" part. I held onto the word as though it was a gravitational pull.

Sway's alarm sounding changed our conversation to her final she was taking today. Soon, we ended the phone call with a plan to talk later today after I got some sleep.

The problem was, I couldn't.

Part of me was focused on Sway saying other guys, the other part, the obsessively selfish side, wanted to kill Blake. Any guy who flouted a women's rejection, deserved to be knocked around. Though I wanted to do it myself, I knew I couldn't. I planned to be in Grand Rapids for the Outlaw race there on Tuesday before flying out to Charlotte on Wednesday.

One rash decision later, I was calling Spencer.

"This better be an emergency?" he said groggily. He couldn't have had much sleep yet, my alarm clock beside the bed flashed 3:45am.

"It is ... well, not really ... no it is an emergency."

Trying to figure out how it was really an emergency, I thought for a second.

"I'm waiting," he pressed impatiently.

"A guy named Blake McCoy is giving Sway trouble at school."

"Blake McCoy?"

"Yeah,"

"I'll take care of it."

"Thanks."

"Yeah, no problem."

And that was that. I knew by "taking care of it" he'd have his police officer friend, Josh Keller, scare him a little.

It took me a good few hours to calm down from the kissing incident but eventually I did and was able to get a couple hours of sleep before I headed to the race shop.

Sunday and Monday I spent preparing both the sprint cars for Grand Rapids. Every track had a different set of rules so we had to make a few changes to the cars, check all the bolt-on parts, and safety equipment before Tommy came by to check setups.

"You know, you should have told me," were my first words to him.

Tommy backed away toward the door. This might have had something to do with the fact that I was holding a wrench in one hand.

"Uh ... told you about what?" his eyes shifted around me.

He knew damn well what I was referring to.

"Blake," I clarified, my inquiring scowl probed for answers.

"Oh, that." He let out the breath he'd been holding. "Well, I was going to but she asked me not to."

"And you listened to her?"

"Like I told her, you scare me. Like hell I was going to tell you another guy had his hands all over her."

"She said he kissed her. She didn't say anything about hands."

"See ..." he sighed heavily opening the door to the fridge in the shop. He retrieved two beers before closing the door and handing me one. I waited for him to answer but it seemed he was taking his time.

"See what?" I pressed opening the beer and taking a drink.

"I don't like getting in the middle of this shit."

He was right, but I would be asking Sway about the touching later. Bile rose inside me thinking of another man touching her. Touching what I wanted badly.

I wasn't *mad* at Tommy, I was *mad* at myself for not being there for her. She didn't deserve to be molested by that douche. No, she deserved to have a man around who would take care of her and not let things like this happen. She deserved someone to worship her in all the ways I did inside. I wanted to be that guy. *God,* did I want to be him.

"When will you two wake up?"

"Probably never," I answered without thinking.

"She is so in love with you that it's revolting to be around."

I smiled. "Nothing about her could be revolting."

"Give me that wrench." Tommy reached for the wrench as I held it above his head.

"Why?"

"So I can smack your pussy-whipped ass."

"I'm almost certain the term 'pussy whipped' ensures you are getting pussy. That's not happening."

Conversation changed to sprint cars after that which was fine by me. Tommy and I ended up changing the weight around in both cars before loading them onto the hauler so Greg, Justin's cousin could drive the truck to Grand Rapids.

"Did you get the new sponsor?" Tommy asked handing Greg and Rusty, one of the mechanics for the team, the directions to the track.

"Yeah, got Ayers as primary sponsor for the No. 19 car."

"The one Tyler is driving?"

"Yeah."

"Look at you, business man," Tommy teased, the guys laughed. "Raking in the sponsors left and right."

"They see the name, Tommy. It has nothing to do with me."

It was true. My name had become somewhat of a household name in a matter of months. I now had sponsors approaching me.

When Wednesday rolled around, it was time to head for Charlotte for the Winston Open. Usually when I flew out to a track, most of the team was already there. Since this race was only thirty minutes from our shop in Mooresville, we all had an extra day. All but me, I had to be there for hospitality events. Simplex Shocks and Springs' headquarters was located in Charlotte so any time we raced there, I was jammed full of commitments for them. When a primary sponsor shells out close $12 million dollars for an entire season, you don't ask questions.

If Melissa, the rep for Simplex, told Alley I would be somewhere, I had better be at that somewhere if we wanted to keep our sponsor.

Puppet strings sound familiar?

All that aside, I don't forget what those strings allow me to accomplish. Racing. So many drivers fight their entire careers to make it to where I am and I'm here living the dream. Controlled to the point that my life right now wasn't even mine, but still, I was able to race.

The Winston (changes names depending on sponsorship) was an All-Star type race prior to the Coca-Cola 600 that consisted of past winners as well as current winners, plus the past five winners of the regular season championship, similar to the Budweiser Shootout before the Daytona 500. Drivers were also eligible if you qualified for it in the 40-lap qualifying run called the Winston Open.

The Winston, as you can guess was held in the heart of NASCAR, Charlotte, North Carolina, at Lowes Motor Speedway. With the nature of the race, much like the Shootout, no points were at stake so the drivers made crazy reckless moves that usually resulted in usually only a few cars finishing the race. On top of that, the winner receives a million dollars. If that doesn't tempt you to lay it all on the line, I don't know what will.

The race, like the shootout, has a different format and changed every year. This year they had a 90-lap segment with elimination. I think they watched a little too much of *Survivor* and came up with this one. This year they ran only past race winners from the previous year, and all former Cup titleholders from the past five years, plus the winner of the qualifying races.

The first segment was forty-laps followed by a mandatory four-tire green flag stop between laps 10-30. Only the top twenty cars advanced to the next segment. The second segment was thirty-laps, only twelve cars advanced to the final 20-lap shootout to determine the winner. And, to make it interesting, they implemented a full-field inversion.

Most of my time there in Charlotte that week was spent with sponsorship obligations.

On Wednesday night, I had a meet and greet at the Ford dealership in downtown Charlotte that Alley attended with me. Being my publicist, we rarely spent much time apart. We both hated this by the way. She couldn't stand me and I personally thought she was a fucking bitch.

The meet and greet had the usual crowd of garage groupies, the girls who were in their early teens and wore enough make-up to appear almost twenty. Then there were the pit lizards with their tits hanging out of their tops and jeans so tight I was sure the seam popped their cherries, and finally there were the older ladies who followed me faithfully to every race and applauded my every move regardless if I called another driver an "asshole" on national television.

Then you had the corporate assholes who hung around for the free tickets to the races and a chance at taking home a pit lizard. They were almost harder to stomach than the actual pit lizards because they thought they were my best friend.

Walking toward the table, the lights seemed brighter than before, the crowd appearing larger. When they introduced me and I stepped forward to sit in front of them, the room erupted in cheers and clapping.

Putting on my game face, I smiled politely for them, taking time to sign everything they pushed toward me, speaking melodiously to the women.

I'll tell you something about this, not that I agreed with it but flirting with them did wonders for merchandise and product sales.

And who pushed merchandise/product sale?

That's right ... sponsors.

They paid me to be available to sell their product so this meant selling myself. As wrong as it felt, it was another part of the puppet game.

I knew encouraging them was wrong because I had absolutely no intention of playing along with whatever ideas they had concocted, but sometimes it was easier to go along and smile. If anything, it made the sponsor happy if let's say that one girl who I spent a few minutes talking to, left and bought a few T-shirts and then her boyfriend, pressured by her, bought shocks from Simplex. That's what Simplex provides the sponsorship for.

So even though I had no intentions with them, it was just business.

Even with all these women throwing themselves at me, I had no desire to leave with them.

It had been since last April that I'd been with a woman physically and though the need was there, the desire simply wasn't. I didn't find them interesting any more. Some peeked my interest, yes, because these pit lizards ran around the track dressed in barely anything, but that was as far as it went. Why did I feel this way? I can only assume because Sway is what I wanted. When I looked at other women, I pictured what Sway looked like.

Even with all those frivolous one-night stands, I can't remember one of them.

I remember every touch and every kiss with Sway. For a long time I felt like a line had been drawn in the sand between us, telling myself: "No way you're crossing that."

But as determined as I was to keep from crossing it, the destructive combers curtly toppling over my line, swallowing my will from beneath me.

I was left with my tenacious side just as equally determined to say: "What line?"

I was up earlier than I needed to be, a consequence of both traveling and nervous excitement of the Winston Open. I loved races like this when I could let loose and race.

Normally on a race weekend, you wouldn't find me in the garage area any other time apart from qualifying and practice runs. Usually I had too many other engagements. Not today, it was Friday, the day before the Winston and I had nothing for the morning or afternoon. Wanting to burn some energy, I went for a run around the track and then headed to the garage.

A few teams were in there but it was mostly calm. Nowhere near what it was like during practice sessions.

Sitting down on a pair of scuffs, I examined the new springs we were testing out. I have no idea how long I stared at those springs, clearly I was thinking about the spring rates or weight distribution, as I should be. My mind was a maelstrom of questions, thoughts and observations. Eventually, my attention was grabbed by my mom opening the door to the garage.

I don't know if my mom is similar to everyone else's but she had this way of always knowing if something was wrong with me, like right now.

"Have you ever stopped to think that maybe she feels the same way?"

"She doesn't," I was only lying to myself. I knew she felt that way.

"Have you ever asked her?"

"No."

"Well, then you don't *know*."

She was right. I didn't know for sure that she did or didn't feel that way. But now, with Charlie being sick, that changed everything. It didn't matter any longer. All that mattered was ... well, I didn't know. I couldn't tell you. That's what had me so confused.

"You can't change your situation, Jameson, or hers. But you *can* change how each of you are dealing with it. That's within your power and always has been."

We eventually started walking back to my motor coach when I caved. "I can't breathe." I told her falling against the couch. My hands in my hair, my eyes falling closed at the admission.

"I know. I've seen this coming for years," she said amiably rubbing my back with slow strokes as she did when I was younger to calm me. "You need to tell her how you feel."

"It's not that easy."

"For a boy who was tenaciously forthright as a child, it's hard to imagine you *can't* tell her."

She had a point, but with Sway, everything was different. "I don't ... what if she doesn't you know ... feel the same way?"

"She does. You know she feels the same way but you're scared she'll break your heart."

No matter how many people told me that, I never believed them. Why didn't I? That's simple, I *refused* to believe it. I knew she loved me, I saw, clear as day.

But I couldn't, for the fucking sake of my sanity, say it out loud.

Why this was so goddamn hard was what I wanted to know. When would the timing be right to tell her? Or would it ever?

Do you wonder how important timing is?

In racing, it's everything as well as in life. People think you're lucky when you win or you were just in the right place at the right time. At least that's what I've come to believe. You never know when your time is right or when lady luck will shine down on you.

I remember when my eyes first met Sway's that summer night at Grays Harbor, that's timing. You could call it fate or destiny but really it was timing. That night we were meant to cross paths and we did. Now here we were, eleven years later, still hanging on so perilously to each other refusing to admit where all that timing had led us.

My mom sat there as I poured my heart out to her. I told her how I felt and that I was scared. But the thing was, even if she told me Sway felt the same way, it didn't change anything. Even if Sway told me, it didn't change anything.

Knowing myself, I knew it would take more than words to prove this to me. It wasn't that I didn't want to believe it either, like I said, I knew she felt that way, but I was scared. Scared of hurting her and scared of her hurting me. For someone who has never been in love with anyone or anything besides racing, you can sense my hesitation here.

"Why do you love her?" she asked finally. I thought she knew but I don't know if I'd told anyone. Up until that point, I had yet to say the words out-loud.

"I love her …" My voice failed for a moment. Clearing my throat, I tried again. "I love her because when she looks at me she doesn't see a famous race car driver or the son of Jimi Riley … she has always just seen *me*. She sees the stalwartly but jaded side that can only think of racing, yet she is still there for me whenever I need her."

Mom offered the only advice she had, which seemed easy but wasn't.

"Follow your heart, honey. Fate has a funny way of sorting itself out."

When the door to my motor coach closed behind her, I fell back against the couch again, left alone with my thoughts.

If only I could escape them, too.

I was beginning to hate myself for the simple fact that this moody, over-analytical asshole wouldn't shut the fuck up.

I didn't pay a lot of attention in school because it didn't hold my interest. No car, I paid no mind. I did, however, enjoy mythology and remember the story of Fortuna, the goddess of fortune and personification of luck in Roman religion and the goddess of fate. Presently life's capriciousness, she would be represented as either veiled or blind as in the modern depictions of Justice. Representing good or evil, fortune or misfortune, *basically*, fucked, or not.

I tend to believe you make your own fortune and your own fate. It's on you, not others. Too bad I couldn't listen to my own advice.

Later that day, before the drivers' meeting and introductions, a few girls hunted me down when my team and I were having lunch at my motor coach.

Usually I never conversed while signing autographs other than simple greetings, but these girls tried hard, so I chatted for a moment hoping they'd leave and I could finish eating before the race.

"How are you guys?" I tried not to look at them, both dressed in barely anything, I didn't want them thinking I was checking them out. "Enjoying the pre-race activities?"

"Now that we met you, *yes*," they both replied with enthusiasm.

Spencer and Aiden started laughing from behind me as the girls clung to each one of my arms, snapping photos.

I thought maybe that would be the end of it after a few pictures were taken but they didn't leave. They hung around at my motor coach as if they were part of the team, mingling with my crew.

"Listen, I signed your autographs but this is my only place to escape," I bit harshly when they sat next to me. If my tone didn't set the mood for them, my glare did.

Let me tell you something. I'm an asshole. I know this for an absolute fact. Always have been. Believe me when I say it's been a point brought up every day by all my family members. So given my permanent status on the asshole bench, I'm never sure when I am being one, but it seemed that way now.

"We just wanted to have a little fun with you," the brunette told me meekly. "You don't have to be mean about it."

I pinched the bridge of my nose before my hand slammed down on the table next to me, glasses and silverware shook on the wooden table. "I'm trying to enjoy a meal. I'm sorry, but I'm not interested."

Some people think drivers should be available all the time. And if you're thinking to yourself, they're NASCAR drivers, not rock stars, how bad can it be?

Let me tell you something here, it is that bad. At the track, and keep in mind this is my first season in Cup and only my second season in NASCAR all together, I cannot walk from my team hauler to the garage without a swarm of fans following me hounding me for an autograph. It never fails that someone is always there wanting me to sign their shirt, talk to me, or get a picture.

So it comes down to where does a line get drawn?

I'm not sure it ever gets drawn.

Emma, who had remained quiet sitting across from me, jumped up knowing I was moments away from throwing something.

"Do you two even have passes to be back here?"

They both looked dumbfounded. Apparently they didn't have passes.

Within minutes, Emma had them escorted away.

"Thanks," I said, when she returned.

"They were even annoying me," she moaned. "You have a meeting with Simplex and Donco in about twenty minutes."

And just like that, my only chance at alone time was now gone.

"Of course I do," I replied standing. "God forbid I have a moment to myself."

For so long I tried not to let any of this break me but whether you want them to or not, pieces of you are broken away, falling away like ash from a fire.

Everyone wanted a piece of me, but I'll tell you something, there was a piece of me they'd never reach. They'd never have that defiant side that was persistently focused on what he wanted, took over to be a champion in the highest-level racing had to offer me, the NASCAR Winston Cup.

Roundy Round – A slang term used in NASCAR to describe an oval track.

With graduation day here, I had little time to watch the Winston. That being said, guess what kind of mood I was in during the graduation ceremonies?

Yeah, shitty.

I couldn't understand the purpose of a damn graduation ceremony. It seemed like a silly waste of time to me. On top of that, I had to deal with Jameson's crush brigade.

Two girls, Amanda Taylor and Erica Ward, were Jameson's crush brigade. Always have been. And these two hookers decided to go to Western, just like me.

Can you guess, me being Jameson's best friend, how they felt toward me?

Yeah, so they hated me. To be fair, I thought little of them as well. Especially Amanda. She had these beautiful blue eyes, blonde hair, sort of similar to Chelsea but more beautiful. Funny enough, she and Jameson had kissed a few times when we were younger so ever since then, she liked to throw this in my face.

The immature side of myself, wanted to say, "Yeah, well, I've felt his camshaft!"

I didn't though because, believe it or not, I was somewhat mature, if you think your average nine-year-old is mature.

Anyway, back to the point here, if there is one. Amanda and Erica caught me before the ceremony. "Hey, Sway," Amanda's eyes glanced around the audience behind me. "Did Jameson make it?"

Again, the nine-year-old in me wanted to say, "Yes, he's waiting for me in my bed." I know what you're thinking here, hello, Sway, a nine-yea-old wouldn't be thinking about a boy in her bed but that's not the point either.

"He's racing tonight in the Winston."

"Oh, right, he's in that NASCAR thing?" she acted as though it was no big deal.

"Yeah ... that NASCAR thing ..."

"Do you talk to him still?" Erica asked running her fingers through her red hair. "I thought you two were friends ..."

"Yes, I talk to him often. And, yes, he's my best friend, we *talk* daily."

That seemed to catch them slightly off guard, but they recovered fast, unfortunately. "If he's your best friend ... where is he today?"

"Like I said ... he's racing."

"Well," Amanda clipped. "I read he's single. He doesn't belong to you."

Where was all this coming from?

I had no idea how to react to them. They didn't teach this at the School for the Socially Challenged where, apparently, I was their valedictorian.

Normally, I would have said something both insulting and mean but I had nothing for them.

I had enough.

Making my way toward the throng of graduates gathered by the stage, I couldn't help but miss him. Knowing he had obligations now, didn't stop it from hurting that he couldn't be here.

I sent him a text: ***Amanda says hi.***

He replied immediately with: ***Who the fuck is Amanda?***

I think I just fell in love with you. I sent it before my brain identified what I typed.

Oh fuck! Nice job Sway! Crap.

I didn't know it was that easy. Lucky me! Who's Amanda?

Blonde, blue eyes, you kissed her your sophomore year...I told her I was carrying your love child.

That's my girl! Still not ringing any bells. Back to this loving me thing...does that make up for not being there today? I'm really sorry.

You don't have to be sorry. It's not within your control.

I know...it's still hard though. I miss you.

I know, I miss you, too. Good luck tonight. I'll be watching.

Thanks honey. Tommy has something from me for you. Talk to you after the race?

Yep!

"Sway?" I heard Tommy call out. He was easy to spot within the crowd with his orange hair.

"I'm right here." I raised my hand. Tommy hugged me in congratulation. Usually me and fire crotch were too busy fighting to hug but I missed Jameson so much in that moment that I returned the hug.

"Here," he said pushing a box at me.

Opening the lid, tears flooded my eyes as I took in the necklace nestled against the black velvet. It was a simple locket, with a delicate silver braided chain. My fingertips brushed across the silver oval keepsake, the oils from my skins left my imprint against the metal. Carefully, I opened the locket to see my favorite picture of us. We were probably thirteen, maybe fourteen.

It was after a race at Elma and we were sitting in a pair of sprint car tires. His arm was draped over mine and I was leaning into his embrace. Both of us had huge grins on our faces. Even at such a young age, unaware to the two of us, a deep emotional bond was being molded between us. One that would remain for the rest of our lives, pure, natural and everything we both needed.

On the other side of the locket was an engraving that read: *Siem-*

pre mi amigo

Recognizing the statement as *"forever my friend,"* I didn't realize I was crying until my tears fell against the metal, washing away my prints made.

Tommy pulled me against his side. "I don't know when the two of you will wake up ... but he loves you."

As much as I told myself he didn't, I think my common sense knew the twist our relationship was slowly taking.

And, as much as I tried, I couldn't deny what was inside me.

I sent him a text again, knowing he might not see it until after the race.

Thank you. It's beautiful.

Unexpectedly, he answered. ***Anything for you.***

I don't know why I hated this graduation so much. Maybe the worst part was that no one was here with me, aside from Mallory, who worked at the track with my dad. Charlie wasn't feeling good so he sent her. Jameson was racing, as was the rest of his family and Tommy had to leave be in Attica, Ohio, later today.

I left graduation as soon as I got my diploma and headed to the bar to watch the race with Mallory. After my run-in with Amanda and Erica, I couldn't wait to leave.

We ordered appetizers, drank beer and had a good time while the pre-race activities started on television.

It was nice to see Mallory again. Mallory Thompson, Mark Kelly's daughter, was currently acting as the Office Manager for the track and took care of things like insurance policies, ticket sales, payroll for the employees ... pretty much everything we wouldn't allow Charlie to do. I'd been assisting her with all this since I was six so I knew the logistics of it all.

"How's Charlie doing with everything?" I asked Mallory chewing my nachos slowly. I spoke to him often but he always talked about school.

She nodded chewing her own food, placing her napkin over her mouth as she spoke.

"He seems good. He and Ryan got into it the other day but all's good."

"Ryan?"

"He drives the water truck for us. You'll meet him. Which reminds me, when do you come home?"

"My lease is up next week so I'm going to move all my stuff during the week and then I'll be out."

"Do you need help?"

"No, Tommy said he'd help. He comes back from Attica on Monday." I reached across the table to dip my shrimp in the cocktail sauce next to Mallory. "The last time Tommy helped me move though, he drank beer while I moved boxes."

"How's that firecracker doing?"

I laughed. "It's fire crotch Mal, not *firecracker*."

"Right—forgot," she giggled.

Mallory was about as green as grass when it came to sex. Mentally, you would swear she was a virgin but her and Bryce had been married for the last three years so I hoped she wasn't still a virgin. You never know though.

"How's Jameson these days?"

"He seems okay, but you know Jameson ... he gets so diligently focused on racing he never bothers to take care of himself."

"I don't know him all that *well* but I definitely saw that side of him." Her soft caramel eyes looked over at me. "So are you two ..." her voice trailed off insinuatingly.

"Oh, no," I waved my arms around, knocked my beer on her and then started giggling when beer came out my nose. Coughing, I answered with a choked out, "Friends."

Mallory laughed as she placed a handful of napkins in her lap to soak up the beer.

"Sweetie, you and him have never been *just* friends."

"That obvious?" I sighed in admission.

I was lying to everyone around me for so long that I had no feelings for him, I almost believed myself.

"It took me a while to figure it out but sometime toward the end of your senior year I uh ... well ... saw you two kissing after a race." I racked my brain trying to think of the specifics she was referring to but I couldn't, so she went on sensing my confusion. "After the Northern Sprint Tour ... he won. Anyhow, I walked into the pits to close up the concession because I wasn't sure if you had already left when I saw you guys in the booth. He had you against the wall ..." her cheeks tinted pink as her eyebrows rose in question. This was her silently pleading with me to remember so her virgin mentality didn't have to continue.

"Oh ... that." I remember all right. That was the night his hands slipped up my shirt and my hands, well they dipped somewhere else. The interesting part about Jameson and me was we *always* stopped. I don't know why, but we did. Believe me when I tell you, I did not want to. There are so many times—I wanted to continue. I wanted so badly to feel his body against me in the most intimate ways. Really though, I wanted to fuck the poor boy senseless.

"So what's with you two then?"

"I honestly don't know," I told her honestly. "When we're together, we can't keep our hands to ourselves. When we're apart, he's the best friend I could ever ask for, always has been."

Cheering down by the bar halted our conversations. Driver introductions were going on for the Winston Open. One of the announcers in the booth, Neil, talked about Jameson while they showed the fans applauding him during introductions. "Jameson has an amazing feel for grip, always has. He can feel the changes to the track and car that ordinarily go undetermined by other drivers. That's where his team benefits," Neil commended. "For only being his second season in stock cars, you better believe this kid has more to offer."

The broadcasters interviewed Darrin Torres, driver of the No. 14, first about the recent run-in at Richmond. His comments were the same each week. "It's hard to respect a guy like Jameson on the track. He has no concern for anyone else."

I wanted to punch this Darrin fucker, having never heard the name until this year; I was not impressed with him.

They interviewed Jameson right after that. I smiled so widely that I thought my cheeks were going to stay that way.

"Wow," Mallory gasped at the television, then back to me with a dazed expression. "He's hot!"

"Tell me about it."

"He's definitely not the same rusty haired little boy, is he?"

"Nope," my eyes glued to the screen as he spoke to the reporter.

"This is your first Winston Open ... do you think you can get a good starting spot?" he asked Jameson. A group of girls, Amanda and Erica included, whistled when they focused on his face.

Jameson chuckled and leaned against his car on the grid. Spencer handed him a bottle of water before he answered.

I wish I was that bottle of water.

"I think we can get a good spot. My Simplex Ford has been great all through practice runs so ... I can't imagine it won't be now," he flashed a smile.

"With this being a 'have at it' race, how do you think the rival with Darrin will pan out?"

Jameson's body visibly tensed. "I guess we'll see."

"Have you guys talked since Richmond?"

"It's hard to talk to him," Jameson said disdainfully. "He doesn't respect anyone around him."

It never changed for Jameson, there was always someone trying to push him to the breaking point.

Why?

Because he is talented. They saw him as a threat and just like any animal, which everyone is whether you want to admit it or not, what do we do when threatened? We attack fighting for survival.

That's exactly what Darrin was doing. He was threatened by Jameson, as he should be.

Here Jameson was a twenty-two-year-old kid with only a few years of stock car racing under his belt and dominating the series as a rookie. Of course, he felt threatened.

Jameson dominated the NASCAR Winston Open and the Winston that night, winning the first two segments, and with stellar pit strategy, he came out first for the third and final segment after the invert.

Darrin fought with Bobby and Tate for the first few laps, allowing Jameson to pull away to a 2-second lead but with three laps to go, Darrin and Bobby had caught Jameson. The three of them battled the last lap taking corners three wide at times (unheard of I might add). You don't take the turns at Charlotte three wide, you just don't. Bobby lifted and darted inside down on the line behind Jameson but Darrin refused to. They bumped, they banged, and bounced off one another until they crossed the line sideways together with Jameson taking the win, but with a destroyed car. The bar was once again in an uproar of cheering and booing.

They definitely put on one hell of a Winston race. Men throughout the bar were cheering and fist pumping each other; women were clapping, the bartenders were nodding in approval, it was a good race and exactly what the fans wanted.

Their cars came to rest on the front stretch in front of the main grandstands where they both got out of their cars and the heated discussion continued, as did the bedlam from the fans. Those fans paid to see a Saturday night race and they got one, with the addition of a brawl.

Darrin shoved Jameson (wrong move by the way), Jameson shoved him and then they were struggling against officials to get at each other. By now, Jameson had tossed his gloves and helmet aside, as did Darrin. His enraged glower at Darrin said it all. They were yelling at one another while the officials fought to keep them apart. With the announcers from the broadcasting station speaking, you couldn't hear what they were saying but I recognized a few choice words like "Fuck" and "Asshole" or "Motherfucker" which was a standard selection of words when Jameson was upset.

They cut to commercial, so I immediately sent a text to Emma.

He's going to get himself suspended!

It took her a moment but she finally responded.

I know. NASCAR is calling them both to the hauler.

When the broadcasting station came back on, they panned to Jameson's car making its way to victory lane as Darrin trudged toward the NASCAR hauler surrounded by officials and crewmembers.

"Darrin," the reporter swarmed him. "Can you tell us what happened there on the last lap?"

"We both wanted the win. It's a big payout and a race where you let go. I wanted to win so I took an opening where I could," he replied with a shrug of his shoulders casually.

"What was the interaction there when you two came to rest there at the end?"

Darrin laughed with intent.

"He flaunts his talent out there like a brat with a trust fund," he told the reporter and began walking again. "There's a reason why he's called 'Rowdy Riley.' He's out of control."

Amazed that asshole suggested that was all Jameson, left me angry as they shot to the view of Jameson now in victory lane pulling himself from the car once again. If you thought this was all by pure luck that they suddenly catch the driver getting out of his car, it's not. That's all planned by the broadcasting stations. The driver gets the cue to get out of the car. If he doesn't listen, he has to do it all over again.

Crossing between frustration, outraged and the thrill from the win, he pulled himself from the car. His eyes were hard, but he smiled despite the scrap he had just been in.

Without a moment's rest, the reporters were there.

"How does it feel to win your first Winston race?"

Jameson chuckled sweeping a towel over his face.

"I don't think it's sunk in yet," he said. "I'm really excited."

I knew he was excited for the win, but I knew him well enough to know the win wasn't what he was thinking about.

"A millionaire now, huh?"

"Yeah, I think that's the payout, right?" he looked around with a grin as the crowd cheered behind him. "Guess so ..."

God did I want to be there to celebrate with them.

"What happened there after the race?"

"I feel bad we tore up the car there but it was racing," he told him. "It's a big deal to win this race. We've been fortunate for a new team that we have the best cars around. These fans wanted a show, they got that."

"Was that planned?"

"No, I never plan to destroy my race car like that," he said. "Tempers flare at these races. We both wanted the win."

"Darrin said you flaunt your talent like a kid with a trust fund," the reporter provoked.

Refusing to make eye contact with the camera, his head shook in a slow vexed movement. "He's just pissed I'm one step ahead of him out there," Jameson bit. "Every move he makes, I've already seen it and predicted what he'll do." He turned after that and faced his crew, evidently done with the interview. Couldn't blame him, they were only setting him up.

The reporter started to sign off when he saw Jameson take the microphone from him. "I forgot to say one thing," he smiled at the reporter. "I need to say hello to my best friend back home who graduated college tonight. Congratulations, Sway ... this win is about fans and you've been my biggest one, thank you, honey!" he winked at the camera and then turned back around to speak with the line-up of reporters waiting for their turn.

Jesus. Way to break my heart.

Mallory turned to me. "That was intense!"

I gasped. "You're telling me."

"Do you think he's in trouble?"

"With NASCAR?"

"Yeah,"

"Oh, yeah, they don't like that sort of thing. Emma said he's been summoned to the hauler already." Before Fox Sports went to another commercial, they caught up with Jimi heading toward the NASCAR hauler himself.

"Looks like Jameson got a little fired up at the end there with Darrin," they hinted probing.

"You can't expect him not to get fired up like that. He's passionate about what he loves." Jimi told them. "For the most part I think he's handling it well considering the way he's provoked."

"So you feel he's being provoked by Darrin?"

"Without a doubt," Jimi said, matter-of-factly. "Each week it's a different track but the same thing with Darrin ... but you have to understand Jameson has been in this game since he was four. There have been times he's pushed to his limit and times he doesn't handle it in the best way. He's a racer. At times, we don't *think* before we react."

JAMESON

I had won the Winston. I was supposed to be happy. But no, fuck no, there I was sitting in the NASCAR hauler defending my actions.

"This is your warning Jameson," Gordon said, his voice hard but controlled. "I don't want to ever see something like that again."

"You should be having this conversation with Torres. He started that shit coming out of turn four!" I shot back slowly rising to my feet.

Once back at my hauler, I forgot all about the fact I won the race, against all the All-Stars in the series.

Instead, I focused on the fact that I was, once again, dealing with a pugnacious asshole on the track. It never ended, every year it was another driver. And though it came with racing, I fucking hated it. When all you want to do is race, this petty bullshit was enough to make you second-guess the choice.

"Goddamn it!" I roared slamming my fist into the side of the hauler. The sheet metal flexed but didn't give the way I'd hoped. "What the fuck is that asshole trying to prove!" It wasn't a question, more of a statement and, as I expected, no one answered. Alley and Kyle stood there staring at me as though I'd lost it again.

Dad walked inside the hauler, slamming the door behind him. He glared at a few team members who had just straggled in to which they scurried right back out.

"What the fuck was that?" he demanded, his voice sharp as he looked directly at me. "Did you hear me, Jameson?"

"Yeah, I heard you." Holding on to the only self-control I had left, my hands grasped the stainless steel counters.

"Do you have any idea what that's going to cost us?"

Refusing to look at him, I nodded.

"I don't want to be the dad who constantly reminds you of what's at stake ... but I think I *need* to remind you at times."

"I already know." Though my voice was unsure, I knew. Believe me I fucking knew what was at stake. I was harked to every word spoken by the media, fans, sponsors, drivers, and friends at what was peril here. I knew. How could I forget when everyone was so unrelentingly reminding me?

"Do you? Do you *really* understand?"

"I understand!" I yelled and turned to face him. "I understand completely. Do you honestly think anyone is going to let me forget how much is at risk? You won't, Simplex won't, NASCAR won't, and Torres sure as shit won't!" By now, I was yelling just as loud as he had been when Alley came back inside.

Her eyes gauged our tempers flaring.

"There fining you five thousand," she told us leaning against the counter beside me.

"Five grand ... are you fucking serious?" This was unbelievable.

"Yep."

"For what?"

"Conduct detrimental to stock car racing."

I wondered if NASCAR found the increased ticket sales from our little brawl detrimental to them? Doubt it.

So, I won the Winston and got fined $5000 for brawling on the finish line in front of a frenzied crowd that NASCAR sales benefited from.

Nice, huh?

I understood NASCAR's position on this. I did. But you'd think a little more slack would be given in this area. These temperaments and aggressive driving did wonders for ratings, that's what I didn't understand. There had to be a line drawn somewhere with them and their penalties.

Was Darrin fined? No.

That right there should have told me something. As a sanctioning body, you'd think there would be a little more fairness.

I was fuming the rest of the night, until Sway sent me a text. ***Congrats on the win.***

Not wanting to say something negative, I stared at the screen for a good ten minutes before replying with: ***Thanks.***

I thought briefly about turning my phone off after that, but didn't.

Don't pay any mind to Darrin or the media. You raced fair and clean, that's all that matters. He's a jackass.

I know.

I hope you do know. And don't just say you know Jameson. You need to actually know because that's the difference here. Knowing and doing.

She had a point. Even clouded judgment could see that—the imperviously manic side of me didn't want reassurance—he wanted to be pissed.

The next morning after I went for a quick run around the track, to calm my impetuosity, I hit the weight room that the track had.

We didn't talk much as we were in there for a reason.

Eventually, Bobby did say something to me.

"That was one helluva show last night."

I simply grunted in return continuing with my bicep curls until I reached my limit. Setting the weights on the floor, I nodded. "Not exactly the way I wanted to end the night though."

"Yeah, so you got fined. I got fined for loose lug nuts during the second segment. It happens."

"He's an asshole. Always has been," Tate added as Andy walked through the doors. We all looked up at him as Darrin shuffled in behind him.

I left immediately. There was no way I could keep from throwing a punch or two at that asshole if he said anything toward me. I didn't plan on starting out my Cup career like this, called into the NASCAR hauler every time I turned around, but no, Darrin ensured I did.

I made my way back to my motor coach in the driver's compound after showing my credentials.

I shrugged out of my jacket not bothering to pick it up from the floor when it missed the coat rack as that would require a little more energy than I was willing to put forth at the moment. Tossing my keys on the counter, I walked past Spencer on the couch watching cartoons with Lane eating a bowl of cereal. Usually, I was the only one who stayed at the track in the motor coach aside from Cal—he stayed there, too. The rest of the team got hotels nearby. Spencer and Lane stayed with me last night though since Alley and Emma drove back to Mooresville.

With the Coca-Cola 600 on Sunday and practice starting on Thursday, I didn't *need* to go back home. It was only a thirty-minute drive so if I needed too, I could go home.

Pouring myself a bowl of cereal, I sat down next to Spencer on the couch, my phone vibrated next to me. Thinking it was Sway, I picked it up to see a text from Spencer.

Wanna go to Williams Grove tonight for the Morgan Cup Challenge?

I don't know why I texted him back, he was sitting right next to me but it was sometimes easier to play along with Spencer antics then to question them.

Can't. Have to be in Concord this afternoon for an appearance.

We'll come with you. We could eat at Longhorn.

That got my attention. Anytime we were in Concord, we ate at the Longhorn Steak House. If there was ever a time where I had to choose my last meal, it would be at the Longhorn.

Ok.

Let's go now.

"I'm sitting right here asshole. Stop texting me."

"It's more dramatic this way."

"How so?"

"I'm not really sure ... but it is," he smiled.

I took his cell phone from his hand and tossed it behind me. "You're an idiot."

Lane glanced up from his cartoons and grinned, milk dripped down his chin. "Who's an in ... it?"

"I said idiot, Lane," I corrected him. "And I was referring to your Dad."

"Oh," he said meekly and returned to his cartoons.

Spencer glared. "Why do you think I text everyone when he's here? He's like a goddamn sponge."

Lane turned around again and opened his mouth before Spencer stopped him. "Don't even think about it little man," he warned in his fatherly tone he had on rare occasions.

Lane, Spencer and Aiden ended up coming with me to Concord that day where we ended with Longhorn. Lane destroyed a plate of cheese fries, we had no idea his tiny three-year-old body could hold that much food. Remaining relatively quiet most of the dinner, I had a lot to muse over.

Penalties, sprint car teams, sponsors, Sway ... and it was just like me to *over* analyze it all.

The more I contemplated the twist our relationship was taking, the more I wanted it to take that twist. It was more than evident she was physically attracted to me. Her body responded to me.

I caught her watching me on more than one occasion, the long lingering glances, and the quick peeks out of the corner of her eye when my shirt was off. And then there were the more discernable responses when we were together intimately. The way her touch set my body on fire, the silent way her eyes pleaded for me to continue ...

even with all this evidence I had, my mind was telling me not to take things further with her.

Then I had NASCAR on my mind. Rookies were supposed to stay out of trouble, respect veteran drivers, and simply gain experience. Though I was gaining the experience and respect of the veteran drivers like Doug Dunham and Steve Vander, I wasn't staying out of trouble. I had Darrin to thank for that.

All this trouble with NASCAR wasn't helping my focus on my sprint car team as well. Our team remained fairly small at the moment so Justin, and now Tyler, needed me as the owner to be there for them. In sprint car racing, it's a smaller operation than these Cup teams. Where Riley Simplex Racing has grown to around a hundred employees now, I had five with JAR Racing. They needed me.

It may not have been the best time to start a sprint car team in the World of Outlaws—a series that had the most grueling schedule in auto racing—but it's where I came from. How could I possibly let that go? I couldn't give that up any more than I could give Sway up.

So there I sat leading up to the Coca-Cola 600, wondering what the fuck went wrong. I was peddled by NASCAR as the next champion in the series, but at the same time found myself in "Big Red" each week. A sprint car team with two of the best drivers on dirt but lacking the guidance of their owner and madly in love with my best friend who had power she didn't even know she had. She could take me down harder and faster than anyone I'd ever known. She had *that* power over me, a power I'd never let anyone have before in fear they'd use it against me. But just like sprint car racing, I couldn't let her go.

It wasn't an option.

The next few days before practice started for the Coca-Cola 600 were spent relaxing and fulfilling several sponsorship obligations.

I devoted some time with my crewmembers and other drivers in the compound. My motor coach was parked right next to Bobby's as it was every week and another rookie in the series, Paul.

Paul was a good guy; he seemed levelheaded enough and also disliked Darrin. I guess he and Paul ran USAC together back in '98.

Paul, Bobby, Spencer and me were hanging around outside Tate's motor coach with him Wednesday night when Spencer decided to embarrass me. His poison for this ... Sway.

I don't know why this happened so often but everyone was curious about us. To me, it was none of their business and I didn't take lightly to discussing it.

Paul, not knowing me well, asked, "What's with you and that small town beauty who comes to see you on occasion?"

I took a big chug of coffee, trying to give myself a minute to think.

But the coffee was fucking hot. It scalded my throat going down, making me take in a gulp of air, which, of course, made me inhale the coffee. I've learned over the years that inhaling is the distinctly suboptimal method of ingestion when hot.

As I tried to reign in my choking gagging and other nasty sounds I seemed to be making, Spencer leaned back in his chair, laughing at me.

Another half a minute of me spluttering like an engine out of gas, he laughed out. "I'm embarrassed for you."

I figured out gasping for life-sustaining oxygen, that I was fucked. Finally I answered with, "She's my friend."

"You are such a fucking liar," Spencer grunted sitting down beside me again and then felt the need to continue. "Those two have been messing around with each other since they were what," he turned to me looking for an answer. I simply glared. This did nothing to addle him. "I think since they were ... fourteen," he laughed. "Caught them dry humping in the movie room one night. She's been on his dick ever since." I was displeased to discover that the quality of his voice increased exponentially in relation to its volume. Now he was practically shouting.

"Shut the fuck up, Spencer!" I snapped punching his shoulder as hard as I could in a sedentary position.

"Friends with benefits ... huh?" Paul said. "I've got one of those. Works out nicely when I can't commit to anything."

"I've been telling him that for years," Spencer added before I punched him again. "Would have saved him years of pain."

"Do you understand what shut the fuck up means?"

"Yes," he laughed. "I'm choosing to ignore you."

"Fuck you." I grumbled making my way around the guys as they sat there laughing.

I went back to my motor coach and locked the door. My mind raced over what Paul said, he had one.

People did the whole friends with benefits thing all the time. It also ruined friendships just as quickly. But if anyone could do friends with benefits with a girl that wasn't complicated, it was us. We could have more, just a less complicated version. It's not that I ever wanted to have her and then the ability to sleep around with others. That was definitely not it. Sway owned me; I only wanted her. This was more about us having what we could have—given the situation we were both in.

Ball Joint – A ball inside a socket that can turn and pivot in any direction. Ball joints are used to allow suspension to travel while the driver steers the car.

"He's being picky," Kyle told me as I stepped on the pit box.

I rolled my eyes because when wasn't my son picky?

"There is nothing wrong with these tires but he thinks they're shit."

"What are his lap times?"

"Enough to break the track record ... that I might add, he already set in qualifying," Kyle sighed and pointed to the laptop in front of him. "These are his lap times for the last fifty laps ... but I can't convince him the car's perfect. Tony says every practice session, 'the tire wear improves. His lines are perfect, his driving is perfect!'"

Jameson poured everything he had into every lap whether it was practice, qualifying, or a race, so, if someone told me he wasn't giving it *everything* he had, I knew they were lying. That wasn't Jameson.

"Let me talk to him." I reached over Mason to grab the other 2-way radio. "Jameson, you copy? It's Dad."

"10-4, what's up?"

"Bring it on in."

"Just give me a few more laps."

There was no convincing Jameson of something unless he believed it to be true. To convince him of something, you had to show him evidence, substantial evidence. You should have heard the conversation we had with him when he found out there was no Santa Claus.

When he brought the car back into the garage, I decided it was time to talk to him. So many times I've tried, but someday I'd get through to this stubborn little shit.

While I waited for him to finish with a few interviews, Nancy approached us.

She was always like a fresh breath of air for me.

"Hey, sweetheart," she stretched up on her tippy toes to place a tender kiss against the stubble of my jaw.

I leaned in robotically. It'd been at least a week since I last saw her.

"Do you want to grab some dinner at Longhorn before the race in Concord?"

"Certainly, my dear ... but I need to speak with Jameson first." Leaning in again, I pulled her closer.

"Oh, well, talk to him tonight. He's racing in the Outlaw Showdown."

I tilted my head in her direction, arching my eyebrow.

"Does Simplex know about this?" Since they found out about his track that was added to his property in Mooresville, they monitored him a little closer.

"Absolutely, they scheduled it."

There's nothing I liked better than racing with Jameson but I feared it as well. What if something went wrong and, more importantly, what if that something was triggered by me? As you can see, my brooding offspring was *just* like me.

Jameson finally made his way over to us, scooped his mother into a tight hug and then eyed me skeptically. "I thought you'd be in Concord already."

"I'm heading there now. I stopped by to see how happy hour was going."

"Shitty, I don't know what wrong with it but I felt like it was lagging there at the end of the run. It's tight on exit coming out of four."

"It wasn't." I told him as we all walked toward his motor coach. We had to stop several times for him to sign autographs but eventually we made it. "Your lap times were enough to break the record you already set."

He seemed to consider this for a moment before smiling at his mom. "Are you staying for the race?"

"Yes, honey," he tucked her under his arm. Though he'd never admit this to anyone, he was a mama's boy. "I'm heading to Concord with your dad but I'll be back in the morning with your grandparents, too."

"Oh yeah? Grandpa and Nana are coming?" Jameson asked shrugging out of his racing suit once inside the motor coach.

We made small talk for a few minutes before heading to Concord for dinner and the race. I knew I didn't have a lot of time but I needed to talk to him before the race tomorrow. If there was ever a chance that I needed him to calm down and think, it was this next race. We couldn't afford another hit in the points like we took at Richmond and Jameson didn't need the added stress.

"Is Sway coming tomorrow?" Nancy asked Jameson when we were eating.

Jameson, trying to hide his smile by looking down, pushed the tomatoes out of his salad along with the cucumbers. Arranging them on a plate he glanced down at them several times as if he thought someone should take them, but his other half wasn't here.

I saw the way my son looked at Sway and I saw the look of pure heartache and remorse when she's not with him. I knew it because I'd been there with his mother. As a racer, you don't want to fall in love in the peak of your career. It's less than ideal when you're trying to balance everything and, without trying to, you can break their heart or they can easily break yours. It's easy to do. They see fame and forgot all about the person underneath.

Even though we live for speed, we have big hearts and when you make it, people seem to forget that. I also knew Sway would never hurt him that way. I hoped at least because, with Jameson, it would destroy him. Out of anything in this world, racing aside, Sway had that power over my son.

"I didn't invite her to come out," Jameson finally said. "She's busy."

"She graduated last week." I said. "How can she be busy still?"

"With the track, she's taking over as General Manager."

Now I understood the change in his personality within the last few weeks. I heard about him flying back to Elma to see Charlie and I had a feeling it had something to do with it. He wouldn't admit this but Jameson was looking forward to Sway graduating. We all were. Jameson was an asshole most of the time with his irascibleness but at least when Sway was around he was somewhat tolerable.

"I'm sure one race won't hurt anything," Nancy said to him reaching for his cucumbers. "I can call Charlie and see if it's all right."

Jameson didn't seem comfortable with the subject but I needed to say a few things to him. "Jameson, I know that you don't understand these feelings you're having for her, but eventually they will make sense." Smiling at my wife, I took her hand. "You can have both. It doesn't have to be one or the other."

Surprisingly, he contemplated this for a moment before his guard came up. "It's not like that with Sway and me," he guarded himself so tightly when the focus switched to her. Even the Russian Army couldn't break through to him.

Nancy and I both laughed, they'd both been denying the love they had for the last few years. There was nothing either of us could say to him to convince him. It goes back to that evidence.

Jameson stood and held up his phone.

"I need to go make a phone call." And, just like that, he disappeared around the corner.

Nancy sighed beside me. "Do you think they'll ever wake up?"

"Maybe," I told her with a smile. "Probably not, but let's hope so."

It took me six *long* months of arguing with myself before I realized I could have both, love and racing. The problem wasn't knowing you were in love. With Nancy, I knew right away that small town green-eyed angel stole my heart the first night I met her. It was balancing the two loves and being able to provide both the attention they deserved from you. Racing could consume your entire life if you let it. Since Jameson was four, he'd let it. But gradually, his interests shifted toward women. I should say one woman, Sway.

Nancy and I feared constantly that his lack of a *normal* childhood had something to do with his indecisiveness with women. Most saw him now as the NASCAR rookie sensation who took his precarious talents to the highest level but none of them knew the boy behind the wheel. There was a boy there, one who had fears but a hunger that outshined it. He was still a boy to me though, one that couldn't see exactly what he needed, the girl.

"What position are we in?"

"You go out twenty-third," Aiden replied wiping sweat from his brow before adjusting his black Simplex hat. Damp blonde curls peeked out from the sides.

Not bad, I thought. Qualifying in the middle was good, got a good amount of rubber down on the track and you also had the advantage of seeing what line was fastest.

I nodded while Aiden and I walked to the hauler. Spencer and Mason pushed the car toward the grid.

The qualifying order for a NASCAR race is similar to what you'd see at a local dirt track, aside from NASCAR using a Bingo parlor setup, whereas dirt tracks keep it simple and draw pills with numbers on them to determine your qualifying spot. It's a tradition with them.

Each team sends a representative to the draw. We usually send Aiden. With his personality, it's entertaining to watch him wait for a number.

Can you understand why we love this so much? He usually spends the entire time trying to foresee the future, so when he comes back it takes him a good hour to calm down.

When qualifying begins on Friday before the Sunday race, one car at a time goes out on the track. We start on pit road, have less than a lap to get up to speed then make two laps. They take the best time out of those two laps to determine your starting spot.

If there is a tie in the time between two drivers, the owner with the highest points gets the draw.

Only two things can send you to the back of the field after qualifying, missing a drivers' meeting or making significant changes to your car such as an engine change or switching to a back-up car.

"You ready?" Aiden asked reaching for his headset. Since last year, NASCAR has required a spotter when your car is on the track. The spotter not only serves as your eyes in the sky but they monitor track conditions, talk to other teams about positions and, oddly enough, calm you down when needed. As you can imagine, Aiden did this a lot.

Entertaining enough, he could make quick decisions on the track but couldn't decide on what socks to wear in the morning.

Pulling out my headphones, I smiled slipping my iPod inside my suit.

"Yeah, I'm ready."

And I was. Throughout the week, I was able to relax and focus on the bigger picture, winning the championship. If I could win the Triple Crown, Chili Bowl and numerous track championships, I could win this as well.

I'd like to think I was relaxed but after snagging the pole, happy hour was a different story. Suddenly I thought my car needed something more, or maybe it was me?

The night before the Coca-Cola 600 was my only free night.

What did I do with my one free evening for the week?

Yeah, you guessed it. I raced at the local dirt track. It just so happened that the Outlaw Showdown was only twenty minutes away in Concord. So Tate, Bobby, Spencer, Aiden, and I piled into a minivan and zipped over to Concord after I had dinner with my parents. Being a team owner now, I had a car ready.

"Why are you adding weight?"

"Because Skip said we were light."

Tommy looked over at Rusty, our mechanic, scratching his orange hair with a wrench. "Take the floor plate out and replace it with a steel plate. Let me know how much weight we're off then."

Rusty and his little helper, his brother, began tearing out the floor plate.

After weighing in again, we were still off by fifty pounds with my car, so I had them add a lead to the Nerf bar on the left side that seemed to take care of it.

It was a blazing hot day and even with the sun setting, as day turned to evening, the track turned dry and slick. Anytime the track crew tried to moisten it up, the sun had it dried out before the water truck had pulled off.

Some of the drivers were packing their suits with ice packs, while others dealt with it. Being used to the high temperatures, I dealt with it.

It was nothing like the race in Texas earlier in the year when the inside of my car was close to 135°.

Before the heat races, I made my way over to the flag stand for an interview with one of their announcers.

Simplex asked that I come, since they were sponsoring the Outlaw Showdown this year. This meant I had a little sweet-talking to do.

Standing there, I had my suit wrapped around my waist with a wet t-shirt clinging to my body. It probably didn't look appropriate but if you've never been on the East Coast during the summer with 103° temperatures and high humidity, you're not missing anything. Nor would you understand why I was standing in front of around five thousand fans sporting a wet see-through t-shirt.

I let out a small chuckle as they recapped my career.

"This young man standing here beside me," Richard's hand

grasped my shoulder shaking me slightly. I smiled wider and the cheering from the crowd intensified. "He started racing at four. By the time he was six, he had won two Regional Quarter Midget Nationals, moved onto the Deming Speedway Clay Nationals at nine ... then the Triple Crown, dozens of track championships ... Chili Bowl ... the list could take up to an hour of our time here but what you all want to know is who this kid is ... right?"

By their screams, they knew me all right.

Richard smiled and pretended to clean out his ears with a quick shake of his peppered hair.

"Looks like they know who you are already?"

"Oh, I don't know about that." I laughed. "Maybe they have me confused with someone else ...?"

"Do you think this is ... *Jameson Riley*?" the fans were literally all standing on their feet screaming. I think I said this back when I won in Rockingham, but I was utterly amazed at how popular of a driver I became overnight.

Richard went on to talk about the Winston race. I kept my comments short and nothing that would come off as rude. When asked about "Rowdy Riley" and Darrin, I simply replied with: "It's just racing. Anytime you put forty-three drivers together, tempers flare. It doesn't go beyond that, it's just racing."

"So you two get along outside of the track?"

"I wouldn't go that far ..."

The crowd screaming dissuaded Richard off subject and I was able to sneak away for the pill draw and then heat races. I ended up one tenth off the track-record, which my dad set. This left me starting on the outside of the front row with him.

It felt good to be out here and still competing competitively still. You can't understand the feeling you get when you can successfully switch to a completely different series, and win.

I loved being around my "dirt buddies" as I called them. Even though I was now technically considered Tyler and Justin's boss, it never felt that way. We were just a bunch of friends going back to our roots that night. Or at least I was going back to my roots, they never left.

And even though I wasn't racing with them anymore, times hadn't changed that much. Justin was still considered "Wicked West" and could pull slide jobs on some of the best on dirt.

Ryder remained the "Beast from the East" and then there was Tyler. His racing had taken off and soon got the nickname of "The Sleeper" because he had the ability of waiting until the last second and then coming on strong like wild fire.

Another kid that caught my eye was Mark Derkin's grandson, Shelby Derkin. He was a sixteen-year-old kid out of Richmond, Indiana. The kid lapped most of the 360 division in his main and could have easily qualified for the B-Feature in the 410 class if he had the power. Part of me wanted to hop into a 360 and see what this kid had to offer. This goes back to the side of me who always wanted to race with the best.

Why?

Because the only way to see how good you are is to race against the best.

After the drivers' meeting we hung around my dad's hauler waiting for the features to begin when a few girls made their way over.

There was one I looked at twice, thinking it was Sway. They could have passed for twins, though I doubted she had Sway's witty traits.

The girl smiled when my eyes focused on hers and she was pretty but was not who I wanted. Returning the smile, I turned away from her silently letting her know I *wasn't* interested.

Next thing I knew, her arm snaked around my waist as she leaned against my side.

"You're Jameson Riley, that NASCAR driver ... right?"

"Last time I checked," giving her another half-smile, I shifted away from her embrace.

"So are you sticking around after the race?"

"Nope," I answered vaguely.

When I looked back at her and her friend, it dawned on me just then who the other woman with her was.

It was Ami, as in Justin's Ami.

"All Outlaw drivers need to report to their cars." The intercom system announced throughout the pits.

Thank God! I thought to myself. It was getting harder and harder to get away from these pit lizards.

Our cars were pushed onto the front stretch and then we walked through the grandstands and down toward the flag stand where they introduced us by our qualifying order. Justin walked past me so I nudged his shoulder.

"Was that Ami?"

"Yeah," he grinned widely. "I saw her about a month ago when I made it out to Elma for that Modified Nationals with Tate."

"So are you guys ..."

"Not sure. But she's here ... that has to be a *good* sign, right?"

"Clearly, you're asking the wrong guy on that," I chuckled adjusting my hat. "Have you not seen me around Sway?"

"Oh, I have," Justin nodded. "But you didn't fuck up the way I did. I broke her heart, and now, well, I couldn't live with myself if I did it again."

"Don't then," I ventured.

He snorted as we filed in beside the stage they set up for us to walk across. "Nice advice."

I didn't get a chance before the roar of the fans and fireworks drowned us out.

"Ladies and gentlemen, you wanted the best, you've got em' here. Let's introduce your starting line-up for the Outlaw Showdown, the heavy hitters of the World of Outlaws!" the announcer drew out in a deep enthusiastic voice. "Starting on the inside of row one, we have the King, your very own, fourteen-time champion ... Jimi Riley!"

"Starting on the outside ... the son of the King and NASCAR's *Rowdy Riley*, none other than Jameson Riley!"

Tipping my head at the crowd, I smiled when they roared to life. Dad turned around, glaring. I'd clearly gotten more cheers than him.

He threw his hands up in the air at the crowd before they admired their champion.

Laughing, he pulled me into a headlock.

Like I said, it was nice to be around my dirt buddies. I considered them my family, yes, my dad technically was, but Justin, Tyler, Ryder, Tommy ... they were all my family in some way.

"How'd the car feel?" Tommy asked sometime after the heat races. He was running around making sure all of us had the right setups.

"When I lift, I got instant stick, maybe too much."

Tommy went right to work on the adjustments.

When we finally started the feature, dad was all business. He was leading the series with Justin a close nine points behind him. He had no room for mistakes and I almost felt bad about being in the mix with the point leaders but I also knew if any of them had the chance to race cup and compete at those levels I had been, they wouldn't question it.

So why should I?

Engaging the coupler, I signaled to the driver, letting him know I would be taking off. The car roared to life. The sound is absolutely addicting. Nothing sounds like or feels the way a sprint car does.

Even my Cup car was nowhere near the consoling meditation that a sprint car provided. I think the best part was the feeling I got just being out here, around the dirt track again. It was exactly what I needed. The dirt, the methanol, even the sunscreen worn by the women, all reminded me of a time Sway was with me, a time when everything was so much simpler, though I'd never taken the time to appreciate how simple it was.

That was until around lap thirty something of the feature and I ended up tangling with Tyler on a re-start. He blew a right rear tire and took me with him.

It was no one's fault, he didn't make it blow. Sprint cars are so temperamental that the tiniest change in that stagger I've talked about sends them flying without a moment of warning.

Being upside down was the least of my worries. I was more

concerned about the methanol pouring onto me. The problem with methanol burning is that it burns invisible, no flame or smoke. If a fire happens, you can't see it to put it out. But you can feel it burning you.

I started thinking of all the ways it could catch on fire. Certainly, it could reach a spark but that wasn't my concern because the engine wasn't idling. My fear was the 800° headers it was pouring onto as well as my racing suit. So while there was no obvious spark for it to come in contact with, the headers were another story. Methanol has a flash point of 385° so the 800° headers were starting to concern me.

Safety crews were scrambling around me, searching for injuries and frantically asking me if I was all right.

"Riley, are you okay?" they repeated that a few times before I could answer.

I nodded and gave them a wave. It wasn't like they could hear me with all the cars running past. Even on pace laps, they produced quite the sound.

Motioning toward the fuel tank behind me, I said. "The fuel is pouring onto me. Can you get me turned over?"

That got them going. The wreck happened right in front of the pit bleachers so both Tommy and Spencer were there to help get the car turned back over. My skin was burning from the methanol that soaked through my fire-resistant suit. It may not have ignited but it was still something you didn't want on your skin.

Knowing me, what kind of mood do you think I was in having a substance on my skin?

Not a good one, but that was all but forgotten when Justin held off the King of the Dirt for the win. My car, a driver I hired and my friend, won that night. The only feeling greater than winning, was seeing a friend win. After celebrating for three hours, I called it a night when that determined pit lizard from before starting hanging on my arm.

"Jesus Christ, you stink!" Spencer grumbled once we were inside the car.

I inhaled deeply. "There's nothing better than racing fuel."

On the way back that night, I drove with the windows down as the methanol was a little strong when confined. With the night's air, the warm summer breeze blew throughout the minivan. The freight truck's hum drowned out Aiden's obsessive talking and Spencer's intolerable snoring.

Being back on the dirt tonight confirmed one thing for me ... I couldn't wait any longer.

My stomach was in knots that night when I made the decision, a decision that was essentially eleven years in the making. Still ... my will wavered and probably would until I saw her again.

I had commitments now, obligations, fans, sponsors, the list endless and if I thought it would get easier, I was in denial.

So when would I ever get a chance for me?

Sure, I loved what I did, this was what I always wanted and worked so hard for. Racing was my life, my passion. Somewhere between the time I left home to chase this dream, and now, I felt something missing and it was her. The one that changed everything I thought I knew with one look.

For the longest time, I ignored the fact that I was in love with Sway for one simple reason, what if she loved me back?

If I didn't want to lose her, how long would I let this go on? I have only ever had physical relationships. How could I have more?

Just simply being my friend came with a price tag, imagine if she wanted more? How would that affect her life and how could I do that to her?

I knew my life would never be normal but I wasn't about to take away any sense of normalcy that she had away from her. How could I? Sway never had a say in anything and Charlie proved that.

Was it fair that she would soon have responsibilities that no twenty-two-year-old should have? No. The difference between her and me was that I asked for this. I knew the sacrifices I would have to make and was *prepared* for them from the beginning. She wasn't. She had no idea of the pressure and opinionative populace that was out there. Being pessimistically jaded, I didn't want her to know that side of the world but I soon wouldn't have a choice and neither would she.

Consequently, I knew my decision was wrong but I also knew that if nothing in life was free, then I was *ready* and *willing* to pay anything for her happiness.

"Who are you calling?" Spencer asked stepping inside the motor coach that night before heading to his hotel.

"Uh ... Sway," I admitted and hung my head waiting for her to answer.

"I'm sure you want to be doing more," he countered with a smug grin.

"Shut up," I kicked him on the way out. Gratifyingly, he fell down the steps. "Hey, wait, get back here." I yelled after him hanging out the door by my arm on the door handle.

He turned to me brushing dirt off his jeans. "What?"

"Did Josh take care of Blake?"

Spencer's eyes lit up like he'd just been told his favorite holiday, Thanksgiving, would be celebrated twice this year.

"Dude, you wouldn't believe how scared that douche was. Even pissed his pants when Josh and his buddy got a fake search warrant,"

"Why'd he piss his pants over a search warrant?"

"Turns out he was growing weed in his apartment and selling to the students at Western."

"No shit?" This turned out better than I thought it would. Even though I would have liked to see him threatened about never touching Sway again, at least he was in trouble.

"Shit." Spencer nodded turning to walk away. "Oh, and, don't sound too eager when you beg her to come out here. Have some dignity."

Chuckling as I swung the door closed and Sway answered. "Hello?" her voice bleary.

"Shit," glancing at the clock on the wall I realized it was nearly two in the morning there. "I forgot the time difference."

"Jameson?"

"Yeah, honey, it's me."

"Oh … good job on the pole,"

"Thanks … hey, I called for a reason." I paused, preparing myself. "Come see me."

"What?"

"This weekend," I clarified. "Come see me in Charlotte. I'll buy the ticket for you to come."

She was quiet for a few seconds, her steady breathing was the only sound before she sighed softly. "I, uh … are you sure?"

"Well, yeah," letting out a soft chuckle, I continued. "I asked—didn't I?"

She was silent so I added fuel.

"I miss you and I got the pole." I softened my tone. "Please, honey …" I begged.

"Fine, I'll come," she sighed with a soft giggle.

My perverted brain was focused on the fact that she said I could come. I blame this on the fact that I haven't had sex in over a year. Hell, I'd barely done any bleeding of the pressure valve these days.

We ended the conversation after that so she and I could both get some sleep.

After I called the airline and got her ticket, I was no longer focused on the fines handed down that had consumed my mind all week. Now I had the pole to the Coca-Cola 600 and Sway was coming.

Oh, goddamn it.

My body had *other* ideas at the thought of the word coming again, so I snuck off to the bathroom before heading to bed.

I woke up feeling both relaxed and energized. For one, Sway was coming to see me and I raced sprints last night. Whenever I got a chance to race on the dirt, I felt better.

Things were looking good, so I thought.

I only saw what I wanted to and had avoided the underlying feelings for too long holding out hope that they'd go away. They didn't. I was determined to do something about it this time. I was done messing around. We needed more from each other and if physical was all we could have, then so be it. The thought both excited and terrified me.

I walked through the paddock that morning, lifting my chin in acknowledgment at the calls from fellow drivers and fans who gathered.

My mind kept considering how I might tell her I wanted more.

I've wanted to tell her so many times how my feelings had changed but I couldn't. This lifestyle was not something I could ask her to adapt to, how could I? That was the part I couldn't get past because in order to give myself to her in all the ways I wanted to, my demanding schedule was what was holding me up.

I'm on the road forty weeks out of the year. Monday through Wednesday, I'm usually doing sponsorship commitments or working on sprint cars for my team. Thursday through Sunday, I was at the track racing and then it started all over again on Monday.

Prior to the team meeting, I stopped by the motor coach where Cal had fixed breakfast for everyone.

"What are you going to do when she's here? You know you need to be concentrating and not thinking of ways to get Sway in bed with you," Spencer asked shoving a bagel in his mouth.

I kicked him under the table we were sitting at. "Fuck off. It's not like that with Sway."

"You're in denial."

I shoved myself away from the table and got ready for my endless amount of interviews today.

On the way there, Sway sent me a text.

Got my ticket, be there at two. Someone had better pick me up, asshole.

I typed one back.

Headed to interviews. Can't wait to see you! Alley will pick you up.

Alley caught up with me after my appearance on Trackside Live.

"Hey, Jameson, you have a meet-n-greet in about an hour." She pushed her curly blonde hair away from her face—the summer heat was blistering today. Her porcelain cheeks flushed from the heat with Lane on her hip.

"Thanks ... hey," I flashed her with a wheedling smile.

My mood was never this good on the day of a race; this wasn't lost on Alley either who looked at me as if she'd never seen me before. "Can you pick up Sway from the airport today?"

She nodded her head looking down at her Blackberry. "Sure, but don't do anything stupid."

"What are you talking about?" Lane squirmed in her arms to reach for me. His bright curious blue eyes scanned around the humming boisterous atmosphere of race day in the garage area.

"With Sway ... just ... *don't*, Jameson," she warned handing him to me.

"Huh?" Lane and I both looked at each other—he squinted into the sun shining on him over my shoulder.

Alley slapped at my forearm.

"I know you ... you want ..." her eyes focused on Lane as she chose her words carefully, "*more* but I'm telling you right now, one of you will get hurt. Just don't."

Lane smiled at me, his expression strangely serious. "Mommy says no."

Great, now a three-year-old is giving me advice.

I knew what Alley was warning me about but I had to know if Sway felt the same way. I knew she had *feelings* for me but I needed to know for myself if there was any chance they might be more. I wanted more. I wanted it so *badly* it's all I could think about right now. Understanding how long it took me to come to this conclusion that I wanted more, do you honestly think I'd be persuaded not to act upon it that easily?

I wasn't sure how it would turn out once she was here but I had to try. I was done wasting time with her, I needed something, anything.

Every race day morning while I did my interviews and meet-n-greets, my car went through inspection at the far end of the garage. NASCAR officials picked over the car on an elevated platform. During various times throughout the weekend, your car was inspected. Usually before the first practice session, before qualifying, after qualifying if you win the pole, and just before the race.

They also do this after the race for selected cars, usually the top five finishers, the first car to fall out of the race not involved in an accident and one random car. You don't know if you're a random car or not until you're pulling onto pit lane and the official tells you. If something doesn't jive after the race, you lose the points awarded for the win and you're penalized. In most cases, you do get to keep the win itself.

They inspect everything from ride height, angle or size of spoiler, weight (they must weigh 3400 pounds with at least 1600 pounds on the right side without the driver), engine specs (the car must adhere to compression ratios and displacement), how the car fits into the templates, and restrictor plates if it's a restrictor plate race.

Now did I mention they check your fuel?

If I didn't, it's because I never thought about it, *until* today.

Our team had no reason to cheat, so why would we?

Each week we were consistent, always had been. I'm not saying we didn't bend the rules from time-to-time because every team did. You push and push until you get handed a fine. Then you know you can't get away with that any longer and you push the next issue. It's racing. With the competition levels the way they were, every team tried to "one up" the other. It was the name of the game.

So, yes, we pushed boundaries, but we never messed with the fuel or tires. Two things NASCAR heavily enforced.

All things considered, when Kyle approached me after inspections and prior to my meeting with Simplex to tell me they found something in our fuel, I wasn't pleased.

"What the fuck do you mean they *found* something in the fuel?"

"I don't know," he threw his arms up. "Mason said they made the crew drain the fuel tank and they took the fuel for testing."

Alley must have noticed my fuse was about out to ignite as Kyle was talking cause she stepped in front of me and her hands gripped my shoulders.

"Jameson," Alley's voice was full of warning. "Don't."

"Don't what?" I was getting angrier and confused.

"Lose control right now," she said sternly. "Just relax."

I grunted and walked away from both of them heading to my meeting with Simplex. This was not the shit I needed or wanted today.

While I was busting my ass through the paddock to make it to the hospitality tents Simplex had set up, Spencer chose now to talk to me.

Catching up to me, he slowed his jog to a fast walk. "Hey, dude, is Sway really coming?"

"Yeah, she'll be here later this afternoon."

"Are you going to *talk* to her?"

This was not a conversation I wanted to have right now or ever for that matter.

Glaring his direction, he grinned. "I'll take that as a yes."

My fist rose to punch his shoulder but he ducked away and bounced on the balls of his feet.

"Good luck, little brother!"

Before I reached the hospitality tent, Alley caught me again with Kyle trailing behind her.

"What now?"

"NASCAR wants to see you, Kyle, and Jimi in the hauler ..."

"I have the ..." I motioned toward the tent as my voice faded when I looked at her. Something was wrong.

She pushed me back the other direction. "That's going to have to wait. I'll talk to them, you go see Gordon."

So there I sat, in the principal's office again. Alley sent me a text when I was sitting there waiting for Gordon.

Whatever you do, don't answer their questions. It's exactly what they expect you to do. Be selective.

I typed my response while Gordon entered the hauler. He didn't look at us as he carried a manila folder inside his office and slammed the door behind him. The water pitcher on the desk outside his office shook from the force.

It's too late for me, they know everything. Get out! Save yourself!

Fucking idiot. She sent back.

I was surprised I was joking around but I had to or else, at that point, I was going to kill someone. Turning to Kyle who was sitting next to me, I asked, "Is there something I should know?"

"What are you talking about?" His eyes scanned mine.

"With the fuel ... did you guys add something?"

Kyle looked offended. "Do you honestly think I'd allow something like that?"

"No, but I'm just checking." I flopped back in the chair wondering how I could get us out of this mess. "I don't want to go in there defending us and then find out it's something we did."

"Our team would never jeopardize something like this." Kyle snapped. "They could impound this car ... you know that right?"

"Why do you think I'm asking?"

Gordon came out of his office after that, looking thwarted. "Riley, can you come in?"

Standing, I tilted my head toward Kyle. "You better be right."

Gordon was silent for a moment before he paced around his office, the room appearing even smaller by his constant movement.

"The officials said they found something in your fuel. They've drained the tank and you will be allowed to race that car with the fuel we tested clean." He paused, his eyes focusing on a stack of papers on his cherry wood desk.

"I'm not sure what's in there Jameson ... but if it's illegal, you better believe this will be *expensive*."

Oh, Jesus ... was he serious? This was just my fucking luck. Where's Fortuna?

Alley was not amused by the time I got back to my hauler. I refused to let this bother me and smiled at her despite my temper boiling under the surface.

She had no reaction at all, other than slowly raising a single finger to me hiding it from Lane. You can guess which one.

Spencer returned right about then from God knows where with more food in his mouth. "Why did we have to change gas tanks this morning?"

"Are you fucking stupid? Or have you not been paying attention?" Alley asked him handing Lane over to me once again.

Aiden walked with a cocky gait, he smiled wide tucking in his shirt. "Jimi's looking for you. He looks crazy."

Even better.

"Why the fuck are you smiling?" I asked heading inside.

Aiden's grin widened.

"Nothin' ..." his expression turned panicked as though I caught him.

Emma, straightening out her skirt, walked past as well but didn't stop. Race days were just as crazy for her as they were for me since she and Alley attended every media event I attended.

I couldn't understand why everyone was acting so strange today. You have Spencer who is in his own world. Aiden who just smiles, and then Emma, who apparently needs to check her attire before she leaves as her shirt was on backward.

Jimi was crazy when I walked inside, that much was evident by his distraught pacing. He reminded me of Gordon. "How'd it get in there?" he asked.

I looked behind me—I wasn't sure if he was talking to me, someone else, or if it was a rhetorical question.

"Marcus asked that we meet with him this morning so we should get going. Gordon informed me they found a mixture of methanol and ethanol in the fuel."

My jaw clenched as I started my own pacing, my luck just got a whole hell of a lot shittier. Like I said, NASCAR is very specific on fuel and tires and adding additives like methanol and ethanol into the fuel they provided was not allowed. If added it increased the oxygen content and, in turn, could make you go faster.

The problem was, how did it get in there if we didn't add it? As I've said before, the car is inspected numerous times throughout the weekend. Not one of those inspections detected anything wrong with the car. Why now? We had been using the same fuel.

"What does this mean?" I asked leaning against the stainless counter in the hauler. Kyle opened the door just then.

Dad looked up at him and then down at his phone he was flipping obsessively in his hand.

"They're fining us $50,000 but we get to keep the starting position since the additive wasn't detected prior to qualifying."

"*Fifty thousand* dollars for a fucking additive?" I yelled. "How the hell did it get in there?"

Dad and I both glanced at Kyle who held up his hands in defense. "We have no idea." His glare was evidence he really didn't know. "Mason and Gentry were with the car all morning."

"What about last night?" Dad asked his face scrunched as he contemplated all the ways something like this could have happened.

"Mason was the last to leave the garage area He said a couple other teams were in there but left right after him."

We had no answers, just that we were being fined $50,000.

Don't get me wrong, I understood the need for rules and respected NASCAR for what they did, but really?

This seemed a little steep for something we didn't do.

My other problem was explaining this to Simplex.

This was not the sort of thing your sponsor wanted to see. When you think about it, without corporate sponsors and fans, we wouldn't have this sport. The money provided pays for us to be competitive, such as buying parts, building these cars and paying the salaries for the team members and myself, oh, and according to NASCAR, buying additives for our fuel tanks.

In turn for this money, the primary sponsor has final say in team colors, uniforms, paint schemes and other team appearances.

What we do for the sponsor is present ourselves in a positive way and advertise for them.

How do you think we looked now?

Certainly not positive ... and when the media catches wind of the fines ... not positive at all.

After a few minutes of silence from everyone, I asked, "Appeal?"

"It was a kneejerk reaction by Gordon." Alley offered. "I think we have a chance with the appeal board on this one."

The NASCAR penalty system is black and white. It just is. They allow you to appeal their decisions and be heard in front of board members of the commission but sometimes this doesn't work in your favor and the fines are increased. If you still aren't happy, you can appeal to the national commissioner for a final appeal but his word is the last say.

My point is, these penalties don't make cheating impossible, just stricter if you get caught. It's like speeding. The ticket isn't going to stop you from, let's say, getting to work twenty minutes faster because you do eighty instead of sixty, but the ticket for reckless driving might make you think twice.

That's what NASCAR was trying to do, I get that. What I didn't get was the severity for something we didn't do.

I didn't break the rules and neither would our team like that. We had no reason to.

"We're appealing the fine," Jimi said, walking out of the hauler.

Alley let out a whoosh of breath before turning toward me. "Is Sway flying into Charlotte Douglas?"

"Yeah, she should be landing soon." Though I was still excited as hell to see her, my thoughts were focused on this turn of events with the fuel.

"Marcus is waiting for you. Just ... be careful what you say."

"Are you sure I should be talking to anyone right now?"

"No. I'm almost positive you *shouldn't* be talking to anyone, especially Simplex. But you're the driver, they want to hear from you." Moving past her she reached out to grab my shoulder, wadding a fist full of my t-shirt in her hand. "Do not, under any circumstances speak to the media about this ... I mean it, Jameson, decline to comment."

"Yes, ma'am." waggling my eyebrows, I asked trying to remain modestly coy. "When will you be back?"

I could not wait for Sway to get here.

"Oh, for Christ sakes, control yourself!"

Lane pointed his tiny finger at my nose, touching the tip of it. "Comtrool youself,"

"I'm not so sure I know what comtrooling is?"

"That not what I said."

"Yes, it was."

"Was not," he argued, his brow scrunched as he glared.

Ruffling his hair, I threw him over my shoulder. "You're definitely a Riley."

Two hours, a meeting with Simplex, and around a hundred autographs later, I was standing next to my car in the garage before they pulled it out to line-up along the grid.

"Did we get it filled up again?" I asked Mason and Trace who were going over their pre-race checklist on the car. Everyone had checklists on race day.

The Car Chief, Mason, had one. The Team Manager, Trace, had one. And the crew, directed by Mason and Kyle, had one. If you're wondering how the Car chief, Crew Chief, and Team Manager had different roles, they all had *very* different roles.

The Team Manager is in essence, the owner's right-hand man. He will oversee the day-to-day administrative duties that keep the team running. Originally, we had Alley doing this but, as you can guess, her double duty of being my publicist as well, she had a hard time balancing the two. Now we had Trace doing this, which worked out well because Trace had previously worked for Leddy Racing the past six years and he had the experience our team needed.

The Crew Chief, Kyle, who worked closely with the Team Manager, oversaw all the hands-on activities related to building and adjusting the car that will race on the track. As you can imagine, the Crew Chief needed to not only know a lot about racing and the setups of these cars but he also had to work well with the driver's personality.

Now the Car Chief, he had the worst job in my mind because he not only took orders from the Crew Chief but also the Team Manager, and me when I felt the need to tell him a thing or two I thought he needed to know. I can be an asshole, but that's nothing new. Mason was good people though, and took it all with thick skin. He handed down the orders during the race that the Crew Chief decided.

So if I said, "I'm tight coming out of four." Kyle would then say, "How about we make a wedge adjustment?" I then say, "10-4." or something similar. Kyle will then send those orders to Mason who directs the crewmembers on what to do.

Some may think that's a lot of passing of orders.

Yes it is, but if Kyle had to concentrate on not only deciphering my cryptic assumption of what my car was doing and worry about the crew doing their job as well, plus try to anticipate what could go wrong on the track and calculate fuel mileage, that's a lot to ask of one person on race day. Hence the need for all these guys.

Gentry gestured toward the official standing next to the car. "He watched us add the drums this time and hasn't moved since."

Mason's voice was harsh and low when he spoke. "Where was he when the additive was placed in there?"

Since the impromptu team meeting we had an hour ago, most of us felt it was added by another team, I had a pretty good fucking idea whose team that was by the way.

"How was the car running in happy hour?" Tony asked approaching us.

Tony, as the tire specialist, kept logs of tire wear, air pressures and temperatures throughout all practices to calculate any changes we may need to make during a run. A run was the distance between each pit stop.

The car was running so I had to speak over the idling.

"I was tight coming out of three but the more laps I made, the more the car came to me," I told them.

Kyle stepped inside the garage motioning behind him. "Looks like someone's here for you," he smiled.

You would have thought I had been shot with the pain that hit my chest when I turned around to see Sway standing there talking to Spencer and Aiden. Her long mahogany waves fell midway down her back and her creamy ivory skin reflected the day's sun like a mass of energy.

For a moment, I couldn't think, couldn't speak as I stared at her. It was if I'd never seen her before. When really, I had never seen her like this before. Over time, she had matured into a woman right before my eyes, but now, the emotions I felt for her only amplified anything I thought I felt for her or saw in her.

When Aiden smiled at me, she spun on her heel, her eager eyes focused on my smiling eyes and ran for me.

Tension built in my chest, stomach and groin when she wrapped her legs around my waist. I wasn't complaining, hell no, I wasn't complaining but it was somewhat awkward having to adjust myself in the middle of the paddock discreetly. My arms instinctively pulled her closer.

"I missed you, Sway, *so much.*"

I felt her shiver at my touch when my fingertips brushed against the sliver of skin peeking out under her tank top. Turning my head, the stubble of my jaw brushed against her bare shoulder, I kissed her flushed cheek.

There were people everywhere around us, but I couldn't stop staring at her, until Alley cleared her throat. Setting her securely on her feet, I kept my arm around her, drinking in her beauty.

"Oh, Jesus, do you two need a room?" Alley snapped.

I wanted to say, "Nope, she'll be with me." but I didn't, instead I laughed.

"I can't believe all this. It gets crazier every time I see you," Sway nudged my shoulder pretending to bounce around like a boxer and then held her forearm to my face. "Will you sign my arm? Or my ass?" she stopped jumping and stood in front of me, waiting.

All I could think about was seeing that delectable skin that I so badly wanted to taste, tempting me. So I licked her arm. "There's your autograph. Want me to sign your ass, too?" *I'll sign every inch of your goddamn body if you let me.*

Rolling my eyes, at myself mostly, I turned toward Alley. "What's the plan tonight?"

She was busy tending to Spencer's eye that was bleeding. "You have the drivers' meeting in an hour."

"What the hell happened to you?" I asked Spencer.

He glared when I chuckled. "You're best friend there decided to try and take my head off with your spring."

"That's my girl," I nodded appreciatively smiling down at Sway tucked under my arm.

"Listen," Alley smacked my shoulder. "You have the drivers' meeting and then introductions start at four. After the race you have to make an appearance at the Howl at the Moon club in downtown Charlotte."

I turned to Sway. "So what ... did you get a hotel room, or do you want to stay in my motor coach?"

She seemed to hesitate for a moment before whispering, "Alley got me my own room."

"Damn," he smirked. "Well, I guess that means I have to return you to your room tonight. Or you could stay in my motor coach."

There was no way I was returning her to her room tonight, not unless I was with her.

Alley smacked at my shoulder. "You're staying at a hotel tonight, dipshit. You leave town tomorrow morning after an interview. Which you better not be late to."

"Am I staying at the same hotel as her?"

"I'm not getting drunk tonight, Jameson," she warned as we walked toward the garage.

"So you say," I pulled her against my side securely before whispering in her ear, my lips grazed her ear. "I bet I can convince you otherwise." I paused before smirking. "Besides, I have another ass cheek that needs branding and so do you." Reaching behind her, I slapped her ass once.

"Is that so?"

"Without a doubt," I replied confidently with a smug lewd smile and then winked to add to the fire (hers and mine). We stopped beside my car, her eyes lighting up. Sway wasn't your ordinary girl around cars, she got the same glazed over expression I got when she heard an engine rumbling, quietude.

As I walked her around the garage, introducing her to the new team members, there was a sense of familiarity between us that was comforting. She was still my girl, the same girl who would blush and punch you at the same time. The same girl whose eyes told a story, but you had to listen to understand them, if you didn't, you would never know the real her. She was the girl who loved ice cream more than breathing, who hated clowns like they were the devil and couldn't walk into a room at night without every light being on. She was my girl.

I watched her closely, inquisitively examining her every movement. It was as if my mind was trying to find a way out of the decision it already made but she wasn't giving me any reason to go back it.

She was responsive to my touch, leaned into my embrace and when I kissed her cheek every so often, she returned the gesture, wrapping her arms around me.

Could it be she wanted something more just as much as I did?

The night was passing with a blur and soon I was heading to the motor coach to get ready. It was funny to me that everything I'd been feeling throughout the day with the penalty, was overshadowed by

Sway being here. She had the power to completely pivot everything hurled onto my shoulders just by being here.

I had a plan for tonight and nothing was going to change that. My mom asked me where that boy was who was so tenaciously determined? Well, I found him. More tenacious and more determined than ever.

Flat-out – Refers to using 100% of the race car and not holding back on the ability of the car in a race.

Leaving Sway with Emma, I made my way to the drivers' meeting.

That's when I spotted someone I thought, hoped, I'd never see again.

Chelsea Adams.

Seeing her, wasn't the most repugnantly unsettling part about it, it was her clinging firmly to Tate's arm that made me want to vomit. She fucking hated racing but she was *here*, with a guy who deserved so much better than her skanky ass.

Don't confuse this with jealousy because that was not it, at all. I *hated* Chelsea and I *liked* Tate. He didn't need that drama any more than I did back in high school.

Bobby noticed my scowl and asked, "You know her?" motioning behind us at them.

I grunted but kept walking toward the media center.

"She showed up this morning," he told me. "Must be his new girl he met in Washington."

"Washington ... what was Tate doing in Washington?"

Bobby looked at me as though I was stupid for not knowing. "The IDC race ... we went out there on the bi-week."

"Oh, right, I forgot."

I wasn't at all surprised when Tate sat next to me at the drivers' meeting. I'm sure Chelsea packed his brain with all sorts of shameless lies.

"I heard you know Chelsea," Tate said conversationally as he sat next to me in a folding metal chair; his hefty arms crossed over his chest. Other drivers and their crew chiefs began filing in behind us, filling the empty chairs on either side of us.

My eyes shifted from my phone I'd been holding, "Yeah, we went to high school together."

"She said you dated."

I snorted slipping my phone inside my jeans. "I wouldn't call it that."

Tate tilted his head in confusion waiting for me to elaborate; only I didn't care to, why should I? I didn't want to remember her any more than I wanted to tell him.

"What do you mean?" he finally asked.

Carefully choosing my words, I replied slowly. "She is not exactly the faithful type."

He seemed to consider this but I also knew Chelsea had a cogent side. She could make you see what you wanted to see. She should have been a politician.

Gordon walked inside the media center after that to begin the meeting. Kyle took a seat next to me, I smiled, he smiled. We both knew what this meeting would contain.

Knowing the events throughout the day with the fines handed down, how do you think the drivers' meeting went?

Yeah, something like that. It was similar to my first few test sessions with Harry, only now I felt angry. I was angry that someone put the additive in the tank and angry that Gordon felt the need to make the entire drivers' meeting about cheating never taking his eyes off Kyle and me.

Staring at my hands, I fidgeted with a callous on my thumb, picking at the skin obsessively trying not to stand up and speak my mind.

My thoughts soon turned to Sway and tonight. We had been apart for far too long and I couldn't wait to hold her, feel her against me, and in the most intimate ways. I wanted to skip the race and be with her, which was surprising. Never in my life had I wanted to miss a race, and now I was thinking with my dick.

Before long I found myself heading for driver introductions, Bobby caught up with me.

"Good luck today, teammate."

"You too," I smiled at him.

"For all the shit that's gone down today, you're awfully cheery." His elbow nudged me. "You feeling okay?"

I waggled my eyebrows adjusting my hat.

"I see your girl's here."

Again, I only nodded with a smug smile. I think Bobby knew I wasn't opening up about Sway so he moved on to talk with Andy and Paul who caught up with us.

Soon driver introductions were over and we were firing the engines up to start the race. I always got a sense of butterflies in the pit of my stomach but adrenaline always outshined to the point I never noticed, until today.

I don't know why this race was making me nervous but it was. Or maybe it was after the race that had me so edgy. Either way, I pushed all thoughts aside and did what I did best—raced.

Spencer leaned inside the car as he always did before the race to wish me luck.

"You got this!" he handed me a picture with tape on it.

Glancing at the picture, I smiled sticking it to the dash where I could see it throughout the race. It was one of me, Sway, Spencer, and Emma after I won the track championship the year I met Sway. Under the picture Spencer had written: This is where you came from.

Without a doubt, that is where I came from.

I may be a NASCAR racer now but I'd never forget how I got here.

"All right, Jameson, two laps to green bud," Kyle said to me as I turned the wheel back-and-forth sharply cleaning the tires during the warm-up laps. "You're pit road speed is going to be 5400."

"Copy that, 5400." I told them glancing at the gauges and then back toward the lines on the track. "When I come out of three ... that yellow line ... is that the line for pit road?"

"Yeah," Aiden replied. "Start breaking after the wall when pitting. You're pitting right after the No. 16 pit."

"Copy," I saw Spencer standing on the wall waving.

Pulling on my belts once more, my heart was pounding—my hands trembled with excitement. The rumbling over the cars provided the right amount of vibration to soothe me. If there's any race you need to stay calm and relaxed for, it was NASCAR's longest night, the Coca-Cola 600.

After a long green flag run, the caution came out. I was leading until we pitted. My car was absolutely perfected. I could run high, low, sideways if I wanted and it went anywhere.

Only problem was going into the stop, I was leading. When I came out, I was fifth.

I have certain expectations from a pit crew and right now, they *were not* meeting them.

I'll admit, I was somewhat fired up but I had good reason to be.

"You guys act as though you've never performed a pit stop before!" I shouted. "What the fuck?" Blending in with the lapped cars, I made me way behind the pace car in my *fifth* position. Not only was I fifth, but I had to fight a handful of lapped cars as well.

"Sorry, bud, there was loose lug nuts on the left rear." Kyle offered.

I understand they had off nights, just as I did. Sometimes a jack man is going to miss his pegs, a tire changer may knock off a lug, or a tire carrier will miss the hang, it's going to happen but it doesn't make you feel any better when you're leading going into the stop and then you come out having lost positions.

Having to spend forty-hours a week working on this, I expected more from them.

Another hundred laps into the race, we were coming up on a pack of lapped cars. "You've got company ahead, hold your lines," Aiden told me.

It literally felt like I'd been inside the car for eight hours, I was exhausted, mentally and physically. Sometime after lap 350, I was mumbling to myself and still leading.

Jesus Christ, where is the checkered flag when you need it. I'd even settle for a caution right now.

Soon the caution did come out but the crew fucked it up again and I ended up seventh, yes— seventh!

I kept my cool on that one but when I made it to the lead again—and then fell back to third on the next stop—I lost it. My screaming into the radio even rung in my ears but honestly, I had a right to be upset. You cannot win these races without all aspects of your team lining up. You need to be on your game, the spotter needs to be paying attention, the crew chief needs to make the right calls and the pit crew, they needed to be perfect.

This time, it was harder getting to the front, with a few laps remaining, every driver steps it up. A move you could hustle in the beginning of the race suddenly wasn't an option and could potentially take you out of the race all together. You had to concentrate and look ahead, anticipating what the other driver was going to do. That was every driver but the No. 14 of Darrin Torres—no one could anticipate him.

"I'm bottoming out in three and four," I told Kyle after the last stop. I was trying desperately to get around Bobby but couldn't once the green flag dropped again. I only had two laps.

Right now though, I had a bigger problem to worry about. My right rear was slipping on exit and Darrin was getting away. That combined with the dragging in three and four, I was losing ground.

"It's the coil-bind. It lowers the ride height so you can get more power but it rubs on the splitter. That's what you're feeling."

"10-4,"

When I made it to Darrin on the last lap, flashes of the Winston finish unnerved me. That was unadulterated sacrilege. You don't fuck with me like that on the track and get away with it and I refused to let him get away. I wanted this win.

"Go for it, bud!" Kyle said when the white flagged waved.

My confidence in my car was there so I pushed as hard as I could. Coming out of four, I held my breath and hung on, praying to God I could catch him in time. I think I may have even closed my eyes but I saw we both crossed the line together.

"Who won?"

Please tell me I won!

Darrin pulled ahead of me on the track, slowing his speed, the radio stayed quiet, so I asked again. "Who won?"

"You did, bud. Nice racing!" Kyle answered with enthusiasm.

"Yeah!" I screamed. I don't think I'd ever been so excited to win a race in front of my entire family. Nope, this was the best one, so far, not the Chili Bowl or the Triple Crown, *nothing*, until tonight. Of all the tracks I raced at, I wanted to win at Charlotte. And it wasn't just the Winston race, I wanted to win the Coca-Cola 600.

Why?

Because that's the heart of NASCAR racing, always would be. The biggest event was the Daytona 500 but to me, winning at a track that most of the purebred NASCAR guys called home; that meant something to me. I could do this. Here I was a dirt track racer, showing these asphalt guys a thing or two about talent.

"Not bad from a dirt track racer from Washington, fuck yeah!" I pumped my fist out the window doing a burnout on the grass and then the front stretch in front of the section where my family was. This was for them.

Reaching for the checkered flag, I could see the grandstands and everyone was on their feet cheering.

Stopping on pit road several times, other drivers, officials, crewmembers from other teams, everyone clapped for me. A few said "congratulations" where others smiled widely.

Tate stopped me and stuck his head in the car. "I'm so *proud* of you, kid!" his hand reached to slap my helmet.

His words held meaning and more implication than he probably understood. A lump formed in my throat, impeding my speech. I simply nodded with a heartfelt smile, trying to control tears from streaming down my face. Once I pulled my car into victory lane, the battle over the tears was harder. My Nana was there jumping up and down, at seventy-two she was jumping. Grandpa Casten who only smiled when he had a flask in his hand, was clapping. My parents were hugging one another, smiling. Sway, Emma, and Alley, who had Lane, were jumping around with Nana.

My entire family was there waiting. Never in all the races I'd ever won, had *all* my family been there to witness it.

Taking my time to remove my helmet, I detached the hoses connected to me and fought the tears back with a smile.

To most, the emotion swelling to the surface could have gone unnoticed, except to my family.

They knew.

I hadn't cried for as long as I could remember, not since Spencer smacked me in the junk with a tire iron when I was fourteen. But now, I was losing the battle; one word could have probably set me off. I prayed my dad wouldn't say anything until I was more controlled. Hearing anything he had to say would have probably sent me over the edge.

Inhaling a deep breath, I ran a towel across my face before placing a hat on. My head fell back against the seat, closing my eyes briefly, I took a deep breath.

"You fucking earned this one!" Kyle stuck his head inside, handing me a beer. "I've never met another driver with the skill you have to handle that beast. Great job, bud."

Looking at the fans gathered, my eyes focused on Sway's.

I winked and then hoisted myself from the car. My heart was racing as I took it all in. Everyone was screaming my name, champagne was bursting, Coke and beer was sprayed. If you have never had the opportunity to have Coke sprayed in your eyes, you're not missing anything. That shit burns.

Provoking the crowd, I beat on the roof of the car before launching myself at my team.

Spencer caught me in his steel embrace. "Way to turn it around for us, Bro!" he pulled back to look at me reverentially. "I can't even tell you how proud I am of you."

Oh, fuck. Thank God for the fucking Coke already in my eyes. At least now, I could blame it on the soda. "Thanks, man," I said, humbly.

The broadcasters were right there pulling at me for interviews but I needed someone.

I motioned with my hand for her to come over but she didn't, so I yelled, "Get over here, Sway!"

Her eyes lit up in a way I'd never seen before, wrapping her arms around my waist.

"I'm so proud of you," she whispered searching my eyes.

For a moment, it seemed as though she could feel everything I was feeling in that moment. My feelings and thoughts were revealed, naked and unprotected for her to judge. Once again, she had power over me. But the girl, the one I grew to love, filled the cracks like bear grease smoothing the imperfections.

No matter how many times I heard the words "*I'm proud of you*" tonight, with each person it was worth something different. I can't explain *why* but each one of them, Spencer, Tate, Kyle, they were *all* proud of me. With Spencer, it meant that he didn't mind that he was forced to give up being with his family every weekend to help his little brother race. Tate, well, he gave me a chance at this dream, for him to be proud of me, well that meant he wasn't disappointed at the decision to help.

Now Kyle, the trust between a crew chief and driver is essential. For him to be proud of me, meant I wasn't just another asshole driver he had to put up with, we respected each other.

When Sway said it, the world stopped, everything stood still. The significance that held was beyond words.

So I settled on, "Thank you for being here. It means everything to me," without reserve, I placed my lips to hers. Now wasn't the time, *later*.

Later, I would show her exactly what she meant to me.

"Jameson Riley, you heard go from Kyle and you did. Tell us what you did there at the end to catch Darrin."

"You know, we had an unbelievable car throughout the entire race. The car wasn't as good on the long runs so we lucked out with the green white checkered. We had some problems with pit stops but we had a fast car to make up for it ... It's pretty awesome to win here on Memorial Day weekend. All my family is here ... even my Nana was able to make it." I paused trying to remember to thank my sponsors. "I need to thank my sponsor Simplex ... all the people that support us, my dad for giving me a chance."

"Let's get him over here." Dad made his way through the crowd toward us.

"Jimi, what do you think of your son here?" he shoved the microphone in his face.

"I knew he had it in him." Dad smiled. I don't think I'd seen him smile that wide since Lane was born. "We're very proud of him," he reached for me.

Pulling him into a tight embrace, he whispered in my ear, "I mean that, I do," he choked. "*Nothing* in the world can come close to seeing you live this dream of yours."

Your whole life, you look to your parents for approval. Even when you're young, so much as taking our first steps, we're seeking approval. Having and wanting are complete opposites and, to me, having is prominence without knowing.

The next hour was spent doing interviews, the hat dance, and kissing Sway a few more times.

This didn't go unnoticed by Lane either when he told me, sternly I might add, "Mama told you no."

"She's not my mother though," I told him standing next to the car.

He was perched on the roof, grinning like a crazed three-year-old who had just had a Coke.

"You still listen," he shrugged.

"No, I don't."

He sighed and looked down at my car we were standing next to before rolling his eyes. "Ne'na says you listen to girls."

"Oh, I listen to *a* girl all right, just not your mother. She doesn't like me."

"I know," he seemed to think for a moment and then sighed again. "Can I sit in the car now?"

"You lose focus quickly, don't you?"

"So do you," Lane grinned widely. "Now hand me that weehd thing."

"The steering wheel?"

"Ugh, that's what I said," he added with another eye roll.

I handed him the steering wheel chuckling that this three-year-old was so damn entertaining to me.

"Does she know your plan?" Spencer asked as we leaned against the bar. It took us half the night to get here, but finally, after all the media, most of my team and family made it out to downtown Charlotte for a scheduled appearance, at the Howl at the Moon bar. The appearance took on a life of its own though with the win.

Turning toward him, I spoke quietly, giving my words a solemnity appropriate to the occasion.

"I have no idea what you are talking about."

He laughed tilting his beer my direction. "That's bullshit."

I honestly believe there comes a point when everything changes for you. You cross a bridge and you can't go back. I've crossed a few bridges. The night I won the Triple Crown, the night I won the Chili Bowl Midget Nationals, or my first Cup win. Those moments changed the direction I was heading in as I crossed over. My life changed.

Tonight wasn't any different. I knew if I acted upon what I was feeling, there was no going back. Did that stop me? No, hell no, that gritty side had taken over and I saw what I wanted, tempting me with each breath she took.

Somewhere between these blurred lines of our relationship, was a trust. A trust that I didn't have with anyone but her, and I knew right then, this *could* work.

"What are you doing?" Spencer asked when I left him standing by the bar.

"Going to talk to her,"

"In front of everyone?"

"I said I was going to talk to her," I smiled over my shoulder, "not rape her."

Approaching her from behind, I wrapped my arms around her waist, pulling her against my chest.

She jumped, her shoulder bumping my jaw.

"Oh shit, I'm so sorry," she sounded genuinely penitent. It wasn't necessary.

Kissing her cheek, I smiled rubbing my jaw, slowly and suggestively. "It's all right, honey," whispering slowly in her ear, I heard the distinct hitch of her breath as mine blew across her neck. "You didn't hurt me."

She didn't say anything as she gaped at me with wide eyes.

I gave up any crazy thought of making a *wise* decision tonight. I had to have her in some way. The need was pulling me beneath the surface I had tried to stay above for so long, consuming and confusing.

My name being sternly intoned broke my reverie. Glancing around the room, I noticed Darrin and his cousin, Kevin, step inside the bar.

"I'll be right back," I told Sway.

Darrin, obviously waiting for me, turned around when I approached him. "You lost?" I asked. "Last time I checked, this was an appearance set up by *my* sponsor."

"Anyone can come into the bar, Jameson," Darrin retorted sharply. From the corner of my eye, I knew who was standing next to him, but I refused to look her direction, refused to even *acknowledge* her presence.

"You should leave," I warned ominously to him and Chelsea. I was so sick of his shit that I wanted to hit him right then. My fists clenched instinctively, anticipating he'd make a scene. I couldn't believe either of them showed up here.

"You act as though the world fucking revolves around your arrogant ass," Darrin stepped closer to me. "Just because your dad provided the ride doesn't mean you're hot shit, Jameson."

Remaining *somewhat* collected, I leaned back against the bar again, trying to appear as though I could give a rat's ass to what he thought of me.

"Darrin," I spoke slowly shaking my head, I kept my tone even and controlled giving it a more baleful hint. "Just because my father owns the team I race for, doesn't mean I can't drive." My chin came up arrogantly. "Who won tonight?"

"By three tenths of an inch, hardly a win," he snorted.

I chuckled with intent.

"Any way you want to look at it Darrin, I won," motioning to the bartender, I ordered another beer. "How's second place feel?"

He stepped closer, fisting his hands in my shirt.

"Listen you little shit," I saw Spencer appear beside me. "Stay out of my way on the track or you'll regret it," he spat.

There are a few things I *do not* like—besides substances on my skin. That includes someone shoving me and someone threatening me.

Within a second, I had a broken beer bottle pressed to his throat, his nose bleeding from where I punched him. "Don't. Ever. Threaten. Me. Again!"

I hated this asshole and for him to come in here and threaten me, on a night I was celebrating with the people who made this all possible for me, made me fucking livid.

Spencer and Kyle had me slammed against the wall. They knew I was moments away from destroying this entire bar to get my point across with this motherfucker.

“Calm down!” Spencer growled in my ear, his fists that were clenching my shirt tightened. “I mean it, Jameson. Don’t do this here.”

“Get him out of here.” I barked at the security guards surrounding me. I’m sure my enraged manic glare was enough for them cause they moved pretty fucking quickly after that.

Equalize – Cars that run at superspeedways are required to run tires with an inner liner. This is a tire within a tire.

It took me a good hour to calm down once Darrin left.

Between the penalties, the race, Sway, Darrin, and my feelings and emotions being all over the place, I drank. Making my way to the bar once again, Marcus, Simplex's president, caught me.

Marcus, who was lit already, stood next to me with his arm around my shoulders, waving a shot of tequila around as he told me, in no certain terms, how he thought I could improve my driving.

Normally, I would have told him I didn't give a shit what he thought but Marcus being my sponsor, yeah, I wasn't going to say that.

After a few shots, I was feeling pretty good and working on my courage to approach Sway.

The bar was full and crawling with pit lizards, all of who I was having a hard time getting rid of. They were always relentless after a race.

"You sure attract the ladies," Marcus deduced after Ashley, the Fox Sports reporter, shoved her tits in my face once again that night.

Motioning toward Ashley, I said. "I'm sure she'll show you a *good* time."

And I mean "good time" by Marcus standards. Marcus thought

he was some North Carolina player, he wasn't by the way. I don't think anyone ever told him that just because the boys in *Men in Black* looked okay, didn't mean he did.

"Oh, yeah?" he elbowed me. "Know from experience, huh?"

I suppressed a sigh knowing I needed to act civilized.

"No, half the fucking industry does though."

Yeah, I slept with Ashley once, but in my defense I was so drunk that night, I ended up sleeping on the sidewalk in front of a Safeway store. I couldn't tell you a single goddamn thing that occurred that night, only that I dimly remember being tangled in the sheets with her at one point. I was also not going to admit this to anyone, it was none of their business who I slept with.

After another round of shots, when I felt Sway behind me.

"Jameson," she sighed. "Don't you leavd me wit you sista again!"

When I looked at Sway, she was gone. Bright glassy eyes, sweet creamy skin highlighted from the alcohol and I had to laugh. She was adorable.

"What the hell happened to you?" I stepped closer to her, pulling her against my side.

She frowned concentrating on her answer.

"Oh ... *you* ... Emma ..." she sighed exasperatedly. She blew a loose strand of her hair out of her eyes, and then braved on. "Spencer he ... I'll tell'd you'd something ..."

"Something?" I laughed.

"What?"

"Huh?"

Without notice, she threw her arms around my neck and kissed me. Not just any kiss, a strong determined kiss. One that I was sure my plan would work well with. My mind was reeling, maybe it was all that tequila but either way, I was spinning.

Breathing deeply, trying desperately to keep my erotic thoughts at bay, I responded with, "Unless you want me to lose control in front of the entire bar, don't kiss me like that." A nervous laugh escaped me.

Sway took that for acquiescence and smiled. "I don't think I'd mind."

This was drunk Sway and drunk Jameson speaking right now and not the two "Grammy Winners" who usually spoke in something similar to morse code when feelings were involved.

"You want me to lose control with you?" my lips were at her collarbone. I kissed softly along the curve and then up her neck before placing a tender kiss below her ear.

"I want you, too," she pressed herself closer as the song *Purple Rain* began.

"Let's dance, honey," I chuckled pulling her toward the dance floor. "They're playing our theme song."

"Team song?" her eyebrow arched in question but followed.

Laughing, I held the Purple Rain drink up.

Sway giggled before nodding enthusiastically, "Yes ... letz."

Whispering the lyrics to her was my way of trying to seal the deal, she loved it when I sang to her.

When I looked into her eyes, she had an expression I hadn't seen before. Love maybe? Lust ... I'm not sure what it was but I'm pretty certain mine mirrored hers in some way. There was a room full of people surrounding us, but I couldn't look away from her in that moment. I'd put my life on hold, telling myself I couldn't, wouldn't have or ask for more than what we had. I failed to realize that I could have *something* with her.

I felt her sigh and lean into my embrace further and then giggle.

"What?" I asked my eyes focused intently hers.

"Nothing," she said, her speech returning to normal; then she winked.

Could she be any more adorable?

"You are the most *beautiful* woman I've ever met," I crooned against her neck as I pressed a tender kiss right below her ear, just as I'd done all night. I couldn't pry my lips away from her skin.

"Yeah, well, you're the most beautiful man I've ever met. And, *Christ almighty,* can you drive a car," her hands reached for mine. "You sure can handle the horsepower, can't you?"

Oh. My. God.

She had to feel my erection against her—she had to. I should have been concerned at the obvious display we were putting on but I couldn't help it. But I cared about none of that as much as I cared about the way my body was responding to her.

Removing my hands from hers, I traced them down the lines of her hips—my fingers dug into the velvety skin and pulled her even tighter against my hips. She gasped and closed her eyes as though the sensation was exactly what she wanted.

"You wanna see how I drive *your* car?"

Sway's cheeks flushed before whispering. "I'd pay money to see that."

She had mocked my words from the night in her room.

"Is that so?" I smirked.

She licked her lips, "Oh yeah."

Dancing seemed pointless, we weren't even moving just kissing and touching.

"Let's get out of here," I finally said.

I couldn't take this teasing any longer. It was different. While I had a plan tonight, she seemed to rouse that plan into action. Instead of fighting with me, she was flirting, instead of taunting, she was teasing.

If she wanted to see how much horsepower I had, I'd show her. I would show her just how powerful these hands could be.

Funny thing was though, she had no idea the power she held in all this.

Back at the hotel, I gave into the desires I had all those years.

Fuck it all. I had to know.

"Stay," I whispered against her calf, placing another soft kiss to her skin before she could sneak away.

My heart pounded because here was the woman I had dreamed about all my life standing in front of me in the most amazing skirt I had ever seen. I waited for her answer and then suddenly I was burning up.

Jesus Christ, is it like a hundred degrees out?

"You're drunk," she told me crouching down next to me.

"So are you." I leaned up on my elbows, trying to make her understand.

I could have tried to blame this one the alcohol that had severely damaged our inhibitions, but honestly, it wasn't that at all. It was the look on her face when I asked her to stay. Everything changed in that exact moment. Our friendship would never be the same with just that one look.

Leaning forward, she kissed me. I couldn't hold back any longer, that tenacious determined side took over, needing anything she was willing to provide.

As our kisses continued, my mouth moved frantically from her ear to her neck and down to her collarbone, then returning urgently to her lips again as if I needed her breath to breathe. Moving against her with more need than I'd ever felt in the past—I couldn't get close enough. Sway gave back, just as stalwartly, fulfilling whatever it was I was seeking. Groaning as I moved from one spot to another on her, I was frustrated that I couldn't get closer.

In return, she clawed at me clinging to me in any way she could. I clenched my eyes shut at the heightening of every sensation that I was already feeling. Some part of me collapsed internally as I realized I had absolutely no idea what I wanted to do. I was on completely unfamiliar territory here. Yeah, I'd had sex before, but I was always mechanical about it, searching for one need and one need only.

Now, here was the woman who meant the world to me laying in my arms, panting against me. Watching her lose control, the same control I was losing, was something I'd never felt before.

Could I please her?

That was certainly a concern of mine. The faded memories of the women in my past, told me that they did a lot of screaming but was this pleasure from my movements? I never took the time to consider that before as I didn't care.

Could I give Sway an orgasm?

Just imagining what she'd look like in the midst of an orgasm was enough to send me over the edge right then. I wish I could say I was fine and *not* scared shitless but that was a lie.

I was unsure and scared. Two more things that were completely unfamiliar to me.

For whatever reason, we seemed to both be letting go, slowly rising with the passion. Letting go of insecurities, boundaries, whatever ties that constrained us before were falling away with each kiss. Everything I had been skeptical of before seemed so silly. If I could have this with anyone it was her, she understood me and understood what I was working for. More importantly, I was comfortable with her and this felt so right.

Complete shock took over at the scene that lay before me. On the center of the bed reclining on a sea of white pillows, was *my* girl. My imagination as to what she looked like completely naked didn't do her justice.

Her dark luxurious hair fanned out on the pillows framing her porcelain face. Her emerald eyes held mine with a burning intensity that had never appeared before. A furious blush bloomed over her cheeks, and my eyes followed its path down to her heaving chest. I sucked in a tortured breath and fought to control the lust that shot through me at the sight of her. Pale moonlight splashed across the flat planes of her abdomen and reflected off the sheen of sweat on her damp skin. My eyes were drawn lower to the bare skin of her slightly crossed legs. All that flowed through me now was a raw desire to claim the woman who lay before me.

Her skin glowed with the slow rising sun and my hesitation got the best of me as I begged her to stop. I know inside this was my way of making this her decision. If she told me to continue, she wanted me just as much.

"Tell me to stop," I whispered gauging her reaction. It took a Herculean act of self-control but I pulled back to look at her, in my arms on the bed of my hotel room. "Please," my voice broke at the end. "Honey ... tell me to stop." My fingertips grazed her soft lips, begging for permission to continue but asking her to tell me otherwise.

Her long legs wrapped around my waist, pulling me even closer.

"Don't," she mumbled softly. "Please, don't stop." Her voice shook with her labored breathing.

I was fumbling and shaky, another part of me that was unfamiliar. But as hesitant as I was, she was acting the same. She was scared.

Resting on my elbows, I looked down at her. "Sway, I ..."

I wanted to tell her so badly that I loved her. Beg her not to break my heart and convince her that I wouldn't knowingly break hers in the process.

She simply nodded as if she heard me, breathing, "I know," Against my cheek. "I want you."

If I wasn't listening close enough, you wouldn't have heard it, but I did.

"I want you, too," I whispered back looking into her eyes.

There was no going back and I don't think either one of us was reasoned enough to understand that right now. All we knew was what we were feeling.

Soon, I let go of everything I'd been feeling, everything I'd been fearing and want bubbled to the surface overpowering and consuming. Feeling her small body underneath me was almost too much to handle. I'd never felt sensations this unbelievably intense before and I still hadn't entered her.

I had to seek her permission though because this was different from all those one-night stands. I knew they wanted it. With Sway, though her body was telling me she wanted it, I had to know. I couldn't do this without confirmation she wanted it just as much.

"Are you okay ... I mean ... are you sure, Sway? We've never ..."

I couldn't believe how badly I was shaking, it was sad.

Stop shaking, asshole, you're not a virgin! I told myself.

He didn't listen, nope, he was far too engrossed in this woman before him offering herself up to him in the most intimate way. Now look at me, I'm shaking like a fool and speaking in the third person.

Pull yourself together! I told him sternly.

"Are you *sure*? We've never ..." My voice was so weak it didn't even sound like me.

Sway smiled shyly, nodding.

"Sway?"

Please, honey, see what I feel for you. Look into my eyes and I'll show you.

"Yes?" she wouldn't look at me, but the nervousness was there.

I wanted to say, *"You're nervous? Hah! How do you think I feel!"* but I didn't.

Instead, I settled on something more simple and vague.

"Are you sure, honey?" my voice was rough. I tried to clear my throat quietly. I don't know why I kept asking but I had to be sure.

"Yes," she croaked softly, her eyes searched mine.

That's all the encouragement I needed, I was naked between her legs, believe me when I say I didn't need much encouragement any more. I was one sigh away from crumbling and telling her how I felt.

Obsequiously crazed by her beauty for years, who knew the night I won the biggest race of my career would be the night I ended up in bed with my best friend.

You'd think at some point, the confident, more stable me would have taken over, but no, I was still fumbling when I reached for the condom, dropped it and then had to search for it on the floor.

Talk about frustrating.

Gathering my wits, I got the condom on and settled between her legs once more.

My hand, yeah, the shaking one, reached between us to guide myself into her. My lips were at her ear, my breathing harsh and staggered. That harsh staggering breathing halted altogether when I pushed forward.

Holly fuck!

I looked deeply into her eyes and saw the apprehension melt into raw unconcealed lust. Her hands slid down the planes of my body and came to rest at the base of my spine. My mind was hazy as I struggled to hold onto what remained of my control. I pulled back hesitantly, shaking with the effort, and slid smoothly in, her wet skin massaging me the whole way. Sway panted heavily in my ear, and the scorching heat of her breath intensified the sensations elsewhere. She pulled at my waist, encouraging my movements and spurring me on. It all felt so good. I wanted more of the pleasurable sensations.

Never in my life had something felt so good as when I entered her. Nothing.

Not even the first time I discovered how good bleeding your pressure valve was when I was thirteen. And never in my life had I imagined this moment to be so intense, so consuming. I never wanted the feeling to end.

It took every single ounce of self-control I could rally not to lose myself the moment I was inside of her—completely lost in it for a long moment, clutching her tightly to me with my hands on her upper arms.

She gasped, her body tensing around me.

I froze, not that I'd moved yet anyway but so much as breathing seemed wrong.

"Are you all right? Should I stop?"

Sway nodded, holding on to me tighter. Kissing her, I poured everything I had into those kisses, wanting her to *feel* the love I had for her even if I couldn't tell her.

I held her hands above her head against the pillow before hitching her leg further, my head dipped down to whisper low and seductively in her ear.

"You don't know how long I've wanted this," I panted as I slowly began to move.

Sway moaned, her mouth finding my own as her chest arched into me, responding willingly to every movement. Her kisses were urgent and full of passion, igniting the burning desire I already had for her.

Trailing kisses down her jaw, throwing her head back, she moaned again while her tiny hands caressed me. It was agony to go slow, but it was the only way. Just the friction, the warmth of her around me was like nothing I'd ever felt before.

"You like that?" I realized right about now, I was panting like a fucking idiot. I couldn't have looked any more out of control. It was ridiculous. Talk about losing all dignity. I could race six hundred miles but I couldn't keep my breathing under control when it came to Sway and being inside her.

"Fuck, yes," she moaned again, her eyes squinted shut in pleasure. "Harder."

Pleasure shot through my spine and between my legs.

I chuckled. "Honey, that I can do," I growled in her ear. "Ride my camshaft," I flipped her over so I could see all of her. The faint light from the rising sun shined down through the break in the curtains. Her skin glowed as if she was on fire. "So, you like car talk, huh?" I asked taking a firm hold on her hips.

"Yes," her back arched at the confession, throwing her head back.

For someone who hated to have anything on his skin, I loved the wetness seeping from her onto me, coating me. "I can tell you like car talk by all this assembly lube."

She started moving faster, I gazed at her wanting this to last forever. This beautiful creature moving against me was mine, for tonight anyway and I didn't want it to end. "Ah, honey, slow down ... *please,* slow down," I moaned nonsensically, fighting my orgasm back. She did thankfully with a giggle, but it didn't stop us from dirty talking.

Once the dirty talking increased, I found it harder and harder not to come. Not wanting this to end, I fought for control. There were no guarantees once this was over. This could be it for us, the only time we'd ever truly share ourselves with one another. I didn't want that to end.

She didn't like the level the dirty talking reached at one point and finally yelled, "Okay, shut up," she slapped me. "Just *fuck* me already!"

Oh, Jesus, that's not helping my control.

I fucked her all right. Judging by her moans and downright screams, I'd say she was enjoying this. My mouth quirked into a small smile as one of my eyebrows rose arrogantly when I was sure her moans could be heard outside this hotel room.

That earned me another slap to my shoulder. "You, shut up."

Every move she made my body came alive, the burning sensation spinning out of control. Beads of sweat were running down my body, the heat was unbearable. Having her that close, all around me, was suffocating me in the most intoxicating way. Gasping for breaths, I was completely overcome by this and annoyed with myself that I couldn't pull my shit together and act normal.

And though we were connected, it still wasn't enough. Moving inside her wasn't enough, I had the urge to crawl inside her and stay there. I could feel emotions stirring inside me that had never been let out before because, really, I'd never done something like this before. As much as it appeared to be just sex between drunk people, it wasn't. It couldn't be. Not with two people who spent their whole lives growing closer and closer until they didn't know each other apart from one another. It could never be just sex.

The way she moved, the sounds, the feelings ... it was too much. When her back arched again, her legs tightening around me, I lost it.

"Oh, God, Sway," I grunted in a loud gasp against her shoulder, "...*fuck* ... I'm sorry ... can't hold on any longer ..."

My orgasm hit me hard, wrenching jerking waves. Dropping my head to the pillow, I let go completely. I faintly registered Sway crying out against me, her fingertips dug forcefully into my skin, holding me against her. The tidal wave washed over me, crumbling, but I could feel *every* sensation. It was by far the best orgasm of my life.

As soon as I pulled out of her, I knew I was in trouble. I didn't want to stop and that was a problem. A strange tangle of emotions ran through me in that moment. I was okay with not wanting to stop. We could have more, right? If anyone, I could have more with her.

Placing kisses against her shoulder, I chuckled. My voice was rough from all that ridiculous panting I'd been doing.

Coughing, I cleared my throat.

"Why were we not doing that from the beginning?"

Sway shook her head throwing her arms over her face embarrassed.

"Because, we were eleven, you pervert," she sighed before looking back at me.

My fingers traced along her cheek and down her neck, our breathing starting to slow. "I didn't hurt you, did I?"

"No," she whispered, her eyes strangely determined as she looked at me.

I wanted to ask her what she was thinking but instead she leaned forward and I kissed her softly losing that train of thought. I don't know if it was all the alcohol we consumed or what we'd just done, but I was exhausted after that. Completely spent from a day of internally debating, racing, and the most intense physical sensations I'd ever felt.

I must have fallen asleep after that because when I came around again, Sway wasn't in bed with me.

I started to panic thinking she left until I felt her slide back into the bed with me. The sun had risen so I got a clear view of her naked body as she pulled the covers over her.

God, she is beautiful.

She seemed nervous and anxious as she stayed on the edge of the bed.

Pulling her against my chest, I closed my eyes thinking of what we'd done and wanting to wash away any fear she had that this wouldn't work.

My brain raced to find a way for this to work but I couldn't get over the idea that we just had sex.

I had sex with my best friend. The best sex of my entire life, but still, it was with my best friend.

Beyond a doubt, in that moment, I was in love with her. If I ever had a doubt, I couldn't deny it now. It was scary, intense, controlling and scary … mostly scary.

Almost exactly eleven years ago today, I met this girl. Over the course of our relationship, I fell, slowly and hard. Now, there was no going back.

"Have you ever thought about this before?" I whispered into the eerie silence of the room knowing she could hear me. My voice soft and soothing as my lips danced across her skin.

"Thought about?"

"This …" My arms tightened around her, kissing her skin once more.

"Yes, and no," she told me.

Closing my eyes, I let out the breath I'd been holding. I wanted to ask her what she felt and if this was something she wanted to do again but my voice failed me.

Though I pretended to, I couldn't sleep.

Instead, I held her close, listening to her breathing, praying I hadn't made a mistake. But I also knew this was Sway and it couldn't have been a mistake. This was us. There should be no reason for anything with us to be a mistake when everything came naturally. Just like tonight, nothing was awkward, well, besides my shaking and self-control, but that's to be expected, look at her. Any man worth his salt would be intimated by this flawless being.

I also knew it wouldn't be enough. I craved her like a junkie. I needed it. My body felt like it was still a parched man in the desert and I could have gallons of water, but I was still able to feel the pain of a dry throat. I had to have more of her.

She had disintegrated me to ash and to be this way with her was the most fulfilling feeling I had ever had.

Action is no less necessary than thought to the instinctive tendencies of the human frame.

-Gandhi

Shey Stahl is the author of the Racing on the Edge Series. She enjoys spending time with her family at the local dirt tracks. You can follow her on the links below.

Facebook: https://www.facebook.com/shey.stahl.9
Website: www.sheystahl.com

Website & Social Media:
www.sheystahl.com
Facebook: Shey Stahl

Novels by Shey Stahl:

Racing on the Edge:

Happy Hour

Black Flag

Trading Paint

The Champion

The Legend

Additional novels coming soon:

Hot Laps

The Rookie

Fast Time

Lapped Traffic

Behind the Wheel - Outtakes

Everything Changes

Waiting for You

Delayed Penalty

Made in the USA
Charleston, SC
15 April 2014